07-2017

The Typewriter's Tale

The Typewriter's Tale

Michiel Heyns

St. Martin's Press

New York

THE TYPEWRITER'S TALE. Copyright © 2005 by Michiel Heyns. All rights reserved. Printed in the United States of America. For information, address St. Martin's Press, 175 Fifth Avenue, New York, N.Y. 10010.

www.stmartins.com

Library of Congress Cataloging-in-Publication Data

Names: Heyns, Michiel, author.
Title: The typewriter's tale / Michiel Heyns.
Description: New York : St. Martin's Press, 2017.
Identifiers: LCCN 2016038740| ISBN 9781250119001 (hardcover) |
    ISBN 9781250119018 (e-book)
Subjects: LCSH: James, Henry, 1843–1916—Fiction. | Rye
    (England)—Fiction. | BISAC: FICTION / Literary. | FICTION /
    Historical.
Classification: LCC PR9369.4.H49 T86 2017 | DDC 823/.92—dc23
LC record available at https://lccn.loc.gov/2016038740

Our books may be purchased in bulk for promotional, educational, or business use. Please contact your local bookseller or the Macmillan Corporate and Premium Sales Department at 1-800-221-7945, extension 5442, or by e-mail at MacmillanSpecialMarkets@macmillan.com.

First published in the United Kingdom by Freight Books

First U.S. Edition: February 2017

10 9 8 7 6 5 4 3 2 1

typewriter

1   A writing-machine [...];
2   One who does typewriting, esp. as a regular occupation.
Oxford English Dictionary

She found her ladies, in short, almost always in communication with her gentlemen, and her gentlemen with her ladies, and she read into the immensity of their intercourse stories and meanings without end.
Henry James, 'In the Cage'

From its inception the typewriter was imagined as a technology that would be especially liberating for women...
    Secretaries are, on the one hand, tools – ideally meant to function as unmediating recorders of another's thought, like the dictating machines they themselves employ. On the other hand, secretaries are, as mediums, never themselves unmediating.
Pamela Thurschwell, *Literature, Technology and Magical Thinking, 1880-1920*. Cambridge UP, 2001

Of course, the great *theoretic* interest of these automatic performances, whether speech or writing, consists in the questions they awaken as to the boundaries of our individuality. One of their most constant peculiarities is that the writing and speech announce themselves as from a personality other than the natural one of the writer, and often convince him, at any rate, that his organs are played upon by someone not himself.
William James, 'Notes on Automatic Writing', 1889

Dearest H – The episode of the message so exactly hitting your mental condition is very queer. There is *something* back there that shows that minds communicate, even those of the dead with those of the living, but the costume, so to speak, and the accessories of fact, are all symbolic and due to the medium's stock of automatisms – what it all means I don't know but it means at any rate that the world that our 'normal' consciousness makes use of is only a fraction of the whole world in which we have our being.
William James, letter to Henry James, 6 April 1906

What I mean to try for is the observation of that strange moment when the vaguely adumbrated characters whose adventures one is preparing to record are suddenly *there*, themselves, in the flesh, in possession of one, and in command of one's voice and hand... what I want to try to capture is an impression of the elusive moment when these people who haunt my brain actually begin to speak within me with their own voices... as soon as the dialogue begins, I become merely a recording instrument, and my hand never hesitates because my mind has not to choose, but only to set down what these stupid or intelligent, lethargic or passionate, people say to each other in a language, and with arguments, that appear to be all their own.

Edith Wharton, *A Backward Glance*

The persons who project, and would fain construct, Channel tunnels know nothing of the art of war, its surprises, stratagems, disappointments and catastrophes... There are some things of such supreme importance that they impose absolute certainty as their only sufficient and adequate safeguard. Nature has provided us with that certainty by placing a barrier of waves between the ambition of Continental conquerors and the liberties of England.

The Standard, June 1890, quoted by Alice James, *The Diary of Alice James*

The Typewriter's Tale

Chapter One
8th November 1907

The worst part of taking dictation was the waiting.

'She found herself for a moment looking up at him from as far below as...'

She waited, Frieda Wroth, watching his broad back retreat to the far end of the room; turning, he resumed the slow tread down the length of the room. She reflected, not for the first time, on the piquancy of her situation, transmitting, through efficient fingers, the emanations of a writer celebrated for his sympathetic recording of just such disregarded lives as hers. Mr James himself had never shown any apprehension of this quiet enough irony: however preternaturally attuned his sensibilities were to the muffled chord of despair as sounded in the elliptical intercourse of his characters, in her he took for granted, apparently, a prompt attention and a cheerful readiness to assist merely mechanically at the slow processes of his deliberations and contemplations.

It had not occurred to her, in presenting herself for this position, that she would be treated quite so much as an undistinguished and indistinguishable appurtenance of the Remington she operated. It was not a matter of her working conditions – these were as pleasant as he knew how to make them – it was, really, only the metaphysical implications of her identity as a typewriter. She could not have formulated any confident theory on the nature and function of the human spirit, but she knew instinctively that it could not have been intended to serve as the animating principle for a machine. There were times when she veritably envied Mr James's fictional characters for the consideration he bestowed upon them, the vivid identities he invented for them, next to which her own pure functionality seemed abjectly utilitarian. To him she did not represent a potential or real subject: she was the typewriter, appointed to that task and confined to that identity.

Mr James paused in front of the fireplace, often but not always a prelude to utterance. Encouraged to 'read something' while he ruminated, she could yet never altogether concentrate on her book, anxious lest in her absorption she might miss the first fine utterance of his deliberations, as she had once done, to his evident but unexpressed irritation. Generally the most equable of men, he tolerated no interruption of his train of expression: for such a slow-moving vehicle, it was surprisingly prone to breakdowns. She thus preferred to amuse herself by trying to predict the outcome of his rumination, though so far she had succeeded only once, when the elusive word had turned out to be *thing*. This time, since it was a simile he was hunting, she knew only that when it came it would be almost exactly the opposite of what she anticipated, but she tried nevertheless to pre-empt this perversity: *from as far below as...* a mountaineer all strainingly shading his eyes against the vertiginous slope of Mont Blanc?... an adventurer beneath some tower sung in legend in which a golden-haired princess is incarcerated?

'...*as the point from which the school-child, comma, with eyes raised to the wall, comma, gazes at the particoloured map of the world. Full stop.*' He resumed his slow, deliberate dictation and she clattered obediently after him, then halted, while he resumed his treading of the carpet. At the window he paused, a slight bow on his part signalling his acknowledgement of a passer-by possibly unaware of the courtesy being extended from the window projecting above the street. His politeness was such that it did not insist on a sentient object: Frieda had once, during a walk on Camber Sands, seen him doffing his hat to a passing ship in mid-Channel.

In the midst of such courtesy and consideration – the chocolate bars left on her machine in the course of his perambulations, the flowers sent to her room whenever George Gammon could spare any of the profusion from the garden – it seemed ungrateful to want for more. In undertaking the task of translating the inspirations of genius into legible characters, it had not been her idea, naturally, that genius should defer to her convenience; but she had dared to hope that it might in a manner share with her the secret of composition, afford her on rare but precious occasions a glimpse into the furnace of art blazing fiercely under the great brow. Subsequent experience had rendered her sceptical of the temperature of that conflagration: it was not, intellectually speaking, a glow at which one could warm one's frozen fingers; one could but marvel that so much light should produce so little heat.

She had ended by asking herself what then she had expected, a question that she at various times answered variously – amongst which variety, however, a family resemblance could be discerned in the form of a small ungrateful subjectivity, a consciousness of a hunger unappeased, like some orphan in legend obstinately refusing to feast on the banquet spread before her by a prince. She was, in short, conscious of being just sweetly disregarded, a state which until recently she would have found preferable, at least, to some others – more particularly to the chronic regard of Mr Dodds, whose placid but persistent courtship she had been fleeing in betaking herself to this small seaside town so far from Bayswater. It was in that unimpeachable part of London that Mr Dodds dispensed his medicines from an apothecary's shop smelling always of tincture of iodine. There hovered about his presence, even in the Kensington Gardens where he took her on fine Sundays, the spectre of tincture of iodine. It was with her a moot point whether she was just where she was most in pursuit of enlightenment or in flight from tincture of iodine.

For the moment, however, this question had to yield before the resumption of the slow and yet fluent dictation: '*Yes, it was a warmth, comma, it was a special…*'

Gift? Grace?

'*…benignity, comma, that had never yet dropped on her from any one, comma, and she wouldn't for the first few moments have known how to describe it or even quite what to do with it…* My dear Fullerton!' The keys of her machine were still rattling, lagging slightly behind the voice, but her eyes were free to take in the sight of the novelist spreading his arms in welcome, a gesture that she had witnessed at the front door of Lamb House, but had not expected to see in the Garden Room. For Mr James to allow, much less welcome, anybody into the inner retreat of his genius was not so much unusual as unprecedented, and his young employee would have been at a loss to account for this deviation from custom had her wonder not been much more actively engaged in contemplating the cause and occasion of it. Of the man standing in the doorway extending in turn his arms to the novelist, it would have been possible to say many things, but none of them as simplifyingly, comprehensively true as that he was beautiful. Frieda had never before thought of men as beautiful. Mr Dodds, she had been told by her mother, was a fine figure of a man, and Mr Dodds was in the habit of stealing glances at himself in the mirror behind the counter of his apothecary's shop with a complacency suggesting that he shared her mother's high opinion; but he had never inspired in her anything other than a guilty but unrepentant sense of not being able to share the public estimate, such as she remembered cherishing on behalf of an aged aunt whom others affected to find Wonderful for her Age, and whom she had found simply Difficult. Mr Dodds was not particularly wonderful for his age, that age being hardly more advanced than her own; but he had Done Very Well for Himself, which was the same thing, morally speaking, in that it placed him beyond light-minded censure, and was assumed to render the size of his nose, which was considerable, irrelevant.

This newcomer, whom Frieda gathered to have returned very recently from America, and who was now with lively self-deprecation apologising for violating the sanctuary of sanctuaries, needed no such excuse for his nose or any other feature. One could admire him without consulting a list of his virtues and accomplishments. She wondered indeed whether he *had* any virtues and accomplishments: it seemed to her that to look like that was to be able to dispense with such things. The blue brilliance of his glance, the strong, humorous lines of the mouth, the very agility of the hands, spoke of a nature quick rather than solid (Mr Dodds was celebrated in Chelsea and Bayswater for his solidity), a temperament attuned to the enjoyment of others rather than to the cultivation of the self. She would have been at a loss to estimate the age of the visitor: next to Mr James he looked very young, too young to have been a friend of the older man's for as long as their mutual familiarity suggested. It was likely, then, that he was not as young as he seemed, and even this reflection enhanced rather than detracted from the interest he evoked in the young woman: anybody, in their allotted time, could be young; to have lived and yet to have retained the freshness of youth was a far rarer achievement. All this Frieda took in, as they say, at first sight; or so it seemed to her later in recalling his so unexpected entry into, as it were, her life.

The two men were too deeply involved in the intricacies of establishing how gratified Mr James was at this proof of the confidence placed in him by his friend, to register the presence of a female typewriter; but having at some length settled the matter, her employer, with his habitual courtesy, introduced the newcomer to the young woman as his 'very good friend, Mr Morton Fullerton,' adding, as if in self-evident explanation, 'Mr Fullerton is from Paris.'

The blue glance was turned upon her, and Frieda felt that she had never been looked at before: he seemed to be taking in not so much an impression of her as an impression of her impression of him, to register by some preternatural agency the confusion which prevented her from making any but the most conventional response to the introduction. There seemed little of force or originality to be said for the advantages of inhabiting the French capital, and Frieda did not make the attempt.

Mr James, perhaps conscious of a certain blankness in his amanuensis, apparently thought that more information would stimulate her to a more intelligent response. 'Mr Fullerton is the Paris correspondent for *The Times*,' he informed her. 'You will often have read his dispatches.'Then, as this still left her mutely gaping, he elaborated: 'The trial of the unfortunate Captain Dreyfus now, no doubt you followed that?That was the work of my friend Fullerton.'

The visitor laughed. 'My dear Henry, I only reported the case, I didn't conduct it.'

Mr James was insistent. 'Ah, but to report so unflinchingly, so... so *heroically*, must have played its little part in the outcome of that tangled affair.'

Upon this Mr Fullerton turned to Frieda. 'You see, Miss Wroth, what it is to have friends who are determined to cast one in the heroic mould!'

His tone was jocular, but to Frieda's sense or fancy there was in the short glance that passed between them more than the acknowledgment of a common social situation: there was the recognition of a shared plight. Through the gaiety of his manner she discerned a consciousness of being confined to a role he found uncongenial, of, in a manner of speaking, also taking dictation.

That, however, was for later reflection. Mr James meanwhile had moved on, and was addressing her with just the slightest blush of consciousness. 'Miss Wroth, since our labours have been so pleasantly interrupted, I find I need not detain you any longer today. Let us declare this a half-holiday in honour of Mr Fullerton's visit.'

She glanced at her watch. It was only twelve o'clock, almost two hours short of Mr James's usual time; furthermore, in the past, on such rare occasions as he had terminated his dictation early, he had always had revisions for her to type. She sensed that the visit was of such import to Mr James that he did not want the distraction of a typewriter rattling away in the Garden Room, an apprehension that Frieda was rational enough not to take personally. Mr James was once again addressing his favoured guest: 'Great as is my pleasure, Fullerton, in seeing you here so long before you were expected, I do regret the loss of the little ceremony of awaiting you at the station. Rye Station has rather a grand little air about it, don't you think, as if it were forever expecting to welcome visiting royalty?'

'Ah, then I thoughtlessly forewent the brass band and the schoolgirls' choir that you doubtless had organised against my arrival. I can offer no excuse other than my haste to see you. My ship docked at Liverpool several hours early; so, sacrificing your convenience to my impatience, I took the first train from Charing Cross.'

The two men passed into the garden discussing the relative merits of the *Campania* and the *Lusitania*, and Frieda gathered her effects for her premature return to her lodgings. To get to the street she had to pass through the door set into the wall separating the garden from the desultory traffic of West Street. She had at first, in her ignorance, passed through the house to reach the street, but had gradually become conscious of the unspoken disapproval of Mrs Paddington, Mr James's housekeeper. The privilege of unlimited access to the house, Frieda was to discover, was jealously guarded, as part of an implication of distinctions and boundaries, differences subtle but strong between 'living in' servants and 'living out': to be the latter was to be a kind of tradesperson, like the coal merchant who stayed only long enough to deliver his wares and then return to his proper setting. Thus, as neither guest nor servant, Frieda moved within firmly if not explicitly drawn margins.

Before unlocking the street door, Frieda paused for a moment to take in, as she often did, the beauty of the garden, which now, in the mild November sunshine, was a blend of mellow tones and soft accents. Her eyes wandered from the varied hues of the vegetation to the rich brick of the house and the old wall enclosing the garden; and then came to rest on the prodigious guest, now arrested on the lawn in conversation with his host. In the sunshine his hair shone a deep black, and when he suddenly laughed, startlingly in the still space of the walled garden, the sound was as a declaration of youth. As she put her hand on the doorknob, she looked back; and she found that he had turned and was regarding her with an expression which she had experienced only once before, on the Underground in London. On that occasion it had compelled her to leave the train at the next station; it now made her open the door quickly and escape into the street.

Chapter Two
1906

Frieda did not have strong views on the question of heredity, which Mr Dodds had denounced to her as the futile fabrication of a godless age. But if the years with her mother in penurious Chelsea, after the inconvenient death of her inconvenient father, had taught her anything, it was that she was, after all, the daughter of the man who had, so her mother grimly assured her, 'done for' them, through 'not having what it takes'. In response to Frieda's queries as to the identity of this exacting force, her mother had replied tersely: 'Life.' As this ominously adumbrated entity gradually took shape for Frieda, revealing itself to be a matter of dark corridors and thin soup, of clothes 'done over' and furniture propped up, of importunate tradesmen and inadequate relations, she concluded that, like her paternal parent, she did not have what it takes. Like him, too, she turned, when she reached the age of discretion, her back upon the fray, and found refuge in Literature, indeed in the very volumes that, as her mother periodically mentioned in an aggrieved tone, were all that he had left his wife and daughter with which, in her phrase, to bless themselves. Whether for the benefit of this benediction or purely for the redoubt it offered, Frieda from an early age took possession of her meagre patrimony, and found there, if not the solution to the many quandaries attendant upon What it Takes, then at least a consolation for not having found it. Literature was at worst less expensive than Life, and at best more amusing.

It had seemed natural then, when the time came for her to 'do something for herself', through the demise of her mother and the consequent drying up of her little pension, to turn her thoughts and her hand to this field of endeavour, really the only one she had cultivated with any assiduity. But as her mother had long maintained, and as soon enough appeared from her own tentative enquiries, literature was not a gainful employment for any but its most successful practitioners. The problem with literature was that short of writing it oneself there wasn't very much one could *do* with it. Writing it herself was indeed an option to which she had addressed herself; but there, too, it transpired that writing was one thing, selling another, and to date she had not succeeded in persuading any buyer of the merit or the commercial viability – she was cynical enough to recognise the distinction – of her modest jottings.

In the midst of this perplexity, it was suggested by her Aunt Frederica, after whom Frieda had been named and who in consequence felt entitled to take an interest in her welfare, that Frieda should qualify herself as a typewriter. 'It's quite the coming thing, my dear,' she explained to her niece, over the cup of strong tea which she favoured, but of which she scrupulously took only one cup, in deference to what she called Frieda's reduced state. Her own state had been assured against reduction by the prudence of her late husband, a bank clerk of such seniority as allowed her, without gross violation of her punctilious regard for truth, to refer to him as *my late husband the banker*. 'It will take the place of hand-written communications forever. Somebody explained it all at my Women's Group. They have courses in it. It's called the mechanisation of the office.'

To Frieda, things in general seemed more in need of humanisation than mechanisation; but Aunt Frederica explained that the aim of the process was exactly for the machines to free human beings for more fulfilling labour and leisure. Frieda remained sceptical, having in childhood listened in wide-eyed dismay to her father's fulminations against the Industrial Revolution, leading her to wonder whether it was too late to reverse a process so self-evidently pernicious. Qualifying herself as a typewriter was clearly a capitulation; but Aunt Frederica's suggestion was at any rate less inconveniently radical than some others that she had ventured – she had once, before the death of Mrs Wroth, advocated emigration to Canada as the remedy to their ills. Besides, typewriting, Frieda imagined, would at worst mean some communion with words. She had the vaguest of notions of what the practice would entail: she thought it might resemble the automatic writing she had witnessed in a darkened parlour in Pimlico, at the behest of her friend Mabel, whose young man Charlie had been killed by the Boers at Mafeking and with whom she sought to communicate through the ministrations of Mrs Beddow.

Betaking herself with consciously heroic resolve to the Young Ladies' Academy of Typewriting, an institution chronically advertised on the back of omnibuses, she was assured that for a very small sum she could be trained to produce a certain number of words per minute, a total which the tone of her informant seemed to suggest was prodigious. The small sum, it transpired, was larger than Frieda had at her ready disposal, but Aunt Frederica, pleased that her advice had, 'for once', been heeded, offered to make a handsome contribution.

Even then Frieda would have demurred. Her design upon the future, though very indefinite, had never included a vision of 'taking dictation', as she now discovered her function would be designated: it seemed so, in its suggestions of mere receptiveness, to deprive her of any independent agency. She might be poor, but she was not abject. But her destiny declared itself, as it happened, during one of the evenings in Mrs Beddow's dingily over-decorated parlour. It transpired that Charlie was a difficult subject: despite Mrs Beddow's ministrations, hitherto so manifestly successful in awaking the departed to the perplexities of the living, the young man stubbornly refused to make known his whereabouts, intentions, or sentiments. Two sessions of Mrs Beddow's fierce concentration produced nothing but a scrawl which even the eminent spiritualist medium herself was at a loss to elucidate, unless one were to take for an interpretation her firm declaration, in a tone less philosophical than aggrieved, 'Well I daresay the dead have their reasons same as us.' She shook her head with such emphasis that her wig shed motes of dust in the lamplight.

Moved to some form of exculpation of her late sweetheart, and yet also put out at the young man's failure to respond to the supernatural soliciting on her behalf, Mabel explained, 'He never did have much to say for himself,' in a tone to which apology and resentment contributed in about equal measure.

For her part, Frieda could sympathise with the reticence of the young man. Whatever the nature of the hereafter – and on this she had no clear idea despite the most earnest efforts of Mr Dodds to explain the teachings of the Methodist Church on the subject – she could not conceive of it as a state in which one was liable to being summonsed, at the whim of one's earthly relics, to account for oneself to Mrs Beddow. Explanations and explications she took to be the stuff of earthly commerce, from which one was exempted at death. If death was not a state of silence, there was very little to be said for it.

One evening, after Charlie had once again declined to declare himself, Mrs Beddow announced that she could feel 'trem\-bulations' signalling, she informed her audience, an urgent need to communicate on the part of one of 'Them'. Taking up her pencil in a shaking hand and assuming the rapt expression of one in the throes of revelation, she submitted to the urgings of her supernatural correspondent. These were of a vigour unprecedented in the generally rather staid proceedings in the little parlour: her arm was slowly lifted in the air and then flung down on the table with a force suggesting some impatience on the part of her visitant, as if it had taken hold of the limb in error and wanted to divest itself of the encumbrance as promptly as possible. The pencil clattered to the table, but Mrs Beddow caught and clutched it with remarkable address, her face under its unrefulgent wig retaining an air of expectant but serene exaltation despite the indignities visited upon her extremities. Frieda, who was constitutionally uncomfortable in the presence of agitation of any kind, feared that Mrs Beddow's *sang froid* would provoke a manifestation of even greater vigour on the part of an agency that had already unmistakably indicated its irritation. But she had reckoned without the force of character that had established Mrs Beddow as the most celebrated medium in Pimlico and Chelsea: her mysterious communicant seemed to have been cowed by her imperturbable mien into tractability and even co-operation, to judge by the large, confident movements of her hand, which was unmistakably forming characters on the blank sheet in front of her – characters with which Mrs Beddow seemed to have as little to do as with the flickering of the flame on the table. The arm, recovered from its recent violent convulsion, moved only enough to allow the hand its free range of expression.

The seizure lasted a few minutes, during which Frieda, whose commitment to the proceedings was at best provisional, weighed up her scepticism against the evidence of her senses. There was of course no effect that a combination of legerdemain and bad light could not achieve; but Mrs Beddow had struck her as the dupe of her own enthusiasm rather than a practised charlatan, vaguely foolish rather than consciously duplicitous. It seemed to the young woman that if the medium had dissembled, she might have done so with more regard to mere aesthetics and with more of the appearance of prosperity than was evident in the threadbare setting and general discouraged air of the dusty old woman. The shabbiness of it all guaranteed its sincerity, if nothing else.

Mrs Beddow emerged from her trance with an air of modest achievement. 'That was an unusually powerful visitation,' she informed her audience. 'It has left me quite drained.' Her audience, though sympathetic, was naturally more interested in the legible evidence of the visitation than in its effects on the medium's constitution; even Frieda found herself hoping that Mrs Beddow was not so devastated as to be incapable of conveying to them the message from beyond. Once again, however, she found that she had underestimated the gumption of their hostess: pushing her wig into place with a determined air, she smoothed out the sheet of paper, and assumed a pair of reading goggles the sheer size of which seemed to confer authority upon the document scrutinised through its bulbous lenses.

It transpired that in straining to summon forth the reticent spirit of Charlie, Mrs Beddow had aroused the shade of Frieda's mother who, identifying herself rather grandly as Agatha (in life she had never been more than plain Aggie), made it known, through much misspelling (an effect, the medium reassured Frieda, of the vagaries of automatic writing rather than of educational regression in the next world), that she was concerned about her younger daughter's welfare, and recommended 'a corse in somthing usful'. Frieda, in spite of her sceptical view of the proceedings, recognised here, disconcertingly, the authentic note of maternal concern, peremptory and vague at the same time. *Something useful:* just so had her mother recommended, in Frieda's youth, 'something cheerful' to relieve the tedium of rainy days, without being able to name, when challenged, any definite activity rangeable under that hopeful rubric. In this instance, though her mother was no more inclined than usual to specificity of reference, Frieda had the advantage of knowing *something useful* that she might take a course in, and that would please Aunt Frederica at the same time. However one looked at it – and our young woman looked at it in a severely pragmatic light – Aunt Frederica pleased was more convenient as a visitor than Aunt Frederica displeased. She dared not, though, divulge to Aunt Frederica her visit to Mrs Beddow: as a member of the Society for Psychical Research, she turned up her nose at mediums like Mrs Beddow, whom she had once denounced as lower-middle class charlatans.

There remained the matter of Mr Dodds, whose views, expressed none the less freely for being unsolicited, proved surprisingly old-fashioned for one usually so respectful of the spirit of trade. Few things roused him to such dudgeon – indeed, dudgeon was not a frequent state with Mr Dodds – as references to Bonaparte's famous slight on the English character, though Mr Dodds was jealous not so much of the English character as of shopkeeping, which avocation, he had been heard to maintain, combined the ideal of service with the noble ambition to 'get on in life'.

Frieda had thus imagined that typewriting, as an indubitably commercial activity, would meet with Mr Dodds's approval; and to hear him say then, 'You don't want to get mixed up with that kind of thing,' was as unexpected as it was, strangely, piquant. She had not yet had the opportunity of demonstrating the limits of her deference to Mr Dodds's conception of things, and the prospect presented itself as possessed of certain distinct attractions. To prove to oneself as well as to any bystanders that, bereft of choice as one was, one was not yet reduced to *that* choice, seemed some compensation for the absence of a larger freedom. Besides, if Mr Dodds objected to typewriting there must be more to it than met the eye.

They were seated in the Kensington Gardens, on the penny chairs that Mr Dodds took when the weather seemed set fair and there was no danger of having to abandon the investment before it had yielded its full value. Her indebtedness to Mr Dodds for this amenity did not prevent Frieda from enquiring 'Why not?' in a tone in which the interrogative was less in evidence than the disputatious. She did not want to hear Mr Dodds's reasons: Mr Dodds's reasons would be reasons only for Mr Dodds.

But whatever there was of the contumacious in Frieda's reply did not perturb this equanimous gentleman. He laughed fondly, as he did when he felt he had caught Frieda in a moment of adorable female weakness of mind. 'My dear girl, you don't know what you're about. Those typewriting machines make an awful racket. You might as well take a job as a mill girl and have done. Besides, you don't want to be one of these... *independent* women who are forever bustling about taking omnibuses and things.'

Frieda wondered how she was expected to get around if not with the help of these useful vehicles; this, however, was extraneous to the question of typewriting, which now presented itself, not in the sober light of filial duty and compliance, but in the lurid glare of an independence of mind repugnant to Mr Dodds's notion of her destiny. She could not have said why, but she realised with a clarity lent sharpness and outline by the brilliance of the morning, that it was important not to accept, and to be seen not to accept, Mr Dodds's assessment of her possibilities.

'The thing is,' she accordingly said, 'that Mama specifically said to do something useful, and I can't think of anything more useful than typewriting.'

'A woman is at her most useful in pleasing her husband,' Mr Dodds complacently replied; then frowned and asked, 'When would this be that your mother told you this?'

'Oh, the other evening. At Mrs Beddow's.'

'Mrs Beddow?'

'Yes. You know, the spiritualist medium.' Frieda was being slightly disingenuous in pretending to think that Mr Dodds knew about Mrs Beddow: she had not told him about her visits to the medium.

'My dear child, you don't want to get mixed up in that lot. They've been proved to be impostors, one and all. Besides, spiritualism is explicitly reprehended in the Bible.'

'I don't see why,' Frieda obstinately objected. 'The Bible is full of spiritualists. What else is a prophet but a kind of medium? Or an angel if not a spirit guide?'

'In those days God chose to reveal Himself to man through human mediums. Today we rely on faith and prayer.'

'When you pray, does God reveal His will to you?'

Mr Dodds looked uncomfortable. As a rule he avoided conversations that were what he described as 'personal'. 'I believe He does, yes.'

Frieda found herself provoked to a spirit of contention by the image of Mr Dodds, no doubt in a kneeling position, his nose pointed heavenward, in communion with his deity. 'How? Does He speak to you?'

'Not as you are speaking to me now, but through – through a subtle influencing of my thoughts.'

'Do you mean telepathy?'

He looked shocked. 'God does not need telepathy. God is God.'

On this incontrovertible note Frieda abandoned the discussion, but resolved quietly not to be led in her decisions by Mr Dodds's strictures and certainties. If she were booked to make a mistake, let it be at any rate her own mistake.

Not so much in obedience to the dictates of her maternal shade, then, as in defiance of Mr Dodds's sense of propriety, Frieda betook herself to the Young Ladies' Academy. This turned out to be an alarmingly thorough institution, presided over by the formidable Miss Petherbridge, who proclaimed on the first day to her shivering gathering of prospective typewriters: 'We women have learnt to our cost that we live as second-class citizens in a Man's World. It is our duty to qualify ourselves to gain access to that world.'

Miss Petherbridge apparently intended a massive invasion of the citadel of male privilege, and her methods of instruction were in keeping with this militaristic ambition. They were, in a word, draconian, and there were times when Frieda wondered whether the price of admission to the Man's World was not higher than the privilege: from what she had seen of men, it seemed a moot point whether one would want admission to a domain so exclusively and invidiously populated by them. But she persevered, if only not to have to confess failure to Aunt Frederica: to brave the regime of Miss Petherbridge seemed less awful than to risk the displeasure of Aunt Frederica. She accordingly submitted to a system of instruction based, according to Miss Petherbridge, on the premise that thought, or what she called cognitive interference, impeded the transmission of information from the eye or ear to the fingers. 'You are an extension of the machine, and your function is to operate it,' she would enjoin her charges. 'Think of yourself as the medium between the impulse and its execution, and you will become an Efficient Typewriter.'

This designation, even when pronounced with all the dignity of Miss Petherbridge's most severe manner, failed to appeal to Frieda's imagination: to be an Efficient Typewriter was not the highest destiny she could conceive. When she mentioned this to Mabel, her friend, always more pragmatic than Frieda, rejoined, 'Well it depends doesn't it? – I mean depends on what it is you get to typewrite. It could be fascinating stuff. All sorts of things are being typewritten nowadays.' When pressed, Mabel was unable to produce an example of such material, and Frieda remained sceptical.

In the event, however, Mabel's faith in the possibilities of typewriting was vindicated. On the day that the Academy grandly called the Graduation, Miss Petherbridge summoned Frieda to her Office, an austere cubicle furnished with a desk and two chairs. Seated in the second chair was a portly, middle-aged man. His air of gravity was oddly contradicted – or emphasised, she couldn't have said which – by his green trousers and blue waistcoat with a yellow check, over which he wore a black coat. As she entered, he got to his feet – he had rather short legs, she noticed – and offered her his chair. She demurred, but he insisted: 'My habits are perambulatory rather than sedentary,' he explained.

Miss Petherbridge introduced the courteous gentleman as 'Mr Henry James, the novelist'.

'You will not have heard of me, my dear,' said the person so introduced. 'I am read by rather a small section of humanity.'

Frieda, who had been taught never to 'show off', wondered whether it would be showing off to claim membership of this select group, then decided it would not. 'Oh, I know,' she replied. '*Daisy Miller. The Portrait of a Lady. The Bostonians.*'

The author looked taken aback rather than gratified. 'You have not *read* them?' he enquired, as if admitting to this might expose her to some regrettable but necessary chastisement.

'Yes, I have,' she admitted, and then thought to retrieve the situation by adding, 'All but *The Bostonians*, that is.'

This seemed but meagre consolation to Mr James. 'Gratified as I am to find that my productions are more widely read than I had imagined, I must confess that in applying to Miss Petherbridge for a typewriter and amanuensis – that is, my dear, a person who writes to dictation, from the Latin *manus*, a hand, though in this case it would be a matter of typewriting, of course, rather than writing by hand – in applying here for a typewriter, as I say, I was hoping for a young person of absolutely no intellectual capacity whatsoever.'

Miss Petherbridge bridled slightly. 'I like to think, sir, that all my young women are above the average in intellectual capacity.'

'I respect your standards, ma'am, but I must confess that for my purposes the blanker the medium the better, in being the less likely to interfere with the process of composition. You see, my dear Miss Wort,' – he attempted to pace up and down while speaking, but the dimensions of the room enabled him only to rotate on the spot like a dog in a basket too small for it – 'you see, my dear, I would not be dictating to you a composition ready-formed and awaiting only to be delivered, like some… *pudding* got up in the kitchen and triumphantly produced in the dining room; I would be creating the composition as I speak, a process which naturally entails frequent and at times lengthy pauses between dictations.' He looked at her searchingly, as if to demonstrate the nature of one of these portentous pauses. He had keen grey eyes, all the more striking for his sunburnt complexion. She nodded, not thinking any response was called for, and he continued: 'Now I have in the past had an amanuensis, a young person perhaps of more abilities or at any rate… *aspirations* than could be satisfied by her position, who thought to improve her usefulness by, on occasion, during these pauses, while I was so to speak considering the various possibilities open to me,' he widened his eyes and lowered his voice dramatically, as if reporting an atrocity too heinous to be breathed out loud, '*proposing to me her own poor helplessly orphaned candidates for adoption.*'

Frieda, finding her eye fixed by the brilliant, slightly bulbous regard of the novelist, and not even quite sure of exactly what the departed amanuensis had been guilty, could think of nothing to say except, 'Oh, I would never do that.'

The great novelist seemed mollified by this reply. 'I would need you to be entirely clear on the... *non-participatory* nature of your function, other, of course, than rendering my spoken words in typewritten form as accurately as possible. You will be, as it were, the medium between my thoughts and the paper.'

'We can guarantee at least ninety percent accuracy in our graduates,' Miss Petherbridge contributed.

Mr James seemed but moderately reassured. 'My dear madam, I am sure that for communications of a strictly utilitarian nature, as between, say, a draper and a haberdasher, ninety percent accuracy is adequate; but a ten percent margin of error in transcribing my novels could mutilate my intentions and quite destroy my effects.'

Miss Petherbridge had some experience of punctilious clients. 'I am pleased to say that our graduates are also trained in the exacting business of reading proofs. Whatever minor errors may intrude in the typewriting process, are invariably spotted and eradicated at the proof-reading stage.'

There was a glint in the novelist's eye as he turned his weighty regard upon Frieda, a slight quivering of the mobile mouth, and she felt that he was extending to her an accord behind the angular back of Miss Petherbridge. 'Well, my dear,' he said solemnly, 'with ninety percent guaranteed and the other ten... *rodent* percent subject to eradication, I need not fear being misrepresented to my public by my typewriter. When would it suit you to commence your employment?'

Negotiating the steep cobbles of West Street, Frieda pondered the unexpected irruption of Mr James's friend into the routine of Lamb House. It was likely to be only a temporary phenomenon: quite apart from Mr Fullerton's own commitments elsewhere, Mr James would surely not allow the tenor of his days to be disrupted beyond this single exceptional occasion. Frieda had been with him for long enough – it had been more than a year now – to know that the claims of even his best friends were relative to the demands of his art. He made it known to them all that he observed, without exception, a working day from a quarter past ten to half past one, and was quite ruthless in declining to be disturbed between those hours. This Frieda respected as the mark of the true artist she believed Mr James to be; and yet there were times when she questioned to herself the human relevance of an art that had to cut itself off from life so decisively in order to flourish, like some exotic bloom that will flower only in darkness.

To her fancy, the stranger with the blue eyes and the ready laugh, making his way unannounced into the Garden Room, represented the quick impatience of life itself at the exclusions of such a concept of art. Most people presuming to enter the Garden Room did so apologetically, like a consciously secular tourist with a Baedeker trespassing in a cathedral; Mr Fullerton had entered like a conqueror taking possession of a subject city. Whatever there might have been of the over-presumptuous in his air had been mitigated by Mr James's own evident acquiescence to the usurpation. Indeed, his entry could, to a fanciful observer, have been seen as a liberation rather than an invasion. The fact, even, that his arrival had released Frieda to indulge in the beauty of the day contributed to her sense of his being a harbinger of freedom.

As she made her way into the High Street to the Warden Hotel, where she rented a room, Frieda wondered how she might best spend the unexpected freedom of the day. Rye, as her employer had warned her, offered no wealth of pastimes for a young woman. 'My situation in Rye,' he had taken pains to spell out, 'though congenial to a man of my age and habits, can promise few distractions for a young person, save those of rural charm and the bicycle.' When he discovered that Frieda could not afford the bicycle part of this combination, Mr James had generously contributed half of the cost of a new machine, and loaned her the other half, to be subtracted from her weekly wage of twenty-five shillings. Rural charm and the bicycle had proved indeed to be an advantage of Rye: if not quite so enthralling as to suppress the need for any other distraction, then at least enough to give her the relief she needed from sitting still at her typewriting for long days, and to give her, in the exertion of her body, relief from the ache of discontent which removal from Chelsea and Mr Dodds had not alleviated.

She could not have expressed in any simple formula the cause or even the nature of her discontent: it was as vague and yet as unignorable as a heavy mist. At times she discerned, through the mist, outlines of things other than the mist, things that could perhaps even dispel the mist if one could get closer to them, give them a name and recruit them to the cause; but they tended to disappear as she approached them, and thus far she had not succeeded in confronting them. Except today, in turning back as she was leaving Lamb House: the way Mr Fullerton had looked at her across the garden figured to her imagination as penetrating at last the mist.

The Warden Hotel was owned and directed by the redoubtable Mrs Tumble, reputedly the widow of the last of the smugglers for which the town had in its little heyday been celebrated. If so, one could only imagine that the late Mr Tumble had married her as a kind of perpetual alibi, a chronic guarantee of righteousness conveniently living on the premises: it was unthinkable that Mrs Tumble could consort or cohabit with any form of iniquity. Be that as it may, Mrs Tumble's fierce respectability had survived Mr Tumble, and had been enshrined in the institution in which Frieda had found refuge and such sustenance as was consistent with its terming itself a Temperance Hotel and Refreshment Bar; its billboard promised, or warned, as if against all kinds of excess, 'Terms Strictly Moderate.' Whatever contradictions it embodied between strictness and moderation, refreshment and temperance, the Warden Hotel did boast amongst its amenities a cycle store which, together with the moderated Terms, had decided Frieda in its favour. Mrs Tumble agreed to accept her after paying a visit to Lamb House to ascertain the propriety of arrangements there. Mr James had good-naturedly endured the visit, declaring it afterwards 'a priceless advantage to have one's premises licensed as decent by the most respectable authority in Rye. She is more valuable than the rat inspector.'

In her dim little garret room, whose sole recommendation was that from it one could see the railway station and smell the Fishmarket, Frieda prepared for her outing by changing out of the coat and skirt she habitually wore while taking dictation. This was a costume arrived at after consultation with Mr James's sister-in-law. Mrs William James, who had pronounced this the appropriate costume for the business of typewriting. For bicycling Frieda adopted the divided skirt recommended by Lady Harberton and the Rational Dress Society. Her Aunt Frederica, who prided herself on her membership of any number of progressive women's organisations, had passed on to her the opinions of Lady Harberton, and though not in general prone to radical notions, Frieda had thought this one sensible; and, upon her aunt offering also to finance this expenditure, had gratefully accepted. This represented one of her few open floutings of Mr James's strictures; he had enjoined her once, when observing one of Rye's emancipated women dressed in bloomers and jacket, 'Glory in your femininity, Miss Wroth.' Though by and large at peace with her femininity, Frieda could not see that it obliged her to risk bicycling in a skirt that could at any moment get caught in chain or wheel and send her sprawling in the dust.

By now accustomed to ignoring the ribald whistles of the potboy at the Oak Inn and the headshakings of Mr Pellett the grocer, she set off down the High Street towards Camber Sands.

This was a favourite outing of hers, especially in such weather as today offered: the wide moist green expanse of the Marsh, stretching on the one side to the clear blue of the sky, on the other to the more uncertain blue of the ocean, sounded in its unfettered expansiveness a note rare in tight little Rye, whose charm lay in the opposite direction, the direction altogether of huddled cottages, dark doorways and narrow passages.

As she cycled, Frieda wondered what Mr Dodds would make of her now, Mr Dodds who had presented her, after a rather one-sided discussion of what he called the new-fangled fashion for female self-locomotion, with an article written by one Dr Cantlie, cautioning the world that active sport in women could develop the shoulders rather than 'the breeding parts of the anatomy'. Mr Dodds, a reticent man in certain respects, had not asked Frieda what she thought of the article, and Frieda had felt free to persist in her acquisition of a bicycle, at whatever risk to the breeding parts of her anatomy, to which, she more and more felt, Mr Dodds had no present or future title.

She could not imagine, as she sped towards the sea, that any occupation so satisfying could be detrimental to either body or spirit; the fresh air, the smell of the sea mingling with the darker odours of the marsh, the bright yet mild sun, the ruined bulk of Camber Castle surrounded by peaceful sheep, the prim little town perched on its hill, suggested an order of nature and civilisation for once in equilibrium. Even the little steam tram bustling towards Camber, absurdly like a toy in the flat landscape, took its place in this order, fussing to and fro between Rye and Camber with no more august purpose than transporting golfers. The mist of discontent dissipated in the sunlight, leaving behind it a sense of present pleasure, only lightly perturbed by a consciousness of Mr Morton Fullerton as both contributing to the radiance of the afternoon and complicating it.

Arriving at Camber Sands, she left her bicycle against the Tram Station where the little steam locomotive, *Victoria*, was puffing as if recovering from its dash from Rye. Rounding the corner of the corrugated iron building, she was momentarily blinded by the sun, at this time of the year low in the south, and she almost collided with a figure emerging from the station. Looking up with a start, she found herself meeting the amused blue gaze of Mr Fullerton.

For a moment she thought that her imagination, fuelled by her wishes, was playing her tricks; but there was no mistaking the smile and then, the voice, as he said: 'Miss Wroth – what a coincidence!'

'Why yes indeed,' she managed to say, 'I – I thought you were with Mr James.'

'I am with Mr James, but Mr James is for the moment otherwise occupied.' He pointed to a low hedge behind which Mr James could be seen, apparently engrossed in studying non-existent cloud formations on the horizon. For a man apparently doing absolutely nothing in the middle of nowhere, Mr James seemed strangely unperturbed.

'What…?' Frieda began and then thought better of it. The slightly mischievous edge to Mr Fullerton's smile warned her not to press for an explanation; and yet to say nothing was in itself an acknowledgement of an awkwardness requiring elucidation.

Mr Fullerton at length undertook to enlighten her. 'I am waiting for Mr James,' he explained solemnly, 'and Mr James is waiting for Max.'

'Ah yes, Max,' she murmured. Having often taken walks with Mr James and his dachshund, she knew that Max's demands were as peremptory as they could be offensive to prim little Rye. Hence Mr James welcomed the larger arena of the Camber Sands for Max's ablutions, and had developed the art of seeming completely dissociated from the activities of the dog to which he was in the most literal of senses attached. This attitude had on occasion figured to Frieda as emblematic of Mr James's connection with reality.

The dog in question now appeared around the hedge, and seeing Frieda, proceeded to bark excitedly and tug at his leash. Mr James, having recovered his awareness of his surroundings, lifted his stick in greeting. Frieda bent down to acknowledge Max's effusions by scratching him behind his ears, relieved to have this distraction from Mr Fullerton's persistent regard.

'You shame us by your self-propelled mode of transport,' Mr James said. 'We were sadly lazy and availed ourselves of the power of steam. We intend, however, to make up for our delinquency by exerting ourselves all the more energetically in our walk on the Sands.'

'Please go ahead, then,' Frieda said. 'I have earned the right to loiter shamelessly. Max would get very impatient with me.'

She was pleased to have this excuse not to impose herself on the two men: Mr James would not have sent her home for the day only to welcome her as a third presence at a reunion that evidently was of some importance to him. The readiness with which he acquiesced to her suggestion seemed to confirm this, and the two men took their leave, Mr James courteously lifting his hat, Mr Fullerton lifting his left eyebrow while frankly surveying her cycling outfit. It was distinctly impertinent. Suddenly, startlingly, Max yapped, as if he too could recognise the impropriety of Mr Fullerton's demeanour.

Frieda deliberately took the direction opposite to that of the two men: she knew that in spite of Mr James's declared intention to take his exercise briskly, they were likely to move very slowly indeed. She had often enough experienced her employer's habit of pausing in his walk while he searched for a formulation, of fingering his watch chain meditatively, of prodding at an unoffending part of the landscape with his stick as if to dig out an elusive word: in short, of dawdling unconscionably. It was for this reason that Mr James liked company on his outings: he needed to talk as he walked. Indeed, Frieda had seen him, on one of his solitary walks, stop and address an imaginary interlocutor.

She privately believed that this was why Mr James had given up bicycling. She had, while he still kept up this form of exercise, been witness to any number of near-accidents as he stopped with no warning and with no regard to what was behind him, the more undistractedly to pursue his topic of conversation. In this manner he had once been collided with from behind by a butcher's boy on a delivery bicycle, who had vociferously and with no concession to Frieda's presence berated the 'silly bleeding toff, who should have eyes in his arse if he's going to up and stop like that in the middle of the bleeding way'. Mr James had offered to pay for the leg of lamb and pork kidney that had been spilled in the dust by the collision, and had not again taken to his bicycle.

Returning from her walk about forty minutes later, she

was thus amused but not surprised to find that the two men had indeed not progressed very far in their chosen direction. What was noteworthy was not their lack of progress, but the quality of attention Mr Fullerton was apparently still able to summon up. Most of Mr James's collocutors, while of course highly appreciative of his conversation, tended to start wilting perceptibly after half an hour or so, during which time they would have covered, topographically speaking, very little ground. Max, through his desultory attention, his evident impatience with the rate of progress of the little party, might indeed have figured forth the attitude of these others.

Mr Fullerton struck her, even at this distance, as different, in having retained his animation of manner and intensity of interest. This conclusion was intuitive rather than empirical; but Frieda had faith in her own perceptions – if one did not have that, what *did* one have? – and even across the expanse of Camber Sands she sensed in him a quality of engagement that set him apart from most other visitors as the rare racehorse is set apart from the common breed by little more than air and attitude. Nobody knew better than Frieda, she liked to think, what an effort of attention Mr James's lucubrations required; but it was one of her inconsistencies that she regarded with some contempt such of his interlocutors as showed boredom or impatience: those worthy of the compliment of Mr James's company were those who appreciated what they were getting in return for their attention. And Mr Fullerton clearly appreciated to the hilt.

Chapter Four
9th November 1907

Mr James usually started dictating at a quarter past ten in the morning, but Frieda liked to come in earlier, at about nine o'clock; he often, having revised a previous day's dictation in the evening, left her the corrected typescript, the emendations written between the lines – she left large spaces for the purpose – as if some pernickety and very literate ghost had in the course of the night presumed to improve upon the Master's labours. This was a time she cherished, not only for the luxury of having the beautiful room to herself with the windows open (Mr James kept the windows shut on all but the warmest days), but for the pleasure of seeing her own mechanical activity reshape the scribbled-over typescript into a clean 'final' copy.

On the morning after her outing to Camber Sands she arrived at her usual time and looked on her typing table for the corrected pages that Mr James as a rule left there for her, even when he had overnight guests. The late night, his 'blessed time of stillness and solitude', was valued exactly for the uninterrupted labour that it made possible. This morning, however, there was nothing, suggesting that Mr Fullerton had occupied more of this cherished time than Mr James normally permitted to his guests. They would have had tea at the golf club – the sole purpose for which Mr James belonged to this institution – and a late dinner, followed, no doubt, by one of the meandering but intense conversations in which Mr James delighted.

Not having corrections to type, Frieda took out a little pile of typescript that she kept in her private drawer: the modest and anxiously secreted evidence of her own ventures into the realm of fiction. If her collaboration with Mr James had not been as directly beneficial as she had hoped, it had yet not discouraged her from her own attempts; indeed, in some respects, the effort of hauling into place the massive building blocks of Mr James's spacious and elaborate structures had reawoken in her a furtive nostalgia for her own little ill-built habitation of brick and mortar. It might not impress, but it was a shelter, or at worst a sign of human industry, in what would otherwise have been a somewhat featureless landscape.

She knew that she was doomed to Mr James's influence, that she could as little escape him in her own writing as she could disregard his looming presence. She intended her story, though, to be in its modest way a corrective to Mr James's methods and assumptions, perhaps even a gentle parody of a style that she knew by now as intimately almost as Mr James himself – indeed, in a sense perhaps more fully, in that to him his style was instinctive, unpremeditated, whereas to her it remained an element knowable all the more sharply for being perceived from the outside. To him his style was like oxygen, necessary but unnoticed, whereas to her it was like an exotic perfume, obtrusive and available to analysis and emulation.

It had ever been his habit, of a morning, to take the air before indulging in such matutinal sustenance as his undemanding system, understood in a physical as well as a philosophical sense, required — if even that were not too grossly imperative a designation for the modest promptings of a constitution that seemed never to want as much for itself as Mrs Blythe was inclined to bestow upon it. It was with him a debatable point whether he nourished himself as a token of courtesy to a system that had served him, by and large faithfully, for more than sixty years, or in deference to the more articulate admonitions of Mrs Blythe, who had with such implacable benevolence presided over the last decade of his uneventful existence. In this relation, as in others, Spencer had learnt that the importunities of kindness were best dealt with in a spirit of compliance, any ill-considered deprecation of solicitude in the sacred name of independence tending to arouse such further demonstrations of concern as quite to constitute an inconvenience.

As she surveyed once more the scanty foundation that was all she had so far been able to put into place, the door of the Garden Room opened, and Mr Fullerton was before her. In the early morning light from the garden, his dark hair and moustache positively shone with health and vigour. Frieda knew, from her visits to Mr Dodds's apothecary shop, that there were more bottled and jarred aids to brilliance than one would have thought marketable to a sex in general so drab; but Mr Fullerton's lustre was all his own, needing no aid from bottle or jar. To this the clarity of his eyes and the whiteness of his teeth testified: his lustre was all of a piece with flawless vitality.

Mr Fullerton did not seem surprised to see her. 'Ah, the modern Penelope,' he exclaimed, with an ease of utterance that Frieda recognised as *aplomb*. She had read about aplomb, naturally, but had never, in her sojourn in the heart of Chelsea, nor even in the so much more socially adept circle surrounding Mr James, met with it so much as a producible and identifiable entity. Mr Fullerton had aplomb as… as Mr Dodds had a large nose, unarguably and unmistakably.

All this she took in almost subliminally, while her conscious mind was occupied in critically examining his choice of image. 'My loom clatters more than Penelope's, I should think. And I am not waiting for an Odysseus.' This last comment surprised her by its audacity, and she wondered if it could be reckoned improper. She had been brought up with a strong sense of what was regarded as proper – by 'people' in general and her mother in particular – and bandying classical references with young men had not featured in that list of permissible liberties. But nor, she comforted herself, had it ever been specifically proscribed.

If there was anything too familiar in her reply, Mr Fullerton was not discomfited by it. He laughed loudly. 'That is all to the good,' he rejoined. 'Odysseus was a rogue and a swindler.'

Not knowing how to pursue this discussion, Frieda resorted to domesticities. 'I hope you had a good breakfast.' Then she blushed, realising that the enquiry implied a proprietary relation to his comfort that might be seen as a presumption.

Mr Fullerton, though, answered as if she had every right

to the question. 'Oh excellent, thank you. And expertly, if rather disconcertingly, served by the silent Burgess Noakes.'

'Why disconcertingly?'

'I find very silent people distinctly unnerving. Don't you find yourself suspecting that they're passing mute judgement on you?'

'Not Burgess. He is silent with everybody except with George Gammon. To him he talks constantly.'

'Is George Gammon the gardener who looks like Ezekiel or Malachi?'

'I should have said like Mr Bernard Shaw.'

'The same man clearly. And what do they talk about?'

'It is more than I would risk, eavesdropping on George Gammon and Burgess Noakes. They probably discuss the unfathomable imbecility of people who spend their time writing books.'

'You sound almost as if you agreed with them.'

'Me? Oh no, I have the greatest admiration for people who write books. I only meant…' She considered for a moment what she had meant. 'I mean that for more practical people it must seem like a fruitless expenditure of time.'

Mr Fullerton was walking up and down in the Garden Room, but not like Mr James, ruminatively; more, she thought, like a fox she had once seen, captured by some boys on a farm on the Marsh, pacing as if it had some obscure purpose frustrated but not quenched by the cage. His manner, though, had nothing of the cage about it; it was as free as a skylark in flight. 'Ah, but when have we ever cared for practical people?' he demanded from her.

Frieda examined the question and found that it did not admit of an answer. 'You talk as if… as if we have known each other for ever.'

'That's because I *feel* as if we have known each other for ever. Don't you?'

Frieda thought it permissible to say: 'Not for ever, no. But for longer than yesterday.'

He looked at her, it was difficult to tell whether with amusement or exasperation. 'Well, if you want to be literal about it! But I thought that was exactly what we agreed we were not.'

Frieda had no recollection of any such agreement, but

to say so would be really to prove herself guilty of literal-mindedness; and before she could reply, he had continued, though with a change of subject so abrupt that it represented a new start rather than a continuation.

'And you?'

'I?'

'I mean do you also write books?'

'Oh, books, no.'

'But you do write.'

'Yes. That is, I try.'

'That is what I imagined.'

'That I try?'

'Well, that you write. I cannot imagine that anybody who is not herself an actual or prospective writer would willingly exile herself to a little village like Rye to take dictation from a novelist as little sensational as Mr James. Besides, there is something in the way you observe the world around you that suggests you are taking notes for a novel.'

Frieda wondered. 'How do I observe the world?'

'It's difficult to describe, but I noticed it straight off, the moment I came into this room yesterday. The way you looked at me told me that you were writing me up for your novel, the insolent stranger who bursts into the artist's retreat, the emissary of the vulgar world shattering the concentration of the great novelist and his devoted assistant. You had me cast as some minor but irritating personage, a brush salesman or a pedlar of religious tracts.'

There was an ironical edge to Mr Fullerton's animation that suggested that this was not in fact a strictly veracious account of his impression of Frieda's impression; but taking her pitch from him, Frieda, too, pretended. 'Say, rather, a disgraced nephew returning home after a foray to foreign parts, come home to his fond uncle, having been disowned by his parents.'

Mr Fullerton laughed, with his perfect teeth. 'Ah, I prefer your novel to my own! It at least provides for remorse and reform on the part of the disreputable nephew.' Then he composed his features, and Frieda wondered whether he was most beautiful when he was laughing or when he was serious. 'But you see, I am right: you are here because you are a writer. There can be no other reason for a young woman like you to hide away in Rye.'

Frieda wanted to ask what he meant by a young woman like her, but contented herself with remarking, 'You must find Rye very quiet after Paris.'

If he found her comment a digression he adjusted to it as easily as he seemed to adjust to everything else. He looked around him at the room serenely admitting the early morning light, as if there and then fixing the exact degree of quietness he could tolerate. 'That is like saying butterflies are smaller than elephants; yes, of course they are, but one wouldn't want them any larger.'

Frieda was not sure that this analogy was valid, but she was starting to recognise that the force of Mr Fullerton's arguments lay in their defiance of gravity rather than in any more weighty virtues. 'One might not want Rye larger and yet not want to spend much time here.'

He stopped his pacing and addressed his reply to her listening face. 'Ah, there you are both right and wrong. I want to spend more time in Rye; and yet it can be proved against me that in the almost twenty years I have known Mr James, and in the ten years he has lived here, this is my first visit. But now that I am here, I want to stay for ever.'

'And will you?' Frieda asked with a freedom that evoked, again, one of Mr Fullerton's smiles.

'Stay for ever? My dear woman, you talk as if we were children before the Fall. *The Times* is a hard taskmaster and recalls me to Paris today.'

'Today?' Frieda was conscious of a certain drop of spirits, which she realised too late must have been all too evident from her tone.

Mr Fullerton adapted his tone to hers. 'Alas, yes. You see, I am taking in Rye on my way back from a visit to the fatherland. I am fresh from America. To that extent your fantasy of the prodigal nephew was well founded.'

'You don't sound American.' It was one of the strange effects Mr Fullerton had on her, that she ventured remarks that formerly she would have regarded as impertinent as addressed to a stranger of the opposite sex.

'That is because I am such a bad American. I came to

London twenty years ago and have not been back except for the merest family visits.'

'Where does your family live?'

'New England, mostly.'

'Like Mr James's.'

'Yes, like Mr James's, and like Mr James I have found the Old World more congenial than the new. America will be tolerable in another four hundred years' time, if it hasn't devoured itself by then, having ingested the rest of the world first.' He turned to her as if he had something very much to the point to say. 'But let's not talk about America.'

He made it sound like an invitation to talk about some alternative, infinitely interesting topic. 'What should we talk about?' she enquired.

He lifted one eyebrow as he had done the day before in regarding her cycling outfit. 'Well,' he said contemplatively, 'we could, for instance, consider the fact that my very good friend Mr James will at any moment have finished his breakfast, and will then demand, first, my undivided attention for leave-taking, and then yours for dictation This consideration might then lead us into a discussion of the fact that in the natural course of things you and I are unlikely ever again to have an opportunity to speak to each other in this way.'

His slightly facetious manner had modulated into seriousness, and he mentioned this last prospect gravely. as if contemplating a personal misfortune of some import. He paused, as if for a reply, but Frieda could not bring herself to say anything; she merely nodded, watching him fixedly: she could not believe that he could be representing such a dreadful prospect without the alleviation of an alternative.

In this she was proved right by his saying suddenly, as if beset by inspiration: 'Unless – unless…'; and then, with uncharacteristic diffidence, he faltered.

'Unless –?' Frieda prompted.

'Well, unless we simply arranged it otherwise.'

'How would we do that?' She appealed to him as if on a practical matter.

'The thing is,' he said slowly, 'that since tomorrow is Sunday, I could, at a venture, delay my departure to France by a day. The further thing is, however, that if I stay here my good friend will naturally expect me to spend the time with him.' He looked at her assessingly. 'Are you totally and completely averse to a certain degree of duplicity?'

Frieda had on occasion asked herself this question, but never in as unhypothetical a form as this. Having now to deal with it as a direct enquiry likely to have practical consequences, she realised that she did not know the answer. To answer in the affirmative would, she recognised, terminate without further ado Mr Fullerton's projected arrangement; to answer in the negative, on the other hand, need not commit her to any particular course of action. Besides, Mr Fullerton had that in his manner that made any equivocation seem callow, an implication that people of the world, as *he* had experienced the world, knew their own minds and acted accordingly. Under these various compulsions and persuasions, she could be prompt. 'No.'

If he was taken aback by her forthrightness, he did not show it. 'Very good,' he said. 'Excellent. What I would suggest is that I depart, as arranged and discussed with my host, for Folkestone this morning. However, once there, I shall not take the first sailing as envisaged, but wait for you to join me either today or tomorrow, as your schedule allows.'

Even Frieda's newfound audacity retreated before this proposal, presented as if it were the most natural thing on earth. But, strangely, instead of withdrawing into the stronghold of established custom, she advanced to survey the field. 'To go to Paris?' she enquired, as if she took trips to Paris every week.

Upon this, he laughed again. 'Upon my word, your imagination outstrips mine. Yes, to go to Paris too, if that is what you want.' Then he checked himself. 'Only… you won't be half as useful to me in Paris just at present as right here.'

Frieda could not imagine how she could be useful to this brilliant man anywhere, but before she could apply for elucidation, he held up a restraining hand. 'I'll explain all that in Folkestone. For the present, we run the risk of being interrupted at any moment. Can you contrive to be in Folkestone tonight?'

At this, at last, some forlorn force of resistance mustered itself, as if in allegiance to the flag after the stronghold has been surrendered. 'Tonight would be difficult. Mr James often works late on a Saturday.'

'Ah yes, we must not disturb Mr James's routine.' It was impossible to tell, either from his tone or his expression, whether Mr Fullerton was being ironical; so Frieda simply, and to her mind rather stupidly, sat staring at her typewriter. But as he also seemed resigned to just waiting, Frieda realised that she was expected to take the initiative. This was something that she was so little used to taking that she had first to take a deep breath. 'But I am free all of tomorrow.'

It seemed to Frieda that this simple declaration was the single most audacious utterance she had ever risked; but Mr Fullerton greeted it with no expression of surprise, simply stroked his moustache in a gesture that she was coming to recognise as a sign of reflection. Before his rumination could issue in speech, however, there was the sound of heavy feet on the steps up to the Garden Room. There were seven steps – Frieda had often counted them – and there would have been time for a brief rejoinder; but Mr Fullerton just stood, stroking his moustache and waiting for Mr James to appear, as he promptly did, bright of waistcoat and cravat, to accompany his guest to the station.

Chapter Five
9th November 1907

'*Well, comma, there had played before her the vision of a...*'
    Refuge? Revelation?
'*...of a ledge of safety in face of a rising tide; semi-colon; but this...*'
    Was doomed to prove an illusion? Could not but disappoint her?
'*...deepened quickly to a sense more...*'
    Profound? Agitated?
'*...a sense more... forlorn, comma, the cold swish of waters already up to her...*'
    Knees? Chest?
'*...waist and that would soon be up to her...*'
    Chin.
'*...chin. Full stop.*'

Upon his return from the station, Mr James, though visibly distracted, dictated more briskly, or rather, less interruptedly than usual. He was now some hundred pages into a story that he had at the outset declared 'a twenty-pager', and he was evidently impatient to reach the end. It was clear to Frieda that the heroine was facing disappointment and disillusion: she could at best salvage from the ruins of her hopes some rags and scraps of dignity with which to bandage her wounded self-regard, or discover perhaps some centre of self independently of what others found it convenient to do with her. Though frequently failing to anticipate Mr James's exact choice of phrase, she could by now predict his larger designs with some accuracy.
    '*It came really but from the air of her friend, comma, from the perfect benevolence and high unconsciousness with which he kept his posture – dash – as if to show he could patronise her from below*

upward quite as well as from above down. Full stop.'

When Mr James was in full spate Frieda had to race to keep up, and it was a while before she realised that he had stopped in front of her desk and was regarding her as if having something particular to say to her.

'Miss Wroth, I make so bold as to wonder, since we lost some hours yesterday, whether it would conceivably suit you to take dictation tonight after dinner – which meal I would of course be honoured if you would take with me?'

This request was by no means unprecedented: Mr James liked sometimes to dictate after dinner, and against a proportionate relief from attendance the following morning, she would stay for that meal and retreat afterwards with him to the Garden Room for another hour or two of work.

She did not mind the relatively late hour; indeed, there was something companionable about the fitfully illuminated gloom of the Garden Room, a quality in the lamplight – Mr James abhorred electric light – that consorted better with her notion of artistic creation than the relatively harsh light that at times penetrated the place during the day.

What she did mind, when there were other guests for dinner, was the ill-concealed surprise of some of these at finding themselves sharing the board with somebody who was, so she believed they believed, paid to be there. It was, she could see them thinking, like going to a restaurant and being joined at table by the cook. Others, however, were charming; but what, in such a situation, could charm *be* but effort made visible, the effort not to remember what the effort made it impossible to forget? She was the typewriter, *tout court*, and persons of quality did not as a rule dine with their typewriters.

At other times she was alone with Mr James for the meal, which had the advantage of not making her feel like a jumped-up servant; but this dinner tête-à-tête, interrupted only by the silent entrances and exits of the taciturn Burgess Noakes, had hardships of its own.

Mr James had, some years earlier, embarked on a regime of Fletcherising his food, which entailed the unrelenting mastication of every mouthful until, apparently, an automatic swallowing reflex mercifully intervened to terminate the process.

Frieda had met the originator of the method, an American named Horace Fletcher (known familiarly but respectfully to his disciples as the Great Masticator), when he had called at Lamb House, dressed in a blindingly white suit, white hat and white boots, and she had wondered at the lapses of genius whereby a man like Mr James could be taken in by a man like Mr Fletcher. She could only think that, much as Mr James professed to deplore the spirit of the age, he had succumbed to the universal promise of mechanisation to regulate everything, even, apparently, the digestive processes.

That, however, was Mr James's affair. What concerned Frieda more nearly was the prolongation of any meal taken with him: the simplest repast could take more than an hour to be Fletcherised. When there was 'strange' company, that is, any guest not intimately known to Mr James, he abandoned the practice in the interests of conversation. Faced with the choice between Fletcherising in silence and speaking to his guests, courtesy and loquacity combined against Fletcher. But when there were only the two of them, Mr James Fletcherised sturdily, leaving Frieda to her own thoughts and meditations.

Given that Frieda had, as she recalled with a pang, turned down Mr Fullerton's proposal to provide for just such an eventuality as this, she should in all consistency have felt vindicated by Mr James's request. But she did not. What she mainly felt was resentment at the assumption, for all that it posed as a question, that she would be available on a Saturday evening to take dictation, an assumption that so transparently denied her a life of her own. Young women in Paris, she felt sure, did not spend their Saturday evenings taking dictation. So to plead, with all appearance of regret, 'a prior dinner engagement', was quite as liberating as if it had been true.

Mr James was too civilised a man to express the curiosity or surprise that he clearly felt; he said only, 'I am pleased that quiet little Rye is not wholly bereft of social intercourse for a young person.' He was on the point of resuming his dictation, but seemed to reconsider and said, 'I would not want to seem persistent, but if by any chance you would be willing to come in for a few hours tomorrow, upon the terms of course agreed with Miss Petherbridge for Sunday work, that would be uncommonly useful to me.'

Frieda felt herself blushing, not so much at the need to compound her lie, as at the recognition of the possibility she was providing for in doing so.

'I am most sincerely sorry,' she nevertheless said, 'to seem so unhelpful, but I happen to have arranged to spend tomorrow with a friend, whom I should not want to disappoint.'

Mr James bowed his assent. 'Of course I would not think of interfering with your social arrangements, and I am grateful to you for your candour. Would you remind me where I was...?'

'Of course: ...*he could patronise her from below upward quite as well as from above down.*'

'Ah yes,' and he resumed his pacing. As if revitalised by the interruption, or perhaps under a sense of urgency sharpened by her refusals, he now dictated more briskly: '*And as she took it all in, comma, as it spread to a flood, comma, with the great lumps and masses of truth it was floating, comma, she knew... she knew inevitable... inevitable...*'

Humiliation? Defeat?

'*...inevitable submission, comma, not to say... not to say...*'

Humiliation? Defeat?

There was a light knock at the door of the Garden Room. Mr James frowned and turned round to glower at the door, his hands behind his back, as if to ward off an attacker with his frown. His belligerent stance relaxed when the door was opened by the diminutive Burgess Noakes.

'Beg your pardon, sir, but I thought it might be urgent, sir.' He held out a telegram. Mr James made as if to take it, but Noakes withheld it. 'For Miss Wroth, sir.' The little butler handed Frieda the insubstantial envelope; she could feel herself blush as she took it. Her instinct was to hide it, but Mr James said, 'As Burgess Noakes says, it may be urgent, my dear. Do feel at liberty to open it,' and, considerate as always, he turned his back to her.

Flustered, Frieda reached for the paper knife in her drawer and slit open the envelope. She fully expected it to contain a cancellation of the appointment, in any case so inconclusive, which she was now conscious of anticipating with some anxiety. When at last the telegram was open, however, resting on the Remington, what it said was: *Trust our arrangement holds good.*

Burlington Hotel, eleven. Come. It was not signed.

Frieda carefully folded the slip of paper and put it into her drawer, with her little pile of typescript. It was literally the first telegram she had ever received, and it catapulted her all at once into a world of intrigue and assignation. 'Thank you, Mr James,' she said. 'I am ready to take dictation. *She knew inevitable submission, not to say…*'

'Ah yes, thank you, Miss Wroth… *not to say submersion, comma, as she had never known it in her life; semi-colon; going down and down before it, comma, not even putting out her hands to resist or cling by the way, comma, only reading into the young man's very face an immense…*'

Indifference? Relief? Opportunity?

'…*fatality, comma, and for all his bright nobleness, comma, his absence of rancour or of protesting pride, comma, the great grey blankness of her… of her…*'

Doom.

'…*doom. Full stop.*'

Chapter Six
9th November 1907

Frieda had not passed twenty-three years in even as unadventurous a milieu as Chelsea without gathering that a young woman dining alone with a gentleman in an hotel thereby rendered herself vulnerable to comment and to misconstruction of the nature of the occasion. It was part of her satisfaction at the prospect of the outing that she felt she could afford to disregard such comment and construction; it was her good fortune as much as it was her doom to be alone in the world, and to have only herself to consider. She knew of course, that such flagrant publicity was taken to signal privacies even more flagrant, and had read enough even to form a theoretical notion of what such privacies might entail. But such notions remained, with her, in the realms of the imagination, the creative imagination of literature or the malicious imagination of anonymous onlookers: the thought of herself actually embroiled in a relation of which such things could be said, lacked reality to her.

And yet, Frieda's own imagination could play her tricks, and fill out the meagre details of quotidian reality with a potential unacknowledged by her conscious self. Getting dressed in her little room on the Sunday morning, she wavered briefly between the more serviceable of her petticoats, which would be more appropriate to a train journey, and the prettier one. She chose the prettier one without examining her motives too closely. Obeying the same obscure impulse, she selected the more jaunty of her two hats, the one that Mr Dodds had pronounced, his simulated jocularity failing to hide his real dismay, 'a bit of a shiner, what?' Peering into the little mirror that Mrs Tumble, in a grudging concession to necessity, had provided, she became aware of her mother's portrait next to her on the dressing-table. Finding the good woman's earnest regard too searching for the occasion, she turned the portrait round to face the wall. As, a few minutes later, she closed her bedroom door, the shutting of the flimsy leaf assumed, to her whimsy, an import like to the closing of a chapter. As she made her way in the brilliant morning light down steep little Conduit Hill to the station, the bells of the Parish Church of St Mary the Virgin started pealing, as if the more emphatically to terminate the chapter.

The train, on a Sunday, was inordinately slow. Waiting on Ashford station for a connection to Folkestone, Frieda wondered at the prosaic nature of her indiscretion, as she now frankly thought of her assignation with Mr Fullerton. Were even chapters of adventure in the end matters of public transport, of train timetables and waiting rooms? The rich, no doubt, with their carriages and motor cars, could take their indiscretions as they took everything else, at their ease and in their own time. What was it, the alleged immorality of the upper classes, but a matter simply of better transport arrangements?

The train, however, eventually arrived, and deposited Frieda at Folkestone station some twenty minutes before the time named by Mr Fullerton. Here she enquired for the Burlington Hotel from a porter who, recognising in her luggageless state an absence of interest for himself, gave her only the most perfunctory of information: 'On the Leas,' was all the help he was prepared to offer, unless one were to take the jerk of his chin leftward as constituting a precise direction.

Relenting, possibly, at Frieda's evident failure to benefit by his information, the porter gave her a second chance. 'You wouldn't be wanting a cab?' His tone was nicely pitched between the respectful and the impudent.

'Not if it's walking distance?' Frieda replied, grateful to be able to make the enquiry in this oblique fashion.

The man did not try to hide his contempt for such an unprofitable means of locomotion. 'Oh, it's walking distance all right,' he said, 'if that's yer way o' gettin' about.'

Frieda found herself wanting to explain that on such a beautiful day as it was… but then bethought herself: there was really no need to ask anybody's permission to walk. It had been one of her mother's cherished tenets that a young woman need not be ashamed of walking anywhere, but Frieda suspected that her mother, in extending such absolute licence, had not foreseen the Burlington Hotel and Mr Fullerton. Her outing to Folkestone was not in any way rangeable under her mother's categories of good behaviour; indeed, it was so egregious as not to have figured even under the categories of the bad.

The Burlington Hotel turned out to be, with only one further enquiry, not difficult to find. It was also, mercifully, large enough and busy enough and public enough, bustling with travellers to and from the Continent, to accommodate without remark one unaccompanied young woman. Here, at last, in the turbulent air of people coming and going, of destinations and purposes extending beyond the horizon, there was the fizz of experience in the making, the flavour of life being lived at such intensity that it had to travel to do so.

Entering the foyer, Frieda suffered a pang of doubt. Hitherto she had simply acted on Mr Fullerton's proposal without committing herself to a final interpretation of his motives. It was only now, faced with the prospect of going up to the superior young woman in the glass cage and declaring her mission, that her intention assumed the character of a definite event. In declaring, 'I am here for Mr Morton Fullerton,' Frieda would be placing herself in unambiguous relation to that event and that personage. She thus felt some relief, amongst a welter of other emotions, to see Mr Fullerton come towards her – he had been reading a paper in one of the deep armchairs that gave the foyer its air of a well-furnished railway waiting room – and extend a hand with an air of such glad surprise as made Frieda think for a moment that she was party to an entirely fortuitous meeting between old acquaintances.

'Ah, Miss Wroth,' he almost exclaimed, such was the exuberance of his greeting, 'well met indeed!'

There was very little for Frieda to say to this; it seemed amongst the range of possibilities of his tone that he might ask her what she was doing in Folkestone and where she was going. She imagined that people practised in such arts could carry off without blushing the feat of seeming at once surprised and pleased at a prearranged meeting, and feared that she managed only to appear neither surprised nor pleased.

However, whatever awkwardness there was in the meeting was easily absorbed in his easy manner, in exclamations upon the beauty of the day, and in a natural enough invitation to walk outside and admire the view of the Channel. Outside, in the hotel garden, from the broad grassy promenade looking across the Channel, the view was indeed splendid enough to cover over any temporary embarrassment. In any case, Mr Fullerton had the gift of dispelling discomfiture by being unaware of it; he took for granted in her, as he so easily took for granted in himself, nothing more compromising than pleasure in the prospect before them.

'We are fortunate,' he informed her. 'It is not always possible to see the coast of France as clearly as this.' And he pointed to the line of white cliffs visible across the expanse of the Channel. 'But you will be used to it, from your snug little vantage point in Rye.'

His manner was so engaging and yet so natural that entering into conversation was as effortless as relaxing into a favourite armchair with a good book.

'Well, it still always gives me pleasure. And yet, it's more the idea, isn't it, of being able to see France, than the actual sight?' she asked. 'I mean to look at it is much less exciting than the thought of something so totally different being so close to us.'

He seemed more interested in this than she had thought likely. 'Do you find that exciting or daunting?'

Frieda considered. She was not used to articulating her reflections on the coastline of France. 'Well, it's both, isn't it? It's exciting because it's daunting and it's daunting because it's exciting.'

Whatever there was of the trite in her reply seemed nevertheless to engage his interest. 'Is that,' he asked, 'because of the possibility of invasion?'

Some instinct warned her not to seem to take his questions seriously. 'I'm not sure that I would find the prospect of invasion exciting,' she laughed.

He was not, however, to be deterred by her levity. 'Then it must be because of the promise it offers of flight, departure, exile…?' And he pointed again at the symbolic coastline. They had strolled some distance from the entrance to the hotel and were now part of the promenading Sunday morning crowd.

'Oh, I don't think of myself as a potential exile. But it's true that there is in the idea of France... well, something of opportunity as well as danger.'

'But opportunity for what?' He asked this as if she could enlighten him as to opportunities he might, in his several years in France, have missed.

'Oh, I don't know... but I sometimes think that somewhere different, somewhere really foreign, not like coming to Rye from London, might give one a stronger sense of... of who and what one really is. Here it's all so mixed up with who one knows and what one does and where one lives.' She paused, conscious of making her own situation sound altogether grander and more inhabited than it was; and then, emboldened by his air of quiet attention, ventured a more personal note. 'Isn't that why you have left America for Paris?'

He nodded. 'Indeed it is, one of the reasons, at least. It is part of the appeal of Paris, that one discovers, as you say, who and what one really is – assuming that one wants to know, of course,' he added, with brief levity, as a way, she thought, of redirecting the conversation. He seemed more interested in her than in himself, which was, for a man, rare to the point of eccentricity. 'But have you really never been to France?'

She shook her head. 'All I know of it is what I've read.'

'Oh, you mustn't believe everything you read!'

'Well, there seems to be a general implication that over there life is more vivid, more clearly outlined than here.'

She pointed at Cap Gris Nez as if it embodied in itself this clarity of delineation, and he also paused and obediently peered across the watery divide. He seemed to understand what she meant, as he understood everything else she meant. When at length he spoke, however, it was to start quite a new idea. 'One day,' he said, 'somebody will build a tunnel under the Channel, and we'll whisk to and fro as easily as between London and Manchester.'

She smiled at his fancy. 'That somebody will have to be American, I imagine. I don't think either the English or the French would be comfortable with such unhindered access. Besides, what would be the point of going to Paris if it were just at the other end of the Charing Cross line? If I went to Paris, I wouldn't want to get there through a tunnel.'

He shrugged. 'Perhaps you're right. The English have lived for so long with the fear of invasion that they can't accept the principle of free access.'

'And can you?'

'Accept the principle of free access? Oh yes, with ease. But then I'm an American living in Paris; I've sacrificed my national identity to a vague ideal of freedom.'

'That seems to me splendid.'

'Sacrificing…?'

'That too, but not only that. It makes a difference that it is in Paris.'

He laughed. 'Oh, I wouldn't sacrifice my national identity to…' – he looked around him – '…to East Grinstead or to Tonbridge Wells.'

They had reached the end of the splendid promenade. There were fewer people here, and in the breezy sunshine, with the glitter of the Channel all before them, they seemed very far away from East Grinstead or from Tonbridge Wells – or from Rye, Frieda recognised with a thrill.

'I could have been typewriting,' she said, to herself as much as to him.

He did not reply, only smiled at her in a manner at once interrogative and reassuring. In the bright autumn sunshine, he looked older than in the subdued light of the Garden Room, his smooth skin showing the first crinkling with which time marks its passage, though the lambent blue light in the eyes, and the lustre of the generous moustache over the full red mouth remained undimmed. By now, the almost blinding beauty Frieda had at first discerned in him had yielded to something less brilliant but more interesting, the appearance of having lived, of still living, with an intensity that could not but leave its traces on mortal flesh, next to which the bland beauty of youth was as bereft of interest as an unprinted page.

'I think you were meant for better things than typewriting.' And this was so exactly what she meant that she took his arm at the exact moment that he extended it, as if she had anticipated his anticipation of her need.

It was over the pleasant little lunch in a windowed alcove of the hotel dining room, against a background of clinking cutlery, the murmur of well-bred English and occasional bursts of French, that she reminded him that he had mentioned, in Rye, a project for her usefulness.

For a moment he looked vague, then smiled deprecatingly. 'Oh yes, that. On reflection I'm not sure that it's worth mentioning.'

'I'm sure it is,' she insisted, wondering if she would strike him as obstinate, 'if it was worth mentioning yesterday.'

'Well, then,' he said, pushing away his empty soup plate. 'It's a delicate matter, and one that I wouldn't inflict on a young woman with an overly fastidious nature.'

Frieda thought she had given, was indeed giving, sufficient proof that she was hardly overly fastidious. 'Oh, I imagine I can deal with a delicate matter,' she said with what she hoped was a cheerful self-sufficiency, emphasised by the firm little movement with which she placed her spoon in her plate.

He just touched his moustache with his starched napkin, and turned his extraordinary gaze on her. 'Well, then,' he repeated, 'it is to do with Mr James.'

The matter, as he said, was delicate, where it was not indelicate, and there were times, during his narrative, interspersed with the arrival and removal of dishes, that she thought that she was after all overly fastidious. She could not, however, say so now; besides, she had long suspected that the world as imagined by Chelsea and Bayswater was not exactly the world as it was lived elsewhere. Now here, in Mr Fullerton's narrative, was confirmation of that suspicion, and she could not retreat before it. She had covered more ground, she felt, in two days than in all her twenty-three preceding years. There remained, however, dusky tracts before which she could but confess to having lost her bearings, and from which, as much as from his insistent blue eyes, she sought refuge in minute attention to her food.

'But what I cannot see,' she informed her fillet of halibut, 'is what these letters of yours that Mr James does not want to return to you have to do with the letters that your landlady stole and is attempting to blackmail you with.'

'Nothing directly. The letters that my landlady stole were from other people and of a different nature altogether. Indeed, my landlady is of a different nature altogether to Mr James, being grasping and vindictive to a degree. But the fact of their being stolen, don't you see, has alerted me to the extreme precariousness of a private correspondence.' He paused, evidently thinking how best to explain himself. 'You see, I have been accustomed, in the eighteen years that I have known Mr James, to confide in him many if not all of the indiscretions that a young man on his own in a foreign country is tempted into. Also, the tone of our correspondence, under the pressure of our long intimacy, is such as to be open to misinterpretation by ignorant or malicious outsiders.'

At this, at last, she looked up at him. 'The tone of your correspondence…?'

He took a sip of his Chablis. 'Well dash it, you know, we live in an infernal age where letters get read out in court and all sorts of constructions are placed upon them.'

Frieda guessed that this was a general principle of which she lacked the particular application. 'I'm not sure that I do know,' she accordingly demurred.

He sighed good-humouredly. 'You do make a man cross his t's and dot his i's, don't you? I'm referring to the infamous trials of the unfortunate Oscar Wilde, and to what, under the spell of that event, can be made, in a public arena, of any exchange between men that seems to the vulgar imagination to exceed the limits of propriety.'

He looked at her, as if for a response, but she could only gaze at him. She was, morally speaking, lost in a strange book imperfectly translated from a foreign language.

'Not, of course, that there was between me and Mr James,' and he smiled at the thought, 'anything like Wilde's relations with his various correspondents. But I'm talking, don't you see, of what can be made of any fairly expressive letter from one man to another in such an age as ours.'

Then, as Frieda clearly still did not see, he asked her, with apparent inconsequentiality: 'My dear child, how old are you exactly?'

'Twenty-three.'

He made a face. 'One forgets how time does pass. You would have been all of eleven years old in '95. I mean,' he added, having apparently decided that her imagination could not be left to interpret his implications unaided, 'that it is unlikely that at that age you would have been exposed to all the details of that case. Suffice it to say, then, that I am concerned about the safety of my letters. You know Mr James's working methods – he does *lose* things, does he not?'

'Well, yes. He's very systematic, and files things very carefully, but then forgets where the file is.' Frieda wondered whether she was being disloyal; but it seemed unlikely that she could tell this man anything about Mr James that he did not know.

'Then there you are.'

She did not, however, follow him in his conclusion. 'But it's not as if somebody... I mean, Mr James has no landlady – and Mrs Paddington or Burgess Noakes isn't going to steal his letters.'

'Yes,' he conceded, 'they probably are safe for the time being. But,' and he paused, 'this is the really delicate part. You know that Mr James's health has not been good.'

'I know that he has been indisposed from time to time, but I thought that was natural in a man of his age. And the family in general is prone to indisposition of one kind or another.'

'That is so. But unfortunately it is also so that in a man of his age – sixty-four, I think – regular indisposition may be a sign of an underlying cause. And in Mr James's case it would seem, it is his heart.'

'How do you know this?'

'He has told me – oh, not as anything to be alarmed about just yet, but as something to take into account. So that is what I am doing – taking it into account. You see, if Mr James were suddenly to have an incident that proved fatal, there is no saying what would happen to his papers. Once dispersed, they can find their way anywhere. And that could be embarrassing for me in various ways.'

As if to ward off the request that she could see looming, Frieda persisted in covering every aspect of the situation. 'But why does Mr James not want to return these letters to you?'

Mr Fullerton hesitated for a moment, then seemed to

make up his mind. 'Mr James is, as you will have noticed, a very tender-hearted man. He cherishes letters from friends as so many tokens of friendship; and he says the act of returning a letter is, in his phrase, symbolic of separation and betrayal. Letters are returned only, he maintains, at the behest of disenchanted lovers and deceived spouses. Also, Mr James was, you may say… '

He stopped as if searching for the right word, and it was a moment before she realised the reason: somebody who had been passing their table had paused, and was now extending his hand to Mr Fullerton.

'Ah, Fullerton,' the newcomer declared, his extreme neutrality of tone betraying neither surprise nor pleasure.

'Ah, Gower,' replied Mr Fullerton, his vestigial American accent lending only marginally more expression to his greeting.

'You are on you way to Paris,' the man addressed as Gower informed Mr Fullerton. 'Unless, of course, you are on your way from Paris.' His eyes for a second took in Frieda, but seemed not to find anything there to detain them.

'To,' said Mr Fullerton, as if to demonstrate that an American, too, could be taciturn. He spoiled this effect, however, by adding, 'On my way from America.'

'Oh, America,' echoed Gower, with the same lack of implication that had marked his salutation. 'Rather from than to, eh?'

'You must remember that it's the country of my birth,' protested Mr Fullerton, though in an accent bereft of all rancour. At this his interlocutor sacrificed his languid manner to an expression of mirth somewhere between a sneeze and a cough. 'My dear Morton, how can we ever forget that?'

'No doubt you never can, my dear Ronald. I, however, don't think of it as my distinctive feature.'

'Perhaps, as poor dear Oscar used to say about himself, you are a citizen of the world. However, I must join my party. I shall see you, no doubt, in Paris.'

Mr Fullerton did not reply to this prognostication, pronounced as it was while the speaker was retreating towards a group that Frieda had noticed earlier as apparently equally at home in the English and the French tongues. To Frieda he said, 'Lord Ronald Gower, an acquaintance of my London days.

Indeed, quite a good friend at one time.'

Frieda felt herself, more and more, surrounded by mysteries. Amongst these was now the question of how a man as incommunicative as Lord Ronald Gower could have been even *quite* a good friend to anybody. She did not, however, comment on this, merely returned to what was uppermost in her mind.

'Am I to understand,' she enquired in what she hoped was a sufficiently businesslike manner, 'that you require my assistance in retrieving these letters from Mr James's possession?'

He seemed to consider, then smiled his leisurely smile. 'That is admirably put. Yes, that exactly: retrieving my letters from Mr James's possession.'

'You mean steal them?'

He grimaced in mock-horror. 'Ah, that is much less admirably put. You see, morally it is a moot point whether it is theft to retrieve, in your excellent word, a letter of which one is oneself the author.'

'And is it your idea that I should deliver these letters to you?'

'Ideally yes; to put my mind absolutely at ease. But failing that, your word that you have destroyed the letters would also contribute greatly to my tranquillity.'

'And if I were to deliver them to you – how would I do so? Would you come again to Rye?'

'That is a detail on which we need not break our heads at present. Unless...' and he looked at her interrogatively.

'Unless?'

He lowered his voice as if sharing a confidence with her, though in the convivial clatter of the dining room nobody could have heard him. 'Unless this might be your opportunity to visit Paris – at my expense, of course, by way of thanking you for your labours on my behalf, but also because of the pleasure it would give me to show you Paris.'

Frieda wondered whether she was being bribed, or merely being offered an incentive. Fortunately this distinction, which was in truth very fine, retreated before a dumb but strong conviction that to see Paris and to see it as Mr Fullerton could show it, constituted an appeal that transcended all conventional categories of judgement. Hitherto her life had been run on lines decided for it by other people; this would be a venture as independent as it was exciting. She would be taking possession of her own life and her own destiny: it would be her own act as a free human being. The fact that she would be doing so at the expense of somebody else was a complication that she would have preferred not to take into account, but that she could not altogether banish from the field.

Mr Fullerton was looking at her if not with impatience, then with a certain clear expectation. 'I would do almost anything to see Paris,' she accordingly admitted. 'But there is obviously a matter also of loyalty to Mr James. However I might represent to myself the justice of your claims on the letters, the fact remains that I would be acting against his interest as he sees it.'

He shrugged good-humouredly. 'Ah, there I cannot help you. I can but put before you my interest as I see it, and ask you to consider *that*. Whatever claim Mr James has on your loyalty is of course not for me to question.' And with that, as the dessert arrived, he seemed to relinquish the matter with a light-hearted wave of his eloquent hand.

'Of course,' he said, as the waiter retreated, fixing her again with his gaze, 'of course, you do realise that it is my intention to make love to you.'

This declaration, coming as abruptly as it did, left Frieda for a moment fairly gaping – not literally, she was later to recall with relief, but spiritually and morally. If the content had not been entirely unforeseen, its form took her by surprise, not only in confessing so frankly to his design, but in imputing to her knowledge of that design. And it was true that to profess ignorance would justify him in asking her what on earth she had thought then, in coming there on her own. This was a question she could not have answered even to herself, unless it were to say that she had carefully refrained from thinking anything at all. Whereas this would serve as an answer to herself, it would not do for Mr Fullerton; such unreflective action could only strike him as hypocrisy or stupidity.

Frieda was aware that for a young woman in her situation there were fates worse than being thought a hypocrite or a fool; and yet, she could not persuade herself that being made love to was one of these. Being made love to was what happened to

young women who went into the great world; and in coming
to Folkestone Frieda had ventured to the portals of that world.
There was, it was true, a distance near-mythic in import
between the portals and the inner reaches, and it was not one
that her education had taught her to negotiate with any aplomb.
She realised that she was giving her pistachio ice more detailed
attention than even its velvety green coolness really merited: this
could not be how women in the great world dealt with such
situations; and yet, looking up, she met only the humorous
regard of Mr Fullerton, which seemed so to take for granted her
acquiescence as a mere detail of his intention. Looking down
again, she found that she had finished her pistachio ice. So,
twirling her empty wine glass, she said, 'Of course.'

Thus committed to a more sophisticated view of their situation
than she in reality commanded, Frieda could not demur at Mr
Fullerton's suggestion that they should repair to his room And
yet, as they entered the crowded foyer, at the far end of which
loomed the grand staircase like some allegorical Road to Ruin,
she stopped. It seemed likely to her that some hotel functionary
appointed and dedicated to the task would identify her, in her
luggageless state, as an impostor or worse, and denounce her to
the assembled crowd.

Mr Fullerton sensed her hesitation and guessed at its
cause. 'Don't be intimidated by the apparent lack of privacy.
Everybody is rushing for the afternoon sailing; nobody has
leisure for idle observation. The trick is to look natural.' And,
setting the example in this respect, he led her up the wide
staircase, making amiable conversation all the while as if he were
accompanying her down the High Street of Rye.

Frieda mentally shook herself, tried to convince herself of
the momentousness of the moment and the precariousness of
her position. She was, according to the best authorities, about to
be ruined. And yet the situation took shape to her imagination,
obstinately, as a conglomeration of material details: the shiny
banister that made her wonder if children slid down it while parents
were at dinner; the dank smell of the long corridor, airless and
lightless; the surprisingly utilitarian character of the room to which
Mr Fullerton opened the heavy mahogany door. By the standards

of the vast foyer and the airy dining room, this room was almost dingy in its proportions; even, in the single ray of sun penetrating the heavy curtains, slightly dusty, the carpet perceptibly worn near the door. The afternoon had become almost oppressively warm, and the room, facing southwest, was close.

Mr Fullerton, who had preceded her into the room, waited at the door and locked it behind her. 'There is a screen in the corner of the room,' he pointed out, 'if you prefer to get undressed behind that.'

'Undressed?' She had not imagined the realities of the situation to be presented so promptly and in so unadorned a fashion.

He lifted an amused eyebrow, and he had never seemed to her more beautiful. 'Why yes, my dear Miss Wroth. It greatly decreases the inconvenience and increases the pleasure.'

Frieda's lack of experience had no choice but to adjust itself to this maxim. It was not for her to contradict Mr Fullerton's certainties. She accordingly went further into the room, to meet as she might her perdition. But still her physical sense of her surroundings was sharper than her awareness of her own moral peril; this extended, as she took off her hat in the small mirror on the dressing table, to herself: she noted with interest that her colour was heightened, either by the morning's walk, or the wine she had had at lunch; she noted even that this made her seem more attractive than as a rule she found herself. Her grey eyes, which she had always found unfortunately neutral, had tints of darker grey, even black, in them.

She thanked the dictates of rational dress: she had several pounds of clothing less to divest herself of than she had been brought up to believe the minimum of decent covering. The screen that Mr Fullerton had considerately pointed out enabled her at least to preserve a last shred of modesty before abandoning it for ever. It also spared her the process of Mr Fullerton's own disrobing. Frieda had not been in the habit of wondering what men wore under their uncomfortable-seeming clothing; she suspected, however, that it was unlikely to minister at all to the passion that the event was, according to report, to unleash in her. She had read, of course, about Emma Bovary and Anna Karenina, and had assumed that they were in the grip of a passion altogether irresistible. She was not, for herself, conscious of any such force; but as Mr Fullerton had proposed repairing to his room with an urgency which she had not witnessed before in him or any other man, she assumed that she was in the presence of that male ardour which her friend Mabel had described to her, as manifested by the late Charlie, as 'awful to behold'.

Emerging from behind the screen, Frieda recollected these words. She had, on visits to the National Gallery with Aunt Frederica, seen depictions of the unclothed male body, and had not averted her gaze from those portions that a young woman was as a rule assumed to be unconscious of. But Saint Sebastian had, in his unclothed martyrdom, carried his sex like an unshelled mollusc, tender and vulnerable; even Mars attending upon Venus had not manifested any unseemly impatience. Mr Fullerton, on the other hand, was very evidently what she had heard described as *aroused*; and it came as a surprise to her to discover how literally expressive that term was. She assumed that the polite thing would be not to notice Mr Fullerton's condition, but in the nature of the situation it was the most salient object in the room, and thus difficult to ignore. She imagined, however, that to gape would be deemed vulgar.

She should have known that Mr Fullerton would smooth over any awkwardness. He shrugged as if ruefully and said, 'You see to what you reduce me – or inspire me.' He then examined her frankly and minutely. 'My dear Miss Wroth, you have been hiding a treasure of price behind your typewriter.'

She wondered whether a more experienced woman would perhaps at this point pleasantly refer to his own treasure, pay it a delicate compliment, or in some other way acknowledge its incontrovertible presence. Mr Fullerton, however, dispensed with further ceremony in a purposeful and knowledgeable manner; he took care of the heavy spread draped over the bed, of the disposition of pillows, and even produced a large towel. If his efficiency in managing the mere practicalities of the situation might be taken to suggest a certain cold-bloodedness, there was, incontrovertibly, the evidence of his arousal to argue otherwise. And if he was, in this condition, less purely beautiful than before, he was certainly indubitably aware of her.

As she submitted her inexperience to Mr Fullerton's

direction, Frieda wondered whether the strange detachment she felt from the experience branded her as deficient in some vital capacity; she could not imagine Emma Bovary and Anna Karenina taking as ironical a view of their own situation. But then, Emma and Anna were created by men, to whose vanity it was probably necessary to believe in the ecstatic transport of their women.

Frieda's essentially literary view of her situation was to be challenged, and not only by the severe pain of her deflowering. Acute as that was, it contended with sensations and emotions that she could not survey from any intellectual vantage point, having no mental categories for an experience at once so painfully invasive and so intimately possessive, so localised in its origin and so pervasive in its effect. Having indeed no desire to categorise the experience, she submitted to the pain and revelled in the possession; a sensation at once fulfilling and desolating. It seemed to her that Mr Fullerton was at one and the same time closer to her than any human being had ever been, and abandoning her to her own extreme of emotion. Her blood on the towel was token of a wounding and a union.

For a while he lay on her breast, his head next to hers. But as his breathing subsided, he raised his head and looked down at her. His eyes were very close to hers. There were little specks of brown in the blue.

'You should have told me.'

'Told you what?'

'That this was your first time.'

'Would it have made a difference?'

'I might have been more circumspect.' At close range, his moustache resolved itself into individual threads, glossy, healthy and separate. She could smell the Chablis on his breath.

'Then I am glad I didn't tell you.'

He smiled down at her. 'You *are* a cool one, aren't you?'

He kissed her, and in the lingering of his lips on hers, the faint brush of his tongue, her last reserve of irony was depleted, and she clung to him anew.

The splendid autumn Sunday, so unlooked for so late in the season, had brought people to the seaside in large numbers; and then, drawing to an end, had abandoned them, sandy and hot, to grubby platforms and crowded railway carriages. Frieda, vying for a seat on the last train to Rye, shared her compartment with a young matron and five children who had reached that stage of tiredness that expresses itself in being disagreeable and unreasonable. The flustered mother was apologetic but ineffectual – 'Their father had to work today, else he would have seen to them,' she explained, 'and when we get home, see to them he will.'

This grim prediction did not have the desired effect on the children; indeed, it roused them to further expressions of discomfort, complaints of tiredness, hunger and thirst, and demands for amenities impossible to obtain on a moving train.

'You always pay for it afterwards, don't you?' the mother asked Frieda. 'For pleasure, I mean,' she added as Frieda stared at her uncomprehendingly.

'Do you?' Frieda enquired politely, disinclined either to take issue with or assent to this gloomy view. She hoped that the fertile young mother had not been sent to her as an awful omen of her own fate.

'Yes, don't you find?' the young woman asked, visibly discomfited by Frieda's uncooperative response to her conversational gambit. 'The moment you have some fun something goes wrong. In my experience anyway,' she added, as Frieda seemed still unreceptive to her confidences.

Frieda, fearing that too receptive an assent to this proposition might encourage the woman to a disquisition on that experience which had apparently so dispirited her, merely nodded vaguely while trying to retrieve her hat, the 'shiner' of Mr Dodds's reprobation, from under the surprisingly capacious bottom of the smallest child. She had unwisely taken it off on entering, thinking it impeded the flow of air in the stuffy compartment.

'Move yourself, Victoria,' the mother admonished her child. 'The lady wants her hat.' Frieda did not so much want her hat as not want it to be squashed, but she could not now seem indifferent to the recaptured trophy, and somewhat self-consciously she placed it on her head.

In the little mirror above the opposite seat she caught sight of herself with her crushed hat at an angle that could only be called undignified; but lacking the space and freedom to rearrange her apparel, she submitted to staring with equanimity at her own dim and disreputable-looking reflection. Is that, she wondered, what a ruined woman looks like? Does it show so soon? It seemed inconceivable that only a few hours earlier she had been sipping Chablis from a crystal glass in a dining room commanding a view of the coast of France, exchanging aphorisms – Frieda liked the idea of exchanging aphorisms, though she could not in strict conscience recall any one in particular – with a beautiful and intelligent man of the world.

The recollection of Mr Fullerton's damp hair on his forehead, the sight of his lean, strong back as he bent down to pick up an errant sock, the sound of his voice as he spoke in her ear: all these were so present to her and yet so remote from the grimy little train bearing her back to Rye, that she looked around her for some intervening medium, some protection of the glamorous past from the prosaic present. But through the dull glass the flat Sussex landscape commanded a view of nothing, and at no point seemed to lead to Paris. At Folkestone there had been, in the bustle of arrivals and departures, in the cosmopolitan blend of French-sounding English and English-sounding French, even the occasional burst of French-sounding French, a sense of connectedness with larger purposes and wider horizons. But here, the very uninterruptedness of the marsh-bound skyline served only to reveal how little amplitude it had – to stretch all the way to the horizon and to amount only to *that* seemed to contract one's notions of the potential of landscape and human effort alike. The little citadel of Rye, rearing its modest hump on the horizon, gave the landscape such point as it had; but for Frieda the stolid little bastion offered no refuge: it had become the stronghold of a secret she was pledged to violate.

Mr Fullerton had not mentioned again the matter of the letters; but he had said to her, as she left, 'When shall I see you in Paris?' and she had replied: 'When I bring you the letters.' Upon this he had pressed her hand as if to seal a pledge – or, she supposed, as a way of not doing anything more than press her hand. A clasp of the hand had always the advantage, for the clasper, of being both eloquent and non-committal.

Amongst the various perspectives on Mr Fullerton's request that she had adopted, its probable effect on Mr James had not been uppermost in Frieda's mind; in the hum and sparkle of the delightful little lunch, and of course in its momentous aftermath, Mr James had seemed at most a necessary and distant abstraction, the keeper of the letters that had been, nominally, the occasion of the negotiations. Now, contemplating her own mission in the dingy light of her railway carriage, with no other distraction than the tired mother and her damp and sticky offspring, she seemed to see it for the first time, in relation to Mr James, as constituting a betrayal. There was that in her which argued against this view, on the grounds that she owed Mr James no greater loyalty than that evinced by a friend as close as Mr Fullerton: if Mr Fullerton did not mind, why should she? But against this another self argued that Mr Fullerton's business was with Mr Fullerton, whereas hers was with Mr James – to which her more pragmatic self replied that her business with Mr James was conducted at the rate of slightly more than a shilling an hour, and he had done little enough to transform that nexus into a more personal bond.

To this inconclusive colloquy were added, to Frieda's fancy, the voices of Miss Petherbridge and Mr Fullerton the former proclaiming, as she had so often done at the Academy, the sacred duty of confidentiality that bound the typewriter no less than the medical man or even the priest; the latter speaking for the claims of her youth against the demands of her profession. Frieda's dilemma was that Miss Petherbridge and Mr Fullerton addressed such different centres of value that one might easily concede both of them their points and be no closer to deciding between them. Miss Petherbridge spoke for training and regulation and discipline, whereas Mr Fullerton spoke exactly for the joy of disregarding these things. He now also spoke with the resonance of the experiences of the afternoon: having yielded to him what she had been brought up to regard as a woman's most sacred treasure, Frieda had appointed him as the keeper of the treasure. Mr Fullerton had established a hold on her exactly in proportion as he had taken advantage of her.

There was yet another voice, weak but plaintive, wanting to be heard: that of her mother, whose observations on the afternoon's proceedings Frieda had no desire to hear; indeed, she wondered whether her mother would have words for such a fate as that befalling her daughter. She had of course had words enough for its happening to other mothers' daughters; but Frieda could imagine her mother only as dumbly shaking her head before a calamity so unthinkable as its occurring to her.

This was fine matter to sift while being jolted by the restless Victoria, and as the little train at last puffed and clattered into Rye station, Frieda wearily resolved, amidst the scramble of the young matron and her children, to postpone the debate to the morrow: there would be time enough to consider her priorities and relive her experiences while Mr James paced the floor.

This, however, was easier to resolve than execute; opening the door to the modest room that, in her haste to make her train, she had left in unaccustomed disarray, Frieda was confronted, as it were, with her previous self: in the serviceable petticoat, discarded, she now knew, as unfit for the amused regard of Mr Fullerton; in the very hairs left in her hairbrush by her vigorous early-morning attempt to impose order; above all in the night-dress with the ribbon at the neck that now seemed girlish to the point of silliness. As if to mark in their fashion the difference, the eight bells of St Mary the Virgin began pealing their evening call to the faithful. Peering once more at herself in Mrs Tumble's dim little mirror, Frieda looked for outward signs of the momentous change in her; but the inadequately reflective surface, so little adjusted to encouraging vanity, showed her only her own effort to see anything at all in the weak electric glow. Henceforth she would have to live with this sense that there was more to her, as they said, than met the eye. It would have been exhilarating, this sense, had it not been so much like deception.

Chapter Eight
11th November 1907

Mr James did not, the following morning, descend at his normal time. Mrs Paddington appeared in the door of the Garden Room with something more than her usual gravity. Though she did not pay Frieda the compliment of a curtsey – that she reserved for Mr James himself – she had respect bordering on superstition for the Remington and the way it could 'turn speech into words': for her, it evidently combined the mystique of magic with the prestige of technology. Frieda's role in this was clearly a second-order function, a kind of priestess of the worship, but still, the fact that she knew how to operate the miraculous machine did reflect some glory on her in Mrs Paddington's eyes, and the housekeeper was always scrupulously polite to her.

'The Master sends word as he is indisposed and regrets to say that he will not be coming down today. He asks will you continue with the corrections as he's left in the usual place, please. He apologises for his absence and hopes you will be comfortable'

Having always enjoyed excellent health herself, Frieda was sceptical of Mr James's chronic concern for his, and privately thought that it might fare better with less fuss; but she had early in life learned that those in good health were for obscure reasons in the debt of those not so blessed, and owed them consideration and attention. She accordingly showed Mr James's delicate health every solicitude. 'Please tell Mr James thank you, I am perfectly comfortable, except of course for being concerned on his behalf. I hope it is nothing serious?'

The housekeeper shook her head gravely. 'There is no saying with the Master, miss. Sometimes he plays up the smallest thing something dreadful, and sometimes he can walk around half dead and not want to go to bed. But he was out of sorts all of yesterday. I wouldn't wonder if it wasn't sitting up so late with that Mr Fullerton on Friday night. Burgess Noakes said he had to trim the lamp four times, and even then the Master told him to go to bed, he'd trim it himself.'

Frieda hesitated. She had been taught that it was vulgar to use servants as informants, but this morning it seemed to her that she had risen above such discriminations, or fallen below them, it hardly mattered which. At any rate, she felt that she now had a right to know what had passed between Mr Fullerton and Mr James. 'Do you think it likely that Mr Fullerton told Mr James something to upset him?'

Mrs Paddington was as aware as Frieda that they were crossing a border. 'I don't know, miss, and by rights I shouldn't be talking like this.' This, however, evidently struck her as a paltry kind of reply, and she relented. 'But I wouldn't wonder,' she added pensively. 'There's something about that Mr Fullerton I wouldn't want to have around me for too long, if you know what I mean, miss. And I'll tell you something else.' She paused for Frieda to prompt her.

'Yes, Mrs Paddington?'

'Max agrees with me.' She announced this with an air of triumph, as if that settled the matter.

'Max? And how has he made his sentiments known to you?'

'Well, the next morning, as Mr Fullerton was coming down to breakfast, Max was lying next to Mr James, as he always does of a morning, and then when Mr Fullerton came in he jumped up like he'd been given a fright and started growling that fierce at Mr Fullerton, you'd have sworn it was a burglar coming in. And you know as a rule Max doesn't budge when there's guests, he's that used to them.'

Frieda, remembering Max's behaviour on the beach a few days before – had it really been only three days? – had to concede, at least, that the dachshund did not like Mr Fullerton. She had not, however, been used to taking her acquaintances from dogs, and she was inclined to think that Max's dislike was Max's business. She had not grown up with dogs – her mother disapproved of their habit of licking themselves and others – and thus could not tell how reliable they were as judges of character, but if Mr James liked Mr Fullerton, as he so evidently did, how could one urge the penetration of a dachshund against that of its master? 'Oh dogs,' she accordingly said, taking her refuge in vague generality, 'they have strange likes and dislikes.'

But Mrs Paddington held to the particular. 'Not Max, miss,' she insisted. 'He's only ever bitten one person, and that was the grocer's boy as was after Alice Skinner.'

This did not seem to Frieda to establish Max's credentials as a judge of human nature as conclusively as Mrs Paddington seemed to believe, but the stately housekeeper retreated as serenely as if she had now made her case incontrovertibly.

Looking at the Garden Room in the gloom of early morning – the bright weather had succumbed at last to the murk of November – Frieda marvelled at the chance that had so promptly put it in her power to ascertain whether Mr Fullerton's letters were kept here. There were two desks in the Garden Room, one at which she sat and that was regarded as 'hers', the other reserved for those times when Mr James chose to sit down to peruse a manuscript. This latter had three drawers, none of which she had ever seen Mr James use, but she knew that he often sat at the desk late at night for letter writing, and it seemed possible that his private papers were kept here.

To walk up to Mr James's desk, however, and coolly search his drawers took more nerve or plain cheek than Frieda commanded, and she persuaded herself that she first needed to settle into her daily routine as a base from which to venture. She collected the corrected proofs from Mr James's desk – he had evidently been working over the weekend – and returned to her typewriter. She worked intently for a while, finding relief from her own indecision in the mechanical labour. She tried to clear her mind of cerebration, as she had been taught by Miss Petherbridge – 'A typewriter's consciousness should never impede the flow of words; she is merely the medium of transmission.'

But as she typed, she became aware that her mind, having been left untenanted by conscious thought, was being invaded by a consciousness other than her own, a matter not of articulate words as much as of images, at first flickering and indistinct, then settling into a single, near-palpable impression of a bundle of letters tied with red tape, lying at the back of a drawer.

This impression was startlingly vivid, and Frieda could not have ascribed any provenance to the phenomenon, had she not, simultaneously with the quasi-visual impression, been suffused with a warmth and well-being such as she had experienced the afternoon before; for a moment she even smelled the sweet rankness of Mr Fullerton's sweat.

She had heard of telepathy from her Aunt Frederica, who believed in being well informed on all manifestations of what she described as 'advanced thought'. On this, as on other of Aunt Frederica's enthusiasms, Frieda had reserved her opinion: with so many people already producing such a superfluity of written and spoken communication, it seemed redundant to establish one more way of burdening others with one's thoughts. But here, now, under the urgency of Mr Fullerton's possession of her, her reservations seemed barrenly academic: what she was experiencing was so direct that it seemed to require no theoretical justification. What she could sense, feel, apprehend with the immediacy of smell, was Mr Fullerton's thought; and what he was thinking of, through her, was the letters.

Frieda got up, still suffused with Mr Fullerton's image, and walked towards Mr James's desk. She tried the top drawer. It opened easily, but to display only a neat array of pens, pencils and chocolate bars, such as Mr James sometimes left on her typewriter when he felt she was in need of sustenance.

The second drawer contained piles of writing paper, and of the bond paper that she used for typing. She lifted the piles slightly, in case there were letters behind them, but she found only a crumpled blank sheet, probably misplaced from one of the piles.

The bottom drawer was empty except for a pair of socks, a bow tie, an eggshell and a piece of string.

These mundane objects drove out, with the sharp edges of incontrovertible presence, the heightened consciousness under the compulsion of which Frieda had acted; and, chastened, she returned to her typewriter. It would seem that Mr Fullerton, whatever his telepathic powers, had no special knowledge of Mr James's storage habits: he was merely impressing upon her a generalised awareness of the letters, or of his need of them. After all, if he had known exactly where the letters were, he would not have needed her help.

There was a tap at the door, and, without waiting for a reply, Burgess Noakes opened the door. He was bearing, again, a telegram.

'Telegram, miss,' he announced superfluously and uncharacteristically, being normally taciturn to a fault. On this occasion he approached loquacity, adding, with a grin that alarmingly suggested a private interpretation of things, 'That makes number two this week, dun't it?'

'Thank you, Burgess,' Frieda said with what she hoped was understated dignity. The little butler smiled cheekily and left, closing the door behind him with exaggerated care.

Frieda sat down and opened her telegram. Was this a rebuke to her scepticism or, on the contrary, a confirmation of it? Did the telegram ratify the communion she had felt earlier with Mr Fullerton, or did it sensibly suggest that if modern people wanted to get in touch with each other there were modern means? The telegram was once again not signed, and said simply '*Arrived Paris but thinking of Rye.*'

The telegram arriving at this moment constituted, Frieda decided, as direct an appeal as was possible at such a distance: Mr Fullerton had apprehended her uncertainty and was sending her this encouragement. His succinct communication was capable of a range of interpretations, but she assumed that, practical as he was, his telegram was intended to contain at least partly a mnemonic function. This was very well, she almost fretfully thought, but of little use in locating the letters. There were so many places they could be... her eye fell on the row of cabinets lining the far wall of the room. She had seen Mr James deposit manuscripts there, after newer copies had been made and sent off, and she had assumed that to be the sole function of these cabinets. Impelled to recklessness by Mr Fullerton's graceful reminder, she went up to the cabinets and opened the first. It was indeed filled with voluminous manuscripts, some handwritten, some typed; a cursory glance sufficed to assure Frieda that there were no letters there. She opened the second cabinet; here, indeed, was a little pile of letters – recent letters, she assumed, from their being unbound.

Faced with an open letter, Frieda's training and instincts combined to make her avert her glance: reading somebody else's private correspondence had ranked very high on the list of reprehensibles her mother had instilled in her, and Miss Petherbridge, too, had stressed the fact that 'to the lady secretary, another person's letters are as inviolable as his personal privacy; only a criminal could contemplate such an invasion'. But Miss Petherbridge's strictures seemed remote from this room and from the charge she was under to find Mr Fullerton's letters. Reaching for the letter at the top of the pile, she felt again the warmth of Mr Fullerton's presence, reassuring her and reinforcing her resolve.

> *The Mount,*
> *Lenox, Mass.*
> *October 31st 1907*

Cher Maître,

> *I write to you thus late in the hope of catching, tomorrow, the same ship – I believe it is the* Campania *– as will bring your – our! – friend Morton Fullerton to you in dear little old Rye, where he tells me that he hopes to pay you a visit en route from Liverpool to Paris. I do so hope that he can manage that, & that he can deliver to you in his own person my grateful regards. If I pick up my pen with more than my usual affectionate impatience, it is to thank you without reserve for encouraging Mr Fullerton, as I gather from him, to extend his visit to The Mount. I have known, of course, how much you have always valued his friendship – but only now, I think, can I say I fully understand your appreciation. He is of the finest grain, as you shd say, & altogether so happily attuned to one's finest moments. I have not had opportunity to see whether he harmonises with equal felicity with one's worse moments – I had no worse moments in the all-too-short two days he spent here – but have no doubt that his way of dealing with them wd have a stamp all his own. He is a true original – for a son of New England to have so the trick of Europe – no, more than the trick, the watermark of the Real Thing.*

> *We went for a drive one magnificent afternoon on snowy roads – he is almost as fond of motoring as you! It is a comfort to know that he will be in Paris, except that it makes the stay here seem all the drearier, beautiful as The Mount is now in the fall – but melancholy too. And what outings, my dear friend, the three of us will have if – when! – you visit me in Paris, as of course you must do as soon as*

I am back in the Rue de Varenne. I had not thought our friendship was capable of enhancement, but I do believe that Mr Fullerton has achieved the impossible, making me more than ever,
    Yrs affly
    EW

PS Teddy is as well as can be expected, which is to say that he is irrational, difficult, inconsiderate and demanding. Mais que voulez-vous? *He is as generous and, when he likes, as sweet–tempered as he ever was. If only he wd 'like' more often!*

Frieda knew EW to be Mr James's friend Edith Wharton. She had met Mrs Wharton more than once, on her triumphant invasions of Rye – tooting her great automobile, jingling her jewels, laughing immoderately, dragging Mr James around the garden as if he were an elderly dog needing exercise, instructing Mrs Paddington about the meals, even advising Frieda about the right kind of ribbon to buy for the Remington: in general, expending so much well-intentioned energy that she exhausted everybody around her. Frieda had read her, of course; had read in particular *The House of Mirth* when everybody was reading it, and had lost patience with the spoilt and suffering Lily Bart. Having had to go out to earn a living at an early age, Frieda had scant sympathy with a social butterfly who discovers at twenty-nine that nobody wants to marry her. As for Lawrence Selden, Frieda wondered whether Mrs Wharton, now that she had met Mr Fullerton, realised what a prig her hero was. *A true original* indeed! How would Mrs Wharton recognise an original, having grown up in the artificial, emulated and emulating world of the rich?

    Frieda wondered whether Mr Fullerton had made love to Mrs Wharton and decided, on balance, that he had not. She was not so simple as to imagine that Mr Fullerton had made love to no other woman prior to doing so to Frieda Wroth; but Mrs Wharton's letter, though fulsome, had none of the complacent satiety that such a woman would not be able to conceal after such an experience. Frieda, indeed, could not imagine the fantastically over-dressed, beplumed, hatted, frilled, laced, furred, booted – especially booted – New York lady ever submitting to the state of undress Mr Fullerton seemed to find congenial. Constituted essentially of appurtenances, she would come apart if you took her clothes off. Her natural element was the motor car, her most profound relation with machines, her emotion a matter of petrol and noise. Frieda was pleased that she had never liked Mrs Wharton, otherwise she would have thought she was jealous, now, of the New York socialite's easy appropriation of her latest 'find', as she could imagine her describing Mr Fullerton to her friends.

Frieda reminded herself that what she was looking for was not Mrs Wharton's effusions, but Mr Fullerton's letters. She peered again into the cabinet where she had found Mrs Wharton's letter. There were a few other loose letters – this was evidently where Mr James put the letters he had not yet replied to – but they were of little import, communications with his agent and his publisher, domestic arrangements, and a letter from Mr William James to his brother – Frieda recognised the characteristic tone and subject matter of the James family communications: '*Peggy is home for Thanksgiving, and in much better tone than ever yet. All thanks to Mrs Newman, the mental curist, who has done heaps of good to Alice as well. (She can't touch me! Alas!) Bill is just out of bed with a real attack of influenza, and looks thin but is cheerful. He has just gone out for a walk in the sunshine up & down the street. Strange liability to catarrhs that we all have! I am just getting over one, the second since I got back.*'

Disquisitions on influenzas and catarrhs did not interest Frieda: she had enough talk of those from Mrs Tumble, to whose discourse on the subject that of the James family was not markedly superior. She opened yet another cabinet. This seemed more promising and at the same time more daunting: all three shelves were filled with piles of letters tied with red tape but, as far as she could tell from a cursory examination, not arranged according to any system, and the writer not identified. Frieda realised that she did not even know what Mr Fullerton's handwriting looked like. It could take her weeks to sort through the accumulation, and she would have to untie each carefully tied parcel.

There was again a knock at the door and, coming up from her stooping position, she caught a glimpse of herself in a pier glass on the wall next to the cabinet – her flushed, flustered features, the furtive glance sideways to meet, with a start, only her own eyes. Had she become a low snoop? Is that what happened to a woman when she was ruined? Did she become as indifferent to considerations of loyalty and gratitude as she had shown herself to be to the dictates of chastity? Why had mirrors started to reflect her so strangely?

It was the housekeeper who, after a discreet pause, opened the door. 'Excuse me, miss, but the Master says to make sure as you have everything you need, and to ask if you'd like tea now.'

'Why, thank you, Mrs Paddington, please tell Mr James that I am very comfortable and that I am getting ahead with the work he left me. And no thank you, I won't have tea just yet.'

'Thank you, miss. And he asked me to tell you that seeing as the weather's turned nasty and is unlikely to turn again, he'll be working in the Green Room when he gets up out of bed. He says if it suits you, perhaps you wouldn't mind supervising while Burgess Noakes carries the Machine' – and she nodded respectfully at the Remington – 'up to the Green Room, so as it doesn't get injured.'

Frieda briefly wondered if Mr James, too, were in touch with her telepathically, and was in this way forestalling her search. Once they were installed in the Green Room, it would be difficult if not impossible to invent a reason to spend time on her own in the Garden Room, which was normally closed for the duration of the winter to save on heating and housekeeping. On the other hand, the Green Room, being in the house itself, was perhaps the more likely repository of personal letters. She remembered, from childhood searches for lost objects, her mother's maxim: 'There's no point in looking somewhere just because it's easiest; you have to look where it's likeliest to be.'

'Of course,' she meanwhile replied to Mrs Paddington. 'I am ready when Burgess Noakes is. Or stay…' she held up a hand to detain the housekeeper, 'I shall need half an hour or so to finish what I am typing and to get everything in order for the removal.' Half an hour was scant grace, given the piles of letters she had glimpsed, but it might give her time to ascertain at least the general type of correspondence stored here – that is, if Mr James's method of storage recognised anything as orderly as a general category. Nothing was more likely than that the letters had been bundled together into the cabinet according to no system whatsoever.

Mrs Paddington withdrew, promising to send Burgess Noakes across after half an hour. Frieda swiftly arranged the Remington for transportation and gathered her own few possessions for the move to the Green Room. Of these last the two telegrams from Mr Fullerton now formed a potentially incriminating part: though his discretion in not signing the telegrams rendered her thus far safe, their contents hinted, she thought, not without a twinge of pleasure, at intrigue and subterfuge. She could not imagine anybody going through her papers, but there was a certain satisfaction in guarding against such an eventuality. She accordingly placed the two flimsy sheets inside the leather binding of the portfolio in which she carried her meagre personal correspondence.

Frieda now had twenty minutes in which to establish whether Mr Fullerton's letters were in the Garden Room. She arranged her effects neatly on her desk for removal to the house, and approached again the cabinet that seemed the most likely depository of Mr James's private letters. She opened the solid wooden door and resumed her search. She worked her way quickly through the few loose letters lying on top, apart from the collected bundles: one more from Mrs Wharton, a short note from Edmund Gosse (Frieda caught only the phrase '*your fabled hospitality*'), a long, scrawled letter signed '*Your ever-grateful Violet Hunt.*' Then, at last, a single letter, signed '*Believe me all faithfully yours, Morton.*' The date on the first page was October 15th 1907, and the address was Brockton, Massachusetts.

Frieda knew that this was too recent a letter to be one of those Mr Fullerton had expressed anxiety about. In all conscience she should have put it aside without another glance, but the inhibition against reading somebody else's letters, once defied, had lost its dominion over curiosity – and over her need for the intimacy of his presence, even in a letter written to somebody else. She felt she had abandoned all scruple; perhaps this, too, was an effect of being ruined.

She accordingly folded open the letter and read it rapidly:

My dear Henry James,
    Having, so to speak, taken heart from your so very kind and insistent adjuration – kindly insistent and insistently kind!

– I have felt free to announce my presence in this country to your friend Mrs Wharton, who has proved herself every whit as gracious as you promised, replying very promptly with an invitation to visit The Mount. I know you take pleasure in your friends getting on well together, and I intend to get on well with Mrs Wharton, even if only for your sake. We shall at any rate have plenty to talk about in recalling your kindnesses – for I assume, you see, that you have been no less kind to her than to me, that being your habitual mode in relation to those lucky enough to call you their friend. I am happy to say that my talk on You, at Bryn Mawr, was a sensation.

The audience applauded me as if I had been You in person, and asked questions that proved not only the depth of their interest but the acuity of their insight. A prophet is not without honour, indeed.

America has proved quite as demanding as I feared, from the point of view of family affections. Quite apart from my dear but querulous parents, you will remember my cousin Katharine, with whom I grew up as brother and sister. That old and comfortable relation has for some time now, however, shown signs, on her side, of yielding to affections less purely familial. In short, my dear Henry, I find myself in a Situation not at all of my own making and yet quite as importunate as if it had been. However, this is not the place for such revelations – we must talk! – to which end I propose, if your kind offer holds good, to spend the evening of November the 9th with you in Rye, after coming ashore at Liverpool that morning. I shall, for the time being, have to limit my visit to one night, as Paris and The Times *beckon peremptorily – the great Blowitz is not to be trifled with – but in future I hope to make a habit of such* escales. *There are also other matters that I hope to advert to in seeing you* tête-à-tête, *matters pertaining to* cette dame là *of whom…*

Frieda paused: she had heard a tread on the steps leading up to the Garden Room; the fact that it was audible suggested that it could be neither the light-footed Burgess Noakes nor the stately rustle of Mrs Paddington. She had time only to fold the letter and place it back on its shelf before the door opened and Mr James himself entered. She was conscious of having no explanation for her presence in front of the open cabinet, but Mr James seemed not to register this as an aberration. If he found it strange to discover his amanuensis just where she was, he did not show it.

'Ah, my dear Miss Wroth, I find you in the throes of the *déménagement* that I have visited upon you so abruptly. You will forgive an old man his whims, but the turn in the weather has caught me unawares, reminding me all too late of the extreme inclemency in winter of this otherwise so hospitable room. I do hope you have not found yourself too much incommoded by my impetuosity.'

'Oh, by no means, Mr James, thank you very much. I shall also be glad to move to more congenial surroundings.' She considered that in spite of his apparent lack of suspicion, it might be advisable to provide an explanation for her presence next to the cabinet. 'I was wondering if we should also arrange to have the contents of these cabinets moved.'

'Thank you, my dear, that is considerate of you. But I shall on a later occasion, when I am feeling more robust, select such of these documents as will be indispensable in the Green Room.' He came to stand next to her, peering at the cabinet as if there and then to distinguish between the dispensable and the indispensable.

'I hope that your presence here means that your health is better than I had reason to fear from your absence this morning?'

'I have somewhat recovered my normal faculties, I thank you, Miss Wroth. It has been in many ways a trying weekend, owing possibly to over-exertion in the preceding week.'

Frieda wondered whether this was an implied reproach for her leaving him on his own for the weekend, then decided against it: Mr James's ponderously hospitable style could accommodate many implications, but not the querulous squeak of self-pity. Before she could think of something to say that would be suitably sympathetic and yet not trite, he continued, 'I trust you had an enjoyable weekend. It seems as if it was the last fine weekend we will be having for some time, now that winter has set in.'

Frieda, not wanting to elaborate on the nature of her weekend, took refuge in his reflection on the weather. 'Yes, I do believe that we'll pay for the unusually good weather we have had up to now. The winter always seems more severe after a mild autumn.'

Mr James, still standing next to Frieda, was not prevented by his courteous attention from perusing, she could see, the contents of the open cabinet. As she turned back to her desk to collect her possessions, he closed the cabinet, locked it, and put the key in his pocket. There was a finality in the gesture that boded ill for her chances of revisiting soon the contents of the cabinet.

Chapter Nine
11th November 1907

In winter, Rye turned its regard inward. Never, on its fortified hilltop, the most welcoming of towns, it yet manifested in summer an agreeable openness to the elements, admitting the sea breeze and the sunshine to its narrow streets, the windows ajar to the scent of the roses climbing up the half-timbered cottages, the doors opening for morning callers and being left ajar for the duration of the visit. Cats sunned themselves on windowsills and shops displayed their wares on the pavement to entice strollers. Door entrances were cluttered with lady artists taking impressions of picturesque corners and alleys, and visitors appeared on the tower of the church to survey the surrounding marshlands, pointing out to each other such features as the unsensational landscape offered to the view.

But in winter shutters were closed, doors were locked, the very dogs seemed to disappear off the streets, as the inhabitants withdrew into dim interiors and vague private purposes. Some visiting persisted, but with a hurried and furtive air as if on clandestine missions; not in fact through any sinister design, but in order to minimise exposure to the icy wind from the sea and the rain driven across the marshes. The sea, for the most part invisible beneath its blanket of mist or behind its curtain of rain, made itself felt only as a salty taste in the damp air.

The move from the Garden Room to the Green Room represented the retreat of the inhabitants of Lamb House from a public presence; for whereas the large window giving onto West Street had enabled Mr James to address directly acquaintances passing by, the Green Room was remote even from such human traffic as persisted in the streets of Rye. On fine days its windows permitted, it was true, a view of Winchelsea to the west, but as a disembodied, distant vision, as unreal as a picture on the wall. Besides, as Frieda had on occasion reflected, a view of Winchelsea was in the end only a view of Winchelsea, not a spectacle to gladden the heart or sharpen the senses. She now had a standard of comparison, in the view of the French coast from a terrace in Folkestone.

It was as if even Mr James's dictation became more introspective, his pacing, circumscribed by the smaller floor surface of the room, more tightly centred on the hearth where a fire burned perpetually. Frieda fancied she could discern a greater inwardness in the dictated matter, an even more obsessively contracted focus of interest.

Into this enclosed world came rumours of a world elsewhere in the form of telegrams, letters, and telephone calls to the little room downstairs where the telephone was kept, and to which Mr James was summoned on occasion by a solemn Mrs Paddington announcing with a deep curtsey, 'The telephone, Mr James, sir,' as if the instrument were being presented at court. Mr James would then descend the staircase at rather more than his usual speed, and conduct the conversation at a volume suggesting some doubt as to the instrument's efficacy, and lending high publicity to these communications. These were usually with Mrs Wharton, as the most inveterately telephoning of Mr James's friends, and the household was as a consequence well informed on that lady's movements. 'My dear Edith!' Mr James would bellow, 'How splendid to hear your voice! But what strange chance or circumstance brings you to *Chichester*?' The perceived need to speak at such abnormal volume inhibited Mr James's normal orotundity, and he achieved a conciseness rare in his spoken or written communications, although his long silences suggested that Mrs Wharton was as unintimidated by the instrument as she was by any other mechanical contrivance. Frieda found it strange that Mr James, who would brook no interruption by any living being of his morning's work, would willingly and without demur interrupt his labours at the shrill summons of the telephone: it evidently presented itself to his imagination as having claims transcending its reliance on mere human agency.

In this season Frieda sensed that Mr James was torn

between his normal delight in receiving his friends, and an impulse to withdraw from human contact. There were times when he paused in dictating, not, as usual, to hunt for a word, but simply to listen to the silence of the house and the little town. 'Ah, Miss Wroth, what price such peace?' he would say, but wistfully, as if he were indeed calculating the price. Into this solitude and this peace irrupted at times those friends who were prepared to adapt to his strict routine and who, as he said 'would not expect from little Rye more than it can offer'.

It was clear to Frieda that Mr James was preoccupied. She saw, in the mornings on the hall table, the substantial letters ready for the post; and she saw the equally considerable replies that the postman brought every morning and every afternoon, and she guessed that serious matters were being negotiated. He had never been in the habit of dictating private letters to her, except once or twice when he had been too indisposed to write; he used, she knew, the long nights to keep up with his extensive correspondence.

On the Wednesday morning after Frieda's excursion to Folkestone, she noticed a crumpled-up letter in the waste-paper basket. This was in itself unusual, though not unprecedented: Mr James deliberated as carefully before committing himself to writing as to speech, and thus seldom needed to discard anything once written. But what most piqued Frieda's interest was the phrase, in Mr James's flowing handwriting, that was just visible from where she sat. The phrase was *My Dearest Morton*.

It was clear from Mr James's abstraction that the writing of the letter, or its destruction, testified to some agitation on his part: the pauses between snatches of dictation were longer than normal, and then quite often not productive of any very remarkable word or phrase.

'*It was all in his*…[pause of five paces] *expression; semicolon; he couldn't keep it undetected, comma, and his shining*… [pause of four paces] *good looks couldn't: colon: ah, comma, he was so fatally much too*…[pause of six paces] *handsome for her, exclamation point!*'

Frieda wondered whether Mr James's discarded letter had been in reply to some communication from Mr Fullerton; perhaps the younger man had been moved to remorse at his appeal to her, and had now had the inspiration of confessing to Mr James – which would, of course, also involve betraying her own part, actual as well as prospective, in hoodwinking her employer. This would explain Mr James's distant manner. She was fully expecting him to make some allusion to his friend's confession, and was but half reassured when, pausing once more in the midst of dictating, he said, 'You must forgive me if I seem but imperfectly attending to the work in hand, my dear, but I have been dwelling, no doubt too obsessively, on a remarkably inconclusive conversation I had this morning with the good but even more than usually obdurate George Gammon.'

Frieda had worked for Mr James for long enough to know that he did indeed at times become excessively agitated about quite trivial domestic matters, though not usually in relation to the venerable gardener, who as a rule was deemed, by none more so than by himself, to know what was best for the garden, and was left to go his way.

'You see, my dear,' Mr James continued, as if sensing the need to explain this aberration, 'I bought, on advice from my friend Mrs Wharton, who as you may know is a great gardener, a young but sturdy walnut tree to replace that rather intrusively and dejectedly sickening balsam-poplar on the lawn next to the studio. Now it has occurred to me, or rather Mrs Wharton has reminded me, that now, when the young tree is entering its period of dormancy, would be the best time to transplant it into its permanent situation, with the least amount of trauma.'

He looked at Frieda enquiringly, as if seeking her approval. Frieda, having known trees only as large immovable objects in city parks, had no opinion on the subject, but gave the reply Mr James clearly wanted: 'It certainly seems as if that would be advantageous.'

'So one would have thought. George Gammon, however, is of the opinion that we should wait until spring to plant the walnut, in spite of my having taken the utmost pains to explain to him that it would be to the young tree's benefit to be firmly rooted by the time it conceives the vernal impulse to sprout, quite apart from the balsam-poplar's avid inclination, if given another spring, to invade large tracts of the garden with its diseased roots.' He looked at her anxiously, as if wishing for confirmation in the face of George Gammon's perversity.

Frieda privately thought that George Gammon, supposing he could arrive at the practical implications of Mr James's tortuous reasoning, was probably reluctant to dig a hole in the cold hard soil, when he could wait for the more amenable medium of spring; but she contented herself with saying, 'That does seem to make sense, rather than have the young tree languish in a container all winter.'

He looked at her gratefully. 'Exactly, my dear Miss Wroth, exactly. Indeed, if you will excuse me for the merest five minutes, I shall convey to George Gammon our combined opinion on the matter.'

Frieda was slightly alarmed: she had no wish to incur the displeasure of the grumpy old man, who had on several occasions compromised his constitutional misogyny by presenting her with flowers from the garden. Still, she could hardly now retract such support as she had given Mr James; besides, he was already making his way down the stairs to the garden.

Getting up from her desk, Frieda could see, through the south window, Mr James in the garden earnestly addressing a manifestly unreceptive George Gammon. Mr James's demonstrations of the advantages of early planting were being expounded at some length without, as far as Frieda could see, lightening the grim old gardener's brow a whit. The debate, if any exchange so one-sided could be called a debate, was likely to carry on for a while, and Frieda, standing next to the window, allowed her eye to wander again to the waste-paper basket.

Having, without quite intending it, read Mrs Wharton's letter to Mr James, she had by now divested herself of her last scruple regarding the privacy of Mr James's correspondence. Besides, committed as she was to plundering Mr James's archives, it seemed a refinement bordering on hypocrisy to distinguish between letters received by him and letters written by him. It was to her a kind of compensation for her seclusion from life as other people knew it, to be admitted, or to claim admittance, to that larger world which Mr James, for all his illusion of solitude, commanded.

Frieda bent down, retrieved the letter, and smoothed it out:

Lamb House, Rye
November 11th 1907

My dearest Morton,

I have once again been pondering your quite overwhelming
confidences, and if I grasp all instinctively at my pen, even after our
so extensive and so recent deliberations tête-à-tête, it is as a poor
spent swimmer clutching all deludedly for salvation at what may
well prove his undoing. What comes over me, as I come up for air,
is my own sense of having been left, all ineffectually gaping, outside
the ante-room of your life, where I was all along fondly imagining I
had been admitted if not quite to the inner chamber, then at least to
a congenial sala from where to survey with you the happily agitated
conduct of that life. To have believed oneself, for these last eighteen
years, more or less an intimate, and then to discover oneself to have
been to such an extent excluded from anything resembling trust or
even hospitality, is to find only a chill chasm where one had imagined
a bridge, and an impostor where one had welcomed a guest.

It did not seem to me, I confess, a matter calling for
congratulation, your having so long ago and with, as you so
oddly insisted, so little effort on your part, attracted the notice of
Lord Ronald Gower; but I can at least see that for a young man
newly arrived in London the attentions of a nobleman with some
pretensions to taste must have appeared a distinction worth having.
Furthermore, in the event no lasting damage seems to have been done,
the connection running the predestined course of all relations posited
upon the interaction of vanity and flattery. Nor can I share your
sense that its nature is now, after the unfortunate fate of the altogether
excessive Oscar Wilde, liable to similar misrepresentation should its
details find their way into the public domain: Lord Ronald, whatever
one may think of his private morals and public manner, has all the
appearance today of a regularised member of society – so unlike, in
the public regard, the associates of the sublime Oscar.

What I complain of, what I protest against as a mortal injury,
is your classing, as a source of peril and insecurity, your letters to me
with those of Lord Ronald to you, not to mention those effusions of
Oscar Wilde which so exercised the moral imagination of the nation
at the time of their being made public.

Here Mr James had stopped writing and crumpled up the paper, presumably to postpone to a calmer moment his response to Mr Fullerton's confidences; Frieda imagined that on reflection he would write in a more conciliatory tone to a friend whom he clearly did not want to lose.

Looking again into the garden, she saw Mr James still remonstrating with George Gammon; his earnestness had something of the passion of desperation about it, as it met the impassive regard of the old gardener. Then at last he must have found some device whereby to penetrate the unresponsive armour of the man's settled opinion, for, with a slight but eloquent shrug, George Gammon took up his spade and started digging in the spot designated by his employer. Mr James stood observing for a minute, as if suspecting this to be but some new manifestation of George Gammon's resistance, but as the soil started flying, some of it indeed coming to rest on Mr James's newly polished boots, he stepped back and re-entered the house.

Frieda took up her place at the typewriter again, her mind full of Mr James's letter. This was the second time Oscar Wilde's name had come up in relation to that past of Mr Fullerton's of which there seemed ever more. In spite of her blankness under the pressure of his questioning, she had indeed heard of the Oscar Wilde affair, though she was only ten or eleven at the time. Her father had fulminated against the bloodlust of the newspapers and the infernal cheek of that man Wilde alike. When Frieda had asked him for an explanation, he had said, 'It's a wretched affair, my dear, for a young child to comprehend, indeed for anybody to comprehend. It makes one wonder what is most rotten, English public life or English private life.' Other than this cryptic comment he had not ventured to explain to his daughter the nature of the case against Wilde, and with time she had forgotten about it: it had appeared so little to impinge on her life. She seemed to remember seeing in a newspaper that he had died in Paris some years earlier. Now to have his name surface again in relation to Mr Fullerton and his connection with Lord Ronald, the extravagantly inexpressive man she had seen in Folkestone, was as puzzling as it was unexpected. She knew, of course, that men were more adventurous in their sexual practices than women – her friend Mabel had had it on good authority from her young man, the prematurely deceased Charlie, that 'there was nothing they didn't do, they got that desperate' – but she had assumed this to refer to wartime conditions, and besides, it was one thing to know something like that in a general way and another to know it as a very particular fact about a very particular gentleman with whom one had oneself recently been in a very particular relation.

Mr James appeared, out of breath from climbing the stairs. 'I trust he saw reason in the end, but it's always difficult to tell with George Gammon whether he is convinced by one's logic or merely indulging one's misguided notions, helpless old fool that he no doubt regards one as. I daresay our servants pass judgement on us quite as feelingly as we do on them, and may well dream of a future in which they will be at liberty to tell us so. Now where was I, my dear? I do believe I was about to finish off the blessed Julia Child. She should have been dispatched weeks ago.'

'*He was so fatally much too handsome for her.*'

'Ah yes.' Mr James resumed his pacing. 'New sentence continue: '*So the gap showed just there, comma, in his admirable… mask and his admirable… eagerness; semi-colon; the yawning little chasm showed where the gentleman fell short. Full stop.*'

'*The point is, comma, however, comma,*'

Here followed a pause and perambulation longer than usual; the *point* being always, with Mr James, more elusive than the circumambient matter.

'*The point is, however, that...*'

Frieda wondered, while Mr James paced, whether he had at last written himself into a corner from which he could not emerge without knocking down a wall or two, a complication which she was perennially half dreading, half hoping for; but he stopped pacing and turned to her as if imparting to her personally a *trouvaille* of some import.

'*...that this single small... corner-stone, hyphenated, comma, the conception of a certain young...*'

Person? Girl?

'*...woman affronting her...*'

Past? Future? Fortune? Family?

'*...destiny, comma, had begun with being all my outfit for the large... building of "The Portrait of a Lady" quotation marks. Full stop.*'

Some young women, Frieda reflected, evidently interested Mr James more than some others – which, she conceded might be only natural. Only, she wondered on what basis he decided.

'*It came to be a square and spacious house – dash – or has at least seemed so to me in this going over it again; semi-colon; but...*'

But I find I have forgotten to install a front door? But I am aware that fashions in houses change from one year to another?

'*...but, comma, such as it is, comma, it had to be put up round my young woman while she stood there in perfect...*'

Indifference? Unconsciousness?

'*…isolation. Full stop. That is to me, comma, artistically speaking, comma, the circumstance of interest; semi-colon; for…*'

Again a long pause; Mr James did tend to set himself up with conjunctions recklessly promising elucidation where elucidation was, in the nature of the preceding material, difficult.

'*…I have lost myself once more…*'

'*…artistically speaking, the circumstance of interest; for…*'

'Yes, yes, thank you, Miss Wroth, but you misunderstand. I am dictating. *I have lost myself once more, comma, I confess, comma, in the curiosity of analysing the structure. Full stop. By what process of logical…*'

Deduction?

'*…accretion was this slight "personality" quotation marks, comma, the mere slim shade of an intelligent but presumptuous…*'

Woman.

'*…girl, comma, to find itself endowed with the high attributes of a Subject capitalised, question mark? Dash – and indeed by what thinness, comma, at the best, comma, would such a subject not be vitiated, question mark?*'

Mr James had, for the last several months, been revising his novels for a new edition to be brought out in New York, and had been dictating new prefaces in which he explored at some length the critical principles that, in the reperusal, seemed to him to be most pertinent to each work. There were many things there that Frieda did not understand, and she wished that it could have been possible to stop Mr James and ask him to elucidate some of the more elusive ideas. But Mr James was as unaware of the intellectual hunger of his typewriter as he was solicitous of her bodily comfort, offering her chocolate bars to sustain her during long sessions of dictation, when what she wanted was sustenance for her spirit. The chocolate bars, she felt at times, were offered in the same spirit in which he fed Max little biscuits from a brown paper packet as a special treat. It was characteristic of him, she thought with unwonted bitterness, that he should lose himself in *analysing the structure* of a story of a *young woman affronting her destiny* and disregard the daily presence of just such a young woman in his own house. She, no doubt, did not qualify for a *destiny*.

Frieda could not have said, if asked, what Mr James could

have done to signal his awareness of her destiny, such as it was, but she felt sure that she would have noticed it if it had been there, this awareness. It was, at bottom, *artistically speaking*, a question of the material on which the artistic sensibility fed: Mr James invoked, as models, Juliet and Portia and Hetty Sorrel and Maggie Tulliver; but what were they to him or he to them, when he claimed his subject was Life itself?

Thus pondered Frieda in the winter of 1907, a period in which she was more aware than ever before of chafing against the envelope of her circumstances. This was, no doubt, partly ascribable to the season: the charms of Rye needed sunlight to quicken them. What glowed mellow in sunshine seemed merely mouldering in the damp, and the romance of lamplight in dark parlours was less evident at three o'clock in the afternoon than late on a summer's night. She did not expect Mr James to provide entertainment for the long winter nights, romps and parlour games and *tableaux vivants* such as she had heard him describe with a shudder as occurring at country seats at this season. She did, however, wish that he could contrive somehow – she scarcely knew how – to admit her to the precinct of that citadel in which his meticulously qualified and amplified ruminations were forged.

But if he remained unaware of her wistful presence peering in at the windows, as it were, of the stronghold of his art, he did show himself more willing to admit her, in a sense, to his private life, by dictating more of his letters. This was a purely practical matter – it saved him time – but she interpreted it also as a greater implication of confidence in her. It gave her a curious pleasure, in the midst of her discontent, to be the medium of communication between this meticulous, talkative man and some of his many equally prolific correspondents. Mr James used telegrams for convenience, but hated their enforced conciseness: ever fastidious as to the selection of the right word, he was reduced to an agony of indecision by a telegram, with its scanty allowance of words – 'Clarity is so *expensive*,' he would wail, 'and economy is so inexpressive.' Hence the rhythm of the typewriter, the liberty to meander, ponder and reflect, was congenial to him in his correspondence; and yet, Frieda came to notice, he managed to compress a good deal of information and comment in a single sentence. He may have been expansive, but he was not empty: '*This is all just now,*' he would say, apparently preparing to conclude a letter to his brother William, only to carry on irresistibly, '*save that I go on the 23rd to Liverpool to meet poor Lawrence Godkin, who arrives there with dear little Katherine G's cold ashes for interment near ELG at Hazelbeach, the so oddly, so perversely fixed little out-of-the-way Northamptonshire churchyard in which their father and husband was (as I feel) so erratically laid after his death near Torquay several years ago.*'

Frieda was proud to think that the compression and complexity which marked Mr James's expression at its best was made possible by her typewriter's capacity to follow without faltering or fatigue the layered patterns of his mind, to accompany with its staccato rhythms the convolutions of syntax that seemed to be spun out by his pacing, to dart into and out of the ever-opening-up and closing-down boxes of meaning, of relations touched upon and left behind in the meandering course of a single sentence: the pathetic little drama of a son travelling from America to bury his mother's ashes next to her husband in an out-of-the-way church in England, the reasons why the father had originally so 'erratically' been buried so far from where he died, Mr James's dutiful travelling to Liverpool to assist at the lugubrious ceremony – all these apparently disparate and discrete elements brought into relation with one another in a single 'situation'.

The visit to Northamptonshire took place over a weekend, and on the succeeding Monday Frieda was left in charge of the Green Room. It would now be a relatively simple matter to gain access to the various places of storage in the room, and to find Mr Fullerton's letters. He had said that there was no great urgency, by which she had understood him to mean that he felt insecure only in the face of Mr James's possibly precarious state of health, and, whereas of course Mr James's health was never particularly good, there was at present no sign of its being appreciably worse than usual. And yet finding the letters had become to Frieda an idea with which she got up in the morning and went to bed in the evening; at such times she could sense Mr Fullerton's presence, not only reminding her of her task, but, more preciously, reliving their afternoon together. It was at times more real to her, this presence, than the sound of the trains or the smell of fish entering her garret room from workaday Rye.

Frieda had often reflected on her experience in the Garden Room, when she had received such a clear intimation of Mr Fullerton's presence, followed by the confirmatory telegram. She understood telepathy as little as she understood the telegram or the telephone, but she assumed that, like those two media, telepathy did not depend for its operation on one's comprehension. She had, of course, remained in touch with her Aunt Frederica, and that lady was gratified at Frieda's sudden expression of interest in a subject in which she had in earlier days tried to involve her without success. '*Oh yes*,' she wrote, '*the Society is establishing new proof every day of the efficacy of telepathy, or thought transference as we prefer to call it, and is attracting some very influential members. You will know, of course, that Professor William James, the brother of your employer, is the President of the Society, and has done much to establish the most rigorous conditions for the verification of thought transference. The American author Samuel Clemens, of whom you have no doubt heard under his pen-name Mark Twain, is an enthusiastic member and writes regularly in support of the Society's work. I have taken out an Associate Membership of the Society in your name, and paid the first year's subscription of a guinea. This will give you the opportunity of deciding for yourself whether you want to continue the membership after the first year. I must warn you, however, that your friend Mr Dodds, to whom I mentioned this, was displeased with me for encouraging you in what he called, rather rudely I thought, irreligious mumbo-jumbo. I told him that scepticism coupled with ignorance was no more than prejudice.*'

Frieda was but moderately interested in the Society's experiments, except in so far as they sanctioned, as it were, her own far more direct experience, and she was completely undeterred by Mr Dodds's disapproval; but she was intrigued by the anxiety of other people to explain to themselves and others a phenomenon the essence of which was surely its private nature. Membership of the Society included a subscription to the *Journal of the Society for Psychical Research*, in which members exchanged views, beliefs, experiences and fears. She was amused to find misgivings being expressed by members about the potential perils of 'mind melding', as one concerned correspondent called it: '...*which is to say the invasion of one mind by another in a form of intimacy more insidious than the physical, because so much more surreptitious. I have known one unfortunate young woman to lose control of her own person through the invasion of her mind by a young man to whom she had been unwise enough to grant access, and to end up on the parish.*' The writer did not make clear how this danger could be guarded against, and Frieda did not consider her own case to be analogous with that of the hapless young woman.

After her initial experience of being entered by Mr Fullerton's consciousness, she had several times experienced something similar. It was not exactly a mental awareness: it was as if, entering her mind, he recalled to her whole body the very feel of his skin and smell of his hair. On a few occasions, in the early morning or late evening in her little room at Warden's Hotel, his presence had been so vivid that she had addressed him, but he invariably withdrew at the sound of her voice, as if he needed silence as a medium. At other times, silence and darkness conspired with her imagination: recalling the afternoon in Folkestone, she could not only recreate the experience, but adapt it to the infinitely more modest but more intimate dimensions of her room. Here, she could instigate and direct, control and guide; she could negotiate from a position of strength the satisfaction of her own body, encounter Mr Fullerton as an equal in desire. After such encounters, his presence remained with her for days afterwards, not only in the dingy light of her room, but also in the larger spaces of her workaday life. Once, even, in crossing Church Square, she had been overwhelmed by a sensation as of his entering her, and she had had to sit down on a bench in the churchyard, to the evident surprise and dismay of the beggars who regarded that corner of Rye as their particular preserve.

She wanted to tell Mr Fullerton that she was committed to finding the letters, and that when she found them she would contrive to go to Paris herself to deliver them to him. Not that her quest was an easy one. The problem, or one of the problems, was that there was a total of eight desks in Lamb House. Of these, Frieda had access to two, dedicated to her use. One other, in the Garden Room, she had already searched. That left five, plus any number of bookcases – in the Green Room alone there were three – which could all serve, in the various cabinets supporting the shelves, as depositaries for letters. As for anything not actually in the Green Room, that was further complicated by the apparently omnipresent Mrs Paddington and the almost equally invariable Burgess Noakes, both of whom had the uncanny capacity to appear unbidden and unexpected at any moment, like inconveniently obliging ghosts.

On the Monday morning, after a disturbed night in which Mr Fullerton had been particularly present to her – he must have known that Mr James had gone away for the weekend – Frieda approached Mr James's desk. She could see Burgess Noakes in the garden talking to George Gammon – they were evidently discussing, with much shaking of heads and gesturing with hands, the newly installed walnut tree – and she could hear Mrs Paddington talking in the kitchen to the housemaid Fanny and the parlour-maid Alice. There was nobody on the second storey with Frieda, and if anybody did approach, she would hear him on the staircase before he saw her. But as she reached the desk, Max, who had been lying next to the fire apparently fast asleep, leapt to his feet and ran towards her, barking shrilly as if possessed by some malign spirit.

'That's all right, Max, it's only me,' she tried to soothe the enraged dog, but he would not desist until Frieda had returned to her own desk and sat down in her habitual place. By this time Mrs Paddington had made her stately way up the stairs and was standing in the door of the Green Room.

'Is anything the matter, miss?' she asked, though by now Max had retreated growling to his place by the fireside.

'No thank you, Mrs Paddington. Max must have been dreaming: one moment he was lying there fast asleep and the next he leapt up as if being attacked by a herd of buffalo.'

Mrs Paddington shook her head. '*Dogs*,' she said sepulchrally. She had confessed to Frieda on occasion that she found Mr James's attachment to Max 'just the slightest bit inconvenient from an *hygienic* point of view. It's not as I mind the dog hairs on the furniture as much as the strange things he brings into the house from his walks.'

For the first time Frieda, who liked Max, was inclined to agree with Mrs Paddington. Max could be a serious nuisance if he barked at her every time she approached any piece of furniture other than her own desk. This was a sad change from his normal behaviour: hitherto he had shown nothing but joyful recognition whenever he saw her, and when not asleep by Mr James's feet, would lie next to her looking adoringly at her.

Frieda knew little about animal behaviour, and had not heard any theories as to their telepathic abilities, but she thought it possible that Max could apprehend her nefarious intentions by whatever instinct dogs had developed to identify miscreants. For whatever reason, though, it seemed that in Mr James's absence Max had appointed himself as guardian of the house.

Not being able to pursue her quest, Frieda resumed her place at her desk. Just there, then, was where she was destined to spend her days, in the keeping of a dachshund, like Danae in her tower, or some Lady of Shalott with a typewriter in place of a loom – and with, on Mr James's return, a benign ogre to circumscribe with his pacing her allocated territory, and dictate to her according to his whim. She reflected with wry irony on Miss Petherbridge's cherished slogan: 'The liberation of women lies in their own hands.' The typewriter, symbol of woman's emancipation, had become a shackle. Only at night, in her cold little room in the Warden Hotel, Mr Fullerton appeared to her, his blue eyes shining in the dark, to whisper in her ear about the beautiful places to which he would take her when she had found the letters.

Mr James returned after four days, tired and depressed by what he called his infernal journey to the other end of England – 'I cannot imagine why people would want to be buried in places they would never have lived in. Miss Wroth,' he added, only half-jocularly, 'I instruct and enjoin you to prevent my ashes from being shipped to America after my death, otherwise I shall certainly importune you from beyond the grave.'

'I hope then that you leave instructions in your will. My word is unlikely to count against the wishes of your relations.'

He sighed humorously. 'I am afraid it would take more than a decree from beyond the grave to convince dear William and Alice that I have not all these years merely dissembled my wish to remain in England. The wishes of the dead are taken to be absolute, and yet they depend for their execution on the good will of the living.'

Frieda felt a twinge here, recalling her own defiance of her mother's will. She had tried to tell herself that she had not violated any express wish or precept of her mother's, but it was no good: she knew that there were certain things that her mother would certainly have proscribed if she had thought her daughter capable of them. Frieda was relieved that she was no longer in a position to accompany Mabel to Mrs Beddow's sessions, for her mother would be quite capable, as she had proved before, of violating spiritual protocol and usurping somebody else's 'turn'. There was nothing to prevent the defunct Mrs Wroth from denouncing her daughter in a full meeting of the Chelsea and Pimlico chapter of the Spiritualists Society.

At this season Mr James renewed his assault upon the stage. Frieda had gathered, she hardly knew how – through rueful references on his part, over-emphatic abstentions from reference on Mrs Wharton's part – that Mr James had, earlier in his career, had a brief and ill-fated flirtation with the theatre. She read into the very slight shudder punctuating such references an aversion to any renewed engagement with the stage, and was the more surprised when she found herself typing, to his dictation, several plays.

She did not verbalise this surprise, but Mr James undertook of his own accord to explain his lapse from absolute consistency. 'I assumed, indeed I resolved, with the bitterness of a spurned passion, that I had done with the theatre,' he explained to her, 'were it not more true to say that the theatre had, in its ruthless manner, done with me, clasping me to its ample but meretricious bosom for just long enough to squeeze the breath out of me before flinging me into the gutter like the veriest impostor. I have always venerated the drama, but feared the theatre – for if the drama is where the deep, deep art of human action finds its most vivid scenic expression, the theatre is ultimately the sum of a certain number of seats that must be filled at a certain price by a certain number of people every night for the poor little drama to survive. It seems, however, according to people whose business it is to keep their fingers on the pulse of the great and fickle public, that just at present there is a demand for the kind of product, as they call it, that I am in a position to supply – something, that is, that appeals to something other than the superficial sensationalism or, heaven help us, the humourless "fun" that has so inexplicably delighted London audiences in recent years.'

Frieda had her misgivings, but kept her own counsel. She could not imagine that the public taste would ever change to the extent of developing an appetite for the kind of product she was daily typing. Mr James's characters were intelligent, they were articulate, they were highly discriminating: they were everything but alive. She had heard Professor William James say to his brother, only half in jest, that no human being had ever spoken like one of Henry James's characters, but this was only partly true: no human being other than Henry James had ever spoken like a Henry James character. And all the men and women so tenuously inhabiting his plays had been created in his image, and spoke like their creator: an idiom adapted to the slow lucubrations and deliberations and considerations of Lamb House, dependent upon the affectionately patient attention of friends content to await the slow unfolding of a sentence as much for the beauty of its sinuous movement as for the elusive insight it guarded jealously in its coils. This could not, Frieda thought, appeal to audiences schooled in the brittle interchanges of Oscar Wilde or the politically weighted dialogues of Bernard Shaw, and she thought that the plays she was now typing represented but a poor return on time that could have been spent writing novels. Nevertheless, Mr James, she guessed, was enthralled by the prospect, as he saw it, of having his fictional characters incarnated, as creatures of flesh and blood who could bleed, laugh and weep.

On the strength of the encouragement of one particularly persuasive actor-manager, Mr James committed himself to the try-out of one of his plays, *The High Bid*, in Edinburgh at the end of March, consenting even to travelling to Edinburgh by special train with the cast, for all the world, he said, like a lion tamer travelling with the animals, or a necromancer consorting with the ghosts he was 'booked' to raise in public.

Frieda was apprehensive lest the Edinburgh audience fail to appreciate the vitality of Mr James's lions or the authenticity of his ghosts, for all that that city had been selected for the try-out on the grounds of its populace being less jaded than the great London public. To her it seemed that Mr James's play required for its appreciation, in so far as it was amenable to appreciation, not the candour of a provincial audience, but the sophistication of the metropolis. In this pessimistic prognostication she was proved wrong, in that she received a short letter from Mr James telling her that '*the Play was an unmistakably complete and charming and rewarding success*,' adding, '*I hope you have passed your days conveniently to yourself.*'

Frieda wondered how Mr James imagined her convenience and what he pictured her doing in his absence, other than the revisions he left her to type; but she concluded that his imagination was engaged elsewhere than with the daily round of his typewriter. He would not, she imagined, have guessed that she was amusing herself by her own venture into composition, which continued haltingly, to her mind limpingly, to fill her pages when there was no other matter to do so.

Such complaisance on Spencer's part, however, yielded on occasion, and with a readiness amounting almost to collusion, to an impulse of resistance prompted by the renewed recognition that in a relation avowedly dedicated to his greater good, he should himself be indulged as final arbiter, albeit only by himself, as the person most concerned with the subject. In keeping with this principle, on the morning that we have occasion here to commemorate, not even the prospect of Mrs Blythe's disapprobation could compel him to abbreviate a walk so sweetly charged with the air of impending spring, as with the promise of a surprise not spoiled in the anticipation nor staled in the repetition. He resolved to prolong his walk as far as the Parapet, a raised level area of ancient origin and obscurely bellicose or defensive purpose, which could be counted on to afford, on a day as pellucid as this, a view of the distant cliffs of France.

Spencer couldn't have said why the remote prospect of
foreign cliffs should so touch upon a consciousness
that was not, as a rule, amenable to the treasonable
cosmopolitan solicitations of mere bootless nostalgia,
a consciousness that had, indeed, cultivated the habit
of regarding it as a matter quite settled that the
rugged amenities of the little marsh-encircled town
would henceforth represent the bourn of his earthly
existence; but it was nevertheless true that nothing
in the small town of Slope, satisfactory as it was in
itself, so pleased, positively thrilled him as this
glimpse of a larger continent. He had in his day drunk
deeply, though with the highest discretion, of the
delights and privileges of this multifarious continent,
of the great capital of culture and pleasure above
all, if indeed it were not more true to state that he
had simply submitted to the burden of pleasure heaped
so copiously upon the unwary visitor, and bringing
with it its own responsibilities and sharp exigencies.
Oh, the exigencies of pleasure! Spencer positively
groaned for them, at this distance of time and across
the sensible void of the chilly Channel, so definitely
and so appropriately, in its uncommunicative dampness,
designated as English.
Spencer had indeed lately received emissaries from the
luminary city across the watery divide, and it was with a
vague ache that he peered across the cool grey haze at the
indistinct extremities of a country so blessed with such
riches; peered as from a comfortable, well-appointed but
sensibly contracted chamber of ease at some distant, dusty
battlefield of life, from which the clash of sabres and
the high alarms of bugles could be heard faintly. Spencer,
if challenged, would have confessed to the greater amenity
of the chamber to a man of his age and temperament; but
neither of these conditions was as yet so absolute as
to suppress wholly the appeal of this intuition of a
life elsewhere, this rumour of unabated strife. His late
communication from the battlefield, moreover, had been
such as to sharpen his interest while increasing his

alarm, as of a report of a loved one wounded in battle.

Mr James returned from Edinburgh 'much emboldened', as he put it, 'by the relative success of my latest assault upon the stage, which is to say my appeal to the discrimination of the stalls and the grand circle, without undue concession to the gallery and the pit.'

Perhaps under the influence of this mood of optimism, he had invested, on his way through London, in the latest model Remington, the Model 10. It was with something of the air of a stage magician that he observed Burgess Noakes uncrating the gleaming machine. When it had been installed on Frieda's desk, he regarded it with undisguised satisfaction but also, Frieda thought, with a certain wariness.

'It is inordinately clever, my dear, and a great advance on the somewhat cumbersome machine you have so valiantly made do with hitherto. It is called the Visible Writer, and has the immense advantage, I am told, of exposing to view the text as it is produced.'

Frieda inserted a sheet of paper and typed some phrases. There was indeed something almost miraculous in seeing the text appear at the same time as she typed it: it gave her as never before the sense of being directly responsible for the formation of the letters. 'This will certainly save time,' she said. 'It did slow us down, my having to open the viewing flap whenever I had to read something back to you.'

'I must confess myself left gaping by all these new inventions. There is no telling where the ingenuity of man will yet take us.'

As winter yielded with bad grace to spring, and the cold winds of March softened into the vernal breezes of April, Mr James started preparing for a visit to Paris. He had resolved, a few months earlier, never ever to cross the Channel again; but Mrs Wharton's fulsome invitations, and possibly also Mr Fullerton's urgings, had moved him to reconsider so absolute a resolution. 'Dear old Paris,' he mused one morning, while peering across at Winchelsea, as if that little port carried somehow the clue to the far great city. 'It is not, I fear, a city for anybody over fifty.'

Frieda waited for him to explain this proposition, but as after several seconds it seemed he was not going to do so, she thought it in order to pry gently: 'And yet there must be thousands of people over fifty living there.'

He laughed at her earnestness. 'Oh, thousands, yes! But only to be aware every day that Paris has nothing to offer them, that she keeps everything for the young, like some spoilt and demanding mistress. A very beautiful mistress, I grant you, of whom everybody is free to admire the beauty, as long as they are prepared to accept her terms.' He paused, and she thought he had concluded his reflection, but he resumed: 'Paris delights in everything that Rye is a refuge from – the life of the senses, the beauty of youth, the extravagance of light, the excitement of conquest; whereas Rye is content with everything that Paris leaves one hankering after: rest, retreat, reflection, withdrawal. To visit Paris at my age is to be made aware of what one has lost, or, worse, what one has never had.'

'And yet,' Frieda ventured, 'to see Paris I would give almost anything.'

He looked at her reflectively, as if it were occurring to him for the first time that she might have such aspirations. 'Oh yes, my dear, you must see Paris. I'm an old wretch for having brought you here before you have seen Paris. For if Paris is for the young, Rye is for the old. You must not allow my selfishness to keep you here: you must go to Paris and you must live all you can.'

This was a stirring injunction, deficient only in not suggesting how it was to be executed by a single woman of limited means. It was a beautiful sentiment, but it was beautifully general. It occurred to Frieda that it would be no very great sacrifice for Mr James to take his amanuensis with him to Paris. From what he had told her, and from what the great lady herself had proclaimed, there was room enough in Mrs Wharton's Paris apartment; and, socially speaking, she knew how to make herself very small. This even Mrs Wharton had noticed: 'One forgets you are here, you are so quiet!' she had once exclaimed to Frieda, as if Frieda's silence were in some sense an imposition on the good faith of the company. Mrs Wharton, never having had to master the art of silence, clearly held it in small regard; but if she did not welcome Frieda as a social asset, she might by the same token tolerate her as a social irrelevance.

But, while Mr James remained so blithely unaware of his typewriter's situation, she had nothing to contemplate but the coming of spring to the little citadel of Rye, and the privilege of taking Max for walks on Camber Sands. Perhaps she might recruit the dog as an ally; and, then, when she had found the letters, she could go to Paris and live, as Mr James had so stirringly enjoined her to do.

Chapter Eleven
April–May 1908

Mr James left for Paris towards the end of April, half apprehensive, half joyful at the prospect of witnessing once more, as he said, nature's miracle collaborating with man's creation. 'Spring in Paris,' he said to Frieda on the morning of his departure, a grey enough morning to give point to his reference, 'is both contradiction and affirmation: her own beauty is so much a matter of glitter and artifice that one would expect her tawdry appeal to be shown up and shamed by the freshness of the season; and yet, the coquettish old city has the trick of turning everything to her advantage, and borrowing from nature the lineaments of youth.'

'I think you will be glad to be there once again,' Frieda said, perceiving an unaccustomed excitement in her generally placid employer; she had on occasion wondered whether his was most a case of having mastered every passion or of having outlived them.

'Why yes, my dear, so I shall. And yet, in Paris one counts one's losses as nowhere else.'

'Not even in Rye?' Frieda permitted herself to ask.

He looked at her in surprise: it was unlike her to question his propositions. 'Oh, definitely not in Rye. Have you not noticed that in Rye one's expectations adjust themselves to the scale of the place?'

Frieda felt a touch of bitterness. 'I cannot say I have. But then, my expectations have never exceeded my opportunities.'

His reply was but half jocular. 'Now that *is* sad. At your age one has no call to be so excessively mature.'

While Mr James was in Paris, Frieda had more than enough

time to reflect on the opportunities offered by Rye and on her own expectations in the light of these. The former, as Mr James had warned her, consisted pretty much of rural charm and the bicycle; but whereas that had seemed sufficient at the time, she now found her expectations informed and suborned by her experience. With April transforming the winter-dreary expanse of the Marsh with the scent of flowers and the sound of birdsong, she longed for more vivid human companionship than that represented by Mrs Paddington and Burgess Noakes, with whatever assistance from Max.

Mr James had left instructions that in his absence the centre of operations was to be moved again to the Garden Room, and this was easily effected with the aid of Burgess Noakes and Mrs Paddington. Frieda felt that she had miserably failed all winter to get any sense of the possible whereabouts of the letters. She assumed, however, that Mr Fullerton would not have wanted her to take any foolish risks. And there was still the possibility that they could be in the Garden Room – a possibility, however, that would have to remain unexplored for the time being, since Frieda found that Mr James had locked all the cabinets in the room.

At this time of Mr James's absence, Frieda frequently found herself in the Garden Room, at liberty to pursue her own interests: her employer periodically sent work or instructions from Paris, but he was evidently kept too busy by Mrs Wharton to generate very much work for Frieda. The young woman turned again to her own novel, shaping and reshaping the opening paragraphs:

Upon reaching the mild prominence of the parapet, Spencer was momentarily disconcerted to find that he had been anticipated by a stranger: a stranger not only to himself but, as he was after twenty years of residence qualified to vouch, to the little town of Slope itself. It was too early yet, in the day as well as in the 'season', for the much-deplored day visitors from London on 'outings'; besides, there was something in the attire of the young man which spoke of his not having arrived by train or char-à-banc or horribly hooting pleasure steamer: an intention to stay over, as they said, signalled by a

certain relaxed air, a matter as much of his easy stance
as of his loose jacket and soft collar — an appearance
of having neither 'dressed' for a voyage nor consulted
a timetable to arrive just where he was, with his foot
resting easily in an embrasure in the low wall edging the
parapet. Not that there was about his manner anything of
the over-familiar taking possession of the place that had
on occasion struck our hero as the mark of visitors of a
certain type, as of people who are at home everywhere and
come from nowhere. The young man seemed, in fine, not to
be 'doing' the sights of Slope as much as lapsing into
harmony with its unsensational oppidan repose. He glanced
at Spencer in a manner that made the latter wonder
whether he were a compatriot from the great democracy,
so little was there in it of the English reluctance to
be 'caught' taking an interest in an unintroduced fellow-
mortal. And yet there was singularly absent from it,
too, any suggestion of the too-avid, the too-unblinking
ocular surface, that at times he deplored as one of the
disadvantages of growing up in a country so bereft, so
suspicious of curtains and draperies and other screens to
vision as his own native land.

'Forgive me,' the young man all hesitatingly
ventured, his tentativeness consciously palliating the
relative boldness of his address, 'but are you not Giles
Spencer, the novelist?'

Frieda amused herself well enough with polishing her phrases
and consolidating her clauses in a manner she thought worthy
of the Master, but she nevertheless felt that the exercise was not
engaging her fully. Sitting at her typewriter, she became aware
of the presence of another consciousness, of her fingers obeying
not the promptings of her own mind or eye, but half-formed
thoughts entering her mind of their own volition. At first she
experienced these irruptions as a disturbance, certainly as a
distraction from her own effort at composition. But yielding to
the impulses of the usurping consciousness, she found that she
could record them as smoothly as if she were taking dictation.
The typewriter, indeed, was eminently suitable for the capture

of such thoughts, and in time she was taking down complete sentences: she needed only to clear her mind of all extraneous matters, and await a tremor in her hands followed by a numbness; then, on her placing her fingers on the keys, they would start executing the impulses of the other mind that she more and more confidently was able to identify as that of Mr Fullerton. The new machine, she had occasion to reflect, considerably facilitated the process by making available instantaneously the text so produced.

Abandoning, for the time being, her own attempt at a novel, she started to make a transcript of what she thought of as her conversations with Mr Fullerton, in the form that she had seen used in the *Journal*. Since her communications with him were not strictly and meagrely verbal, she had, in transcribing them, also to translate their content from the kind of intuitive apprehension that was the form in which she received them, to a verbal equivalent. This was at first difficult, since some of these communications were almost purely physical in nature, a heightened awareness and increased sensitivity in some parts of her body; but with time she learnt to sublimate those into more tractable verbal constructs, or otherwise to filter them out of the transcript.

Her own replies to him she also typed: as newspaperman he would abhor slovenliness or imprecision of expression, and typing was a way of ensuring that she was focusing and shaping her thoughts coherently and systematically. In time she found, indeed, that with the aid of the typewriter she could achieve a fluency of communication that was impossible in any other way, probably because, as Mr James said, the clicking of the keys stimulated the mind and facilitated thought. The exchanges were at first rather stilted, as both of them struggled to adapt to the unusual means of communication, but with time it came to seem almost natural, the speed and rhythm of the typewriter again aiding the illusion of fluency and immediacy.

She had gathered from her reading of the *Journal* that thought transference by no means took place at will: the two people concerned had both to be in a receptive state of mind at the same time, which was, of course, difficult to arrange where she had no other contact with Mr Fullerton; and there were times when she sat at the typewriter to no effect. He, too, seemed conscious of this problem, for one morning, when she was sitting in the Garden Room waiting for some sign of his mental activity, her fingers went unbidden to the typewriter:

```
This time of morning, before I go to work, is generally
the most convenient for me to make contact with you. I
hope you can contrive also to be free at this time.
```

Thus there was established between them an understanding and a routine that became the most important part of Frieda's day. She adopted, in recording these thought-transference sessions, the terms *Receiver* and *Transmitter*. She realised that this was not strictly speaking accurate, since both of them were in fact receiving as well as transmitting, but she could not escape the illusion that the Remington was in some way instrumental in receiving Mr Fullerton's thoughts. It pleased her, too, that this form lent an air of scientific objectivity to her transcriptions. She knew that there were all too many sceptics ready to scoff at anything violating their barren notions of rationality, and though she had no intention of ever publicising these communications, she felt proud to think that, if challenged, she could have produced these proofs of impeccable documentation. These were not the wild ravings of old women in darkened rooms; these were the properly attested records of technologically aided thought transference.

```
April 30th 1908, 8.35 a.m.
```

```
Receiver:       Have you seen much of Mr James since his
                arrival?
Transmitter:    A certain amount. He is staying, as you
                probably know, with Mrs Wharton in the
                Rue de Varenne.
Receiver:       Have you seen him there?
Transmitter:    Yes, on occasion. He likes the comfort
                and amenity of Mrs Wharton's quarters,
                otherwise I should prefer to meet him at
                a café.
Receiver:       Do you not like the Rue de Varenne?
```

Transmitter: Oh, it's a charming street! It's even a
charming apartment. (Pause) It's perhaps
just a tiny bit too full of Mrs Wharton.

Receiver: The apartment?

Transmitter: Well, the apartment, to start with; but
the Rue de Varenne, too; indeed, all of
Paris, all of France. Mrs Wharton fills
any available space, as you may remember
from her visits to Lamb House, and her
forages into the surrounding countryside.

Receiver: I had imagined Paris could accommodate
her more readily than Rye.

Transmitter: Oh, Paris can accommodate anything.
But it brings out false notes the way
a beautiful frame shows up a too-garish
picture.

Receiver: You are not kind. I'm sure Mrs Wharton
finds your company very pleasant.

Transmitter: So she tells me, and so Mr James tells
me, and of course I am flattered that an
American writer of such eminence should
pay attention to me. But, to be honest,
I'm just the least little bit bored
with it, too. She hardly discriminates
between me and one of the numerous
lapdogs she seems to have forever about
her person — and they in their turn
are distinguishable from her equally
multitudinous furs only in being more
noisy and more smelly. And her hats!
— they are like strange little animals
perching upon her head. I am in constant
fear of being pounced upon.

Receiver: Mrs Wharton dresses very well.

Transmitter: That depends on what exactly you mean
by well. She is dressed well as a leg
of lamb is dressed well, that is very
completely. I have seen nothing more
complete than her boots, for instance.

If she had not so obviously been the possessor of a motor, one would have assumed she was planning to cross the Alps in her boots.

Receiver: Mr James is very fond of going on motor trips, is he not?

Transmitter: Yes, the dear man is as excited as a child whenever an outing is proposed — or announced, since Mrs Wharton does not propose things.

Receiver: Do you accompany them on these trips?

Transmitter: When I can't come up with a reason not to — that is to say, a reason acceptable to Mrs Wharton, who does not measure reason as other mortals do. For her, her preference constitutes a reason that outweighs any other consideration.

Receiver: I would have thought you would enjoy the opportunity of seeing the French countryside in such comfort.

Transmitter: Comfort? I grant you, the seats are as comfortable as upholstery can make them, and the India-rubber tyres do deal with the bad roads admirably; but comfort? — to be blown about by the wind, suffocated by dust, choked by gasoline fumes, and deafened with the rattle and clanking and hissing and tooting of the infernal machine? — no, Miss Wroth, for comfort give me a spacious, airy terrace overlooking the Channel any day. And apart from one's personal comfort, spare a thought for the poor French countryside, being invaded as if by a victorious army, the lives of people and animals endangered, its country inns commandeered to produce meals for a horde of exacting foreigners — it's the most impudent thing since the Goths overran the land.

Frieda was at first rather shocked at Mr Fullerton's outspokenness on the subject of his distinguished compatriot. She had been used to hearing that lady spoken of with the greatest respect, or otherwise good-humouredly celebrated as a force all but irresistible and a benign but absolute power. Mr James, in particular, referred to 'the all-imperative Mrs Wharton' in terms that expressed awe and admiration in about equal measure. Frieda, having cherished her own impressions of the lady in question, found Mr Fullerton's irreverence, after her initial surprise, congenial to these impressions, though she avoided the vulgarity of too exuberantly seizing upon his strictures for her own sustenance. She did not have to share Mr Fullerton's reservations about Mrs Wharton; it was enough that he shared hers.

Mr Fullerton's communications were not the only ones Frieda received from Paris. Mr James sent almost daily directives about particular points in the Prefaces to be attended to in his absence, and on one occasion a handwritten manuscript for her to typewrite. Occasionally his letters contained a more personal note, which provided an instructive counterpoint to Mr Fullerton's more critical accounts:

Whereas Paris remains a great glittering bauble of pleasure and visual effects, the countryside for its part – dear old part! – remains imperturbably, stolidly rural, with here and there, as the influence of the church or the moneyed classes dictates, monuments to a larger view of life and death. Yesterday we went – I say we, meaning Mrs Wharton and I and Mr Fullerton, whom I am sure you remember from his single visit to Rye last year – we, as I say, always under the able and peremptory direction of Cook, the chauffeur, motored to Beauvais, there to feast our eyes and in a manner our spirits on the splendid old cathedral – and to feast our bodies no less sumptuously on the most delightful little déjeuner a French inn can produce. I toured in my ruminative, not to say ruminant, fashion – the whirlwind never being, as you will remember, my preferred medium – the ambulatory of the great building, and marvelled afresh at the spiritual impulse capable of such immense material gesture. Mrs Wharton and Mr Fullerton pleaded fatigue and waited outside with their customary patience, for if I am a prisoner of ease and a captive of luxury, I am a much indulged prisoner and captive, kept in gilded chains and gorgeous bondage…

*When I am not being whirled around the countryside in motor-goggles, I am sat down (*sans *goggles!) and stared at and talked at, on the whole quite brilliantly, by M. Jacques-Émile Blanche, while he takes, no less brilliantly, my portrait. From what I can see, he is making me seem very fat and rich and brainy and substantial. It is something at my age to discover oneself to this extent,* representable, *to be capable of forming, in one's shapeless way, a competent subject for an artist so accustomed to the most august of subjects (M. Blanche comes to me fresh from a most victorious rendering of the so eminently angular Thomas Hardy). But his figuring forth of me may be a proof the more of his competence, that he can transform the most helplessly unpictorial of subjects into something, as who should say, monumental.*

Frieda wondered whether Mr Fullerton would comment on this outing; she did not want to ask, lest she should seem to be prying; and yet, one would have expected his communication to arrive before Mr James's, which had to rely on more conventional means of transmission. She was thus relieved, when she sat down to the Remington the following day, to feel almost immediately the impulse she had learnt to recognise as a signal from Mr Fullerton.

Transmitter: I have been recruited to form part of Mrs Wharton's Invasion of France once again, this time to take by storm the cathedral at Beauvais.

Receiver: Mr James mentioned it to me in a letter. He seemed to find it very beautiful.

Transmitter: I imagine he did. He at least was allowed to see it.

Receiver: And were you not?

Transmitter: Well, only enough of it for Mrs Wharton to evolve a theory about it, after which I had to sit on a stone wall and listen to her propound the theory.

Receiver: I hope it was a good theory.

Transmitter: Good for what? A theory is a good one

if it enables its holder to justify his
or her actions in the light of it. By
that criterion, Mrs Wharton's theory is
an excellent one: she maintains, on the
basis of the beauty of Beauvais, that
the artistic expression of spiritual
sublimity needs material conditions in
order to flourish, and by extension
flourishes best in conditions of material
prosperity. Ergo, it is good to be rich,
ergo Mrs Wharton is a good person.

Receiver: Are you as satirical when you are with
Mrs Wharton as when you tell me about
her?

Transmitter: My dear Miss Wroth, the truth must ever
be tempered with mercy, and whereas I
do not of course enter whole-heartedly
into the good lady's speculations and
assumptions, I do give them at least the
attention that good manners require.
Otherwise where would we be?

Receiver: Do good manners require insincerity?

Transmitter: Only in cases where good manners stand in
for more meaningful intercourse. People
who truly understand each other do not
need good manners — nor, of course, bad
manners. Manners belong to the drawing
room, understanding to other areas of
human activity.

Mr Fullerton, Frieda thought, was strangely silent on the subject of Mr James. He mentioned him, of course, as making up any number of excursions, but whereas on the subject of Mrs Wharton he expressed his opinions with a freedom bordering on the reckless, he did not venture a judgement on Mr James's actions. Frieda respected this: she knew that there was between the two men a strong bond of affection, and the younger man clearly venerated the older. And yet she felt that Mr James was, after all, apart from being the august senior novelist, also embroiled in human relations in which his conduct might be as open to scrutiny as that of any mere fallible mortal. Thus, on the last morning before Mr James's return, she touched on the subject as delicately as was compatible with making any impression at all.

May 9th 1907

Receiver: Do you think Mr James has enjoyed his stay in Paris?

Transmitter: Assuredly! He has been fêted and feasted and painted and pampered and taken about like visiting royalty.

Receiver: He told me that Paris was a city in which one felt one's loss of youth.

Transmitter: That is as it may be. But he seemed to me to recover quite soon the zest of youth if not, admittedly, its agility.

Receiver: He said to me before he left that he felt guilty at bringing me to Rye before I had seen Paris, that the proper time to see Paris was in one's youth.

Transmitter: If he felt that way, why did he not bring you with him, as he very well might have done?

Receiver: I imagine he did not want to be lumbered with a paid typewriter on his holiday.

Transmitter: It is true that Mr James has been in England for long enough to have absorbed their curious notions of propriety, as if the nicest people one met weren't either a class above one or a class below one — and you'll understand, of course, that I'm using the terms above and below as the English understand them, which is to say as referring to a fictional but real line drawn horizontally across English society according to whether one works for a living or not.

Receiver:	But Mr James works for a living; he works very hard.
Transmitter:	So he does, but to such small effect, measured in vulgar monetary terms, that it almost counts as amateurism. Mrs Wharton makes money; Mr James produces art. Be that as it may, and reluctant as I am to criticise any aspect of the conduct of my old friend, it does rather occur to one to wonder at his denying you such an opportunity. As for the proper time to see Paris being one's youth, I don't know: the proper time to see Paris is whatever time one has.
Receiver:	But after a certain age, it is surely better to see Paris sooner rather than later?
Transmitter:	Oh, I grant you that, the sooner the better! Which is why, my dear Miss Wroth, we must contrive to get you here before you are very much older.

This rather broad imperative was the only reference Mr Fullerton made, for the time being, to her finding of the letters and its conceivable sequel. She had wondered at his indirectness, but it occurred to her that he might have a delicacy about seeming to urge her against the dictates of her conscience. He clearly had but imperfectly taken the measure of her conscience; but there would be time enough to correct his impressions.

Chapter Twelve
May 1908

Mr James returned from Paris late on Saturday afternoon, and Frieda saw him only on the Monday morning following. She endeavoured not to compare invidiously his exuberant reports on his fortnight in Paris with her own sojourn in Rye, and managed a tolerably sincere show of interest and pleasure in his accounts of Mrs Wharton's formidable hospitality.

'It is something,' Mr James said, in the bright light of the May morning, 'between a force of nature, an act of God and a steam express; only it acts always and miraculously to one's benefit. If I had not *wanted* to see Beauvais I might have found Mrs Wharton's insistence that I should see it inconvenient; but as I very much did, and she literally smoothed the way with her India-rubber Juggernaut, I was merely being, you might say, helped to a proper understanding of my own needs.'

He beamed, looking indeed much healthier than Frieda had seen him for a long time, more like the bronzed sea captain she had originally fancied him resembling.

'But what if she were to make a mistake?' she nevertheless found it impossible to resist asking. 'I mean, if she were to misinterpret one's need?'

To her surprise, he chuckled, a rich, cynical near-guffaw. 'Oh dear, yes, if Edith made a mistake it would be on a scale quite unimaginable to more cautious mortals like you and me.' Then he collected himself. 'But fortunately Mrs Wharton's determination is well matched by her sagacity. She makes fewer mistakes of that kind than anybody I know.'

It was a matter of some satisfaction to Frieda that she had, in her privileged insight into Mr Fullerton's appreciation of Mrs Wharton's bounty, the advantage of Mr James. The good lady did make mistakes, after all.

Mr James had returned from Paris with a strong sense of arrears of work. He was now intent upon completing the proofs of the revised edition of his novels and their Prefaces. 'I must confess to a certain weariness, as the end looms,' he said, looking around the Garden Room as if seeking some bolthole or perhaps some secret source of inspiration. 'I am satisfied that I shall leave behind me a body of work as perfect as I can make it; but perfection is an exhausting quest, and achieving it akin to a little death. Now that the end is in sight I wonder what is beyond it.'

He took up a sheaf of paper from a pile on his desk awaiting his attention. 'But this is not the time for the weak wail of despair. If Paris has the tendency to make almost any alternative to herself seem comparatively futile, she does at least condescend to receive tributes. My own little tribute to her has been much in my mind, in *The Ambassadors* – a novel you may of course not be familiar with.'

Frieda felt a spasm of irritation with Mr James's modesty, which would have been admirable had it not also reflected its drab light on her. 'I am very familiar with it. You may not remember that it was the novel from which I took dictation in order to demonstrate my fitness for my present position.'

'Ah yes, so you did, so you did. As I was saying, then, the novel is set in Paris, a city to which I feel I have in a sense rededicated myself for a last time by my visit. What has come to me with a singular felicity on this visit was how exactly Paris is the place for my fable and, if I may so put it, the moral that I wished to draw from the place.'

As he spoke, he started to pace the floor, in which Frieda recognised the signs of imminent dictation, and she readied herself at the Remington.

'If you would be so kind, my dear… ah, I see you have anticipated me with your usual prescience. *Nothing is more easy to state than the subject of "The Ambassadors" quotation marks…*'

Frieda was amused at the implication that anything could ever be *easy to state* for Mr James, but in fact, as her fingers raced across the keys to keep up with his dictation, she realised that he was more than usually fluent. His own novel had evidently acquired a new clarity and vigour for him, and he could recall it with extraordinary minuteness.

'*The whole case, comma, in fine, comma, is in Lambert Strether's irrepressible outbreak to little Bilham, that is B-i-l-h-a-m, on the Sunday afternoon in Gloriani's garden, comma, the candour with which he yields, comma, for his young friend's enlightenment, comma, to the charming admonition of that crisis…*'

For Frieda this dictation, so fluent, so assured, seemed to emanate from a different source than the usual painfully considered, anxiously pondered, weightily accented periods of Mr James's prose; he seemed almost to be drawing upon a well of personal inspiration, as if possessed by the vigorous spectre of his own youth.

'*The remarks to which he thus gives utterance contain the essence of "The Ambassadors", comma, his fingers close, comma, before he has done, comma, round the stem of the full-blown flower; semi-colon; which, comma, after that fashion, comma, he continues officiously to present to us. Full stop. Open quotation marks, "Live all you can; semi-colon; it's a mistake not to. Full stop.*'

At this point Mr James came to a stop, standing directly in front of Frieda; and instead of pacing as he dictated, he fixed her with his remarkable acute stare, and dictated as if he were addressing her.

'*"It doesn't so much matter what you do in particular so long as you have your life. Full stop. If you haven't had that what have, underlined, you had, question mark?*'

He resumed his pacing. '*"I'm too old – dash – too old at any rate for what I see. Full stop. What one loses one loses; semi-colon; make no mistake about that. Full stop."*'

At this Mr James paused again, and consulted the sheet in his hand, whether to draw breath or to refresh his memory of his own writing. But now that he was in full spate, he was as persistent, as continuous, as at other times he was hesitant and sporadic, and the pacing resumed.

'*"Still, comma, we have the illusion of freedom; semi-colon; therefore don't, comma, like me today, comma, be without the memory of that illusion. Full stop. I was either, comma, at the right time, comma, too stupid or too intelligent to have it, comma, and now I'm a case of reaction against the mistake. Full stop. Do what you like so long as you don't make it. Full stop.'"*

Here again Mr James stopped at Frieda's desk, and again she had the strange sense that he was dictating not so much to her as at her. It was possible that this sense owed its origin merely to the fact that so much of what Mr James was dictating was in the imperative mood, a mood which naturally seeks to attach itself to an object.

"'For it was, underlined, a mistake. Full stop. Live, comma, live! Exclamation point! Close quotation marks.'"

At this, at last, he stopped. He seemed fatigued, and betrayed a certain consciousness of having been carried away by his own fervour, in the deprecating manner in which he said, 'Thus far *The Ambassadors* today, which I wanted to commit to paper while the experience of Paris was still present to me. There is so much else I have to do in the next few days.' He looked at the sheaf of paper in his hand as if that represented the task awaiting him; before repairing with it to his desk, he paused again.

'I foresee a much invaded summer,' he told Frieda. 'My brother William, whom you have met, is at the moment in Oxford delivering the Hibbert lectures, and I shall be called upon to grace the proceedings with my largely uncomprehending but infinitely supportive presence. Indeed, I leave for Oxford tomorrow, and shall probably spend the better part of a week there.' He sat down at his desk, but he had not concluded. 'After Hibberting, my brother and various members of his family will spend the summer in England, using, of course, Lamb House as their European *pied-à-terre*. I am as honoured as I am delighted, but I am aware of the need to prepare in some measure for their presence in advance, to earn myself some credit upon which to draw when there are other demands upon my time.'

For her part Frieda felt no call to be either honoured or delighted. Though she had the greatest respect for Professor James's intellectual properties, she did not consider that they translated well into social graces. She had always taken for granted, in social situations, a certain mild hypocrisy, as concession to the always more or less incompatible views of any but the most feeble-minded of companies. Professor James, on the other hand, treated each conversation as a matter of conscience, and was honest to the point of brutality. When Mr James had introduced her as his 'invaluable amanuensis', he had looked at her piercingly and said, 'I hope you can understand my brother's lucubrations, because I'm damned if I can.' Nor had he intended it as a joke. The Jameses of Boston, Frieda gathered, did not joke, or if they did, it was a heavy affair, a dutiful concession to levity, a pious festivity, a kind of conversational Thanksgiving Dinner. Mr James, to give him his due, had shaken off the family gravity, or had retained it only as a medium for his irony: his own humour needed to pretend to take the solemnity seriously in order to make fun of it.

All this, though, Frieda naturally kept to herself. She had gathered from the letters she now and again typed to Mr James's dictation that his tone to his elder brother was unfailingly respectful, and she had no desire, even if she had had the courage, to reflect the least little critical light upon a relation so strong and yet so delicate. Having been an only child, she did not understand the sibling relation; in particular, she did not understand male siblings. She would have to ask Mr Fullerton for an explanation.

As for Mrs James, Frieda's limited acquaintance with her had inclined her to the view that she too readily allowed too many of her views to cross the Atlantic with her: opinions that might have been suitably vigorous in their native element in Cambridge, Mass., appeared rather raw-boned and ungainly in the more confined and circumspect space of Lamb House. She was silently gratified to find her sentiments shared, with adjustments to that lady's area of concern, by the august Mrs Paddington, who muttered under her breath about 'folks as have mighty high notions of cleanliness and don't mind who they tell them to. It comes from having slaves to do the work, I shouldn't wonder.'

The housekeeper nevertheless proceeded, once Mr James had left for Oxford, with a spring-cleaning of Lamb House so thorough as quite to constitute an inconvenience. Every room was invaded in turn, and all but voided of its contents. Frieda wished that she could offer to help Mrs Paddington: it would be a useful opportunity to find out where the letters were kept. But Mrs Paddington had strict notions of the proper stations of servants and non-servants alike, and treated Frieda's tentative enquiries as if they had been the Communist Manifesto: 'Thank you, miss, but I always think if we all did what the Lord saw fit to give us to do, the world would look more like His idea of it and less like the devil's.'

This seemed to imply that the Lord had seen fit to make Frieda a typewriter, a theory that had the virtue at any rate of according with Mr James's view of her. Just at this time, indeed, her employer did have greater need than usual of her services, and while he was away in Oxford she spent her days checking endless proofs of the endless New York edition, and retyping revisions of revisions of the Prefaces. It occurred to Frieda that at the end of this process she would be the person on earth most closely acquainted with the Novels and Tales of Henry James.

In the midst of this demanding and solitary labour, it was a welcome diversion to receive Mr Fullerton's communications, as she was now able to do almost effortlessly, by sitting down at the Remington at the time agreed upon with him and concentrating her attention.

May 15th 1908

Receiver: Mr James has gone to Oxford to be with his brother.

Transmitter: Ah yes, the Hibbert lectures — and then you are to have the pleasure of a visit from Professor James and his family?

Receiver: I believe they will be using Lamb House as a base for their travels this summer, yes.

Transmitter: An invasion by the James clan is not a prospect to be contemplated lightly.

Receiver: Do you know Professor James?

Transmitter: I have met him from time to time. A brilliant man.

Receiver: And his wife?

Transmitter: A proper wife for a brilliant man. I have noticed that the wives of very clever men often achieve something of the effect of profundity by assuming extreme

seriousness about all matters both
trivial and momentous.

Receiver: Mrs James does not have very much humour,
I think.

Transmitter: As much as a clam on a rock at low tide.
But William does not notice and Henry
pretends not to notice, and both spend
an inordinate amount of time deferring
to her. It is a fiction as necessary
to Henry as to William that she is
wonderful, a kind of genius of domestic
virtue, and they are forever assuring
each other of this fact, when they are
not proclaiming it to her face.

Receiver: Why did you say it is necessary to Mr
James to maintain a fiction about his
sister-in-law?

Transmitter: Because if he didn't he would hate her.
She has appropriated William's life
and moulded it in her image; she has
reduced him to chronic hypochondria by
declaring his health to be in need of her
ministrations; she treats the intellect
as a secondary adjunct of the bowels.

Receiver: The whole family is much concerned about
health.

Transmitter: The whole family is obsessed with health,
and as a result suffer from a variety
of ailments unheard of in the annals
of medicine. It is my theory that they
positively bring on ailments in each
other. To hear two brilliant men like
Henry and William natter on about their
digestion like a pair of constipated
dowagers is too tragic for words. But it
is Mrs James who presides over all like a
queen over a fractious empire. She rules
over the lower bowel like Queen Victoria
over the Punjab.

Mr Fullerton's disrespectful animadversions upon the James family made the prospect of their sojourn more tolerable to Frieda, as if she would have a companion in her silent spectatorship with whom to exchange glances of mutual understanding whenever the perfervid consanguinity of the Jameses threatened to close in upon her. In the past she had had to make do with stroking Max, who was banished from the company on suspicion of inducing catarrh, but the little dog was disappointingly forgiving, running up to the Jameses whenever they ventured outside, eternally expecting his inexhaustible goodwill to be reciprocated. Mr Fullerton, it had to be said, had nothing of the dachshund about him.

Mr James returned from Oxford less exuberant and more tired-looking, Frieda thought, than from Paris, though he declared himself more than satisfied with the proceedings.

'My brilliant brother swept all before him; he conquered the haughty citadels of Oxford and took their best minds hostage; he laid siege to their most cherished beliefs and mercilessly decimated the children of their intellect.'

Frieda thought this sounded unpleasant, but knew to make allowances for Mr James's metaphors, which were frequently more bellicose than their originator. She contented herself with enquiring after the health of the family – 'Tolerable, thank you, only as many catarrhs and grippes as are to be expected in a mediaeval town in an English spring' – and the probable date of their arrival.

'They want first to see the Lakeland – my sister-in-law has heard that the lakes are unhealthy later in summer – and will then make their way down here.'

With Mr James's return, Frieda's opportunities to commune with Mr Fullerton were curtailed, the Remington naturally being under requisition for Mr James's dictation. But the time that she had always found most conducive to establishing contact was at nine in the morning, which was earlier than Mr James's habitual appearance: that arrangement could thus remain undisturbed by his return. There was an anxious moment while Mr James debated with himself, at some length and with excruciating reversals and revisions, whether it would not be advisable, all things considered and in the light of the extreme pressure of work to which he had returned, to commence his labours say a half an hour, nay even an hour earlier in the morning than had been his wont these last ten years... But fortunately Mrs Paddington decided the matter by declaring respectfully but firmly that desirous though she was to cater to Mr James's every whim, and she did not think it could be proved against her as she had ever declined any reasonable request, for her to produce breakfast an hour or even half-an-hour earlier would throw out her settled routine to that extent that she'd never recover it for the rest of the day.

Thus it was decided that Mr James would continue to start dictation at a quarter past ten as hitherto, and Frieda, by coming in at nine, had the Garden Room and the Remington to herself. Mr James showed no curiosity as to her reasons for doing so. He knew that she caught up with some of the work he left her the night before, but he must also have known that she was doing her own typing. It was entirely characteristic of both his kindness and his blindness that he allowed her to go her way without wondering where that way led.

Chapter Thirteen
August 1908

The James family arrived in August, pleading exhaustion from their travels, but otherwise more cheerful than Frieda had yet seen them as a family. They brought with them their daughter Margaret Mary, known as Peggy, and their son Henry, known as Harry. Frieda thought that *Peggy and Harry* suggested a childlike jollity and chumminess altogether absent in the bearers of these names, and preferred to refer to them as Miss James and Mr Harry respectively.

The son had inherited all his father's confidence with little of his sensitivity or intelligence. He was a successful man of affairs, and treated his uncle with the condescension of a young man consciously more capable of dealing with life than an elderly bachelor who spent his time writing books that nobody read. Frieda guessed that he took his tone from the family dinner table, where the impracticality of Uncle Henry would be a frequent subject of good-humoured head-shaking. There was, in the way the young man settled into Lamb House and its amenities, something assessing and critical, as if he were already taking possession, it being presumably a made-out case that as eldest offspring of Mr James's eldest brother he would in the natural course of things inherit Lamb House. He irritated George Gammon by proposing improvements to the garden, which the gardener dealt with by affecting not to understand 'American'; he infuriated Max by pretending to throw sticks for him to retrieve and then producing the stick from behind his back after the dog had dashed off into the empty distance yapping excitedly. He was, as a man of affairs, elaborately interested in his uncle's system of dictation, and asked if he could be present at the sessions in the Garden Room. Mr James, who in the past had treated the Garden Room as an inviolable sanctuary from even the most favoured guests, found it difficult to refuse his brother's family anything, and reluctantly agreed. Harry assured his uncle that he would not be an obtrusive presence, but as he was a rather large young man, and blessed with the family catarrh, he blocked the path of Mr James's circumambulations and sounded like a marine mammal in distress. This caused Mr James's dictation to be even less fluent than usual, more prone to long pauses and revisions.

Apart from this literal invasion of his sanctuary, Mr James had to bear with any number of other calls on his time. A bad headache on Mrs James's part, for instance, to which she was much prone, would necessitate the offices of Dr Skinner, the local physician; or an enquiry on Mr Harry's part as to the guest facilities of the golf club would impel his courteous uncle to accompany him there in order to introduce him. And whereas Harry's golf was conceivably, unlike his mother's headache, a matter that could be deferred to the afternoon, the young man's manner did not provide for that possibility. All the minor inconveniences occasioned by his own consideration Mr James revelled in even while he groaned at them; indeed, the more he groaned at them the more he revelled in them, as proof that he could, in refutation of his family's estimate of him, be of use.

Miss James took up less space than her brother, or did so less aggressively: her presence suffused rather than asserted itself, but was difficult to ignore, like a slight but damp draught. She was pale and serious, prone to nervous exhaustion, the subject of endless solicitude on the part of her parents and ill-concealed impatience on the part of her brother; this in spite of being alleged to have benefited greatly from the ministrations of Mrs Newman, the mental curist. She attached herself to Frieda whenever an opportunity offered, even on occasion coming into the Garden Room in the early morning, before Mr James came down, in the time when Frieda would normally have made contact with Mr Fullerton. Frieda was sorry for her, because she seemed rather lonely, but did not like her morning intruded upon; besides, Miss James was a strenuous conversationalist, incapable of pleasantries or trivialities, and tending to hold her interlocutor captive with her pale stare. Whereas Frieda, too, avoided when she could the rattle of empty sociability, Miss James's unrelieved solemnity made her long for superficiality; indeed, at times she feared that she herself might break out in unbridled frivolity and out of pure exasperation tell a joke or dance a hornpipe.

Occasionally, when Frieda had finished her typing for the day, Miss James asked for her company on a walk, which Frieda preferred to the rather intense sessions in the Garden Room: on the walks there was at least the chance of breaking Miss James's unremitting grip on the conversation by a greeting to a passer-by or an admonition to Max, whom Mr James pleaded with them to take along: 'I'm afraid the poor little dog has been let down scandalously by the increasingly sedentary habits of his master.'

On these walks, Miss James, expressing admiration for what she called Frieda's *independent state*, liked to discuss the Condition of Women. She had seen the suffragette demonstration in front of the Houses of Parliament on the day after her arrival in London, and had been deeply impressed, although a certain ambivalence was evident in the tenor of her comments. 'I am told there were a hundred thousand women,' she said to Frieda, 'and some of them made their way to Downing Street and threw stones through the Prime Minister's windows. More than twenty of them were arrested and sent to Holloway Prison. It is rather extreme, of course; in America the ladies have better manners.'

'I think the suffragettes would argue that manners are just a way of keeping women in their places.'

Miss James twirled her parasol a trifle tetchily. She evidently did not like counter-arguments: it was possible that she experienced them as contradictions. 'Well, as far as I can see, men also have manners. American men are known for their manners.' She bethought herself; Frieda wondered whether she was aware of a contradiction between her feminist sympathies and her patriotic loyalties. 'Of course,' she conceded at length, 'you might say that men defer to us on silly things so we shouldn't ask for the big things, like the suffrage.'

'Are you a suffragette, then?'

Miss James laughed rather self-consciously. 'I daresay I seem rather outlandish to you. Is the idea of women's suffrage so foreign to you?'

'Not at all. My aunt, to whom I am very close, has been for some years a member of the WSPU.' Frieda had never been as pleased with Aunt Frederica's radical sympathies as in being able to put down the condescension of Miss Peggy James.

'The…?'

'The Women's Social and Political Union. Mrs Pankhurst's group.'

This caused another vacillation in Miss James's opinions. 'Well, we do things differently in America. I am not sure that Mrs Pankhurst's methods will win her many friends. There are those who see in this kind of demonstration only proof that women do not know how to use political power responsibly. The cause of women's suffrage has been much agitated in Boston, of course, that being one of the most advanced cities in America, but in a much more reasoned way, with meetings and speeches.'

Frieda wondered at Miss James's faith in the power of meetings and speeches, but she contented herself with saying, 'I believe there will be a suffrage meeting at Mrs Dew-Smith's house next week. She is a great friend of Mr James's; perhaps he will take you there.' This was an over-simplification of a delicate social negotiation. Mrs Dew-Smith had for a few months declined to know Mr James, after it had been reported to her that he had described her unfortunate albino Pekingese as *emetic*, but the social resources of Rye were not such as to allow anybody the luxury of ostracism for very long, and Mrs Dew-Smith had recently invited Mr James to tea as token, he said, of his readmission to the circle of the little old ladies of Rye.

'Oh, I should like that!' Miss James exclaimed. 'But Uncle Henry is opposed to women's suffrage, is he not?'

Frieda wondered if she could explain to Miss James how inadequate her understanding of her Uncle Henry's mental processes was, in assuming some crude partisanship on his part. 'I don't think he would join a demonstration in its favour,' she attempted, 'and I know he is also a friend of Mrs Humphrey Ward's – you know, one of the leading lights in the League Against Woman Suffrage. But he tends not to take sides, and I am sure he would be happy to take you to the meeting, if only as a compliment to Mrs Dew-Smith.'

'And, I should hope, a little as a compliment to me.'

'Oh, that of course. I meant that even without that...'

'Of course you did. You must not take me so seriously, you know. I do have a sense of humour, though I do come from New England.'

Frieda consented, through her silence, to take Miss James's word for her sense of humour. She guessed that the young woman's determination was such that she would prevail upon her obliging uncle to accompany her to the meeting at Mrs Dew-Smith's house, and was accordingly not surprised when Miss James announced that Mr James had duly secured her and Frieda invitations to the event.

On the evening in question, Mr James accompanied them to 'The Steps', Mrs Dew-Smith's house, a place Frieda knew he was fond of visiting, partly because, he claimed, on a clear day it afforded the best view in Rye of Cap Gris Nez. The meeting being in the evening, there was no question of viewing the symbolic promontory. Mrs Dew-Smith's little sitting room was in any case so crowded that there would have been no room for the kind of negotiation required for viewing distant prospects from a confined space. Having found a seat, one had to remain seated in order not to inconvenience one's neighbour. The atmosphere – hot, close and expectant – reminded Frieda of the séances she had attended in Mrs Beddow's over-decorated parlour, though the audience was rather better dressed and less vocal, made up of a dozen or so retired gentlefolk. The only outsider, as far as Frieda could see, was Mr Chesterton, whom she knew to be staying at the Mermaid Inn, just round the corner from Lamb House: Mr James had earlier that day enjoined her to peep through the curtain of the Garden Room as the other writer, hugely corpulent, red of face, and greasy of hair, passed by – 'How tragic,' Mr James had remarked, 'that a mind like his should be imprisoned in such a body.' The malignec albino canine had a seat with its mistress in the front of the room, next to the small table and chair reserved for the speaker.

It fell to Mrs Dew-Smith to introduce the speaker. Her style was plaintive rather than argumentative; her large brown eyes seemed permanently reproachful which, together with her tiny figure, gave her the air of a disappointed child. She was reputed to have psychic powers, and indeed apparently held, from time to time, spiritualist sessions, about which Mr James had confessed himself curious: 'It would be singularly instructive to determine whether spirits under the somewhat frail aegis of Mrs Dew-Smith were themselves of more robust substance.'

It appeared, however, that Mrs Dew-Smith acquired considerably more presence when confronted with a roomful of people than when having Mr James to tea. Getting up to introduce the speaker, she displayed, for such a small person, much point; or it is possible that her point was all the more salient for being concentrated, as it were, into such a small circumference. Her tiny feet were shod as if for strenuous feats of equestrian daring and endurance; her eyes had, behind round glasses, a glint as of steel or frost, and when she spoke, her voice was like the point of the engraver's tool on his plate. She announced, by way of preliminary caution, that she was 'not here to bring homage to the Angel in the House', a mistake which by this time none of her audience would have been likely to make. There was nothing angelic in Mrs Dew-Smith's mien.

'The purpose of this meeting is to bring to this secure little village, this stronghold of conservatism and tradition, a consciousness of the struggle being waged out there in the name of all women, not only the women of the metropolis, not only the women in the factories and fields of England, but also the women of the towns and villages of England; not only in the kitchens and nurseries, but also in the drawing rooms. Our speaker tonight, Mrs Mabel Tuke, one of Mrs Pankhurst's most trusted lieutenants and comrades, Joint Honorary Secretary with Mrs Pankhurst of the Women's Social and Political Union, has distinguished herself in that battle which, every day, is being fought with increasing fierceness, even ferocity, as the powers of conservatism, resistance and reaction close ranks against the forces of progress and change. She has magnanimously condescended to give us an address on the policies and aims of the Women's Social and Political Union, policies which, as you will know, have of late taken on a much more forceful complexion.'

The assembled audience applauded politely their own imminent harrowing by the emissary of change, and Mrs Tuke rose to her feet. If Mrs Dew-Smith tended rather too much towards unmediated point, Mrs Tuke at first sight erred in the other direction, in seeming to have a deficiency of point – indeed, to lack any sort of precise outline. It was in the first place a peculiarity of her hair, which stood out from her head half-heartedly, as if uncertain whether it shouldn't rather lie down, and resolved the matter by doing neither. Her excessively pale face contributed to the effect of ambivalence, in combining remarkably large, mournful eyes and a prominent chin with an almost total absence of nose and mouth, causing her expression when in repose to be not so much inscrutable as self-contradictory. She seemed fretful rather than forceful, fidgeting distractingly while Mrs Dew-Smith was talking, and looking warily at her hostess's Pekingese as if anticipating an attack. Apparently within the ranks of the WSPU she was known as Pansy, but to Frieda's mind she looked more like a small over-bred terrier than a flower. Frieda had, of course, seen pictures of the celebrated Mrs Pankhurst, and thought that nothing could be further from that lady's air of indomitable resolve and unswerving purpose than the nervy apprehensiveness of Mrs Pansy Tuke.

But if Frieda wondered how a woman apparently so irresolute could be reckoned a power in the land, she was soon to be instructed. As Mrs Tuke, disdaining the table and chair provided for her, rose to deliver her address, it was curiously, as she took a deep breath, as if she expanded: one might have fancied one heard her stays cracking under the strain. Quite a small woman in repose, in action she seemed gigantic.

She started speaking in a thin, colourless monotone, explaining why the WSPU had decided on adopting a policy of 'greater visibility'; but as the simple enumeration of those reasons modulated into a more impassioned rehearsal of grievances, it was as if Mrs Tuke shed whatever was undefined in her manner and appearance and assumed an altogether sharper and more vigorous identity. Her very hair seemed charged with the electricity of her passion; her eyes, hitherto so unfocused, seemed to be penetrating the walls of Mrs Dew-Smith's house to behold some shining goal beyond; from the small aperture of her mouth issued forth a voice out of all proportion to its source. She was as if possessed by another presence – presumably that of the redoubtable Mrs Pankhurst, speaking through her lieutenant.

'I speak, as Mrs Dew-Smith has told you, not for woman in her role of angelic comforter, rather for Woman in her new role as Warrior, Conqueror, and if need be, Enemy of All that Is. For too long have we served our husbands and our sons in the capacity of helpmeet, and sacrificed our own gifts at the domestic hearth; for too long have we been rewarded with praise and gratitude calculated to keep us in perpetual durance and prevent us from claiming our rightful place in the government of the country. Every compliment that we are paid by a man, every expression of gratitude, nay every profession of admiration, is as a confirmation of that inferior status to which such lip service condemns us. We are gentle, they tell us, we are nurturing; it is our pleasure to sacrifice as it is our duty; we have no higher calling than to bring forth children and bring them up in the image of their parents: if they are boys, to rule and condescend, if they are girls, to obey and submit.

'The new policy of the Women's Social and Political Union is no longer to ask for favours, no longer to plead with our leaders, but to demand a political voice as our right, and to express our dissatisfaction by invading, if necessary, the very seat of power. Our methods have been called militant, and we are proud of it; they are militant as the church militant is militant. Sage commentators tell us we have sacrificed the goodwill of the public by our late actions; we say where, in fifty years, has the goodwill of the public brought us? Our motto is "Deeds not Words", and the words of sympathisers have proved empty and worthless; nay worse than worthless. That so-called goodwill was merely a comfortable shelter from which to patronise us as harmless eccentrics; for us to be taken account of we have to invade not only the seat of power and public office, but the consciousness of the fickle and superficial public.'

It was evidently not part of Mrs Tuke's programme to flatter her audience, including it with a large gesture of her arm in this invidious designation; and Frieda sought comfort for the lady campaigner's aspersion in the reflection that insofar as it included her, it included also Mr James: to be fickle and superficial in his company had, after all, its own distinction. Frieda glanced at his large head, tilted attentively to one side in his habitual listening attitude; there was nothing in the gravity of his regard to give any hint as to his opinion of these views. But on Frieda's other side, the rapt expression on Miss James's face, the lips slightly parted, even at times apparently mouthing certain phrases in empathy, left one in no doubt as to the young woman's transport. If Mrs Pankhurst was speaking through Mrs Tuke, she was, through that medium, entering the consciousness of the young American.

'If you ask me tonight, as I have been so often asked before, why we have chosen to adopt means so little calculated to appease those in power, I reply the time of appeasement has passed; we are in a time of war, a civil war, and I speak to you as a soldier in that war. There are those who believe that Woman is the bringer of peace; but I say to them there can be no peace while there is no justice. If I be permitted a personal note: I am proud to recall here that my family motto is "My soldiers are many", and I exult in being the latest soldier of my line.'

Mrs Tuke's address was long, and Frieda found her attention wandering. She thought that Mrs Tuke was right – she knew only too well that for a woman the price of being reasonable was being ignored – but she wondered whether the good lady had ever, at a rate of a shilling an hour, earned her own living. She, Frieda, had in a manner penetrated the male stronghold, only to find there barriers more subtle and more insurmountable than those around the House of Commons. Perhaps, she reflected with a smile, she should one morning arrive with a few stones in her bag and break the windows of the Garden Room, if only to witness Mr James's bewilderment.

Looking up, she found Mr James's gaze on her, smiling at her smile. There, then, was the enemy; and as that thought crossed her mind, Pansy Tuke closed her peroration 'And we believe that in our pursuit of our fair portion of life, we are justified in any measures short of taking life. But though the WSPU shall take no life, those lives which we have to give, our own lives, we have pledged in the cause, and have vowed that *we shall have freedom or we shall have death.*'

This last declaration, delivered in tones adjusted to the streets of London rather than Mrs Dew-Smith's drawing room, left Mrs Tuke's audience not so much stirred as flattened. In some perplexity as to whether applause or perhaps some more militant manifestation was called for, they compromised by remaining silent and staring at the tips of their boots. Mrs Dew-Smith alone showed some presence of mind by rising to her feet, which set off the albino Pekingese in a fit of yapping that made up in volume if not in articulateness for the stricken silence of the assembled humans. This proved a useful cover for the rest of the meeting to disperse in vagueness and mutters, all but Mr James and Mr Chesterton, who engaged immediately in an exchange of views. Mr James introduced Frieda to Mr Chesterton, to her irritation, as 'my indispensable amanuensis and typewriter', which gave Mr Chesterton an opportunity to deliver himself, with a practised air suggesting that it was not the first time he had done so, of the reflection that 'In recent times, millions of young women have risen to their feet crying "We will not be dictated to", and proceeded to become stenographers.' He laughed immoderately at this witticism. Mr James, Frieda was pleased to see, looked pained; Miss Peggy looked puzzled.

Seeking out Frieda for a walk the next day, Miss James returned to the subject of the meeting; she had been deeply impressed with the need for women to assert their rights, given that men were not going to grant them voluntarily. But there was something almost perfunctory in her rehearsal of Mrs Tuke's arguments; she evidently had something else on her mind. To Frieda's surprise, she herself seemed to be the object of Miss James's interest.

'I think you have mentioned that you are a member of the Society for Psychical Research,' she began, as they were walking through St Mary's churchyard and idly reading the inscriptions on tombstones. It was, for Miss James, an unusually tentative opening, and Frieda confessed readily enough to her interest in psychic phenomena, without finding it necessary to explain the nature and origin of her interest.

Miss James's next statement seemed, at first, quite divergent. 'I am fascinated by your typewriter,' she declared. 'It is in a manner, is it not, a kind of automatic writing?'

Frieda had no intention of sharing with Miss James her own experiences in this regard. 'Well no. I do have to hit the keys.'

'But is it not so that after a while that becomes automatic?'

'In the sense that one no longer thinks which keys to press, yes. One's fingers... yes, I suppose one could say that they automatically form the words being dictated to one.'

'Then that is very much like automatic writing.' Miss James was very definite. 'Have you not tried real automatic writing... typing out communications from the spirit world?'

Frieda remained evasive. 'I think one has to have special gifts to receive such communications.'

'But if you were to work through somebody who has such gifts...?'

'Do you mean a medium?'

'Yes, though I don't necessarily mean ancient foreign women in darkened rooms. My mother knows Mrs Piper rather well.'

'Mrs Piper?' Frieda had heard the name somewhere but could not for the moment remember where.

'Yes, the medium from Boston, don't you know? I believe she is celebrated even in England. My mother attended a sitting, during which Mrs Piper relayed a message from my grandmother to my Uncle Herry.'

'And how did Mr James receive this message?'

'How did he receive it? Oh, you mean, how did he react to it? Apparently he was very much moved, because the message contained a reference to a matter known only to himself and his mother. Mrs Piper, you know, is in touch with a spirit control called Rector who facilitates the contact.'

'Are you interested on your own account? I mean, do you want to make contact with your grandmother?'

'Oh, not my grandmother, please no... I mean, I am sure she was a very worthy woman, but I don't think she would have anything to say to me. One is given two parents on this earth and I find they suffice to most human needs.'

They walked for a while and then Miss James said, 'No, it is my Aunt Alice who is trying to reach me, I think.'

'You had an Aunt Alice?' asked Frieda, not entirely candidly; she in fact knew about Alice James, but did not want to admit to her knowledge too readily.

'Yes, didn't you know? Of course, it was long before your time. I myself was only six when she died. She was my father's younger sister, never in very good health, and then died at the age of forty-four – here in England, as it happened, languishing in dreary lodgings in Leamington Spa and Kensington. She had a very good friend, a Miss Katharine Loring – Kath – who looked after her, much of the time, and who has spoken to me about her. She says I remind her of my aunt. But my parents do not encourage me to speak to Miss Loring; they see very little of her. Uncle Henry and my father rather hold it against her that she had my aunt's diary printed, which they think too private for public dissemination. But I've read the diary in my father's library – there are only four copies in existence, or perhaps three – I think Uncle Henry burned his copy.'

Frieda was in a position to know, but not to say, that Uncle Henry had not in fact burned his copy. She had come across it on his shelves during one of her book-borrowing visits in his absence, and had read it, but without telling Mr James; she had guessed that he would not have wanted anybody outside the clan to have access to the comments of the invalid, which were frequently of an outspokenness possible only to those consciously about to depart this world. So she murmured something non-committally, and Miss James continued, 'She was a very unhappy woman, I think, although in her diary she keeps on saying how happy she is; she talks of the strange people who have the courage to be unhappy, but I can't see how she could possibly have been happy, confined to her bed for most of her last years.'

This seemed to Frieda like a misunderstanding of the strange, self-centred, sardonic stoicism of the bed-ridden diarist, revelling grimly in her own superfluity and yet taking pleasure in such small matters as presented themselves to her interest. It did not surprise her that Miss James, who was as deficient in humour as an ironing board, should have read past the fierce pleasure of her aunt's sarcastic aphorisms; but she was now condemned to the silence of the guilty, and could only listen to the younger woman's opinions.

'And now,' said Miss James slowly, with a certain self-conscious ponderousness, 'I think my aunt is trying to get in touch with me.'

'Why do you say so?'

Miss James hesitated, visibly uncertain. Then she blinked quickly, a sign apparently of having made up her mind. 'It came to me so sharply last night as I was listening to Mrs Tuke, that my Aunt Alice had been a victim of exactly the situation she was describing. It could have been meant especially for me, that address, to remind me of my duty to my aunt. And then, you know, I have dreams. That is to say, I have a dream. It is always the same dream. My aunt comes to me, looking as she does in the portrait my father has of her, and she holds out her hand as if she's trying to give me something; but when I hold out my hand, she opens hers, and it's empty, and she tries to take hold of my hand. I think she wants something from me.'

'But what?'

'I don't know. But she did not have much of a life, you know, for all that she was always saying how fulfilled her life was, and it is possible that she left something undone that she wants me to do. She was the only daughter in a family of four sons, like me. And you know when there are four sons... I've often thought that she must have understood what I feel sometimes, surrounded by people who are so sure of their purposes in life, all these men who are born into their destinies. Poor Aunt Alice had no destiny, so she became a professional invalid; she could not appeal to her family's imagination, so she appealed to their charity. My father says she accepted death nobly – she wrote a beautiful letter to him that he gave me to read. She says her approaching death is *the most supremely interesting moment in life, the only one in fact, when living seems life.* Isn't that beautiful?'

Frieda considered – they had paused by a relatively recent grave, as if reading the inscription – 'I don't know. It *sounds* beautiful, if you know what I mean, but when one thinks about what she is really saying... how can death be the most interesting moment in life? Isn't it just... the end?' She pointed at the inscription: *Caroline Mary Bushby, born 1821, departed this life 1838.* 'Doesn't that mean simply that poor Caroline Mary Bushby had seventeen years of life and then... nothing?'

'That is what we don't know, don't you see, and what I don't believe, that death is just the end. And Aunt Alice may be able to tell me.'

'But how could I help you? I'm just a typewriter, not a medium.'

Miss James blinked again. 'I was hoping, don't you see, that if you and I just sat down, you know, with the machine, and you made yourself receptive, then perhaps she would speak to me. I know you've been reading about it, so you must know how to do it, and I have also been studying my father's material.'

For a moment Frieda considered mentioning her experience with thought transference to Miss James, but a certain instinct warned her not to involve her own life too much with the troubled existence of the young American. Miss James had an emotional hunger that would feed on any morsel of sympathy. But while she was considering these matters, Miss James seized her hand and said, her normal blandness breaking into an almost anguished appeal, 'Oh please, won't you just try? It's keeping me from sleep and work, this thinking all the time that somebody is trying to get through to me, and experiencing somebody else's pain, don't you see?' Then, as if conscious of having exceeded the limits of her self-revelation, she withdrew again into her daughter-of-the-professor mode. 'And I'm sure you'd make a good medium, you're so used to, you know, transmitting somebody else's words without perhaps even understanding them – I mean, not many people do understand Uncle Henry's novels, you know.'

Frieda did not relish Miss James's condescension, but she now had a clearer idea of the uncertainty it was designed to mask. And she had become accustomed to the assumption – Mr James, for instance, betrayed it all the time – that she was an efficient typewriter because she was too stupid to understand what she was typing. It intrigued Frieda that in their different ways all the members of the James family saw her only as an extension of the Remington. The theory at Miss Petherbridge's had been the converse: 'Through the machine your powers will be extended and your influence will be felt far beyond woman's sphere.' She was averse to serving as instrument of communication between two more members of the James family, even if one was dead; but there was, in spite of everything, something touching in Miss James's appeal, a kind of despair that Frieda could understand: it was the cry of an undernourished soul. And there was a difference here, from her usual function as passive mediator of information: in this girl's appeal was an acknowledgement of her power. No longer merely an obedient conduit of other people's creations, she was assumed to be able to control the passage of communication between the living and the dead.

'Are you suggesting that we should have a séance?' she accordingly asked, as mildly as if Miss James had proposed an outing to Rye Harbour.

'I guess that is what I am proposing,' the other woman laughed, a bit breathlessly, trying to make light of it. 'But no darkened rooms and table-rappings, just you and I and the typewriter – perhaps tonight after dinner, you know. I could easily say you're typing a letter for me, as you did for father yesterday. And then nobody will disturb us.' Miss James had evidently thought it all through. She had even decided in advance that Frieda would willingly lend herself to the project.

Then Frieda remembered where she had come across Mrs Piper's name. In her diary, a few days before her death, Alice James had written: *I do pray to Heaven that the dreadful Mrs Piper won't be let loose upon my defenceless soul.*

Mr James acceded readily, even eagerly, to his niece's request. As host he was often confessedly at a loss as to how to amuse young people, and he welcomed any expression on their part of a wish that it was in his power to grant.

'Excellent, excellent,' he said. 'Only in that case Miss Wroth must be appealed to to share our meal, frugal as it may well be tonight.'

Frieda's heart rather sank, not at the prospect of a frugal meal – Mr James's meals, though seldom lavish, were never really frugal as she had known frugality in her youth – but at the thought of dining with the whole phalanx of Jameses, a family quite formidable enough in its non-dining state, and likely to prove more so at repast.

In the event, they proved not so much formidable as ruminant. Frieda had often been silent witness to Mr James's Fletcherising, a process relatively painless once one had accepted the essentially unsociable aspect of prolonged mastication, and conducive, if nothing else, to quiet reflection. She had not realised, though, that both Professor and Mrs James were Fletcherisers, whereas their children were not, a divergence that produced some conversational awkwardness. On her own with Mr James Frieda could simply pretend he wasn't there, but that fiction became more difficult to sustain in the midst of three masticating adults, the more so that Mr James was clearly interested in whatever passed amongst the three normally chewing members of the company, and seemed to expect them to delay their conversation to await his contribution, which in the nature of Fletcherising was slow in coming.

On this occasion Mr Harry, possibly out of sincere curiosity, more probably out of sheer boredom, took up the subject of the little terracotta bust on the mantelpiece.

'I've often wondered who that perplexed little boy is,' he said, to no-one in particular, since the person best qualified to tell him had just commenced Fletcherising a morsel of boiled lamb – which, in the tradition of Lamb House cuisine, was not tender.

Frieda felt it incumbent upon herself to say, 'It is the Count Bevilacqua, I believe.'

'Yes, so the inscription informs us,' Mr Harry replied. 'But I mean who he really was, to merit his place on our mantelpiece.'

Mr James had by now finished Fletcherising his mouthful – Frieda suspected that under the pressure of wanting to speak he had surreptitiously swallowed the food prematurely – and intervened with more than his usual authority. 'The young count owes his place on my mantelpiece not so much to the historical person who is there so memorably immortalised, as to the circumstance of his creation, and of course to the sweetness of the thing in itself. I bought him in Rome from the sculptor, a young friend of mine who happens, so I fancy, to resemble the little count – if not in the individual features of his face, then in his youthful expectancy and openness before life.'

With a slight gulp Mrs James also terminated her current spell of Fletcherising. 'Oh, that very dear Mr Andersen who visited us in Cambridge – don't you remember Harry? No, I think you were away from home. I do believe I wrote to you, Henry, at the time to tell you what a very pleasant impression he had made upon William.'

Professor James swallowed decisively and said, 'To be perfectly accurate, my dear, *I* wrote to tell Henry what a more than pleasant impression the young man had made upon *you*.

Not that I did not share the sentiment – he was a delightful young man indeed.'

'And, as is evident from that little work, a consummate artist.' Mr James sighed. 'That is, if he allows himself to be. He has of late conceived some notion of doing something on a heroic scale, a composition made up quite… *extravagantly* out of a complication of gigantically and, as it were, *insistently* unclothed figures. You will remember, William, seeing the kodaks of some of these… *uninhibited* figures, having been subjected to them, I believe, on his visit to you in Cambridge.'

'Yes, and I thought them rather fine, in that style.'

'In that style exactly – the heroic style, the largely gestural, the aspirational, the near-apocalyptic – the style that is everything to do with Style and nothing with Life.'

The professor was not to be intimidated by his brother's absoluteness. 'I thought they had a certain robust presence.'

'They have presence, as much as you like, they have execution, they have substance even in excess; all that they lack is life, that precious quality which not to have is to doom a work of art to futility.'

'They seemed lively enough to me, with their bare-bottomed cavortings.'

Mrs James looked pained and glanced at Peggy, but the young woman was gloomily pushing her food around on her plate and seemed not even to have noticed her father's assault upon her modesty.

Mr James smiled at his brother. 'Cavortings indeed, lacking in all proportion, excessive in all respects – except, by the by, that of their lower limbs, which are all, inexplicably, too short. The athletically intimate or intimately athletic ladies and gentlemen are indistinguishable in terms of amplitude of chest and stoutness of limb, and all too distinguishable in respect of other matters usually less… *rompingly* offered to the public eye.'

'Are you saying, Henry, that these statues are indecent?'

'I care little, as you know, for decency or indecency as judged by the guardians of our public morals; but I do care for proportion in the doing and for some close relation to some immediate form of life, which these writhing and stomping immensities utterly lack, for all their rapturous expenditure of energy, not to mention their so almost distressingly plentiful supply of infants.'

Mr Harry looked as if he was sorry that he had started the subject; Miss Peggy was clearly preoccupied, presumably with her project for later that evening; Mrs James seemed vaguely ill at ease with the subject of Mr Andersen, and took refuge in another bite of boiled mutton. But Mr James, having firmly laid by his knife and fork, had taken fast hold of his subject. 'That little head with as you say, Harry, its puzzled appearance contains more real life in its left eyebrow than all the gigantic Tributes and Symbols in all their collected and contorted limbs and appendages. Young Andersen will come to his senses one day and produce more things of that exquisite quality. He has it in him, I know. I am only afraid that he will be spoilt for the small gesture by reaching too avidly for the monumental. He made a bust of me in Rome last summer that fell woefully short of the quality of that exquisite thing, even allowing for the comparative grossness of the subject. Not being able to represent me in any… *athletic* aspect, he attempted to render me as one of the Caesars, as the nearest approximation to the heroic still open to me, and succeeded only in making me look unpleasant in a senile sort of way, like a death mask of Caligula.'

Frieda was surprised at her employer's heat: she had known he was fond of the little terracotta sculpture, but had not realised what apparent atrocities its maker had since committed, nor how much it mattered to Mr James. As if guessing her thoughts, he went on, 'And if you feel that one artistic abomination more on earth is a trivial matter, consider that it is an exquisite talent spoiled, a divine gift spurned, for the hurdy-gurdy and hoopla of the fairground. It is the reckless expenditure, in sheer megalomania, of the rarest thing on earth, the only true immortality.'

Mr James had clearly not finished his disquisition; but Miss James, who had been prodding at her remaining morsel of boiled mutton in evident boredom, interrupted without ceremony. 'But why should it be the only true immortality? There are so many witnesses to testify to the immortality of the soul, are there not? An immortality not dependent on marble and canvas and paper?'

Mr James regarded her with his head at the slight angle he adopted when considering a point of view other than his own. 'I don't know, my dear. That is the province of your learned father. I pretend to speak only as an artist, with no doubt the limitations of vision implied by that. To me the immortality of the soul is something I cannot understand; but the immortality of *that* – and he gestured towards the little count – '*that* I can speak for.'

In the lamplight the little terracotta figure shone serenely, the little count seeming to glow with this assurance; but Mrs James, having completed another mastication, asked through the last shreds of boiled mutton, 'And yet, who knows who the Count Bellivacqua was?'

'Ah, but there you have exactly the nature of artistic immortality. The count will be forgotten, or will be remembered only as the subject of young Andersen's study. It is Andersen who will survive.'

'By that logic,' Miss James objected, 'only artists have immortality. What happens to ordinary people when they die?'

'If we knew that, my dear Peggy,' her father intervened, 'we should have far fewer philosophers and almost no theologians.'

'You say you can't say anything about the immortality of the soul, Henry,' Mrs James rather reproachfully said, 'and yet you remember that message that your mother sent you two years ago through Mrs Piper and Rector, and that you said contained a reference that nobody else could have understood.'

'I remember being very much struck with it at the time; I think, William, you said that whatever else it meant, it suggested that the world our normal consciousness makes use of is only a fraction of the whole world in which we have our being.'

'Yes, that much I am still prepared to vouch for. But after twenty-five years of research into the matter I don't have very much more than that to say with any real belief. I find myself believing that there is *something* in these never-ending reports of psychical phenomena, although I haven't yet the least positive notion of the something. It has become to my mind simply a very worthy problem for investigation.'

The professor took a bite of mutton, and his brother took advantage of the opening in the conversation. 'To this day I cannot dismiss my sense of some strange continuum between this world and the next, which enabled mother's message to reach me from there; but can it be said to constitute *life*, producing oneself at Mrs Piper's behest? Is it not just a hitherto unsuspected aspect of death? And if it does not constitute life, can it constitute immortality?'

Professor and Mrs James, being occupied with their mutton, could not respond to this rhetorical question, and Miss Peggy having apparently withdrawn from the discussion, it was left to Mr James to conclude, to his own satisfaction, with the observation that, after all, the immortal Shakespeare had said as much as could be said, perhaps, about the matter, through Hamlet's observation about there being more things in heaven and earth than are dreamt of in your philosophy.

Chapter Fourteen
10th August 1908

After dinner Frieda and Miss James excused themselves from
the conviviality attendant upon three talkative people reclaiming
the communicative function of their jaws. It was still light in
the Garden Room, the serene summer evening prolonging itself
luminously against the warm brick of the garden wall, and it was
not necessary to light a lamp. Frieda sat down at the Remington,
suddenly apprehensive. She understood but imperfectly the
power she called up through her machine: having discovered it
through her communications with Mr Fullerton, she had no idea
whether she could at will summon up, as Miss James expected her
to do, a particular person from the beyond. The *Journal*, it was
true, seemed to suggest that the process of thought transference
was essentially the same, whether between two living people or
one living and one dead, but to Frieda's more sceptical mind the
difference seemed far from negligible. It also seemed unlikely
that Alice James, given her views on mediums, would consent
to being interviewed by her niece. Indeed, Miss James's sense
that her aunt wanted to get in touch with her went contrary to
everything that the diary suggested about the reclusive invalid,
fiercely independent of all but the few chosen intimates whom
she bound to herself with hoops of steel.

'What must I do?' Miss James asked, evidently at least
as tense as Frieda. Frieda was about to confess to her own
ignorance, when a sudden impulse resisted this abject course.
Miss James evidently regarded her as a kind of supernatural
typewriter, appointed to take dictation at her convenience. But
she need not accede to this instrumental view of her function:
she could demonstrate to Miss James, and for that matter to
the whole spirit world, that mediating between the living and

the dead was an active process, involving certain choices and particular procedures.

'Sit down behind me where I cannot see you,' she accordingly improvised, 'but where you can read over my shoulder. It spoils my concentration if I have to read to you the communications that come to me.'

'Will you also use Rector? He seems to know our family, through having put my grandmother in touch with Mrs Piper.'

'I cannot speak for Rector or for Mrs Piper,' Frieda rather grandly said. 'I have my own conduits of communication.'

If Frieda had wanted to impress Miss James with her spiritual connections, she had now evidently succeeded. Miss James blinked in surprise. 'You didn't tell me that you were in touch with a spirit control.'

'I prefer not to talk about it. A spirit control is, as the term indicates, a powerful force that invades one for the duration of a sitting, and that one does not want to invoke idly outside of the conditions of such a session. So if you would sit quite still where you are, or perhaps slightly to the right, like that, I shall attempt to contact your aunt. I shall need you to concentrate very hard on her, and I shall do the same, with my hands on the keys. If she does come forward, you may ask questions, which I shall convert into type.' Frieda thought she had better provide for the possibility of a total lack of response. 'Remember, beyond a certain point it is your own attitude that determines the co-operation of the subject.'

'I think Aunt Alice wants to speak to me. I can feel it.'

'Then she will come forward when invited. But we shall have to remain very quiet now and concentrate very hard.'

Miss James blinked as if she wanted to say something, but reconsidered and settled herself in her chair, staring grimly ahead like an unmusical person preparing for a virtuoso musical performance.

Frieda typed the date at the top of a blank page; she rested her fingers lightly on the familiar keys and closed her eyes. She was in all conscience as uncertain as Miss James – indeed, even more uncertain, in that she did not share the young woman's belief that her aunt would be willing to have her niece, in her phrase, *let loose* upon her.

The still warm late summer evening was quiet, except for a few seagulls flying overhead and a single pedestrian passing by in West Street. The light was mellow with the drowsy heat of a room at the end of a hot day, and Frieda was conscious of a pleasant languor stealing over her.

Miss James leant back rather heavily in her chair. Frieda could hear her breathing – she evidently had her share of the family catarrh – and even smell the perspiration generated by her tension. She forced herself to shut off her senses to these distractions, and placed her fingers on the keyboard again. A fly settled on her left hand. She waved it away and composed herself again. She closed her eyes and tried to imagine Alice James; from what she had read in the diaries, she pictured her as sharp-nosed and pale, but with vivid red cheeks prone to a hectic flush.

Her hands felt numb, even disembodied. The keys clattered suddenly, a brief, irritated burst.

Transmitter: Whatever happened to the concept of
               resting in peace?

There was a sharp intake of breath from Miss James and Frieda lifted her right hand to signal to her to be silent, before typing her reply.

Receiver: Who are you?
Transmitter: I take it you have not disturbed me only
               to tell me you do not know who you want.
Receiver: No, indeed, we were hoping to make
               contact with Miss Alice James.

'She died in eighteen ninety-two,' Miss James whispered; she had involuntarily leant forward and was reading over Frieda's right shoulder. 'That may help to identify her.'

Receiver: Miss Alice James died in eighteen ninety-
               two.
Transmitter: I think I can be trusted to remember the
               date of my own death.

Miss James suppressed an exclamation and even Frieda felt a surprise bordering on panic. She succeeded in controlling her actions, however, sufficiently to type a collected reply.

```
Receiver:          Your niece is anxious to contact you.
```

'Her niece Peggy,' whispered Miss James. 'William's daughter.'

```
Receiver:          Your niece Peggy. William's daughter.
Transmitter:       Peggy was a nice enough little girl, and
                   poor dear William meant very well. I will
                   answer questions as long as I don't have
                   to act as a district messenger for the
                   dead. I will not convey messages to my
                   parents or any other person. With those
                   reservations, I will answer Peggy's
                   questions if she is sure she wants to
                   hear what I have to say. I have no
                   uplifting messages of good cheer to the
                   living.
```

'Oh yes, of course I want to hear her,' whispered Miss James.

```
Receiver:          Miss James would like to hear what you
                   have to say.
Alice James:       I can receive Peggy's questions without
                   your machine, if you will be so kind as
                   to mediate my replies. I have always
                   wanted to dictate to a typewriter as I am
                   told my brother has taken to doing.
```

Miss James composed herself on her chair, and spoke at the typewriter, as if her aunt's spirit were lodged inside the machine. 'I am grateful for this opportunity. I have been troubled by the apparent discrepancies in various descriptions of the afterlife, and would like to know whether death is truly a state of bliss.'

```
The best thing about death is that one does not have to
```

drag around a bundle of shawls and pillows. The next best thing is that nobody asks one how one is feeling, as if it were one's moral duty to feel well. I don't know if that is bliss.

'What would you do if you could have your life over?'

I would decline the opportunity.

Miss James, evidently checked by this uncooperative reply, was silent, and for a moment Frieda thought that Alice James, who struck her as curt to the point of being ill-tempered, had withdrawn into the everlasting rest that was surely now her prerogative. But her fingers remained poised over the keys, and after a few seconds resumed their activity.

If you are looking to me for advice, I can tell you only what I could have told you if I had known you while I was alive, which is to get on with your life as best you may, and not to expect death to make up for what you miss in life. I am now in a position to say that it does not. Don't believe anything the newspapers say about the world or the Church says about the hereafter. Cherish your friends and malign your enemies.

'How am I to deal with the fact of having four brothers?'

Fratricide is one possibility. The other, which I chose as less sensational, is invalidism. The power of the weak is in being so weak as to appeal to the chivalry of the strong.

'But is there no chance of proving myself their equal?'

Not if two of them happen to be geniuses whose equal you never can be, and the other two are failures whose equal you never want to be. In any case, you will have to fight your so-called privilege in being born a James. History is intent on reducing you to a footnote in the

149

James family history; you will have to clamber out of
the footnotes and write your own story.

'How do I do that?'

I don't know. I'm a footnote. But there is something I
should like you to do.

Frieda could hear the sharp intake of breath as Miss James said:
'I knew it. I sensed it.'

I want you to help Kath.

'Miss Loring?'

Miss Loring. Kath. She has been trying to have my diary
published, but has not met with any encouragement from
my brothers, who seem to believe that it would be
immodest for me to enter the field that they have made
their own so magnificently. They have also chosen to
take offence at Kath's private publication of a few poor
copies, and have prevented them from achieving any kind
of public circulation. All I ask from you is that you
should assist Kath in getting my diary published.

'Of course I would be only too happy – but what should I do?'

She will manage the practical details, which she is more
than capable of doing. But she can't manage the human
aspect. That is to say, my brothers. It will be your
task to persuade your good father and your Uncle Henry
to give their co-operation or at any rate their blessing
to this modest enough venture. It will not be easy. They
prefer me as a footnote.

'Of course I will do that. Only… why does it matter to you now
whether your diary gets published?'

I want to be remembered as something other than William

and Henry James's problem sister who took to her bed
because she was too stupid to do anything else. I spent
my life preparing for death; the one thing I left undone
was to prepare for immortality. But you must excuse me
now. I am as prone to fatigue here in my disembodied
state as I was in life. Both the advantages of death and
its terrors have been exaggerated by the living.

The machine clattered into silence, leaving Frieda staring at her
own hands, as if to make sure that they still belonged to her.
As the sensation gradually returned to her fingers, she touched
the warm grain of her desk for its reassuring familiarity. She
knew, from the relaxation of tension in her hands and spine, that
whatever power had possessed her had relinquished control.

Miss James was leaning back in her chair, pale, but with an
expression almost of ecstasy on her face. 'Thank you,' she all but
whispered, 'thank you very much. You have given me something
to live for.'

Frieda thought, but did not say, that in recruiting her niece to
her cause, Alice James had shackled her to her own footnote. The
appropriation of the living by the dead was an old enough tale.

Whatever esteem Frieda gained in Miss James's eyes through her successful summons of Alice James was, for Frieda herself, secondary to her own sense that she was evidently to some significant extent in control of her powers of invocation. And these spirits that rose in response to her summons and offered their testimony, were they, after all, so different in kind from the characters Mr James called forth and set in motion? If her typewriter was doomed to remain an instrument of mediation, then mediation could itself partake of the exhilaration of creation.

None of this Frieda could impart to Miss James or anybody else. The special consciousness that Miss James now seemed to think existed between them was not easy to maintain at a pitch commensurate with the young woman's evident expectation, feeding as it did on significant glances exchanged over dinner plates or pregnant references veiled in commonplaces. Frieda soon felt that they had exhausted the expressive possibilities of this means of communication; the regrettable but incontrovertible fact was, as far as she was concerned, that she and Miss James now had nothing new to say to each other, having exceeded in one evening the limits of such intimacy as their acquaintance justified. Also, if Miss James really were going to appeal to her father and uncle to allow Miss James's diary to be published, she had no desire to be present, or even invoked as the mediator of the request.

Hence, when, soon after the sitting, the James family departed for a visit to the Low Countries and France, Frieda was relieved. Mr James did not say so, of course, but Frieda could sense in him a relief at least equal to her own. She read it in the sprightliness of his morning greeting and heard it in the sharpness of his concentration as he dictated. Intensely as he loved his family, it was all the more of a liberation not to have them to consider. Although he had, as was his wont, endeavoured to keep to his daily routine even while his family was staying, that routine had inevitably been disrupted by such intrusions as will assume licence in any closely-knit family. He needed now, quite literally, to work in order to pay for the bread and butter that his family had consumed in such large quantities.

For Frieda, too, this was a time of consolidation and recuperation – not in any physical sense, for her constitution remained as strong as ever, but in spirit and intellect. She had not realised how taxing the constant presence of an unremittingly serious person like Miss James could be. Mr James, though the least frivolous of men, guarded against solemnity by elevating misfortune or inconvenience to the level of catastrophe, a vantage point so extravagant that it was but a shrug away from the saving perspective of irony. Whatever was, lost its power to disconcert or overwhelm when measured against the possible, the calamitous other case.

There were times, indeed, when Frieda was moved to a kind of awe amounting almost to horror at the operation of this principle. Responding to an account from an old friend of accompanying his mother on a harrowing visit to a dentist, Mr James's compassion did not deter him from a certain satirical hyperbole at the expense of the poor old lady: '*You wring my heart*,' he dictated to Frieda in a tone and with a countenance altogether unwrung, '*with your report of your collective Dental pilgrimage to Boston in Mrs Howells's distressful interest. I read of it from your page, somehow, as I read of Siberian or Armenian or Macedonian monstrosities, through a merciful attenuating veil of Distance and Difference, in a column of* The Times.'

The Macedonian monstrosities were to remain with Frieda as an image of Mr James's slightly bemused Distance and Difference from human suffering. The merciful attenuating veil, she could not help feeling, screened Mr James from agonies less dental than those of Mrs Howells. There was something inhuman and yet admirable, a kind of callous courage, in the novelist's detachment from the sufferings he perpetrated for his unfortunate characters; and this in spite of the most extreme, even excessive, solicitude for misfortunes more nearly home, like Mrs James's chronic headaches, or Professor James's digestive problems. The price of Mr James's artistic interest, Frieda seemed to see, was his human concern.

The summer of 1908 was a brilliant glow of windless warmth, mellowing gently into the riper shades of autumn. To Frieda the routine of the Garden Room, interspersed with long walks on Camber Sands and bicycle rides across the marshes, was restful in its very uneventfulness. Mr Fullerton's communications were regular enough to be reassuring and yet irregular enough not to become predictable; if the price of this was disappointment on many a morning, the reward was the delight, all the greater for not being depended upon, of the by-now-familiar sensation of being entered by his presence.

Before Frieda and Mr James had had time to catch up the arrears of work accumulated during the early part of their visit, the James family returned from Europe for another instalment. They were sunburnt and ebullient, Professor James full of the names of obscure Flemish painters, Mrs James full of the many bargains she had struck in the acquisition of lace, chocolates, rugs, and whatever objects of consumption had presented themselves to her as indispensable. All of them were triumphant in not having succumbed once to any of the considerable list of ailments that made travelling for the James family so much more hazardous than for other families.

To Frieda's relief there was now a certain distance in Miss James's manner, as if she, too, wanted to avoid overly familiar reference to their joint communion with the spirits. Frieda guessed that she had not made much progress in her resolve to persuade her father and uncle to the publication of her aunt's diary, and that she did not want Frieda to tax her with her delay. This did not prevent her from asking Frieda to accompany her on walks, Frieda imagined because she felt rather helplessly blank when on her own: in what Frieda thought of as the American way, she seemed to exist only in relation to other people.

One day, returning from an outing to the Art Pottery Galleries on Landgate, where Miss James had hoped to find some cocoa mugs to take to her friends at Bryn Mawr, they passed Ypres Castle, which Miss James, who had studied French at college, pronounced after the French fashion.

'They call it Wipers here,' Frieda said, glad to have a piece of local lore to impart to the well-informed young American.

'Do they?' asked Miss James, evidently interpreting and resisting Frieda's comment as a correction. 'I am surprised. One would have thought living so close to France they would have mastered French pronunciation.'

'The castle was built to ward off invasions from France,' Frieda ventured; then, as her companion looked at her blankly, 'I mean, just because they live close to France doesn't mean they identify very closely with the French.'

Miss James shrugged impatiently. 'You'd think that by now people would have stopped fretting about being invaded, wouldn't you? What would be the *point* of invading England? It's so much smaller than France.'

'Well, there was William the Conqueror. *He* seemed to want England. But you never can tell, with the French, what they want, can you?'

Miss James was as oblivious to irony as one of the seagulls perching on the parapet before them in the hopes that the two ladies with parasols would prove to be visitors with sandwiches. 'Well, I guess it helps if you speak the language. We had a few days in France on our way here, and I found I could make myself understood tolerably well. Do *you* speak French, Miss Wroth?'

'No, I'm afraid I don't.' Frieda found condescension most easily dealt with by entering fully into the other person's limited estimate of her. 'And I've never even been to France, though I have been living within sight of it for the last year and more.'

'Well, isn't that a shame? I mean, for a young woman to be... to live here all the time? You can't be much older than twenty-five?'

'I am twenty-three.'

'Are you really? Well, all the more reason then for you to see the world. I'm sure I've learnt more in these last few weeks than in two years at Bryn Mawr.' She looked critically in the direction of the French coastline, which was not, however, visible in the hazy light of the September afternoon. 'Not but that the New World could teach the Old a few things. I must say, I found Paris inferior to Washington in point of planning and design, less *monumental* somehow.'

Frieda was unmoved by Miss James's patriotic strictures on Paris, but for reasons of her own she was interested in the city itself. 'Did… did you see many people in Paris?'

'More than I was comfortable with. My father seems to know so many people wherever we go. Even in Amsterdam people were coming up to him all the time.'

'But in Paris… did you see Mr James's friend Mrs Wharton?'

'No, I do believe she is still in America; she has a most magnificent property there, you know. I was sorry to miss her, for I do think her the most interesting novelist of her generation – taking her generation to be the one after Uncle Henry's, of course.' Miss James's distinctions were nothing if not precise: she had a mental map of her preferences open in front of her at all times.

'Did you meet many of Mr James's other acquaintances?'

'I hardly know, we were there for such a short time and met so many people.' Miss James seemed as little interested in following up Frieda's conversational lead as Frieda was in hers, but unexpectedly, after a brief pause, she added, 'Except for Mr Fullerton, of course.'

'Mr Fullerton?'

'Yes, I guess you won't have met him, he's so firmly settled in Paris. He was very attentive to us: he is a great admirer of my father's work.'

'And of Mr James's, I think. He did in fact come here once on his way to France.'

'Did he? Perhaps we are not talking of the same person – a Mr Morton Fullerton? I do not recall that he mentioned visiting Rye.' Miss James seemed anxious that Mr Fullerton should not have visited Rye, as if that would somehow compromise her proprietary interest in him.

'He may well not have had occasion. We must allow for the very many other things he will have wanted to discuss with Professor James.'

'That is possible, though I cannot help thinking… however, that does not signify. He showed us around Paris most delightfully and most obligingly, I must say. He has a the aplomb of the Parisians without their indifference to the common courtesies. I am pleased that I can take back good reports of him to Bryn Mawr. He is engaged to be married to one of our teachers, you know.'

Frieda was to remember later, in recollecting this moment, that she had been staring at one of the field guns pointing bravely but ineffectually over the marsh to the Channel. She was glad that she had not been facing Miss James as she made her bland announcement; as it was, she had time to gather her reserves before repeating, with no more than polite curiosity: 'Mr Fullerton is engaged to be married to one of your teachers?'

'Yes, but… oh dear, I suspect it may still be a great secret. You see, Miss Fullerton, or Miss Katharine as we call her, grew up as Mr Fullerton's sister, though she is in fact no relation at all, having been adopted as an infant by Mr Fullerton's parents. But there is apparently some sensitivity about its being known just yet. *We* know about it because Miss Katharine told her best friend, Miss Connelly, and Miss Connelly told her niece, who is in my cocoa group. It happened last October, on his last visit home. It is considered very romantic. I must admit, though, that I find it less so; I mean, if I were to discover tomorrow that I had been adopted by my parents, I cannot imagine wanting to get married to Harry.'

Frieda's perturbation sought refuge in the irrelevant reflection that she could not imagine wanting to get married to Harry either; but insofar as this offered a distraction, it did so only for a moment, after which she had to confront again the startling allegation that Miss James had so blandly placed before her. Mr Fullerton engaged to his own adoptive sister, a fortnight before making love to Frieda, almost immediately before visiting Mrs Wharton and making his impression on that lady… it was surely some strange infatuation on the part of Miss Katharine Fullerton, or some tangled chain of miscommunication that had issued in this announcement.

Miss James ventured no further information; it was clear that she had only the information of her cocoa-drinking chums to support her belief. On the whole, Frieda was not inclined to believe a story as unlikely as this one was in every respect; she refrained, however, from comment, and was relieved when

Miss James found a change of subject in the behaviour of two children quarrelling over a stale bun given to them by a well-meaning but short-sighted shopkeeper.

On reflection Frieda decided that there was only one way of finding out the truth about Miss James's bizarre rumour. Mr Fullerton himself was the only person who could be relied upon to have absolute clarity as to his intentions *vis-à-vis* his adoptive sister; and Frieda accordingly broached the subject with him the following morning.

September 9th 1908

Receiver:	I heard an interesting rumour yesterday regarding your sister Katharine.
Transmitter:	How rumour does travel, all the way to Rye. Let me guess — your informant has lately been to Paris?
Receiver:	Yes, Miss James. She says they saw a good deal of you while there.
Transmitter:	A good deal? Well, let us say twice. I paid them every respect I thought was due to such close relations of Mr James. And I admire the work of Professor James. Mrs James and Miss James I must confess to have been but moderately charmed by.
Receiver:	And yet Miss James found you exceedingly pleasant and helpful.
Transmitter:	And so I hope she did, after the quite exceptional trouble I took to be so - helpful, that is; pleasant I left to emerge as it might. Mrs James is essentially a bourgeoise married to an intellectual, and Miss James is the unfortunate progeny of the mismatch, with all that one would expect as a consequence in the line of insecurities and unassimilated culture. But you have not told me what the rumour is that she brought with her from Paris.

Receiver: Not from Paris — from Bryn Mawr. She says
that you are engaged to be married to
your adoptive sister.

Transmitter: And you believe this wild rumour?

Receiver: Not if you declare it to be wild.

Transmitter: I do declare it to be wild, the product
of the over-heated imagination of a crowd
of college girls with nothing to occupy
their minds. I should have thought that
one's own sister would be safe from
the romantic speculation of impudent
spectators. I am very fond of Katharine,
of course, and have made no effort to
hide that fact, which no doubt excited
the prurient impulses forever awaiting
their opportunity in the thickets of the
Puritan mind.

Receiver: That was what I thought, but I judged it
better to tell you what is being said
about you.

Transmitter: Thank you for that. I shall take care in
future how I behave towards my sister in
public; that is, I shall act even more
affectionately than hitherto towards her.

To Frieda's mind this was a more plausible account of events than Miss James's. It was likely that the rumour had started as an idle speculation at one of their cocoa parties, and that Miss James, who at the time did not know Mr Fullerton, had retained a false memory of the exact import of the rumour. Frieda had the vaguest notion of what a cocoa group entailed, but thought it probable that an unexpressed aim in its constitution was the generation and dissemination of just such speculations as this.

After this, Frieda was more impatient than ever that the James family should make their way back to their native element: quite apart from the sheer distraction of their various needs, wants and preferences, she judged that she had delayed for long enough in finding Mr Fullerton's letters and restoring them to him in Paris, and the presence of four ubiquitous and inquisitive

Jameses rendered it impossible even to attempt a search.

It was with an inner sigh, then, not loud but deep, that she listened to their plans for departure, early in October. There were interminable discussions of every aspect of the journey, but in particular the James family's choice of route and hence of ship, Mr James recommending the Liverpool-New York route with its newer and faster ships like the *Lusitania*, the Jameses favouring the more direct Liverpool-Boston route with the slow but familiar old *Saxonia*. The latter prevailed, amidst much good-humoured head-shaking of Mr James: 'Why anybody would choose to spend ten days aboard a wave-tossed plank when for the same money they could do it in six days escapes my comprehension,' he remonstrated. The professor no less good-humouredly pointed out that it was not in fact for the same money, quite apart from the extra expense and inconvenience of travelling from New York to Boston at the other end. Mrs James added that the Boston route attracted a better type of passenger than the more 'cosmopolitan' New York route.

Frieda privately cared very little whether the Jameses went back via Vladivostok or Shanghai, as long as they went; and it was with something like disbelief that she saw them actually depart, with all the high publicity that departing Americans are capable of, and with a grumbling George Gammon and a taciturn Burgess Noakes carting piles of luggage to Rye Station in the little handcart that Mr James claimed to have bought with the royalties from *The Wings of the Dove*. Mr James, of course, accompanied them to the station: Frieda watched from the window of the Garden Room the progress of the little procession down West Street, Mr James frequently stopping the better to make a point, to the evident impatience of Miss James and Mr Harry, who, Frieda imagined, had by now had their fill of quiet little Rye and their expansive uncle alike. They disappeared at last into the High Street, leaving Frieda to reflect on the miracles of modern transport that made possible such a promiscuous wandering on the face of the earth.

Mr James returned from the station with something of the same consciousness. 'Isn't it wonderful,' he asked Frieda, 'how people, in this modern globe-life, *recur*?'

Frieda must have looked rather blank at his appeal, for Mr

James undertook to elaborate: 'In an earlier age people went to the antipodes and remained there, or returned in extreme old age, strangers in a world altered beyond recognition. Now they go there only to be back three months later, to a world changed as little as they themselves. This is, of course, splendid in the case of those one loves; but the process is as indiscriminate as every other aspect of the age we live in, and one is beset by people whom one had thought safe in Schenectady or Buffalo. I do believe I have never had a summer as unrelievedly hospitable as this one.'

'Are you expecting any more visitors this summer?' asked Frieda, thinking it best to seem to assume that Mr James's reflection was unconnected with his lately departed kinsfolk.

'Not to my knowledge, my dear, and certainly not with my consent. Mrs Wharton, of course, arrives on the fifth of next month, and that cannot but rather *loom* – but her I am always delighted to see. I was thinking more of stray Americans *hovering* at one as if expecting to be invited to *descend*, on the strange assumption that on foreign soil all Americans are brethren under the skin. They are only to be repelled at the price of a certain brusqueness that is foreign to one's nature. Diplomacy has never been a deterrent to invasion, I fear.'

There had now appeared several volumes of the Collected
Edition of Mr James's works, enough for him to start looking
for evidence of the world's appreciation in the form of increased
royalties. He had invested, as Frieda knew better than anybody,
considerable time and trouble in the painstaking revision of
almost all his works, in accordance with the better judgement
that he considered he had gained in the almost forty years since
the publication of his first novel. Not everybody considered
these revisions to constitute improvements: Frieda herself
thought there was a kind of disingenuousness amounting almost
to deception in presenting to the world a revised product as if
it were the first fruits of one's inspiration. She knew that there
was no such duplicitous intention on Mr James's part: indeed,
the Preface conscientiously appended to each volume generally
reflected at considerable length on the process of revision itself,
but she yet felt that a novel, once sent out to make its way in
the world, had better make it without such a radical change of
complexion as some of these revisions constituted.

This, however, was naturally not Mr James's view of the
matter, and he was looking forward with some eagerness to the
reverberation of the critical tribute that he regarded as due to
the immense effort represented by the Edition. There had in
fact so far been little acclamation to greet the first few volumes
issued, other than polite expressions of gratitude and admiration
from the select few favoured with complimentary copies of the
handsome and expensive volumes. Frieda knew that Mr James
was harbouring some anxiety on this score; and when, early in
October, after reading his morning post, he confessed to her
that he was feeling too unwell to dictate, she assumed that he

had received bad news regarding the Edition.

'It's nothing to alarm yourself about, my dear; it's a spiritual rather than a physical ill; only I find it occupies my mind to the extent that I cannot attend as I should to my work. You will oblige me greatly by typing up the corrected proofs of *The Golden Bowl*, while I take my poor aching head to my darkened room.'

This resolve, however, lasted for only an hour, after which Mr James dispatched Mrs Paddington to ask if Frieda would be so kind as to come and take dictation in his room, as she had on previous occasions done when he had been too ill to get up. Burgess Noakes conveyed the Remington with due care and ceremony up the stairs, and Frieda took her place at the desk in Mr James's room, while he reclined in his bed, looking more than ever, with his great head and mournful gaze, like some disappointed potentate. Max lay on the floor by the bed; he lifted a wary ear at Frieda, and then signalled with a slow oscillation of his tail his acceptance of her presence.

'You will understand, my dear,' Mr James said, 'that circumstances oblige me to entrust to your confidence matters that normally I should not have the impertinence to subject you to.'

'I understand perfectly, Mr James. It is part of the training of a typewriter to deal with confidential material with the utmost discretion.'

'Of course, of course, I have never doubted that. I am merely in a manner perturbed that you should be drawn into matters that you may regard as unprofessional; indeed, in this instance it is a quite personal... *perturbation*, being a letter to a dear friend in some distress. I do not want to delay the letter until I am better able to deal with it manually, as she is about to sail from America, and I am anxious that she should receive my letter before doing so.'

Frieda was by now established behind the Remington, with the paper in place and the margins set as Mr James liked them. She thought it redundant to reassure Mr James once again; her manner should speak for itself. Whereas in assuring him of her professional discretion she was entirely sincere, this did not prevent her from speculating on her private account that the correspondent about to sail from America would be Mrs

Wharton – not that a good many of Mr James's friends were not chronically about to sail from America, but there was about Mr James's manner a subdued histrionics, an incipiently flamboyant emotionality that Frieda associated with his dealings with the florid American lady.

Mr James was clearly at a disadvantage in having to dictate without being able to pace. He fidgeted with the bedclothes, and cleared his throat several times before starting. *'My very dear Friend,'* he intoned, almost as if addressing the absent friend from a considerable height, some promontory or desert outcrop. Following somewhat ponderously upon this theatrical salutation, the opening paragraph fussed and rumbled anti-climactically about sailings, and worried redundantly, Frieda thought, about the likelihood of the letter not reaching its addressee in time after all, if it did reach her before she sailed, there would have been no point in expressing the anxiety, and if it did not reach her, there would have been no point in writing the letter.

After this, though, Mr James was, for him, remarkably direct. *'I am deeply distressed,'* he almost groaned, as if indeed in physical pain, *'at the situation you describe and as to which my power to enlighten now quite miserably fails me.'*

Having made this admission of defeat, Mr James lay in silence for a moment, his eyes closed, his hands clasped on his chest, and Frieda wondered whether, unprecedentedly, he was at a loss for words. This could be the shortest letter Mr James had ever written. But in so far as he was defeated, he was so only for a moment: he could always make matter out of his own helplessness. *'I move in darkness,'* he began, and then, gathering momentum, and regaining the ringing quality in his voice and the ruminative energy of his pursuit of precision, *'I rack my brain; I gnash my teeth; I don't pretend to understand or to imagine.'*

It had not escaped Frieda's notice that the letter was addressed to an anonymous recipient, and that the subject was being referred to in the most circumspect of terms, so as to conceal its content from unenlightened outsiders like herself. She did not take this personally: she knew that Mr James harboured dark suspicions about posterity, and was determined to foil the impudence of later generations sifting through his correspondence for clues as to matters that they had no title to. Besides, she flattered herself, she had penetration enough to arrive at a tolerably coherent interpretation of the situation: Mrs Wharton had evidently shared with Mr James her perplexity in the face of, presumably, the conduct of a common acquaintance, and had possibly asked Mr James for elucidation. Mr James, on his part, was pleading incomprehension, even helplessness; but, unwilling, no doubt, to be reduced merely to a failure of understanding and imagination, he ventured, after all, some advice: '*And yet, incredibly to you doubtless – I am still moved to say "Don't conclude!"*'

Mr James, it would seem, was resisting some conclusion that Mrs Wharton had adumbrated: '*Anything is more credible – conceivable – than a mere inhuman* plan. *A great trouble, an infinite worry or a situation of the last anxiety or uncertainty are conceivable...*' Mrs Wharton, then, had been haunted by the possibility of the mysterious stranger's acting in terms of some design, *a mere inhuman plan*; against which Mr James was positing *a great trouble.*

Mr Fullerton, of course, was never far from Frieda's thoughts, and her ingenuity had little trouble in finding in this mysterious situation veiled references to his situation. Like Mr James, but presumably unlike Mrs Wharton, Frieda knew, after all, of the *anxiety or uncertainty* that Mr Fullerton was facing in the person of his presumptuous landlady. Unlike Mr James, Frieda knew that Mr Fullerton was less enamoured of Mrs Wharton than she evidently was of him, though, no doubt, she would have represented her infatuation to Mr James as no more than deep friendship, hurt at a lack of reciprocity.

Frieda, calculating rapidly, thus felt herself the most privileged of the three: if Mr James knew more than Mrs Wharton, she, Frieda, knew more than Mr James. Mr James meanwhile, knowing but imperfectly, was giving advice of the most general kind: '*Only sit tight yourself and go through the movements of life. That keeps up our connection with life – I mean of the immediate and apparent life, behind which, all the while, the deeper and darker and the unapparent, in which things really happen to us, learns, under that hygiene, to stay in its place.*'

At times like these Frieda did not know whether she was most enthralled by or exasperated with her employer: with such unerring instinct could he describe her situation, and with such sublime blindness fail to notice its application to her. She stored away, nevertheless, the notion of *the deeper and darker and the unapparent, in which things really happen to us* as his unconscious gift to her. What did Mrs Wharton, that most expressive and voluble of women, know about the deeper and darker and the unapparent? Frieda's way of going through the movements of life, meanwhile, was to type the letter as if her only interest in it were professional; but the unapparent in her was alert to any suggestions as to the ramifications of Mrs Wharton's quandary. '*I have had but that one letter*,' Mr James dictated, '*of weeks ago, and there are* kinds *of news I can't ask for.*'

As Mr James referred to the *one letter*, Frieda noticed his glance flicking to the other desk in the room on which, indeed, she noticed an unfolded letter – presumably, then, the letter from Mr Fullerton.

There was, after this, not very much more, Mr James still being anxious that he was wasting effort on a letter that would arrive too late to offer even such limited support as its wails of helplessness, its guarded exhortations and its cautious consolations could render. Not that this anxiety prevented him from a closing affirmation of *aboundingly tender friendship*, the exact constituents of which – *the understanding, the participation* – took him some minutes to assemble; and it was while he was hovering over these that Frieda noticed, in the reflection of the mirror on the dressing table, that the top drawer of the other desk was open. It was only very slightly open, but it told Frieda that the letter had probably been taken from this drawer; and it was accordingly here, presumably, that Mr James kept his letters from Mr Fullerton.

Frieda wondered whether it would be a breach of her professional duty to Mr James to mention to Mr Fullerton the matter of Mrs Wharton's distress. She decided, regretfully, that there was no plausible manner of interpreting such a disclosure as consistent with that undertaking of discretion she had given her employer. There *was* a rationalisation available to her, in the circumstance that Mr James had in fact not confided in her, had left it to her ingenuity to discover for herself the identity of his correspondent and the subject of her distress, but that would be a barren technicality of which she scorned to avail herself. Having committed herself to a very large betrayal, she needed to make the most of small loyalties.

It was thus a relief to Frieda when, the following morning, Mr Fullerton himself introduced the topic.

October 14th 1908

Transmitter: I have had several letters from Mrs Wharton accusing me, bafflingly, of a dereliction of duty to her.

Receiver: What duty?

Transmitter: Well may you ask. She calls it the duty of friendship, but it is surely not in the province of friendship to be so very exacting as to the number of letters each party to the relationship finds time or opportunity to write the other.

Receiver: It is possible for a friend to feel neglected.

Transmitter: My dear Miss Wroth, by what criterion is my neglect measured? What moral or social authority obliges me to satisfy Mrs Wharton's epistolary requirements?

Receiver: That would depend on what undertakings you gave her when you spent time with her.

Transmitter: That would indeed, and if I tell you that I gave her precisely no undertaking as to my future conduct towards her, you will understand why I feel perplexed. I am even concerned, from something she let slip in her last letter, lest she should address her grievance to Mr James.

Receiver: How would that advance her cause?

Transmitter: Not a whit. But she might in her extremity imagine that he would intercede on her behalf; and I would naturally not enjoy being calumniated to Mr James,

	whose good opinion I value above all else.
Receiver:	And since he thinks very highly of Mrs Wharton...?
Transmitter:	I should also think very highly of Mrs Wharton? Oh, I assure you, I do think very highly of Mrs Wharton; I only do not commit my high opinion to paper as often and as warmly as she apparently expects.

Frieda thought she had evaded with commendable adroitness the question of how much Mr James was in Mrs Wharton's confidence. She had no desire to take unfair advantage of that lady's indiscretion; besides, there was a certain satisfaction in being the only member of this so oddly established coterie to command a total view of the situation. The fact that she was not regarded as a member at all by the other associates gave piquancy to this consciousness.

The month of October was not a happy one for Mr James. A week after he had dictated to her his reply to Mrs Wharton's distressing letter, Frieda found him one morning, on arriving for work, in the Garden Room, pacing up and down with a letter in his hand. It was unusual for him to be in the Garden Room before her, and for a moment she thought she must be late; but a glance at the clock on the wall reassured her.

Mr James looked up as she entered, as if he were surprised to see her. He was as impeccably, even jauntily, dressed as always, but his manner was, for him, distraught. 'Ah, there you are, my dear. I was not expecting you so early. I have been reading the morning post over breakfast, and have found this letter unusually agitating.'

Frieda assumed that there had been another communication from Mrs Wharton, and did not know what to reply. Certainly she could not say what she thought, which was that quite enough emotion had already been expended on the adolescent infatuation of a middle-aged woman. Poor Mrs Howells having all her teeth extracted, or conceivably even the latest Macedonian monstrosity, was surely a worthier object of compassion than Mrs Wharton fabricating a grievance out of the fact that Mr Fullerton did not write to her by every post.

But Mr James did not expect a reply: he was too engrossed in his own distress – which, in the event, turned out to be nothing to do with the amatory anxieties of the lady novelist. 'I have here,' Mr James explained, 'a letter from my agent, Pinker, enclosing statements from the Scribners who, as you know, have undertaken publication of the Edition. It seems, as far as I can make out,' and here Mr James gave her a look at once perplexed and outraged, 'that there is *absolutely nothing*, not a single American cent or English penny, not a *sou* or… *drachma* due to me in respect of the sales so far of the Edition.'

'But how can that be? If they sold anything at all, there must be something due?'

'So, in one's blessed innocence, one would have thought, and so, in one's blessed innocence, did one calculate. But I find now that everything is swallowed up in paying out the original publishers who have retained, it seems, a right in my work even where it has been as substantially revised as these have been. In short and in sum, I have to pay to have my own works published.'

He threw the letter he had been holding onto her desk as if he wanted to get rid of it. 'My dear Miss Wroth, pray to heaven that you will never labour so hard and so long to so little effect.'

Frieda was sorry for Mr James, but also disappointed. What did he mean by *so little effect*? She had watched with admiration mixed with exasperation the extreme care with which he had revised works that were, to her mind, already perfect of their kind; she had recognised in him the urge to perfection at any price, and respected the desire to leave behind a monument of the highest quality. 'I certainly want no other,' he had said to her. 'If I am going to be remembered at all, it must not be for my mistakes. If I have opted to live for my art, thereby foregoing so many of the satisfactions that the vast majority of people seem to find indispensable to Life, my art must justify my life, or the life I never had.'

Frieda could see that what Mr James wanted was a kind of immortality: just as his brother was searching for some key to the existence of life beyond death, Mr James was, in his own more practical way, trying to ensure his survival beyond the grave. This endeavour and its effect seemed to her independent of the financial reward to be reaped from the process. 'At least it is a consolation that the Edition will be there, and that it will be as good as it is,' she accordingly said.

He looked at her, his gaze unenlightened by such comfort as she had to offer. 'A consolation, yes, my dear, but there are times when we cannot make do with consolations. From a purely practical point of view this has been, as you know, a most... *hospitable* summer, with a corresponding increase in household expenditure. In a word, Miss Wroth, I need the money to live, and was looking to the Edition as the means to provide some of it.'

Life as a creature requiring a certain sum of money per week to sustain itself was an apparition that Frieda was acquainted with of old, from the dank little house in Chelsea with its careful little meals served in chipped heirloom china that could not quite conceal the meagreness of the fare. Now to confront again that dour familiar in this little mansion of plenty was like fleeing the country to get away from an undesirable relative, only to find he had stowed away in the ship carrying one to freedom.

'You may, then, no longer require my services,' she offered, more in this spirit of unwelcome recognitions than of sacrifice. But whatever there was of the ungenerous in her offer escaped Mr James.

'My dear, you shame me with your example. I am touched beyond words by your unselfishness, but I had no thought to involve you in my own financial difficulties. Had I known that you would attempt to make them your own, I should not have breathed a word to you; I would not dream of putting you out into the street because I am suffering a temporary embarrassment. Apart from any other consideration, the time you save me through your miraculous dexterity more than pays for itself in increased output.'

Spurred on, it would seem, by his mistaken interpretation of her example, Mr James made an effort to rally his forces. 'Let me turn my mind, with whatever diminished expectation, to the Edition. I must confess I have quite lost my spring for it; but there is no stopping now, I suppose. My dear, if you would be so kind as to remind me... the Preface to *The Golden Bowl*, was it?'

'Yes, Mr James, you had just started... *what most stands out for me is the still marked inveteracy of a certain indirect and oblique view of my presented action...*'

There were, after all, few things as consoling, as revitalising, as his own prose. He listened intently, and, listening, started to pace: he had recovered his spring. 'Ah yes, thank you, I recall my train of thought. '*I have already betrayed, comma, as an accepted habit, comma, and even to extravagance commented on, comma, my preference for dealing with my subject matter, comma, for quote "seeing my story," comma, end quote, through the opportunity and the sensibility of some more or less detached, comma, some not strictly... involved, comma, though thoroughly interested and intelligent, comma, witness or...*'

Mediator?

'*...reporter, comma, some person who contributes to the case mainly a certain amount of criticism and interpretation of it. Full stop.*'

In November Mrs Wharton spent the better part of two weeks at Lamb House, as preliminary to what Mr James called the Descent of the Angel of Devastation upon the British Isles. Frieda was sorry for Mr James, knowing that he had had more guests all summer than even his habitual hospitality found congenial or convenient, especially in what he confessed to having been his worst year, financially speaking, for twenty-five years. Mr James himself, however, professed nothing but pleasure in anticipating the visit.

Frieda privately thought that in his secret heart he must regard the extravagant, generous, all-consuming Mrs Wharton as a mixed blessing: while providing him with the inexpensive exhilaration of being whisked about the countryside in her huge motor car, she was naturally used to eating well, one of the apparently considerable number of things she found indispensable to Life, like draping herself in the furs of animals less fortunate than herself.

Frieda winced on Mr James's behalf at seeing him trying with so little success to dress up his relatively meagre fare to appeal to the sophisticated New York palate of his guest. There was a painful little scene when a pie was produced for lunch that had already, the night before, been served for dinner. Its lack of allure on that occasion had apparently caused it to be returned to the kitchen but barely broached; and the frugal Mrs Paddington, having made the most perfunctory of attempts to repair the unenthusiastic depredation of the previous night, had returned it to the luncheon table.

Mr James placidly presided over the distribution of heavy wedges of the unappreciated steak and kidney pie, but Mrs Wharton could contain no longer her suppressed sense of the unfitness of things. 'Honestly, my dear Henry,' she exclaimed, 'have we not endured this particular pie once before? I do believe I recognise the very kidney I have upon my plate as one I sent back to the kitchen last night. It is very peculiarly shaped.'

Mr James looked bewildered. 'I imagine it is kidney-shaped, Edith.'

'It is peculiarly shaped even for a kidney, Henry. I would recognise it anywhere.'

'I do not imagine the pie is trying to impose upon us, Edith.' Mr James waved his fork vaguely in the direction of the now devastated crust. 'It confesses quite guilelessly to its identity.'

'It is its guilelessness that I presume to criticise, Henry. Do you not think that cookery, as much as any other amenity of life, needs art to make it palatable? Now this is the most artless pie I have ever seen; it positively boasts of its disreputable origins and revels in its ravages. Surely, Henry, we have not come to such a pass that we need eat for luncheon a dish that was deemed unsuitable for dinner, as if it could miraculously redeem itself by spending the night in the larder?'

Mr James seemed amused rather than embarrassed at Mrs Wharton's diatribe. 'I think, Edith, Mrs Paddington assumed that it was lack of appetite rather than a failure to appreciate her pie that moved us, last night, to decline the meal set before us. She would be too proud to serve up a second time what was spurned on the first offering.'

Frieda was not convinced of this: she suspected the old housekeeper of taking a certain delight in confronting Mrs Wharton's sensibilities with solid English home cooking. It was her form of passive resistance to the invasion of automobiles, chauffeurs and Frenchified affectation, and it was, in its way, as eloquent as a Martello Tower or cheval de frise.

But Mrs Wharton, not content to let the matter rest, persisted. 'My dear Henry, what on earth *is* lack of appetite if not a failure to appreciate?'

Frieda was sorry for Mr James and angry with Mrs Wharton. It was easy for an American heiress to talk of the amenities of life as if they were a matter of disinterested connoisseurship to be had for the asking. Frieda knew that the amenities of life had a price, and that lack of appetite was a problem only for those who had never suffered hunger.

In lamenting to Frieda the invasion of his home by friends and relations, Mr James was, she judged, entirely sincere; and yet she sensed also, in the sheer extravagance of his lamentation, a perverse satisfaction in the inconvenience of being so persistently visited. Frieda, in her relative inexperience of friendship, had imagined it to facilitate one's existence and alleviate one's cares; but for Mr James it was evidently most itself when most requiring trouble and even expense.

From this point of view the many young men whom Mr James befriended were admirable, in chronically involving both trouble and expense. Amongst these, the sculptor Hendrik Andersen was supreme in demanding very large quantities of both. The little bust of the young Italian nobleman that Mr James had bought in Rome gave him such pleasure that Frieda could not in all conscience count that as an unreasonable expense, though it had cost a considerable sum; but the bust of the Master himself, which the young sculptor had made the year before, was like a funeral monument to a dead friendship: cold, aloof, fleshy and yet cadaverous. There was a sad irony in the fact that Mr James, so addicted to the art of representation, should himself be so grossly misrepresented. Though Mr James seemed to have forgiven the young sculptor this atrocity, and blamed only himself for the failure, Frieda found it difficult thereafter to regard the young man's photograph with anything but the revulsion she felt for his creation.

Then there was young Mr Persse – though she had heard it said that he was not as young as he looked – with his exuberant laughter, his refusal to be intimidated by the conversational heavyweights he was likely to be confronted with at Lamb

House, and his total absence of any kind of intellectual or artistic aspiration. Frieda noted, not without pleasure, the twinge of slightly pained toleration on Mrs Wharton's well-regulated features when Mr Persse joined her and Mr James in their slow perambulation around the garden of Lamb House; it was an expression Frieda had seen on her face once before when Max, whom she adored less than her own dogs, had rushed in fresh from digging up a muddy patch of garden and leapt on her lap.

Refreshing as Mr Persse's juvenile energy indubitably was, Frieda wondered a little at Mr James's readiness to spend long hours prattling – about what? – with such an unlikely conversationalist. She had always judged inarticulateness to be the one state that Mr James could not negotiate: a certain simplicity he could delight in, a wrong point of view eloquently defended he could attack with gusto – but sheer dumbness in the face of experience left him helpless. Not that Mr Persse was dumb – far from it – but his conversation was like the incessant patter of raindrops, conducive to nothing but puddles and muddy patches.

Frieda, in short, wondered at the principle of selection whereby Mr James tolerated, even welcomed, conversationalists as limited in range and depth as Mr Andersen and Mr Persse – Mr Fullerton of course was another matter altogether and required no explanation – while making so little of other opportunities, such, for instance, as offered by his young female amanuensis. But if there was to Frieda something invidious in Mr James's cultivation of such stony ground and shallow soil, she still found this element more congenial than the undeniably more fertile loam of Mrs Wharton's social manner. The young men took Frieda in their long stride, whereas Mrs Wharton seemed always, intellectually speaking, to pause and regard her with polite puzzlement, as if she were a strange and possibly disreputable roadside object. One never knew whether she was going to tell one to move on or offer one a shilling. To do the good woman justice, the eleemosynary instinct was in her more strongly developed than the expulsive; but both were in their way equally the privilege of conscious power.

So, somewhat inconsistently, Frieda preferred the relatively gormless young men to the scintillating, shimmering, tintinnabulating Mrs Wharton. It so happened that another one of these young disciples made his appearance not long after Mrs Wharton's departure to a house party in the Midlands for, as Mr James put it, further furious feasting. The young man was preceded by a letter, as Frieda knew thanks to that latitude that she now allowed herself in respect of Mr James's correspondence. The letter had been lying on Mr James's desk in the Green Room, amidst a clutter of other material: he had obviously, the night before, been perusing the letter and might well have replied to it. Something about the letter – the paper, the glimpse she caught of the handwriting – suggested to Frieda that it might be from Mr Fullerton, from whom, to her knowledge, Mr James had not had a letter for at least six months.

She listened to the morning sounds – the swish of Mrs Paddington's dress as she carried a tray from the dining room to the kitchen, the knocking of Alice Skinner's brush as she swept the fireplace in the drawing room. Mr James was evidently still at breakfast, 'munching and mumbling alone', as he liked to describe his solitary bouts of Fletcherising – and even Max was absent, presumably fast asleep in front of the dining-room fire.

Had the letter been folded, Frieda might have hesitated, but, open as it was, it seemed to invite perusal, and it was the work of a moment to retrieve it from the desk. Her first impulse was a disappointment: it was not from Mr Fullerton at all. The handwriting was neater than his, rather anxiously formed, and lacking the characterful sweep of his penmanship.

7th December 1905

Dear Mr James,

Emboldened thereto by the recommendations I enclose from Messrs AC Benson and Percy Lubbock, I address you thus as one of your most ardent admirers. I have but recently completed my first novel – The Wooden Horse *– which is due to be published in the new year, and would not presume to address you thus had I not been assured that your kindness is as great as your genius. I cannot pretend to believe that a young man of twenty-four, as I am, can have anything to offer a man of your experience, other than the most sincere admiration of your craft and an intense desire to get to know more closely the mind capable of such consummate masterpieces. I* *is no small thing for somebody setting out on a career in writing – I have recently established myself in a modest way in Chelsea, hoping to make my way in literary journalism, and have been fortunate in being asked to review several books – to address one of the...*

Frieda heard the unmistakable tread on the staircase too late to replace the letter – she suddenly couldn't remember exactly in what position it had lain on the desk – and in a gesture of panic she stuffed it into the pocket of her jacket. Mr James, entering with his usual urbane greeting and enquiry after her welfare, and settling at his large desk, seemed not to notice that the letter was missing. Frieda could only hope that his rather haphazard system of filing would be held responsible for the disappearance of the letter.

No alarm being raised, she forgot about the letter in her pocket, and when she got home to her little room in the Warden Hotel, she found it there, by now too hopelessly crumpled to be returned to Mr James's desk without causing even this most unsuspicious of men to wonder where it had been and what had happened to it in its absence. Frieda glanced at the rest of the letter to ascertain its likely importance to Mr James: it was a fairly standard obsequious letter of introduction from an aspiring writer, of which Mr James received several every month. This was from one Hugh Walpole, and Frieda imagined that Mr James would not be greatly put out at what he would regard as his mislaying of the letter, though he generally did insist on the courtesy of a reply to such approaches.

She was interested, then, and reassured, when she noticed, a few days later, a letter on the hall table for taking to the post, addressed to Mr Hugh Walpole, care of Mr AC Benson – Mr James's expedient, then, to reply to the insinuating Mr Walpole. She assumed this letter was one of Mr James's beneficent but firm brush-offs, and was accordingly all the more surprised when, several months later, he announced that a Mr Hugh Walpole was coming to spend the weekend.

'He is a young writer,' Mr James explained in his measured way, 'whom I have had occasion to see in London, most recently during the all too brief run of my play, and whom I find most... *attaching*, in the most favourable sense of that word. He is of a freshness and candour that does one good in one's mildewed dotage. I fear, however, that I do not hold out any great hope for him as a writer; he has presented me with the firstling of his pen, a production entitled *The Wooden Horse*, in which the quality of woodenness is not, alas, confined to the equine characters.' Mr James paused, his head at an angle, as if reconsidering; but only with the effect of reinforcing his judgement. 'Indeed, the manner of the whole thing speaks of carpentry rather than of architecture or composition, held together somewhat desperately with a visible excess of nails and glue.' There flitted over Mr James's mobile features the hint of a smile that at moments signalled his enjoyment of his own acerbity, and then he recomposed his countenance. 'Still, this does not prevent him from being one of the most charming young men it has been my good fortune to meet, and I look forward to a most congenial visit. You shall meet him at luncheon on Saturday, if you would honour us with your presence.'

Frieda had no particular desire to meet yet another young man whose ambitions were larger than his talents, there being in her experience but a thin line between freshness and callowness; but it had been a long and bleak winter in Rye, and she felt the lack of variety in the company she saw. She also guessed that Mr James needed, more than usually, the kind of reassurance that he derived from the admiration of his youthful disciples; the London run of *The High Bid*, which had gone so well in Edinburgh, was a disappointment, being curtailed to a few matinees to make way for a triumphant play by a Mr Jerome K Jerome, about, according to Mr James, 'Jesus Christ himself, or somebody purporting to be or suspected to be or aspiring to be Jesus Christ himself; not the kind of competition my poor little play about ordinary mortals could very well expect to contend with.'

If Mr Walpole could serve to persuade Mr James that whatever the tastes of London audiences, he still had the ear of youth, he might lighten the slightly melancholy atmosphere of Lamb House. Frieda was thus better disposed than she might otherwise have been to the aspiring young man, and repaired to the dining room, on the Saturday promised, with even a hope of forming a new relation.

She was at first sight disappointed. She thought Mr

Walpole rather colourless, his manner not enhanced by the awe
in which he clearly held Mr James: one felt excluded from it, as
from the private devotions in the side chapel of a large cathedral.
But his features were strong, with a prominent chin and full
mouth, and he had probably, when not on pilgrimage, his
own little personality. His eyes were kindly, slightly unfocused,
possibly nearsighted. He seemed about her age or slightly older,
but his manner had a premature gravity about it that was yet not
humourless; one could imagine him having grandchildren but
not children. He was very taken with Max, and seemed anxious
that Max should be taken with him. Indeed, in his earnest
contemplation of Mr James and his exuberant delight in being
noticed, Mr Walpole was not unlike a dachshund himself. This
could only please Mr James, and even Frieda, liking Max as she
did, could not find it in her heart to dislike the young man.

It transpired that Mr Walpole's affinities with Max
extended also to wanting to be taken for a walk: he proposed,
or requested, an exploration of Rye, which he had never seen.
Mr James pleading arrears of correspondence, it fell to Frieda
to accompany Mr Walpole, a substitution that he accepted with
good grace if not alacrity. Frieda assumed that Mr Walpole liked
her well enough, given that she had hardly been the object of
his pilgrimage, and she was prepared to like him in turn, given
that he was not Mr Fullerton. Only Max seemed perfidiously
indifferent to being bought off with a substitute, and was
unreservedly overjoyed at being taken for a walk.

Rye was now, in late April, shaking itself out of its winter
gloom, but the spring was as yet tentative rather than exuberant.
It was as if the damp had not dried out of the dark little streets,
and the houses, standing open to admit the weak sunshine,
exuded at the same time the mustiness of winter. Mr Walpole
declared himself charmed with the comfortable scale of things,
enthused properly over the view across Romney marsh, and was
polite about the more insalubrious aspects of Church Square,
though decently outraged at the fate of the poor dancing bear
belonging to a lodger at the Jolly Sailor – 'It is sad, is it not, that
to many people the height of art and entertainment can consist
in watching a poor animal stagger around on its hind legs?'

From a discussion of the non-existent rights of animals the

conversation moved naturally enough to the topic of women's suffrage, in which Mr Walpole had a lively interest, pronouncing the increasingly militant policies of Mrs Pankhurst and her followers 'jolly plucky, though extreme, you know'. But it was clear that all he really wanted to talk about was Mr James. He was not so vulgar as to angle for intimate insights into the daily habits of genius, but he was naively eager for any information pertaining to Mr James's writing methods, as if the knowledge would enable him to emulate the Master. He was particularly intrigued with Mr James's use of dictation, and once again Frieda saw herself assume, in the regard of her interlocutor, a special status as the operator of the machine. He asked Frieda solemnly if she looked at Mr James while he was dictating – presumably thinking that she might be blinded by the sheer luminosity of his genius.

'Well, that depends,' Frieda replied thoughtfully, guessing that Mr Walpole would not like to hear the truth, which was that she had never given the matter any thought. 'I think Mr James finds it helpful at times to be made aware of a sympathetic audience.'

He sighed, as if he could imagine nothing more blissful than to be a sympathetic audience to Mr James. 'How extraordinarily fortunate you are, to spend your days in such proximity to genius. Taking dictation must be like accompanying a great singer.'

Frieda was for the moment occupied in discouraging Max from barking at a cat sunning itself in a cottage window, and did not want to shout her reply above the canine fury. Succeeding at last in calming the passion of the dog, Frieda asked, 'Given a choice between writing your own novels and spending your days taking dictation from genius, which would you do?'

Mr Walpole, half lost in his own imaginings, blinked at Frieda through his round glasses, clearly surprised at her question. It took him a moment to consider his answer. 'I have no illusions about the quality of my writing – Mr James is the most forthright of critics–' he said ponderingly; then, with sudden candour, 'But no, if it were a matter of choosing between writing my own third-rate productions and recording his masterpieces, I do believe that I would opt for doing my own little thing.'

'Then there you are,' Frieda said. She expected him to

express surprise at the idea that she, as appointed typewriter, might harbour her own literary aspirations, but he was too polite or too sensitive to do so, and merely said, 'That does put a different complexion on things.'

He had not, however, exhausted the topic of Mr James. 'I take it you meet many of Mr James's visitors?'

Frieda wondered whether he intended this as a consolation, but reverted to the politely non-committal tenor of their earlier conversation. 'Yes. Mr James very kindly tries to include me in some of the social occasions at Lamb House.'

'He must have many friends; he is so extraordinarily kind and hospitable.'

'Oh yes. But I do not get to know very many. Only his more particular friends like Mrs Wharton and Mr Fullerton.' She wondered later why she had mentioned Mr Fullerton: possibly only for the pleasure of sounding his name as if she had a right to it.

A brief clouding of the young man's clear brow suggested that he was at that stage of a new relation where he was jealous of all earlier claimants. 'Mrs Wharton I know of course by reputation and through her novels, but Mr Fullerton...? I don't think I have heard of him.'

'Oh, he is one of Mr James's oldest friends, though he is himself relatively young. He is an expatriate American now working for *The Times* in Paris.'

The cloud flitted across his countenance again. 'Ah yes, I have after all heard him spoken of. Rather more of a boulevardier, I seem to have gathered, than I would have thought Mr James would find altogether congenial.'

Frieda did not feel called upon to defend Mr Fullerton against Mr Walpole's aspersions. 'I couldn't pronounce on that,' she accordingly contented herself with saying, 'All I know is that Mr James has the highest opinion of his judgement.'

'And he is a frequent visitor?'

'Oh yes.' Frieda did not mind chilling Mr Walpole's slightly exasperating fervour. 'That is,' she nevertheless added conscientiously, 'he was here only a few months ago and I think Mr James is expecting him again soon.'

Mr Walpole looked so forlorn at this information that

Frieda almost felt moved to reassure him that it would not be difficult in that respect to catch up his arrears. By the end of the weekend he would in fact have spent more time at Lamb House than Mr Fullerton had done in all his years of acquaintance with Mr James. And she found that she quite liked Mr Walpole, partly because she realised that he quite liked her, almost in spite of himself – all his instincts were attuned to admiration of the Master, and he had not provided for an inconsiderable presence like herself. And yet he had taken note of her, and not only because she was the Master's amanuensis; there was a warmth in him that was more human than his ambition. But between his taking note and Mr Fullerton's there was again a world of difference, and she was loath to seem to minimise Mr James's friendship with Mr Fullerton. Mr Walpole's jealousy could not do him or anybody else any harm.

Chapter Eighteen
June 1909

Frieda did not think of herself as callous, but she had a healthy person's scepticism in the face of what she regarded as other people's exaggerated concern with their health. She found it incongruous that two people as intellectually gifted as Mr James and his brother should spend so much of their time talking about and writing about and pursuing cures for the ailments that they fancied themselves suffering from. The family's absurd dedication to the practice of Fletcherising, she judged, formed the perfect image of the gaping imbecility to which this pursuit of health could reduce normally intelligent people. She could see how the practice might be conducive to the comfort of Mrs James, who could hold her own in this relation more effectively than in more articulate discourse, but Mr James and Professor James, she felt, were sacrificing to their digestion their God-given talent of inspired speech. In her irritation she suppressed a more dispassionate voice arguing for the James family's concern with their health as a tribute, in its ungainly fashion, to life, a recognition, after all, that it has no other home than the fallible body.

When, then, in the winter Mr James reported several *cardiac incidents*, as he called them – none of which, as it happened, Frieda witnessed – she was inclined to regard these, too, as probably a symptom of the James family malaise rather than of anything more life-threatening. But as the dark months extended themselves, Frieda had to concede a difference, evidenced by Mr James's abstraction and his lapses of attention. She had not known him before to lose concentration while dictating, as he now not infrequently did. The depth of his concern was evident also from his decision, in February, to give up Fletcherising, which had hitherto been a cornerstone of his faith in modern medicine. The local man, Dr Skinner, whom Mr James described as *careful and kind but not other than very moderately intelligent and perceptive*, prescribed digitalis and strichagen, in addition to more exercise, which Mr James had given up as redundant when he started Fletcherising, claiming that the time normally spent on walking could now be spent on reading. For him, then, to exchange Fletcherising for walking suggested a level of alarm so extreme as to be based on more than fancy. Of course, it could mean merely that Mr James was more than usually convinced of his own decrepitude, but it was also at least possible that he really was not well. Even hypochondriacs, after all, did get ill.

Frieda's sympathy with Mr James in his evident distress was, once it had been aroused, sincere enough, but not unmixed with other sentiments. It was impossible not to think of Mr Fullerton and his concern about the fate of his letters, should anything *happen*, as they so ominously said, to Mr James. It now seemed possible that something might indeed happen to Mr James; and were it to do so, it would prove invidious, to say the least, to retrieve the letters, in a manner of speaking, from under his death-bed. Therefore Mr James's condition, while increasing Frieda's sympathy with her employer, also reinforced her resolve to rob him.

It was thus with a sense of moral relief that she heard, early in April, from an urbanely rejoicing Mr James, that he had received complete reassurance about his condition from a most excellent physician in London who, while seconding Dr Skinner's prescription of more exercise, saw no harm in Fletcherising, indeed confessed to being an adherent and proponent himself of what he called, never having heard of Mr Fletcher, *complete mastication and insalivation.* The combined blessings of exercise and Fletcher restored Mr James to a condition of health, he claimed, that he had not enjoyed for years. Frieda, for her part, was relieved of the burden of feeling that she was conspiring against a dying man: whereas Mr James would presumably not feel less conspired against for being in relatively good health, the difference was greatly consoling to Frieda.

The doctor's reassurance, reinforced in no small measure by the introduction of Mr Hugh Walpole to the list of regular guests to Lamb House, heralded in a time of renewed activity for Mr James; having now sent off the last of the revisions to the New York Edition, he felt free to return to the writing of new fiction. He expressed mild impatience, though, with the fact that this new freedom coincided with an unprecedented onslaught of social engagements, taking him all over England in response to pressing invitations, when it did not keep him at home in hospitable durance to visiting friends. There was, of course, always the remedy of refusal; but, as he put it to Frieda while contemplating yet another invitation to be elsewhere, 'Accepting an invitation always entails, except in the cases of the most direly predictable boredom, an element of the unexpected, which I find extremely difficult to resist. Refusing the invitation, on the other hand, has but one result.'

When Mr James departed on these sociable forays, he left Frieda on her own, to get on with such work as he left behind for her. He did not usually think to tell her whom he was going to see or what he was going to do, unless he considered it would particularly interest her, or needed her to perform some aspect of his arrangement for the expedition. She realised that he was considering what he regarded as her indifference to his social engagements, but she quarrelled exactly with this assumption: she thought that she had abundantly demonstrated, when given the opportunity, the level and extent of her interest in what was, after all, the raw material of Mr James's fiction.

It was then almost by accident that she learned of a social engagement that interested her greatly. 'May I ask you to send a telegram as you walk down the High Street?' Mr James asked her one afternoon, early in June, as she was preparing to leave for the day. 'I would ask poor little Burgess, but Mrs Paddington has dispatched him to Winchelsea, I believe, in search of fresh tomatoes, a commodity apparently inexplicably unavailable in Rye at present. I need to settle an arrangement for supper on Friday evening with an old friend – Mr Morton Fullerton, whom I do not expect you to recall meeting, his visits having been so infrequent. He is nevertheless a constant and valued friend, and as he is about to leave for America on a short visit, we, that is Mrs Wharton and I, whom you will of course remember, from her frequent manifestations here; indeed, to be strictly veracious,

Mrs Wharton has suggested, and I have gladly fallen in with her plan, to arrange a little farewell meal at his hotel, the Charing Cross Hotel, that is – a hostelry more functional than festive, I fear, but convenient to the trains.'

As Mr James seemed in danger of losing sight of his own purpose in his enumeration of the various constituents of the projected occasion, Frieda judged it in order to remind him. 'Will you be wanting me to take the telegram now?'

'Only if absolutely convenient for you, my dear. I am well aware that the duties of an amanuensis do not extend to the menial task of dispatching telegrams, so I am asking you as a favour from friend to friend, and am well aware of imposing upon your goodwill.'

'It's the smallest of favours, I do assure you. I walk right by the telegraph office on my way home.'

'That is very kind of you, Miss Wroth. I have become sadly spoilt with having poor little Burgess always at hand; I make a hardship out of walking half a mile to the post office. I shall just write down the message for you here, with the address.'

Mr James took a sheet of paper and started writing with his customary assured flourish; but having written a few words, he paused, and Frieda guessed that his fluency had abandoned him after the inditing of the address: nothing inhibited Mr James as painfully as the need for conciseness in a telegram. She resigned herself to waiting, under pretence of rearranging the contents of her handbag, and at length Mr James extended to her the fruit of his deliberations with a sigh – 'Forgive the delay, my dear, but telegrams are so *constricting*. This is not even yet as expressive as one could have wished, but I trust it is clear enough for its purpose.'

Frieda folded the sheet of paper and put it in her bag. She judged that it would be indelicate to read it in front of Mr James, though they both knew that she would have to read it in order to transcribe it to the telegram form.

The message was, as Mr James had hoped, clear enough, at any rate to anybody versed in Mr James's various appellations for Mrs Wharton:

To Fullerton, Charing Cross Hotel, London. Expect to see me at seven on the fourth. Angel of Devastation to meet us there. Henry James.

Frieda paid Mr James's shilling and sent his telegram. She could recognise the occasion as one of Mrs Wharton's making, in which Mr Fullerton would have been consulted only in being informed of the arrangement. She was nevertheless curious to glean from Mr James some indication of his sense of the farewell feast; but she was fated to wait for even such oblique light on the evening as his circumspect manner would afford. Immediately after seeing Mr Fullerton off on his way to America, Mr James was booked, as he put it, to accompany Mrs Wharton on another of her automated forays, this time to friends in Windsor and thereafter to Wallingford – unless it was Wallingford first and then Windsor: Frieda had little sense of any geographical coherence in the great flights of the Angel of Devastation. She wondered, indeed, if Mrs Wharton herself conducted her life on the basis of any plan other than the determination to be elsewhere in the shortest possible time with the largest possible entourage and the most possible publicity. She wondered at Mr James's willingness to be bundled up and carted around the English countryside like a large but amenable household god; she could only think that to him it offered a respite from the burden of unaccompanied exploration, the essential loneliness of the creative process. Here, too, she believed in all humility that she had a role to play in alleviating that loneliness; but it was of the essence of that role not to obtrude itself. Frieda thanked heaven that she knew how to be inconspicuous; it was an art that Mrs Wharton, for all her multifarious talents, would never master.

Mr James had in this period preceding the projected farewell meal an invitation unusual enough to prompt him to divulge its nature to Frieda.

'It is quite extraordinary,' he said, perplexity and amusement contending with each other in his face. 'I would seem to have had for a while now, all unbeknownst to myself, a little band of youthful admirers at Cambridge University.'

He looked at Frieda as if expecting some response. Her first emotion was, indeed, surprise that Mr James should number amongst his admirers anybody younger than fifty, but she reminded herself that, quite apart from her after all not inconsiderable self, there were also Mr Fullerton, Mr Walpole, Mrs Wharton – all of whom, nevertheless, struck her as *established* in a manner which one could not think of a group of Cambridge students as being. She tried to express something of this: 'One would have thought of students as being more superficial in their literary taste.'

'I don't know if I would have called it superficial, my dear, but I suppose I imagined, or would have imagined if I had given it a thought, students of that age reading Mr Wells and Mr Bennett, or even Thomas Hardy's more luridly lugubrious productions in preference to my own relatively rarefied lucubrations. However, it would seem that I would have done them an injustice: there are at least three of those currently pursuing enlightenment at Cambridge who profess themselves to be inveterate admirers of my work; so much so that they invite me to pay them a visit there.'

'And shall you go?'

'I do believe I am tempted. Quite apart from the pleasure, uncertain as that is, of communion with the young mind, there is the beauty of the place itself, which I well remember as one of the supreme things England has to show. It is an unlooked-for honour, indeed, to be invited to such a place on one's own terms, even if only by three relatively insignificant burghers of the town.'

While Mr James was away from home complying with all these demands on his time and person, Frieda, left largely to her own devices, felt at liberty to complete the exploration of the Garden Room initiated so tentatively so many months ago. All the drawers and cabinets had by now been trustingly unlocked; if Frieda felt a qualm about availing herself of the confidence so displayed, she muffled it in the reflection that she was acting at the behest of somebody in an even closer relation of trust to Mr James than she.

The unlimited freedom of access, however, and the moral justification Frieda negotiated for herself with her conscience, availed her but little, except in enabling her to establish beyond a doubt that Mr Fullerton's letters were not held in the Garden Room. They must have been of the very few not held there, for Frieda went through more letters than she had thought it possible for a single human being to receive in a lifetime, especially assuming that each letter would have been precipitated by or replied to by a letter from Mr James. As a record of a life it was both remarkable and disheartening: remarkable in the sheer volume of it, the variety and calibre of correspondent, but disheartening in not, in the last analysis, amounting to more than a finite number of dusty pages. To anybody wishing to write a history of English and American letters in the late nineteenth century, the Garden Room contained a treasure of incalculable worth; Frieda rubbed her eyes at many of the names, names she knew from the spines of venerably bound volumes, here unassumingly and often familiarly placed at the foot of humble missives. But for her own purpose the room yielded as little as if it were the cell of an illiterate hermit: there was not a scrap of paper from or about Mr Morton Fullerton. Mrs Wharton's correspondence, too, was missing, presumably being stored with Mr Fullerton's. Frieda returned to her theory that the letters were kept in the drawer she had glimpsed once in Mr James's bedroom; and of course, at this time of year, with no call to be in the Green Room, there was no excuse to be in that part of the house at all.

Reconciled to a routine of simple usefulness, Frieda contented herself with typewriting revisions that Mr James had left behind. With Mr Fullerton in America, her communication with him ceased: not, she imagined, that the Atlantic presented too wide a barrier for telepathic contact, but probably because of Mr Fullerton's many commitments and, of course, the difference in time between the continents.

In the afternoons she took Max for a walk, in spite of the wetness of the season: the summer was proving to be so unrelievedly rainy that there was little point in deferring outdoor exercise to a sunny day. Max's pleasure in these outings was so extreme and demonstrated with such exuberance that Frieda felt almost ungrateful in not finding a like satisfaction in the occasion; but try as she might to adopt a canine perspective, she could not blind herself to the dreariness, if one were not a dachshund, of an existence enlivened only by such variety as their walks provided: the variety of walking either towards Winchelsea or towards Camber, of following the course of either the River Tillingham or the River Rother; or, on very wet days, of deciding whether the Gungarden and the Landgate or Watchbell Street and The Strand would be less conducive to wet boots. There were times, admittedly not her best times, when even the Kensington Gardens with Mr Dodds planted in the centre of them like a large-nosed exotic presented themselves to Frieda as preferable – as preferable, for instance, to yet another exchange of pleasantries with Mrs Sims, guarding the doorway of the family confectioner and umbrella hospital in the High Street. Mrs Sims was an excellent woman, but Frieda had now several times declined the honour of an invitation to a performance of *The Yeoman of the Guard* in the Bijou Theatre, in which Mrs Sims's daughter Dora was billed to play a small but vital role, and the young woman feared her own weakness under yet another appeal to her 'artistic inclinations'. She dreaded the thumping tunes and the hilarity, the general conspiracy to *romp* that such an evening represented. Mr Dodds, as it happened, had once taken her to a performance of *The Mikado*, which had given her a headache, but which he had pronounced the equal of anything done anywhere, a claim so large as to be irrefutable.

Thus, when Mr James returned from what he termed his peregrinations, Frieda welcomed him back with unfeigned pleasure. However exasperating some of his assumptions and attitudes, he represented a larger world than was open to her anywhere else in Rye; and, for all his blindness to her real needs, he evinced a level of concern for her wellbeing that nobody else on earth felt, with the possible exception of her Aunt Frederica.

Mr James, for all the delight he professed and no doubt felt in the excursion, seemed relieved to be home. 'Magnificent as it always is to be carried in such comfort for such immense distances, there is something distinctly... *disquieting* about a motor car driven at speed in heavy rain along an exceedingly muddy road. Mrs Wharton's excellent chauffeur, the good Cook, is as a rule utterly to be trusted; but I am not convinced that he perfectly understands our English roads in combination with our English weather. There were times when I feared we would capsize in the most ignominious fashion by the roadside, and have to be extricated by a team of horses, as I am told not infrequently happens in the more rural areas of England. It is fortunate, perhaps, that where the roads are least well adapted to the rapid passage of motor cars, horses are most readily to be had, but it is not a coincidence by which one would choose to benefit. I refrained, of course, as much as I judged prudent from expressing my misgivings, having noted a certain touchiness in Cook as regards well-intended advice; but on several occasions I was moved to alert him to particularly muddy patches in the road, and I am convinced that had it not been for my cautionary ejaculations, we might all have *come to grief.*'

This last dread possibility was whispered melodramatically, Mr James's large eyes rounded to their fullest extent, he was relishing his own alarm as much as he had clearly enjoyed the whole expedition. Frieda was sorry for Cook, but considered that Mrs Wharton had got what she deserved: if she wanted to cart Mr James around as a hostage or a spoil of war, she needed to be reminded that he had an equivalent centre of self with its own concerns and anxieties.

Frieda was curious to hear Mr James's account of the dinner in London, but found to her surprise and exasperation that there were other excursions uppermost in his mind, notably the visit to Cambridge, which for once Mr James had been permitted to pay without Mrs Wharton. It was, after the terrors of the muddy roads, the topic to which he most frequently returned.

'An extraordinary few days, quite extraordinary,' he exclaimed, pacing as intently as if he were dictating a particularly absorbing novel, 'not, I am abashed to admit, on account of my young hosts, who were remarkable in the main alike for their admiration of my work and their inability to express it in any strikingly intelligent way. Oh, I liked them quite sufficiently for the occasion – the occasion being, as far as I could make it out, a matter of bringing elaborate homage to me as a kind of Pasha of the fictive art. They were pleasantly gaping and touchingly juvenile, like a nestful of hungry fledglings; that is, all of them, with the exception of one quite remarkable youth who was selected, I was told, for his skill with a punt, it being his appointed duty to take me out on the river, an outing which I confess I rather dreaded as likely to have, in its flat-bottomed manner, all the inconvenience and none of the *sprezzatura* of a gondola. In the event he lent the occasion an almost mythological allure. Although, as I say, he was young, he was not juvenile; and though he was attentive, he was not gaping. He was simply the glamour of youth personified and intensified to a pitch almost wasteful in a setting itself so beautiful.' Mr James paced awhile, evidently lost in recalling the scene; but he had not concluded. 'It is something, after all,' he continued, 'for the Old World to have produced such a happy conjunction of scene and character; not only the venerable old buildings in their hodge-podge of all the ages next to the unhurried little river, but the splendour of such youth – not merely the producing of it, but the... *cherishing* of it that such a place bears witness to. To see such a golden youth in such a place on a summer's afternoon is to understand, I think, what life is capable of at its magnificent maximum. Surely the world that has as one of its possibilities the bringing forth and the *appreciating* of such beauty is a better place, with whatever attenuations, than that into which we were born? I speak of *we*, my dear, meaning my generation rather than yours; you, no doubt, will live to see much greater marvels.'

'This young man – was he one of your hosts?'

'Not nominally, no, in that his name was not amongst those appended to the invitation originally extended. But he was so good as to express admiration of my work. I am told he is a poet, though one of my hosts expressed reservations about the quality of his productions – indeed, if it be true, a fortunate falling-short: for one young man to look like that *and* be a good poet would be more than any mere mortal is entitled to without exciting the jealousy of the gods. His name, I believe, is Brooke, Rupert Brooke, and I am confident that we shall hear his name again triumphant in some context in which youth, beauty and enthusiasm are blessedly conjoined.'

Frieda, having heard Mr James express a somewhat similar enthusiasm for Mr Hendrik Andersen, the sculptor, whom she had found rather vapid and vain, was inclined to suspect that Mr Brooke was similarly overrated; besides, she had an interest of her own to pursue. 'And I trust your dinner in London was... satisfactory?' she at last permitted herself to ask.

'My dinner...? My dear, I have had at least twenty dinners in London since I last saw you. Dining is really what London is best at, which is surprising, given the general standard of the cooking.'

Mr James was in an unusually expansive mood, possibly from having spent long periods confined in a motor car with Mrs Wharton, and Frieda thought it best to refocus the subject of conversation. 'I meant the dinner for which you originally went to London, the one in the Charing Cross Hotel.'

'Ah, the Charing Cross Hotel, yes indeed. These great cosmopolitan caravanserais combine in the most absorbing way in the world an air of cynical lawlessness and extreme fastidiousness: one feels they would countenance everything except one's being late for breakfast. Not, of course, that I have had occasion to put the matter to the test one way or the other, even if I had been inclined to, preferring, as you know, to make my home at the Reform Club when in town; but one reads the general tone in the rigour with which the tablecloths are starched and the salt cellars are filled. The large questions are disposed of by the meticulousness with which the small ones are observed. It is a kind of morality after all, in its concern for the amenities of life.'

Frieda, on the basis of her one experience of such an institution, could neither privately dissent nor publicly concur. She was not, indeed, primarily interested in an exchange of views on the nature of large hotels, but saw that if she wanted things named she would have to name them herself. 'Will it prove possible for your friends Mr Fullerton and Mrs Wharton to visit Rye again? I think Mr Fullerton called here on his return from his last visit to America?'

'So he did indeed, though I wouldn't vouch for that having been his very last visit to America; it could well have been his penultimate visit. However, that is not material to your enquiry, which is very pertinent, since indeed, I am delighted to say, Mr Fullerton expressed every intention of returning to Paris by way of Rye. Mrs Wharton understandably seemed less confident of coinciding with Mr Fullerton; as a married woman, a successful author and a much-courted guest, her time is not her own to dispose of as she might wish, and just at present she seems much intent upon establishing, as it were, a presence in this country by taking by storm as many strongholds of social prominence as possible.'

Frieda placed a sheet of typing paper in her typewriter and rolled it briskly into position, as a subterfuge to hide the impatience with which she asked, 'But Mr Fullerton…?'

Mr James turned to her, his attention at last arrested by the slight sharpness which she could not altogether banish from her tone. 'Mr Fullerton, I venture to say, though not without trepidation, we may count upon.'

Frieda imagined, with a certain grimness, that Mrs Wharton could in her turn be counted upon to arrange her complicated social, professional and personal life so as to make it possible, after all, to coincide with Mr Fullerton; but she confined herself to a simple enquiry: 'Did Mr Fullerton mention a date? Will he be very long in America?'

'I am happy to say that we can look forward to seeing him in something less than a month from today. He intends his visit to America to be as short as he can make it without offending such friends and relations as are naturally eager to detain him.'

Frieda wondered whether Miss Katharine Fullerton, the supposed fiancée of Mr Fullerton, counted amongst this number of friends to be considered; poor Mr Fullerton, she reflected only partly in irony, had an inordinate number of people to please.

Chapter Nineteen
12th July 1909

Unlike Mr James, Frieda conscientiously refrained from regarding Mr Fullerton's projected visit to Rye as anything other than provisional: if, in the past, she had explained to herself the infrequency of his visits by recourse to a sense of the many demands upon his time, it would be inconsistent now to count on his being master of his own movements. She did, however, remember to note the date on which he would arrive if indeed he did arrive, and it was in fact almost exactly a month later that Mr Fullerton, triumphing over time and circumstance, paid his second visit to Lamb House.

Frieda was alerted to his imminent arrival by Mrs Paddington, who bustled in one sunny morning, while Frieda was arranging her papers preparatory to her day's work; the housekeeper was carrying, as usual, an arrangement of flowers for the Garden Room.

'I'm sure I'm sorry, miss, as this is such a poor bunch this morning, but it's all that George Gammon could spare after I'd made up three bunches for the house. It's been that cold and wet for July, the flowers haven't really been up to standard. As it is, I've had to steal a few more when George wasn't looking so as to make a halfway decent bunch for this room; I always say if you're going to have flowers there's no point in a few bedraggled blooms, it just looks dismal.'

'Is Mr James expecting guests again?' Frieda enquired. She knew that Mr Jocelyn Persse had been spending the weekend at Lamb House.

'Yes, miss, one's hardly left when the other arrives, or the others I should say, since this time there's likely to be two of them, and she with her dogs all over the furniture.'

'Is it Mrs Wharton you are referring to?'

'Yes, miss, her with the motor car and the hats. Very civil she is always, and Burgess Noakes says she always tips him most handsomely, but she fills a house all on her own, with her luggage enough for Napoleon's own army and as I say her dogs taking liberties as poor little Max wouldn't dream of doing. She wasn't going to come originally, Mr James just said to get a room ready for that Mr Fullerton, but then this morning early the telephone rang and I had to get Mr James out of bed for it, and all it was was her saying she'd changed her mind and would be arriving tonight after all.'

'With Mr Fullerton?'

Mrs Paddington glanced up from her flowers at Frieda, and the young woman wondered whether she had betrayed too pointed an interest. But all the housekeeper said was, 'I believe not, miss. Mr James said they'd be arriving separately because Mr Fullerton is coming from London and she's coming from somewhere else where she's been visiting in her motor car.' Mrs Paddington firmly removed one particularly bedraggled bloom from the arrangement and, as if emboldened by this decisive step, continued: 'Her problem, if you ask me, miss, is that she can't be in one place for more than a day or two without her getting restless on account of having that big motor car standing there and of course that driver of hers Cook sitting around with nothing to do when he's not driving her around.'

She looked critically at the remaining flowers in the vase. 'I can't seem to get them right this morning, with this sorry lot of flowers. It comes from being American, I suppose.'

'The flowers…?'

'Oh no, miss, I mean Mrs Wharton's restlessness. These Americans never seem to be at home, do they, forever turning up here? It makes you wonder, between us, miss, what Mr James *sees* in them Americans, when there's any number of nice English people he could be seeing.'

'That may be because Mr James himself is American.'

'Bless you, miss, I never think of him as American, I'm sure he doesn't sound American does he, and just because he was born over there, that doesn't make him one of them, does it?'

'I think it does, Mrs Paddington. I think that's what makes you an American, being born in America.'

Mrs Paddington did not reply, merely shook her head as if mystified by this perversity. She stepped back again to assess her own effort with the flowers. 'I'm sure that's the best I can do, miss, with all the best flowers gone into the guest rooms.'

Frieda, wanting more than anything else to be left alone with her thoughts, felt that she wouldn't have minded or even noticed if Mrs Paddington had brought her an arrangement of two cabbages and a Hubbard squash, but the normally reticent housekeeper was clearly having one of her rare bouts of garrulousness, possibly under the provocation of having two Americans to prepare for. 'Take that nice Mr Perse, who left this morning, and a nicer young man you couldn't hope to find between Land's End and John O'Groats, and that Mr Walpole, too, ever so quietly spoken and polite, both of them, you wouldn't catch them carrying on like Mrs Wharton and Mr Fullerton, would you?'

Frieda was aware of looking blankly at Mrs Paddington. 'Carrying on?' she asked, before she could reflect that this could be taken as encouraging gossip – which, indeed, in the event, was how Mrs Paddington seemed to interpret Frieda's question, because she carried on. 'I'm sure it's not for me to repeat stories, miss, but Cook does say as he's forever driving around Mrs Wharton and Mr Fullerton to all sorts of places, and spending the night too, that he wouldn't like his wife to go to with another man all on their own like.'

'They're not all alone, are they, if Cook is with them?'

'Bless you, miss, you know how these people are, they think anybody they pay a salary to doesn't have eyes and ears just like them. And tongues, I could tell you, miss, if I hadn't been brought up not to carry scandal around like a cat that's caught a mouse and doesn't know what to do with it.'

Frieda thought that Mrs Paddington had, in spite of her education in discretion, delivered herself of a sizeable enough mouse. 'American women are allowed freedoms British women would never take,' was all that she permitted herself to say, in a tone that she hoped conveyed stern finality; she dreaded to give the impression that she had somehow courted the kind of confidence that she had just involuntarily elicited.

'That's as it may be, miss,' the now unstoppable Mrs Paddington remarked, as she swept past Frieda on her way out, 'but Cook's an American and he should know what's allowed and what isn't over there.'

Frieda felt unclean and angry; angry in the first place with Mrs Paddington, for thinking that she would want to be party to her confidences and speculations; but angrier still with Mrs Wharton, for exposing herself and others to that kind of speculation. It was all very well for her to affect indifference to public opinion; but she was splashing others with the mud that she kicked up in her wake. As for the substance of Mrs Paddington's tale, when looked at coldly, it meant only what Frieda already knew, which was that Mrs Wharton liked taking people to places in her motor car, and that she liked above all taking Mr Fullerton. She also, to Frieda's knowledge, took Mr James, whom nobody thought to link with Mrs Wharton in any connection other than that of passenger. Frieda concluded that Cook had too much time on his hands, and too few qualms in disseminating the inspirations that came to him in his hours of idle imagining. It was not that she imagined a man as evidently experienced as Mr Fullerton to abstain from relations with all other women; but it had come to matter to Frieda that he should abstain from Mrs Wharton.

It was particularly provoking that Mr Fullerton's first visit to Lamb House in two years should now be diluted by the presence of a woman who could and did visit Mr James at will and who could and probably did demand Mr Fullerton's presence in Paris at almost any time. Frieda would not have expected it to occur to Mrs Wharton that her insistence on making part of Mr Fullerton's visit to Lamb House could affect Frieda in any way, but the merest mite of natural tact should have whispered to her that Mr James might prefer to see as close a friend as Mr Fullerton on his own on the rare occasion of that friend's sojourn. Frieda wondered anew at the amount of brutal presumption that could, under certain conditions, flower and flourish under the cover of a universal urbanity.

In the meantime there was the day's work to attend to as best she might. A few minutes after the departure of the housekeeper, Mr James appeared, looking more spruce than usual, wearing, with his green trousers and blue waistcoat, what seemed to be a new cravat, certainly one Frieda had not seen before, in a bright marigold. His manner, too, was what one would have described, in one less congenitally dignified than Mr James, as *buoyant*.

'Such a brilliant day as this is almost enough to reconcile one to all the abysmal days the rest of this summer has visited upon our defenceless heads. I had almost given up expecting to see the sun again.' He picked up from his desk some sheets that Frieda had typed and glanced at them, but she could see that his attention was less focused than usual; there was a restlessness in his manner that she could ascribe only to excitement at the impending visit.

'Mrs Paddington tells me that you are expecting a visit from Mrs Wharton,' Frieda ventured. As a rule she would not interrupt his reading, and he fixed his regard upon her with such penetration that Frieda feared he might be offended by her departure from custom. But his reply, when it came, lacked all rancour. 'Yes, is that not part of the brilliance of the day? And I imagine Mrs Paddington did not tell you I shall not say the best part of the news, since I have no desire to make invidious distinctions, but certainly the most *unusual* part of the happy event, which is that Mr Fullerton will be accompanying her – that is, not accompanying her, since he will be arriving by train from London, having only just landed at Plymouth, and she will be motoring here from whatever seat of distinction she has been gracing with her presence – as I say, not *accompanying* Mrs Wharton, strictly speaking, but arriving at the same time, or indeed I believe even slightly earlier.'

'I am very happy for you if you are happy. I had feared that you might find such a succession of visitors exhausting, with Mr Persse only just having left.'

'Bless you, my dear, for your concern, but the truth is that Mrs Wharton and Mr Fullerton I count as no trouble at all. That is, to be candid, I do not find Mr Fullerton so; Mrs Wharton, I concede, is a strenuous guest, but only in the sense that her enjoyment of life is such that one is driven, or it would be more accurate to say *enticed*, to share in it as if one were oneself blessed with her eternal youth and boundless energy. I call her the Firebird, you know, after the brilliance of the Diaghilev creation.'

Frieda felt but limited interest in Mr James's appellations for Mrs Wharton. 'Will they be staying for long?'

'There you have exactly Mrs Wharton's youth and energy. I had hoped she and Mr Fullerton would avail themselves of the opportunity to enjoy for a few days the tranquillity of Lamb House, but Mrs Wharton, to whom tranquillity is as treacle to a dolphin, has decreed that we shall devastate the counties of Sussex and Kent for two or three days, sweeping in like a westerly gale from Chichester to Canterbury. I do believe that thanks to the marauding instincts of Mrs Wharton I shall soon have visited every cathedral in England with the exception of Peterborough, which has hitherto escaped her long reach, being situated, I believe, in one of the duller counties of England.'

'So you will be leaving again tomorrow?'

'So I have been informed. It seems likely that I will have but little time permitted me for the rest of this week to pursue my poor little avocation, so you and I, Miss Wroth, must avail ourselves of the few hours vouchsafed to us before the descent of the Firebird.'

Mr Fullerton arrived in the afternoon, while Frieda was typing revisions and Mr James was in the garden, making use of the rare spell of sunshine to direct George Gammon on the tying back of the espaliered pears against the south wall: ' – and just so, my dear man, one would strive to secure the branch so as to expose, in a manner of speaking, the bashful cheek of the fruit to the impertinent but beneficent caress of the sun.' The headstrong old gardener, having learned that resistance only prolonged Mr James's demonstrations, was refraining from comment, but would, Frieda knew, in the end consult only his own wisdom in the matter. On this occasion, in any case, he was spared even the rudimentary hypocrisy of pretending to concur in Mr James's recommendations, because Mr Fullerton appeared at the door of the drawing-room.

Frieda, drawn to the window of the Garden Room by Mr James's exclamation of joyful welcome, had time only to register that the almost two years that had passed since she last saw Mr Fullerton had not dimmed his brilliance: stepping into the sunlight on the lawn to meet the wide embrace of Mr James, he was as much as ever a happy combination of grace, energy and pure animal vitality. He was as pliant to the older man's embrace and yet as self-contained as a healthy cat.

The two men disappeared into the house. George Gammon shook his head and returned to tying up the pears as he had been doing before interrupted by Mr James. Frieda taking her lead from George Gammon, returned to her Remington, and saw no more of Mr Fullerton that afternoon. She assumed, however, that he would have asked after her and that Mr James would have mentioned her presence; if today, with the flurry of arriving, he could not make an occasion to see her, he would surely do so on the morrow before the departure to harrow the South East of England.

Frieda, departing for her lodgings, left through the gate in the garden wall leading to West Street. She could have left through the house in order to bid Mr James farewell, but she judged that he would not welcome the obligation, imposed upon him by his inveterate courtesy, of reintroducing his guest to his typewriter. She had a sense, nevertheless, as she crossed the lawn to the garden wall, that she was being watched – not with the benign indifference of her employer, but with the alert attention of his guest.

As Frieda walked down West Street, she met, coming the other way, the gleaming Panhard, filling the narrow street with stench and noise. In the back, apparently conversing animatedly with the little dog she was holding in her arms, was Mrs Wharton. She did not notice Frieda, who had to cower in a doorway in order not to be flattened by the machine.

On the Tuesday morning, Frieda went to work earlier than usual. Surely Mr Fullerton would, like the previous time, come to her in the Garden Room at the time that she now regarded as 'their time', the hour when she had found it easiest to make telepathic contact with him. She opened the windows of the Garden Room: it was going to be a warm day, probably building up to a further bout of storms. There was an oppressive yellow tinge to the sunshine that presaged another spell of what Mr James called diluvian weather.

At the time, almost exactly, that Mr Fullerton had walked into the Garden Room on that momentous day almost two years earlier, he appeared again, coming out of the drawing room; and this time, because she was expecting him, Frieda was watching for him. She paused at the window for the pleasure of seeing him taking in the bright morning and stroking his moustache as if it partook in the electrically charged air of the morning. He seemed, for a moment, almost at a loss for direction, which was odd; but then she realised that it would not do for him to be seen, by anybody who happened to glance out of the house, heading too purposefully to the Garden Room. As if demonstrating, then, his uncommitted state, he put his hands in his pockets and strolled across the lawn with an air of merely taking the air. Frieda wondered whether she should retreat to her typewriter so as not to seem to be waiting for him; but then she felt ashamed at this coquettish impulse: when an understanding had reached such a pitch of completeness, it was surely a form of treason to pretend otherwise. She did not mind his knowing that she had been waiting for him; she wanted him to know it, for the pleasure it would give him, as it gave her pleasure to see him advance, obliquely but unmistakably, across the lawn towards her redoubt.

It was with a near-physical shock, then, as if witnessing some sickening act of gratuitous violence, that Frieda saw appear, in the door of the morning room, with every appearance of strong purpose, Mrs Wharton. She was evidently, from the urgency of her step and from her hatless state, in pursuit of Mr Fullerton. He had not seen her, and she did not cry out – not wanting, evidently, any more than her quarry, to betray to invisible watchers in the house the strength and direction of her purpose. But he was walking slowly, maintaining the pretence of taking the morning air, and she was gaining on him in her booted and purposeful stride. He did not hear her: on the thick summer lawn her boots made no noise, and as she had not yet assumed her panoply of jewels, she did not clank and rattle in her normal manner. From Frieda's vantage point she could measure the decreasing distance between them, and she had to suppress an impulse to lean out of the window and shout to him to walk faster, to run, so as to reach her before Mrs Wharton could catch up with him. Once inside the Garden Room, Mr Fullerton would be safe from Mrs Wharton's entreaties; for even she, surely, would respect the territorial dominion of the other woman. But as Mr Fullerton reached the steps to the Garden Room, Mrs Wharton put out a restraining hand, rather like a constable taking into custody some miscreant, and Frieda was close enough to hear her say, 'I have been waiting for you for ever.'

'This morning?'

'This morning too. But more literally, I seem to spend my life waiting for you to turn up somewhere, to write, to say something…'

'Well, here I am now,' Mr Fullerton said, turning round to face Mrs Wharton, and Frieda could read into his tone his renunciation, his resignation to the demands of Mrs Wharton. Frieda felt that he was renouncing also on her behalf, and there was a moment when she verily toyed with the idea of running down the steps and demanding his attention, demanding Mrs Wharton's withdrawal, insisting that she, too, had a claim.

'Here you are, indeed. And instead of making the most of your presence on this sunny morning in this lovely old garden, I complain and harangue and remonstrate.'

The two had paused just outside the window. It was now too late for Frieda to make her presence known; she could only withdraw into the dim coolness of the Garden Room and hope that they would not find her there. Not, she reflected, that it would signify if they did. She had not planted herself in the Garden Room in expectation of their appearance: they had trespassed on her space, not she on theirs; that is, Mrs Wharton had. Mr Fullerton had free access.

The two interlocutors, meanwhile, had seemed to find it convenient to remain just where they were, looking around them as if they were admiring the wisteria, in truth by now a scraggly relic of its early summer glory.

'You say you complain; but I cannot see, Edith, what it is that you complain of. You asked me to meet you in London, and I agreed. Then you changed the rendezvous to Rye, and I agreed to *that*.'

'That is my point exactly. You agree so easily because you

don't care. It's all the same to you. You're the easiest man on earth to please, which makes you the most difficult to know.'

'Would you like me to be difficult as a way of proving that I care?'

'I should like you to demonstrate that one aspect of our friendship matters more to you than another, that it matters to you to meet me in London where we can be alone together rather than here, where we have all of Lamb House and its functionaries and appendages to consider.'

'I thought it was your point that you wanted to see Henry.'

'Oh, I always want to see Henry, but don't you see? I always *can* see Henry, whereas you… for all that you live around the corner from me in Paris, I have to travel to England to see you on your own. And now that we're in England… well, you bring us *here*, after having invited Henry to share our last evening together before you left for America. For two people of independent character and means we seem to find it inordinately difficult to spend time alone with each other.'

'You forget, my dear Edith, that it was you who suggested that we meet here rather than in London; just as, if I remember correctly, it was you who proposed that Henry dine with us in London.'

'You should know that a woman intent on being unselfish sometimes wants to be saved from herself. As I say, it is the very readiness with which you agree to my every suggestion that makes me suspect that you have no preference of your own. It is like being agreed with by one's milliner. Besides, if you hadn't so shamelessly neglected Henry, I shouldn't have felt obliged to make up for it.'

Mr Fullerton laughed. 'How you do talk of shameless! Would you have preferred me to neglect him even further and not come down here at all?'

'Yes, I would, beast that I am. Don't you see? In you it would have been only consistent; in me it would have been a betrayal.'

'Your logic is impeccable, once we grant that I am a blackguard and you are a faithful friend.'

'I am not appealing to your logic, I am appealing to your charity. Oh, but what's the use of these reproaches? *Et alors, je n'ai plus de volonté.* We are here and we have three more days of each other's company…'

'And of course Henry's.'

'How could I not invite him? He dotes on these motoring trips; in fact he was the one who suggested it. And what would he think if we set off together without him?'

'*Il faut choisir*, my dear Edith. You cannot have Henry's company and yet see me on my own.'

'I know I can't; that's why I wanted you to arrange it. You know that I hate myself for thrusting myself at you: and yet there are times when you leave me no choice, when you seem to withdraw from our shared comradeship into some private enclave of indifference or worse, leaving me to batter at the door and peer in at the window.'

Frieda understood the situation. Mrs Wharton was trying to arrange a tryst with Mr Fullerton, and he was too polite to tell her that he was not interested. He might indeed, with more credit to his manliness, have been more direct in his expression of his unwillingness; but Mrs Wharton was evidently a woman whose voluble vulnerability made it impossible for those she depended upon to be honest with her. As woman to woman, Frieda should have felt something for Mrs Wharton – felt, that is, something other than the slight impatience with which she heard the older woman give herself away so thoroughly.

'You wrote to me in Liverpool,' Mr Fullerton was saying, 'I gathered with the express purpose of denying, in your words, any alarming determination to take possession of my time.'

'I know I did; and from the time I said that, I was waiting for you to demur, to say *but what do you mean, ma chère, you cannot take possession of something that is as freely yielded as I cede my time to you*, some such wondrously implausible pledge of your dedication of three miserable days to me.'

'If I understand you correctly, you accuse me of having taken you at your word.'

'Let us not talk, between us, of accusing. What I am gently and I concede illogically complaining of is the readiness with which you accept any suggestion of mine that will curtail the time we spend together, whereas any proposal tending towards bringing us together is treated with the greatest circumspection and caution. I would, in a word, like you to be less damned self-possessed. just once to fling caution and logic and restraint to the winds.'

'To be possessed with you, you mean.'

'Why not? We are free, we are privileged, we are not obliged to be timid and conventional like... like a bank clerk and a typewriter on a Sunday outing to Battersea Park.'

Anger was not an emotion Frieda often felt free to indulge: she had such a small basis of entitlement on which to rear her indignation, so little territory for others to trespass upon. But she had, somewhere, her private sense of appropriateness; and that sense told her now that it was monstrous that a New York heiress should undertake to pronounce on the Sunday outings of typewriters. Let her write her novels about creatures as spoilt as herself, but let her not presume to look down on wretches who had to work for such little pleasures as they were vouchsafed.

Without reflecting any further than this, Frieda stepped out of the door of the Garden Room onto the first of the steps leading down into the garden. She was to think of it afterwards as the only occasion in her life on which she had made, as they say of great actresses, an entrance; except that to her mind the image was rather that of a chieftain striding out onto the ramparts of his beleaguered stronghold, to cow the enemy with the very fact of his presence.

Mrs Wharton, with her back to the steps, did not see her, but Mr Fullerton, sensing the movement, looked up, and said, under his breath but quite audibly to Frieda, 'Let up, will you? We are not alone.' Frieda noticed again, in the bright light, the slight wrinkles around his eyes, the intelligent curve of his mouth even at such a relatively unpropitious moment as this.

Mrs Wharton now also looked up, and Frieda was gratified to register her blanching with dismay. With the scene thus set for her, Frieda could have expressed her sense of the other woman's impertinence, could have told her about the Sunday outings of typewriters, could have brought home to her the life that even typewriters, in this respect indistinguishable from lady novelists, were doomed – or privileged, it hardly mattered which – to feel and endure and somehow make the best of. She could have denounced the presumption of people who believed that life was something reserved for those who could afford to pay for it, and she could have spoken for the equal intensity with which the inferior orders lived their lives and confronted their destinies. She could have howled her outrage at having to countenance, in her own stronghold, the other woman's grasp at what she had no title to, not being, to Frieda's knowledge, divorced or separated from her legitimate husband; she could have claimed to have known the joy of the uncoerced passion of Mr Fullerton.

All this and more Frieda could have said, and reproached herself later for not saying; for, finding Mr Fullerton's blue gaze upon her, and Mrs Wharton's ghastly stare of shock, all Frieda could do was stand there in the sunshine at the top of the steps and allow her presence to be taken in and to speak for itself.

Mr Fullerton was the first to regain his composure. 'Good morning, Miss Wroth. I fear you come to tell us that we are disturbing your labours with our idle chatter outside your citadel.'

Frieda knew that he wanted to know whether she had overheard their conversation, and for a moment it seemed that the sweetest revenge upon Mrs Wharton would be to let her know that she had; but a subtler instinct told her that it would be a greater torment for Mrs Wharton not to know. So she smiled in what she hoped was an enigmatic manner and contented herself with saying: 'I find I have to fetch something from the house. Please do not let me interrupt your conversation.'

She descended the steps, still with a certain consciousness of dramatic effect. As she passed the other two mutely observing her, she smelt Mrs Wharton's perfume, something heavy and expensive, and Mr Fullerton's pomade, fresh and sweet. She avoided, with an effort, his eyes – she knew she would find there the sardonic contraction of irony – and walked towards the house with such dignity as she could muster. As she entered the dining room, she heard Mr Fullerton say: 'I say, Edith, what an unfortunate simile, under the circumstances, don't you think?'

In the dining room Mr James was placidly Fletcherising his breakfast. Frieda, realising that she had no excuse at hand for her flight into the house, took refuge in the typewriter's privilege. 'Will you excuse me for a few minutes please, Mr James? I find I need to replace the ribbon of the typewriter, and I shall just step out to the stationer's for a new one.'

Mr James swallowed heavily. 'Certainly, my dear. You will of course ask Mr Adams to charge it to my account. And we shall,

I believe, be departing almost immediately after breakfast for our subjugation of the south-eastern counties, to take advantage of this unusually fine weather that Mrs Wharton assures me will last for the duration of our little tour, so this is also an opportune moment to take my leave of you. I shall peregrinate the more easily for knowing that you are ensconced in the Garden Room guarding over my poor neglected utterings.'

Frieda took her leave as quickly as Mr James's courtesy and solicitousness would allow, and left by the heavy front door. As she stepped around the pair of lady artists positioned in front of Mr James's door, taking an impression of the view of the church, she was thankful that she had provided herself not only with an excuse but also a destination, somewhere to get away to from what she now, as her anger subsided, saw as the ignominy of her little performance. She had not, as she had fondly imagined, made an entrance: she had made a spectacle of herself, had *produced* herself like a cuckoo emerging mechanically from a clock, and what she had found to say was scarcely more intelligent than the moronic two notes of the wretched bird. If only she had emulated the bird also in retreating into the oblivion of her clockwork, she would not now be abroad in the streets of Rye.

But she had now, with the aid of the only fragment of intelligence she had managed to summon up, secured for herself a respite: she had something to do and somewhere to go, and by the time she returned, Mrs Wharton would surely have had the decency to retire into the house, there to chuckle good-humouredly with Mr James about her lamentable but after all quite amusing, if looked at in a certain light, *faux pas*.

As for Mr Fullerton, it was clear that he was under some kind of pressure to be at least civil to Mrs Wharton: as one of Mr James's closest friends, he could not be seen to be rude to such another, the more so that they were fated – or arranged, by Mrs Wharton's design – to spend three days together. Frieda was prepared to make allowance for the small hypocrisies of social living, but could not but think that Mr Fullerton could have been more outspoken in his strictures on Mrs Wharton's invidious reference to typewriters.

There was a step behind her and a light hand on her elbow.

'Miss Wroth – if you have a moment.'

Frieda stopped, and the sensation so familiar to her from her mornings at the typewriter suffused her: Mr Fullerton was next to her, pressing, in the morning traffic of the High Street, lightly against her. She could see the individual threads of his moustache, and the light specks of brown in the blue of his eyes. He was slightly out of breath from having followed her. 'You were magnificent.'

'Magnificent?' She tried to imagine what he was referring to. 'When?'

'Now; there: emerging from the Garden Room like Electra from the palace at Mycenae.'

'Why Electra?' was all she could think of saying.

'The vengefulness of your mien, the purposefulness of your stride, the high drama of your exit.'

'I was angry.'

'And with good reason. Mrs Wharton wants me to say how sorry she is that she spoke so thoughtlessly. She did not know of course that you were within earshot.'

Frieda had little attention for Mrs Wharton's apology. 'But you… you must have known that I was there.'

'Must I? Of course, I might have remembered from our previous time – but how was I to warn Mrs Wharton? How, for that matter, was I to know what she was going to say?'

They had now reached the stationer's shop in the High Street to which Frieda was nominally making her way. She stopped, and on the narrow pavement, with carts passing in the street, there was hardly room enough for both of them. 'I must go in here,' she said.

'And I must return to my duties as guest. But I had to express something of what I felt.'

Frieda could express, in her turn, only a fraction of what she felt. 'I am glad you did. I was hoping to have an opportunity to talk to you.'

He smiled his brilliant smile. 'Ah, opportunities to talk! How we waste them when we have them and miss them when we don't! Was there anything in particular that you wanted to say to me?'

'Only about… what you mentioned last time. I have not

forgotten it.'

'I should very much hope you haven't.'

'And I have been planning how to go about it. I should be able to give you what you want very soon.'

Mr Fullerton was looking at her with an intensity that yet had something questioning about it, as if he were concentrating very hard to figure out what she meant. But he must know of course. 'That is excellent, then,' he said, with every appearance of pleasure.

'You must have wondered what I was about all this time.'

'Oh, I trusted you to know what you were doing,' he said comfortably.

'That is all I wanted you to know – that I know what I am doing.' She did not want him to go, but did not know what to say to make him stay.

'Then there we are.' And still he smiled at her, his beautiful smile, his warm, intimate smile that expressed everything and committed him to nothing.

'You won't mind if I just squeeze past you here, will you, Miss Wroth?' said a sharp little voice next to her. 'This pavement is rather narrow for folks to be having conversations all over it.' It was Mrs Tumble, her landlady, fixing her with a stare in which curiosity vied with disapproval and lost. Mrs Tumble did not approve of young women talking to unknown young men in public; Mrs Tumble did not approve of young women talking to young men at all. To demonstrate this point she waited with conspicuous patience for Frieda to move out of the way, and then bustled past as if, having been detained, she was now disastrously late for an urgent appointment.

Frieda grimaced at Mr Fullerton. 'My landlady,' she informed him, behind the upright retreating back of Mrs Tumble.

'Indeed? And where are your lodgings?'

Frieda pointed at the Warden Hotel. 'There.' In the sharp morning light the dour little establishment looked so helplessly charmless that she felt impelled to defend it against what she was sure Mr Fullerton would think of it. 'It is not very beautiful but it is clean and of course it's very decent.'

'Oh, eminently decent, I'm sure. A Temperance Hotel! It cannot help but be decent.'

On that note, inconclusively, they concluded. 'I just wanted to urge you,' he rather awkwardly brought out, 'not to attach undue importance to Mrs Wharton's unfortunate formulation.'

'Oh, I attach no importance to it whatsoever,' Frieda said, with a touch of grandeur. 'We all speak without thinking at times.'

He looked at her with his most ironical contraction yet. 'I don't believe *you* ever do, Miss Wroth,' he said, and left her there in the High Street.

The fine weather bravely prevailing for two days proved, at the end of that period, to have been only a respite from the otherwise unrelenting savagery of this summer. The Panhard had barely been packed with its human and animal cargo, Mr James reassured about everything being provided for in his absence, and the whole contraption set in noisy motion by the inscrutable Cook, when the baleful yellow light of the early morning thickened into cloud. Within the hour a south-westerly gale was driving torrents of rain across the sodden lawn outside the Garden Room.

Frieda did not as a rule seek pleasure in the misfortune of others, but there was room in her breast for the reflection that Mrs Wharton could, after all, not control every aspect of her universe. She wondered, as she gazed out at the opaque curtain of rain, whether the travellers would not now sensibly return to the comforts of Lamb House: it seemed impossible that even Mrs Wharton could delight in sightseeing in conditions that, as Mrs Paddington informed her, kept even the fishing boats confined to their berths in Rye Harbour.

But Mrs Wharton proved more hardy than even the seasoned fishermen of the Cinque Ports: by Wednesday evening the little party had still not returned from its expedition, although there was no sign of the weather letting up; indeed, if possible, the rain seemed to beat with greater energy and the wind to blow with greater force.

On Thursday morning, however, Mrs Paddington rustled into the Garden Room with an air of having something to impart: Frieda recognised this in the great care with which the older lady placed the vase, barely filled this morning with a few storm-tossed blooms, on the mantelpiece, moving it several times as if to find exactly the right spot for it.

'Mr James telephoned this morning,' she announced at last. She hesitated for a moment; Frieda knew that a certain minimum of encouragement was expected from her. 'Are they enjoying their excursion?' she accordingly asked.

'He did not say anything about that one way or the other, miss, and it's more than one would expect from Mr James to give one a clear opinion on something like that in less than ten minutes, but he did say as how they were in Canterbury now but it was raining so yesterday they couldn't find the Cathedral even though they were right next to it and they were making their way back today and would I light fires in all the bedrooms straight away. I should think they'd be wet and cold enough by now,' concluded Mrs Paddington, not without a certain grim satisfaction.

'And will Mrs Wharton be staying for a long while?'

'Not if she has a choice in it. Mr James said she was wanting to cross the Channel from Folkestone tomorrow.'

Frieda dared not ask whether Mr Fullerton would also be crossing on the morrow, and was silent. Mrs Paddington concentrated hard on making the most of the few battered-looking flowers in the vase, then added, as if in afterthought, 'And that Mr Fullerton too.'

'Mr Fullerton too?'

'He's also wanting to cross tomorrow, Mr James says. With Mrs Wharton, I suppose.'

This was not a line of speculation that Frieda wanted to encourage, and she tried to change the direction of the conversation. 'With the weather as it is I can't imagine there'll be any crossings for a few days, surely?'

'No, I imagine not, miss. They'll just have to wait for the weather to clear in its own good time. Mind you, it always does, doesn't it? There's a lot of talk now about building a tunnel under the Channel for a train to go through, but I say if God had wanted the French to come and go as they please he wouldn't have given us the Channel to keep them on the other side. It's only the other day we were building towers to keep them out – my own grandfather worked on the Martello towers – and now they're wanting to build a tunnel to let them in.'

Frieda's short meeting with Mr Fullerton two days earlier had confirmed and deepened her sense of an unusual rapport between them; he understood her even when she was unsure of her own feelings, had seen her demonstration on the steps of the Garden Room in its true light even when she had wanted to disown it. He recognised the spirit of resistance in her, and admired it, where other men saw only a spirit of compliance and made use of it. He wanted her to be an equal, even an accomplice, not a gaping admirer.

It was in this assurance that Frieda sought comfort, while waiting for the travellers to return. But she found little repose in a certainty that was, after all, so vulnerable to contradiction, so covetous of verification. There was a time when she could have rested content in the security of her own conviction, but renewed contact with Mr Fullerton had left her unsatisfied, greedy for more. She could accept absence as an interruption of intimacy, but not as an absolute state.

It would not do, however, to lurk or hover, to hang about like some moonstruck maiden: if her rapport with Mr Fullerton was as complete as she imagined it, he would not need her physical presence to apprehend her need of him. To advertise that need would not only be redundant: it would risk attracting the notice of Mrs Wharton, whom Frieda suspected of possessing the preternatural perceptions of a woman in love.

Frieda accordingly kept to her post in the Garden Room when the Panhard's heavy throb, unmistakable even through the noise of rain and wind, announced the return of the expedition. She refrained even from looking out of the window, a simple discipline that yet cost her more than she could have imagined. She could hear Mrs Wharton's high-pitched chatter – 'Henry, I do believe you have been sitting on my muff – it looks like a squashed cat!' – and Mr James's measured and resonant reply; but if Mr Fullerton was with them he did not betray his presence by speaking. There was an opening and closing of motor car doors, the sound of the front door opening, of luggage being unloaded, a few yaps from one of Mrs Wharton's dogs, the excited staccato bark of Max greeting Mr James, and then silence, as Lamb House absorbed the arrivals into its dignified hospitality.

Upon the hour when Frieda normally went home, she carefully arranged her papers, as she always did, and left on Mr James's desk the typing she had done in his absence; she assumed that he would look at them only on the morrow, but he did sometimes work late in the evening after his guests had gone to bed. She was surprised that he had not come to the Garden Room to greet her, as he usually did when he had been away, but she ascribed this breach to the demands on his hospitality of both Mrs Wharton and Mr Fullerton.

It was still raining hard outside, and as Frieda crossed the lawn she could make out only that the curtains of the house were drawn against the elements; there was smoke coming from the chimney and the glow of lamplight behind the curtains; it was difficult to imagine that this was a summer's night. She shivered, meeting the wind and the rain head-on; her boots sank away in the soft turf of the sodden lawn. She reached the door in the garden wall, and as she did so, she looked back, as she had done on the day she first met Mr Fullerton. The curtains of the drawing room parted; at the window, peering out into the dusk, was Mr Fullerton. For a few seconds he was looking straight at her, as she stood at the open door. It was impossible to tell whether he saw her; he gave no sign. Then he released the curtain and it fell back into place. She closed the door behind her and returned to her lodgings.

Frieda had her dinner in the barren little dining room where Mrs Tumble served her guests the precisely portioned-out repast included in the cost of a room. There was the usual constrained and unconvivial blend of transient 'commercials' and settled 'regulars', the latter having the advantage of knowing which of the proffered dishes to avoid ('English meat only and two vegetables'), the former having the consolation of knowing that they would only be staying for one night. There was a smell of smoke, wet mackintoshes and cabbage. Mr James often invited Frieda to stay for dinner when he had guests; she assumed that tonight, with two such close friends, he would have preferred to keep the domestic circle unbroken by outsiders. For this Frieda was grateful; she did not think she could have countenanced Mrs Wharton's condescension in the presence of Mr Fullerton, or known how to behave towards Mr Fullerton in the presence of Mrs Wharton. She wondered how long Mr Fullerton was still staying; since he had not made an opportunity to see her today she trusted that he would do so the following day.

Frieda normally took a walk after dinner before retiring to her room, in spite of Mrs Tumble's dark prognostications about the fate of young women wandering around after dark on their own. Frieda reasoned that if, on those evenings that she worked late, she could walk from Lamb House to the Warden Hotel on her own, there was no reason why she could not walk from the Warden Hotel to any other part of Rye. Tonight, however, the weather was too violent even for the normally venturesome Frieda, and she decided to have an early night.

She read for a while by the inadequate electric light, aided by a candle next to her bed. She had borrowed Thomas Hardy's *Jude the Obscure* from Mr James, and had at first been entirely engrossed in its account of a young man's attempt to better himself through education. Tonight, however, its chronicle of blighted hopes and failed relationships seemed too bleak, too congruent with her little room and her situation. She switched off the light and blew out the candle. She lay listening to the wind and the rain, to the creaking of the rafters in the roof and the rattling of her windowpane, and she imagined Mr Fullerton's presence, as it had been in the languid warmth of the room in Folkestone. It did not seem possible that in one lifetime one could be two people as different as the inexperienced and expectant young woman in the sunny room in Folkestone and the shivering, deprived person in this cold, rain-battered room in the Warden Hotel. She drew the bedclothes closer to her and pictured Mr Fullerton gazing at her as he had done that day; this merged with the more recent but vaguer memory of his standing at the window of Lamb House, staring unseeingly into the rainy dusk…

She must have slept, for she did not hear her door open. She became aware of a presence next to her bed only when a hand touched her shoulder and a voice said: 'Is there a light?'

She was awake instantly, and knew who it was. 'There is a candle next to my bed,' she replied, and put out her hand for the matches. But his hand was there first, and took up the box. There was a scratch and a flare; the candle flame guttered and then burnt up strongly, wavering slightly in the draft from the window.

In the half-light, in his overcoat and with a cap on his head, she hardly recognised him. In Folkestone his manner had been whimsical, ironical; there had been the air of an autumn afternoon's dalliance about it. Now he seemed to have brought the storm with him: he was a thing of darkness and stealth. He took off his cap; his eyes seemed black; his moustache sparkled with drops of water.

'You're wet,' she said. She was strangely calm. It was as if, in coming to her room, he had not so much invaded her territory as consented to inhabit it on her terms.

'Only my boots and overcoat,' he said, and took off his overcoat. Underneath he was dressed as if for dinner.

'How did you find me?'

'I remembered where your lodgings were from your pointing them out to me the other day.'

'But my room…?'

'There was a night clerk downstairs, a very sleepy young man. I said I had an urgent message from your employer.' He held up an envelope. 'The same letter that served as my excuse to quit Lamb House – I told Mr James I had to get it to the post.'

'That's Fred Tumble. He'll tell his mother.'

'Do you mind?'

She shook her head. 'No.' She did not want to discuss Mrs Tumble. 'Mrs Tumble doesn't matter.' She was now sitting upright in bed.

He took off his overcoat and jacket. 'Can I take off my boots?' Without waiting for an answer, he sat down on the single upright chair and tugged off his wet boots. He got up from the chair and, hooking his thumbs through his braces, slipped them off his shoulders and unbuttoned his trousers. Then he came across to the bed. Holding his trousers with his left hand, he extended his right hand to Frieda, wanting to draw her nearer, but she shrank back from him.

'What's the matter? You're not going to deny me now, after I've…?' and he pointed at his half-undressed state, which did indeed reveal a certain readiness on his part.

She shook her head. 'No, I won't deny you. You can stay.

But not... like that.'

'Like what?'

'Fully dressed.'

'My dear Miss Wroth, I am hardly fully dressed; it's just that under the circumstances to get fully undressed would take more time than I have, apart from being damned cold.'

He put his hand on her shoulder again but Frieda still held back. 'I don't think that's right,' she said.

'Not right? What do right and wrong have to do with it?'

'I don't know. But I... I don't want to make love to a man who's wearing a collar and tie.' In the memory of him that she had cherished he had a strong back, slim hips and dark hairs on his chest; now he seemed merely a cluster of male appurtenances.

He shrugged and smiled, but the smile was less brilliant than usual. 'I don't normally ask my partners to dictate to me the proper apparel for the occasion.'

Frieda noted the careful cynicism of the reply without being hurt by it. She had imagined this scene so often that she knew every detail of it; she could not accept the substitute he was offering her. 'Last time you made me undress.'

'Last time it was considerably warmer.' In the candlelight his smile looked strained. 'But I can see you are going to insist.' He took off his tie and collar and unbuttoned his shirt. Before taking off his shirt, he paused. 'Hang it,' he protested, 'it's a bit damn embarrassing, stripping to the buff in front of an audience. How about you, then? That rather severe nightdress?'

Frieda got out of bed, turned her back to Mr Fullerton, and took off her nightdress. She did so as slowly as possible, to give him time to get rid of his complicated male apparel. When she turned around, he was as she remembered him, except that he had his arms clasped around his chest, shivering.

'And now do you think we could get into bed?'

In Folkestone Frieda had submitted to his will and his directions; now, she knew not only what he wanted from her, but what she wanted from him. In the half-light of the candle, with the noise of the storm outside, there was a kind of anonymity to her actions: she felt no compunction about directing his actions, controlling his movements by her own, increasing the intensity of the experience by pressing him into her, at first adjusting her movements to his thrusting and then gradually luring him into a slower, more rhythmical movement. She explored his back and buttocks with her fingers, felt his smooth tight skin under hers; she took his hair and brought his mouth round to kiss her. In Folkestone the fruity aroma of Chablis had lingered on his breath; now the darker bouquet of Mr James's claret filled her mouth as he kissed her. She clasped her legs around his middle and clenched him to her. Possessed, she was possessing; taking, she was being taken; entered, she was entering: unmediated, direct, naked, they were as close as two human beings can be in this life or the next, communicating through touch, taste, smell, and the mounting rhythm of their joint passion and motion, body and mind and spirit expending themselves as they were fulfilled.

Mr Fullerton's eyes looked black in the candlelight. 'You have learned a lot in two years,' he said. 'May I ask who taught you?'

'You.'

'I...?'

'I imagined,' Frieda said, 'how it might be.'

'The Lord be praised for the imagination. Some people learn less from a lifetime of experience than you have gleaned from your imagination.'

He kissed her lightly, then got out of bed. 'I must get back to Lamb House. It's possible that Mr James will have sat up for me. I'll have to invent a long walk in the rain.'

'Will you be staying in Rye for a while?'

He fumbled with his shirt. 'Alas, no. I have to return to Paris tomorrow.'

'In this weather?'

'In this weather. That is, there may well not be a crossing tomorrow, but I'll have to go to Folkestone in case there is one after all.'

'Will you be returning to Rye soon?'

He sat down to pull on a boot; concentrating on getting the wet thing onto his foot, it took him a moment to reply. 'What do you mean by soon?' he then asked.

'I don't know. Within a year, perhaps.'

'I don't know from one month to the next where I will be,

so I cannot answer for a year. But I seem to have been coming to Rye with increasing frequency.'

Frieda hoped he would now urge her to come to Paris, but he seemed preoccupied with a bootlace, or perhaps only with the need to get back to Lamb House. So she only said, 'Well, there are other places – I mean where one might meet.'

He got to his feet, now fully dressed. 'There are indeed. You and I have found that.' He leant over, kissed her, and left, closing the door as soundlessly as he had opened it.

Frieda lay listening to his careful tread on the stairs, more audible now that the rain had abated for a moment. She felt, more vividly than anything else, regret that he had to leave so soon; but what was the regret at his absence posited upon, after all, if not the delight she had taken in his presence? He had been less demonstrative, less gallant than the previous occasion, but this she interpreted as his recognition of their essential equality in passion. She was no longer an inexperienced young girl to be wooed and instructed. Had he not likened her to Electra?

The following morning, at breakfast, Mrs Tumble personally brought Frieda's tea, a chore normally performed by the maid-of-all-work Betty.

'I'm told as you had bad news last night,' she said, as she put down the pot.

'Bad news? No, indeed.'

'Fred says as he was woken up by a gentleman who said he had bad news from your employer up West Street.'

Frieda carefully poured herself a cup of tea into the thick white cup, adorned with the crest of the Warden Hotel, a strange device featuring a sheep's head and a fish in intimate concourse. 'No, that was not bad news, just a very urgent piece of work Mr James wanted me to have a look at before going to work this morning.' Then, as the suspicious old lady showed no sign of departing, Frieda added, 'But thank you for your concern, Mrs Tumble.'

'It's not only bad news as I'm concerned about. Miss Wroth, it's also about the reputation of my establishment. I can't have gentleman callers at all hours of the night, and I'll thank you to tell your Mr James that.'

Frieda took a sip of her over-sweet tea. It struck her

that her landlady herself combined in the strangest ways the qualities of a fish and a sheep; she wondered whether this was an effect of dwelling one's whole life half-submerged between sea and marsh. 'I shall convey your message to Mr James. I am sure he will be mortified at having jeopardised the reputation of your establishment.'

Mrs Tumble, having invoked Mr James, could now not redirect her complaint to Frieda herself, where she clearly thought it belonged; she had to make do with sniffing loudly and saying, 'And so he should be, and all as have anything to do with him.'

When Frieda arrived at Lamb House, there was no sign of the Panhard, though the weather was if anything worse than it had been the day before. Mrs Wharton, no doubt, had decided that she would rather wait out the storm in Folkestone than in Lamb House, and it would follow that she would take Mr Fullerton with her. It had been gradually becoming apparent to Frieda that Mr Fullerton, for all his strength of character and power of presence, was to a lamentable degree under the well-shod heel of Mrs Wharton, held there no doubt by a misguided impulse of guilt for not reciprocating her voluble passion. His return had confirmed to her what she had suspected, namely that he did not care for Mrs Wharton other than as a friend of Mr James's. Allowing even for the more adaptable emotions of men in general and Mr Fullerton in particular, it was not to be credited that a man would leave behind, in the drawing room as it were, one woman for whom he cared in order to go and make love to another. That, however, was Mr Fullerton's business and, in a different sense, Mrs Wharton's; she, Frieda, had to do only with her own designs upon destiny. These were not yet fully formed, but they had been brought into sharper focus by her experience of the night before; what was clear to her, at least, as she sat down to her Remington, was that typewriting was not an element in them, and taking dictation not a feature.

Mr James appeared at his usual time. Frieda thought he looked tired and pale, but he greeted her as briskly as ever, though he was floridly apologetic for not seeing her the day before. 'I have treated you most rudely, Miss Wroth, really unforgivably rudely, in spite of which I nevertheless do entreat you most humbly to forgive me. The truth was that after our two days of more or less waterborne sightseeing – if indeed it be accurate to talk of sightseeing where there was so little of any sight to be seen through the impenetrable medium of a positively diluvian downpour – the truth was, as I say, that I was simply too... *depleted* to show a civil face to anybody except poor little Burgess, who by now is hardened to the very worst face I can show him. So I selfishly huddled by my fireside, mumbling and muttering like some ancient crone, too decrepit even to contribute anything to the conversation of my guests, who found me as a consequence, I'm afraid, a sad companion.'

'Have your guests now left?'

'Why yes, my dear. The irrepressible and indomitable Mrs Wharton was up at daybreak, or at what would have been daybreak had anything resembling a day ever broken upon us today, intent upon getting to Folkestone in time for the morning sailing. It is difficult to imagine, for anybody as habitually timid as I am in the face of elements at all unruly, that there could be any sailing whatsoever in weather as tempestuous as this; but both Mrs Wharton and Mr Fullerton, quite apart from being far more intrepid than I, have reasons to be in Paris as soon as possible, and do not want to miss the chance, however small, of sailing.'

Mr James seemed so exhausted after what he termed his *virtually sub-marine exploration of Sussex and Kent*, that Frieda was mildly surprised when he announced the Friday following, that he had invited Mr Hugh Walpole to stay for the weekend.

'It is true,' he conceded, 'that I have had what some may term a preponderance of congeniality of late, of indeed a particularly vigorous kind, given the talent for life which both Mrs Wharton and Mr Fullerton bring to bear on all their exploits, and consequently also upon those poor less talented creatures intended by nature to wallow and flounder feebly in the tepid medium of their own mediocrity, drawn in spite of themselves within the orbit of these brilliant apparitions – as I say, it is true that just recently I may have over-taxed my powers in pursuit of the flight of the Firebird; but it is exactly in proportion to my prostration, socially speaking, that I look to Mr Walpole to revive me, as with a cup of warm milk after an over-indulgence in champagne. I know few people who are as soothing without being soporific as Mr Walpole.'

Mr Walpole duly arrived on Saturday morning, and Frieda was invited to share the late luncheon that Mr James's working habits dictated. She was amused to note, again, the almost abject veneration on the part of the younger man for the Master, as he quite unselfconsciously called him; and conversely, the urbane ease with which Mr James took for granted the reverence of the younger man. Frieda could see the force of Mr James's image of warm milk: Mr Walpole was so unabrasive, so emollient and so wholesome that one could picture him as ministering to stress or irritation without, as it were, hovering anxiously by the bedside with a damp cloth. He was an excellent listener, as indeed all

Mr James's friends of necessity were or soon became; but he was also a very good talker and, more exceptionally, knew when to listen and when to talk. He acknowledged Frieda's presence without patronising her, and did not solicit her opinion, assuming sensibly that she would offer it if she felt the need. Mr Walpole being still by way of a new acquaintance, Mr James in his honour forbore Fletcherising, and the meal was, for Frieda, much more enjoyable than many a repast with more brilliant company. Even Mrs Paddington's steak and kidney pie was consumed without comment as to its appearance or constituents: at Mr James's table Mr Walpole would have consumed hay and sawdust and considered them nectar and ambrosia.

Sunday morning dawned clear and sunny, mildly cooled by a soft west wind; it was the first such morning in almost a week, and Frieda resolved to put it to use by walking or cycling some distance. She wondered whether she should stop at Lamb House, as she often did, to collect Max, but decided that Mr Walpole, even unassuming as he was, might suspect her of courting his company. She was the more surprised, having fixed on a walk as her chosen form of exercise for the day, to find Mr Walpole and Max approaching down the High Street.

Max yapped in shrill recognition, and Mr Walpole raised his hat in a gesture almost as expressive as the dog's bark.

'Ah, Miss Wroth, well met! I was hoping to persuade you to come for a walk with me, and was going to apply at your lodgings for an interview with you, but I must confess I was rather apprehensive, Mr James having warned me of the fearsome respectability of your landlady.'

'I think Max would have vouched for the purity of your intentions. But this is a fortunate coincidence, in that, as it happens, I was just setting out for a walk.'

'Oh, excellent. I was hoping that Mr James could accompany us, but he pleaded arrears of correspondence, apparently quite distressingly so, to his brother.'

It seemed not to have occurred to Mr Walpole to go for a walk on his own. Frieda guessed that he found it difficult to be alone; indeed, Frieda could not imagine what converse he could ever have with his own spirit, his energy being so much a matter of engaging others, his nature being so naturally receptive. The thought crossed her mind that it might prove to be taxing, supplying such an eager mind with sustenance for an extended period, especially since the involuntary comparison he would be making would be with Mr James's substantial fare.

In the event, she need not have been concerned – or she could have spared herself that particular concern. Mr Walpole, it transpired, had something quite specific to say to her. They had taken the footpath across the marsh towards Camber Sands, that being the route that afforded the best views of Rye from a distance; but Mr Walpole, formerly so attentive to any detail of local import, seemed indifferent to the view. Frieda noticed a certain reticence in his manner, and was not wholly unprepared when he said, somewhat abruptly, while she was pointing out to him the peculiar behaviour of two sheep, which seemed to be trying to upend their water trough: 'Miss Wroth, I wonder whether I can recruit you to my cause.'

Frieda abandoned the sheep to their own short-sighted pursuits. 'You will of course have to tell me what it is.'

'Of course.' Mr Walpole stopped and looked back at the low profile of Rye, as if his cause had some connection with the town. 'It concerns Mr James.'

Frieda involuntarily recalled a not dissimilar opening to a conversation with Mr Fullerton, and hoped that Mr Walpole was not also about to ask her to retrieve letters he had written to Mr James. 'You are concerned about Mr James?'

'Yes, I am, though not in any way that is easy to explain. I mean, it's not about his health or anything like that.'

There was something almost comical about a man so young, so almost boyish, expressing concern about a man as infinitely mature as Mr James. Frieda carefully composed her features, and said, 'If you feel that the problem is one that I may be able to help you to solve, I should be only too willing to listen.'

'Oh, I think you can help – that is – yes, I think you can. It's only not very easy to explain.' He paused again. 'You see… you know, of course, of Mr James's friendship with Mrs Wharton and Morton Fullerton.'

This was so wholly unexpected as a source of solicitude in Mr Walpole that Frieda consciously gaped for a few seconds before meeting, after a fashion, his approach. 'Indeed I do. They spent some time here only last week.'

Mr Walpole looked grave. 'Yes; and you may know that Mr James met them in London last month for a meal at the Charing Cross Hotel.'

'I do happen to know that, yes, but I fail to see how this could be a source of concern to you.'

'You feel, no doubt, that it is none of my business, and I daresay it is not. Only, you see, a man can't stand by without saying anything while a man like Mr James is made a fool of.'

'Mr James? Made a fool of?'

'Yes – not deliberately, or at any rate not designedly, but they must *know* what they are doing.'

'And what is it that they are doing?'

At this Mr Walpole displayed, for the first time in her acquaintance with him, evidence of anger: it failed to imbue him with dignity, tending instead to make him seem like an agitated child. 'They are simply making use of Mr James's goodness and gullibility, with not a thought for what happens to him in the process.'

'I wish you would be more specific.'

'Yes, of course, I'm being wretchedly inarticulate. You see... people are talking.'

Frieda felt an impulse of impatience such as she did not often allow herself. 'Oh, people always talk. Do you mean they talk about Mr James?'

'Yes, about him and Mrs Wharton and Mr Fullerton... that is, not as...'

'Perhaps you should tell me what people are saying.'

'Yes, of course. You see, on that occasion, when Mr James had dinner with Mrs Wharton and her friend, they were seen by several people.'

Frieda stared at Mr Walpole: if this was his revelation, it was mild indeed. 'Having dinner together? Can that signify?'

'Yes, in that... you see, people are assuming that Mr James is condoning, for reasons of his own, the relationship between Mrs Wharton and Mr Morton Fullerton.'

'The relationship...?'

'Yes, the... irregular relationship. You see, on this occasion, a friend or at any rate acquaintance of mine also happened to be staying at the Charing Cross Hotel preparatory to crossing to France, a Lord Ronald Gower…?'

'Lord Ronald…?'

'Yes – do you know him?'

Frieda recollected herself. It would not do to admit having seen Lord Ronald at Folkestone. 'No, I'm sorry. Please continue.'

'Yes, well. Lord Ronald is very much a man about town, and it so happens that on this particular evening he chose to spend the night elsewhere than in his hotel room. It so happens further that he was returning to his room at about seven in the morning when he met Morton Fullerton coming out of what he knew to be Mrs Wharton's room.'

Frieda bent down and adjusted Max's lead, which Mr Walpole had in truth fastened too tightly. The movement gave her the time she needed to recover her composure; as she lifted her face to Mr Walpole, she could ask in a tolerably neutral tone: 'Is it not possible that this Lord Ronald is motivated, in his making public of this anecdote, by some personal malice?'

Mr Walpole nodded. He had regained his air of rational deliberation. 'That is almost certainly the case; I gather that he feels he has reason to resent Fullerton's treatment of him. But that does not necessarily invalidate his story, you know.'

Frieda felt that it did; she had been taught by her mother to distrust the merchandise of dishonest tradesmen. But she did not want to get involved with Mr Walpole in a barren exchange of contradictory assumptions; besides, she had other questions. 'But how does this… what does this have to do with Mr James?'

'Well, you see, Lord Ronald of course made it his business to pass on the little incident to his London *monde*; only, to add piquancy to a not unfamiliar tale, he is suggesting that Mr James is in a manner… an accomplice in the affair.'

Frieda stared again. 'It is difficult to imagine quite how, in such an intrigue, Mr James could figure in that capacity.'

'Oh, in no direct way, of course. But don't you see, while Mr James is seen in public with them, that extends a kind of respectability to their relationship. He is known to be so very scrupulous in his observance of the forms that his mere presence is a kind of licence.'

'But is that not exactly your point, that his presence is no such thing, that people are spreading gossip in *spite* of his sanction?'

'Yes, but that is only because of Lord Ronald's little discovery. Without that, the two could have kept up appearances. But now that Lord Ronald is circulating his story, Mr James is being subjected to the ridicule of the whole London set – either for his ignorance of what he is condoning by his very presence, or worse, for what is seen as his vicarious, even salacious, participation in a relation that in the nature of things excludes him.'

Frieda pondered this for a while. Her whole moral nature rebelled against the ghastly implications of Mr Walpole's story, but she took refuge in a practical objection. 'I can see that that is a most unfortunate position for Mr James to be in, but I am at a loss to see what it is that you imagine I of all people could do about it.'

'Well, don't you see, Mr James must be made aware of the situation in which he is being placed by two of his closest friends.' He bent down absent-mindedly to release Max, who was pulling at his lead.

'Excuse me, I wouldn't advise that. He chases sheep.' Mr Walpole restored the disappointed dog to confinement, and Frieda continued. 'Have you not considered telling Mr James yourself?'

'Oh, I have. I have more than considered it.'

'You have told him?'

'I have tried. Last night, to be precise, after dinner. It was rather painful.'

'For Mr James?'

'Well, mainly for me, I think. I quite badly miscalculated my effect. Mr James, to his credit, took gentle but very articulate umbrage at my confronting him with aspersions on the conduct of two of his most intimate friends, based on the gossip of someone he called one of the more garish flowers produced by a near-tropical climate of decadence. He refuses to accept that the pure water of truth may gush from a polluted source. He also very affectionately but no less articulately let me know that he regards my intervention as touching proof of a misguided concern for his reputation. I think what he was saying was that he thought I was jealous of his friendship with Fullerton.'

'And are you not?

Mr Walpole took this without flinching; he had at least the courage of his own prejudices. 'I suppose I am – but only because I think he is not worthy of Mr James's high regard. I do not consider that anybody who really cares for Mr James would want to see him exposed, by the two people whom he regards as his dearest friends, to the kind of moronic speculation that is doing the rounds in London.'

With a conscious effort of detachment Frieda said, 'But is it clear that Mr James would mind so very much being associated with their… attachment?'

'My dear Miss Wroth, surely, to anybody who really knows Mr James, as clear as daylight. He has a horror of public indiscretion; and for him to be made part of it, in a cynical attempt to purchase respectability, is to make use of him in a way that he would find extremely hurtful – that is, he would find the association painful in any case, but he would be devastated by what he would certainly regard as a betrayal. That, indeed, was the burden of his refusal to countenance my suggestion: he said that for him to believe my allegation, as he called it, would mean accepting that the two people dearest to him on earth had knowingly deceived him and exposed him to the gossip and ridicule of the world. He maintains that their friendship is, as he terms it, a virtuous attachment.'

'Then is it kind of you to want to force him to accept anything as destructive to his peace of mind as your allegation?'

'Do you mean we should leave him in a state of blissful ignorance? Is that not in its way as presumptuous – to argue that one must protect Mr James from the truth because he is not robust enough to tolerate it?'

'You still assume, you see, that what you have to convey is the truth. All you have to go on are appearances, and the London world's interpretation of those appearances.'

Mr Walpole flushed slightly; he had, after all, a personality of his own. 'Miss Wroth, forgive me if I call things by their name, but when a man is seen emerging from a woman's bedroom at seven in the morning, appearances would seem to urge themselves upon one with a certain air of reality. One might even say that, in the eyes of the world, such an appearance *becomes* the reality.'

He peered at her through his round glasses, and for the first time since she had met him, Frieda found him rather ridiculous, with his solemnity and his veneration and his little quiff sticking up. Frieda looked about her, at the flat expanse of marsh in the unsparing light of summer, extending to a watery horizon in one direction, interrupted by the brave little mound of Rye in the other. It was extraordinarily as if she, with her faith in Mr Fullerton and Mr James, were alone in the world with this man and his belief; and there was a moment during which she asked herself if his belief were not, after all, more rational than her faith. But the moment passed, leaving her all the clearer on the grounds of her faith.

'I think you are wrong,' she accordingly said to Mr Walpole, 'and your mistake surely does you no credit, as it does no credit to the people you implicate in it. You have not known Mr James for long enough to understand that he is incapable of such a grotesque mistake as you ascribe to him. He could not spend such long periods of time in such close proximity to the two people he knows best on earth, without guessing that they are dissembling the nature of their relationship. As for Mr Fullerton, I cannot claim a long acquaintance with him, but I think I can answer for his indifference to Mrs Wharton in any relation other than as a friend of Mr James's. And Mrs Wharton – well, once we have accepted Mr Fullerton's indifference, she is condemned by that token to loyalty to her husband and to Mr James alike.'

As Mr Walpole seemed disinclined to reply, merely pondered the walking stick that he was somewhat absent-mindedly swinging, Frieda continued. 'Can you really think,' she demanded, 'that a man of Mr James's penetration and knowledge of human beings, somebody whose very profession is dedicated to understanding human motives, could live so close to such a secret and not guess it?'

At this, Mr Walpole was moved at last to speech. 'I grant you, that is puzzling,' he conceded. 'But is it not true that even the wisest amongst us interpret events in the light of our desires?'

The young man advanced this unoriginal proposition with all the gravity of a newly-discovered verity; and it was likely that he thought he had originated this generalisation. He had been capable of that: what he was not capable of was seeing how it might apply to himself. It suited his need to think that Mr James was being misled by his two dearest friends; his need was to take their place in the Master's regard. Frieda could have felt sorry for him in his delusion, and sympathised with his concern for Mr James, had his delusion not been essentially so selfish and his concern so much a function of his need.

'I don't really know why you are talking to me like this. I don't think I can help you, even had I wanted to. If Mr James did not listen to you he is very unlikely to want to listen to me.'

'But he has known you for so much longer.'

'Yes, in my capacity as typewriter. Mr James does not listen to his typewriter; he dictates to her. But I wouldn't want Mr James to listen to me saying things like that, things that make him out to be a dupe and a fool.'

'I am sorry, then, that I spoke to you like this. I can see that I have upset you.'

'Oh, I am not upset on my own account. I am only angry that you should seek out Mr James in what I know he regards as a sanctuary from exactly the vulgar speculation of the world, and confront him with the fabrications of a malicious imagination. I don't mean you, of course; I believe that you are only too well-intentioned. But good intentions can serve the purposes of malice quite as effectively as the most calculated ill will.'

If there was anything over-explicit in Frieda's little speech, Mr Walpole gave no sign of taking umbrage. He mildly enough prodded his stick at a mole hill, and said, 'I repeat, then, that I am sorry that I burdened you with my concern. It is possible that I am over-solicitous for Mr James's welfare; he strikes me as so unworldly as to court all innocently the machinations of a fallen world.'

Frieda consciously moderated her manner so as not to seem to grant Mr Walpole's suspicions the dignity of a rational position worth her opposition. 'Mr Walpole, I do not think we should quarrel over matters concerning really only Mr James and his friends. You have surely done your duty as you see it in making known to Mr James your suspicions. I must do my duty as I see it, which is, as I have said, in the first place as typewriter. I must also pay Mr James the compliment of believing that his own judgement and discretion are his best guides.'

Mr Walpole silently nodded his assent. It was more than Frieda could answer for, of course, that she had actually convinced him; it would have to suffice that for the time being he seemed to be reconciled to taking no further action in the matter. They walked further, commenting desultorily on such aspects of the landscape as obtruded themselves upon their notice, and exchanged views on the hunger strike of one of the imprisoned suffragettes, one Marion Dunlop, which had that week led to the woman's early release; the authorities, however, were now taking to force-feeding hunger strikers to close that avenue of escape. Mr Walpole expressed horror at this perversion of the age-old idea of feeding the hungry, 'physical violation masquerading as nurturing'. It was a topic in which Frieda had some interest, but her mind was preoccupied with Mr Walpole's allegations. She thought the young man in his way as much mistaken as Mrs Wharton. They had, both of them, too much at stake to see Mr Fullerton clearly. For the greater credit of all involved, Frieda believed that Mr Fullerton had for Mrs Wharton at most the regard of a common friend of Mr James's; by this interpretation, Mr James was not being misled by Mr Fullerton, and nor was Frieda. It was true that by the same token Mrs Wharton was being duped, but more by herself than by any other human being. One could feel sorry for her, but one could not admire her perspicacity.

A corollary, if not a precondition, of Frieda's interpretation was her faith in Mr Fullerton's interest in her. She knew, of course, that as a man of the world he had more claims on his time and attention and even affections than she, in quiet little Rye, could begin to appreciate, but she could make, she believed, allowances for that immense difference. Within the limits left to him by the claims of that world, she believed that he cared for her; if not *only* for her, then as he cared for nobody else. Recalling the afternoon in Folkestone, and the evening when he came to her room, she could believe nothing else: it was impossible that anybody could dissemble such closeness and such warmth. And did their telepathic contact not in itself prove a meeting of minds more profound than mere telegrams, telephones and motor cars?

It was strange, then, given Frieda's certainty on this matter, that she derived so little comfort from it. She could find no fault with her premises nor with her conclusions; but it was as if they left uncovered a whole dim area of emotion, of mystery, of intrigue, she hardly knew what to call it; she was like a general who had drawn up all his defences along the lines familiar to him, only to be told that the front extended beyond his ken into terra incognita. She sensed rather than saw that whole dusky territory of error and illusion, occupied by she knew not what dim shades and strange desires, beyond the realm of her reason and her experience. She had no desire to venture into this obscure region; but she could not rid herself of a premonition that it was from there that her security would be threatened.

On Monday morning Frieda woke to a sense of hovering on
a threshold in her relations with Mr James. She had angrily
rejected Mr Walpole's allegations, and on balance she still
believed that she had been right to do so. Quite apart from
her own assessment of Mr Fullerton, she placed her faith in
Mr James's judgement. Surely the sexual relation with all its
subterfuges and disguises was the territory that he explored
most assiduously in his fiction: however beguiled by his own
affection for his two friends, it was not credible that he could be
so wholly mistaken in them and the nature of their attachment
as Mr Walpole chose to suggest.

But the fact remained that she now knew that Mr James
had been confronted, as she had been, by a rumour that he,
no more than she, would be able simply to disregard. Even
if he believed, as she believed he did, that there was no solid
foundation to the rumour, the mere existence of the rumour
constituted an affront: she knew that to Mr James there was
something dishonourable in the very circumstance of being
the subject of vulgar speculation. And in going to Lamb House
she knew that she would be facing him across the abyss of the
knowledge that she could not confess to sharing with him.

It was thus almost with relief, though promptly qualified
by concern, that Frieda received the news from Mrs Paddington
that Mr James would be remaining in his room.

'Is Mr James ill?' she enquired of the housekeeper.

'Not so's you or I would notice, miss. That is, he *looks*
as well as he ever does, only he complains of indigestion, and
feeling tired, which between us doesn't surprise me one bit,
miss, with those Americans last week, and then Mr Walpole this

weekend. There's such a thing as seeing too many people all on top of each other, to my way of thinking. It's not as if Mr James rests when he has guests, is it, miss? He *will* talk, and you know as well as I do, miss, how much he puts into his talking.'

Frieda thought Mrs Paddington's theory quite sound. Mr James had spent the months of June and July in a constant perturbation of sociability, whether visiting or being visited; and Mr Walpole's revelation, coming so hard on the heels of the visit of the two people most concerned in it, must have added to a general exhaustion the strain of a particular anxiety. Mr Walpole's concern for Mr James, then, had been as counter-productive as such short-sighted solicitude often was.

'Oh, and Mr James says, miss, not to feel obliged to sit in here all day, with such a lovely day as it is again today and not likely to last, and he's not been able this weekend to work, so there's not much for you to do around here. He says if you want to take Max for a walk later on he will take that as quite sufficiently, as he says, meeting the terms of your employment.'

'Thank you, Mrs Paddington. I shall avail myself later of Mr James's kind permission. I do, though, have a few things that I should like to complete first.'

As Mrs Paddington took her dignified leave, it occurred to Frieda that she now had an opportunity, such as she had not had for a long time, to establish communication with Mr Fullerton, and elicit his comments on Mr Walpole's theory. But the idea of telepathic contact with Mr Fullerton had little appeal for Frieda this morning: it was now too vivid to her what such contact had always been a poor substitute for. Besides, she did not want to seem to be giving even such credence to Mr Walpole's rumour as to seek Mr Fullerton's refutation. There was something unworthy in the anxiety that sought such reassurance.

Taking Mr James at his word, and being assured by Mrs Paddington that her employer was 'tolerably comfortable', Frieda recruited a delighted Max for a walk. It was indeed again a shining day, full of the colour and vigour of summer, and Frieda decided to venture as far as Camber Sands, for the freshness of the sea air and the prospect of the distant coast. It was a longish walk, and it took Frieda, walking more slowly than was her wont, the better part of two hours to reach her destination.

She crossed a dune and there it was, the shimmering sea, the placid Channel, the open sands. It was on a day much like this that she had found Mr James and Mr Fullerton here in earnest converse: she could call up without effort the image of the older man explaining, the younger man listening, the particular glint in Mr Fullerton's eye as he caught sight of her, perhaps even his relief at having the colloquy interrupted.

Max tugged at his leash, impatient for the freedom of the Sands and the pursuit of seagulls. She bent down and released him, and the little dog rushed with joyful yaps at a nearby colony of gulls. They scattered noisily, and he circled the sand either in disappointment at their disappearance or satisfaction in chasing them away.

The morning was held suspended in the hush of sand and sea and emptiness; apart from a few children engrossed at the far end in digging for bait or some other treasure, Frieda was, on this Monday morning, the only human being on the whole long stretch of sand. The shiny summer's day was yet too hazy to permit a view of the coastline of the great country across the Channel, but it was as if the haze formed a medium connecting her more directly, bridging the divide that on a clear day the Channel demarcated so unambiguously.

She walked towards the children, enjoying the freshness of the air and the warmth of the sun. But gradually her sense of connectedness with a larger world dissolved into a consciousness of her isolation in her dilemma, as she now frankly recognised it to be. She was in the strange position of being in love – and she did not shy away, now, from calling it by its name – with a man desired equally, in one sense or another, by arguably the two leading novelists of their respective generations. How Mr James and Mrs Wharton between them arranged their common infatuation was, of course, their affair entirely – or their affair and Mr Fullerton's, which made it Frieda's again, because she would be dealing with him across, as it were, the space occupied by their concurrent claims. Whereas she could answer for her own strength in the face of the mute – or possibly not so mute – appeal of the others, she could produce no certainty on Mr Fullerton's behalf. He had shown himself to lack force in his accommodation of Mrs Wharton's demands; it seemed unlikely that he would choose to brave in any direct way the incredulity and outrage of the older woman and the more dignified but no less deeply-felt disillusionment of Mr James, if he were to confess to either or both of them his relationship with Mr James's typewriter.

Her thoughts were not, as she had hoped, clarified by the exercise and the change of setting; she seemed to herself to be going around in the same issueless circle again and again, retracing old arguments, revisiting old rationalisations.

In the shadeless light of midday, there was no latitude for tone or nuance; the empty sky seemed to demand the sharp outline of an absolute certainty, and to bleach into insignificance the wavering shape of approximate conclusions.

She walked for a while, aimlessly following where Max was led by the teasing of the gulls. The glare was proving too strong for her eyes, and was bringing on a headache. Max's barking was too shrill for her. She felt alone; and not just alone here, on the beach, but alone in all eternity. The empty sand and sea, the blank horizon, presented themselves to her not as local incidents but as so many images of her life. She smiled wryly as she tried to fit Max into a metaphoric scheme of her emotional life: he was too much intent upon his own purposes to figure at all in hers. Perhaps there was, after all, a metaphor in that.

As she stopped again and looked about her, she became aware that across the sands a figure had been slowly approaching, materialising out of the mist. Coming closer the image resolved itself into that of two people walking very close to each other. It was a young man and woman of about Frieda's age, oblivious of or indifferent to any presence outside their charmed conjunction. Approaching Frieda, they stopped; the man was saying something urgent to the woman, and she was looking up at him warily, but with a smile playing on her lips: one could imagine some ironic reserve in her amusement. Then he leant forward and kissed her; she stiffened slightly, as if in resistance, then relaxed and gave herself to the kiss. Max, returning from yet another unsuccessful foray against the seagulls, trotted past the two lovers in silent embrace and barked at them sharply, just once, as if to see whether they were alive. They took no notice.

Here, Frieda recognised, neither her metaphorical bent nor

her irony could find any purchase: the two lovers, engrossed in each other, had nothing to do with her and nothing to say to her, except to speak to her of her own exclusion. She watched the young man's hand explore his young woman's body, impatient with the barriers of cloth. She was fascinated with the strange blind purpose of the hand, moving as if independent of the body of the young man.

The young woman, less single-mindedly absorbed in the embrace than her lover, said something to him, and he disengaged himself for long enough to look searchingly at Frieda. She felt rebuked and yet unrepentant: she had not invaded their privacy, they had chosen to pause in her little area of the beach. She nevertheless turned her back on them and faced again the misty ocean.

There was now, in the luminous haze, a strange clarity of outline: the more indistinct her surroundings, the sharper Frieda's perceptions seemed to grow. Staring dry-eyed into the haze, she could verily see her own lack, register it precisely as a want of what the two young people had in having each other. It came to her as a knowledge that preceded intellect and an awareness that transcended her senses: she wanted the simple physical presence of Mr Fullerton. And for this presence no substitute would serve; there *was* no substitute. In the end all the theories that sought to turn absence into presence broke down here: the claims of mediums to 'bring back' loved ones, the chronicles of 'contacts' with the departed, the documented reports of telepathic communication over long distances, the so-called consolations of separated lovers faithful unto death and beyond. Even the miraculous modern means of effecting contact over vast distances broke down into the ludicrous: a squeaky voice emerging from a tube, a few meagre words unsyntactically pasted on a slip of paper.

They could none of them, these vaunted substitutes, reproduce the glint of Mr Fullerton's moustache, the sound of his laugh, the feel of his skin, the taste of his tongue or the smell of his body. She stood amazed: why was it that nobody had pointed out this obvious fact before? She thought, for the first time in months, of her friend Mabel, who had said, one evening after Charlie had at last put in an appearance in Mrs Beddow's parlour to announce that he was fighting in the armies of paradise: 'That's all good and well, but where I want him is in my bed, not in ruddy paradise.' At the time, Frieda had been shocked, but she now could see that Mabel had put her finger on the flaw in spiritualism, on the simple fact that it had to deny in order to produce its attempt at a consolation. It tried to compensate for the loss of living flesh by denying its importance. The truth was that there was no substitute and no consolation; Life, if it meant anything, meant the presence of a living body. However profound the spiritual understanding evinced by telepathy, what was it but a pale phantom of physical touch? No wonder the poor spirits returning at the behest of Mrs Beddow and her tribe rapped and knocked and slapped and pinched: they needed to demonstrate by force the physicality that they knowingly lacked. And all the ridiculous efforts to bring back the dead: why on earth, when there were so many living people to engage our energies? Poor Miss Peggy, wanting to dedicate her young life to the spirit of Alice James, was doomed not to realise until it was too late that Alice herself had been able to sustain her own life only by becoming a kind of vampire, demanding, coercing, at whatever price, the physical closeness of another human being. Poor Mabel even, suffocating in Mrs Beddow's parlour for a word from Charlie, when she would be far better off walking out in Hyde Park with a new young man.

Two children ran past Frieda, the one chasing the other with a dead sea creature that he had dug out of the sand; there, too, was life, in the pursuit and the flight, and the poor corpse could serve only to frighten the living.

Frieda shook herself. What was the point of this insight if she did not act upon it? If what she wanted was the physical presence of Mr Fullerton, she would have to arrange it somehow; he had sufficiently demonstrated the limits of his own desire to do so. He would come to Rye only when his multifarious other interests permitted it; whereas, apart from operating the Remington, there was nothing and nobody that required her presence in Rye. If she wanted to see Mr Fullerton she would have to go to Paris; and there was nothing to prevent her from going to Paris. The claims of Mr James and Mrs Wharton, even Mr Fullerton's own vacillations, were as nothing against her certainty that, for her, a life of typewriting in Rye was no life at all, and that in Paris she would live at last, to experience, almost certainly, the pain of hardship with, possibly, the joy of fulfilment. All that she needed was to find the letters.

She turned again to the coast, and as if in response to her new clarity, the haze shifted, revealed for a moment the outline of Cap Gris Nez. She had put it off for long enough. She called to Max; he reluctantly gave up the pursuit of the gulls and submitted to being put back on the leash. She turned her back on the lovers, who did not notice, and walked, briskly now, to the tram station where the little steam train was preparing to return to Rye.

Arriving at Lamb House, Frieda found Mrs Paddington waiting for her in some agitation. 'Oh, Miss Frieda, thank heaven you've come at last. Mr James has had such a queer turn!'

'Why, whatever's the matter with him?'

'I don't know I'm sure, miss, but I'm sure it's very bad. He was feeling a bit better, he said, and went downstairs into the garden to give George Gammon some instruction about tying up the pears, and he was just reaching up like to show George what he meant, when he sort of fell back and complained of a bad pain in his chest and all over, and then he just collapsed like, and Burgess Noakes had half to carry him to his room which you can imagine, miss, wasn't half difficult, what with Burgess being that small and Mr James of course not being what you would call light, it was like a mouse trying to drag a loaf of bread upstairs, no disrespect intended, miss…'

'Quite, of course, Mrs Paddington, but have you called the doctor?'

'Yes, of course, miss, as soon as ever I could I telephoned, but they said Dr Skinner had gone to Winchelsea so I sent Burgess off there on the bicycle, and now they've telephoned to say somebody said they saw Dr Skinner on his way to Playden, so I'll have to go home and send my nephew off to find him there, but I don't want to leave Mr James all alone, just with Alice Skinner to mind him, so if you wouldn't mind sitting with him, miss, I'd feel a deal more comfortable.'

'But of course, Mrs Paddington, though there's little

enough I can do.'

'I know that, miss, but he may come to and want something and find there's nobody around. The thing is, you see, miss, he takes them dynamite pills when he's taken bad, and I know he doesn't have any of them, because only Friday he said to remind him to ask Dr Skinner come Monday, which of course is today.'

'Is he unconscious, then?'

'Not really, no, miss, just in bad pain I think, but he lies there without opening his eyes, looking all blue in the face.'

Frieda went up to Mr James's bedroom. He was indeed lying with his eyes closed, looking, Frieda thought, just very very tired. She spoke to him gently, calling him by name, but there was no response. For a moment he seemed so still she wondered if he was beyond any help; but as she approached, she saw the heavy chest lift with the effort of breathing.

Frieda sat down next to the bed on the chair presumably placed there by Mrs Paddington. As she had said to the housekeeper, she did not feel that she was in any way useful sitting there, but there was no doubt a kind of decorum in watching over the sick.

As Frieda waited for Mrs Paddington to return, she pondered the coincidence – or was it something other than that? – that today of all days, just after her moment of lucidity on the Sands, Mr James should, as it were, make her opportunity for her. For there was no doubt that it was an opportunity; Frieda had not forgotten that the top drawer of the second desk in this room was where she had concluded the letters were to be found. That drawer was now not five yards from her.

Mr Fullerton had said that if Mr James were to die the letters might end up in the wrong hands; and how could one know that he would not die? And if he truly were dying, indeed even if he were not, was it not just and fair that she should avail herself of the means to life? People said that it was a heinous crime to steal from the dead and dying; but was it not a worse crime to steal from the living? Had Mr James not said to her himself: *Live all you can; it's a mistake not to*?

So Frieda thought in all conscience while she sat by Mr James's bedside watching the pale countenance. Her mother had had a poor and honest woman's respect for other people's property: knowing so intimately the value of things from lacking them, she magnified to herself and her daughter the enormity of appropriating what was not one's own. And Frieda had learnt her lesson well, at that time of life when such lessons have no countervailing arguments to contend with; she was enough of her mother's child to know that stealing was stealing.

It was possible that this near-religious sense of the sacredness of property in general would have prevailed against Frieda's excellent reasons for feeling entitled to this particular sheaf of property, had not Max at this moment entered the bedroom. Frieda assumed the dog was in search of its master, and was apprehensive lest Mr James's condition should distress the animal; but she need not have concerned herself, for, coming into the room, Max walked, not to his prostrate owner, but to the desk that had been so vividly on Frieda's mind. The young woman stared in a kind of dread of superstition as the dog walked up to the desk, sat down, and yapped sharply at the very drawer that Frieda had been contemplating.

Frieda tried to distract the dog by calling it to her, but Max's only response was to yap again, even more peremptorily than before. Frieda got to her feet and walked to the desk; there was no doubt that Max's attention was fixed on the drawer. She moved towards it to open it, and Max got up, in evident expectation, wagging his tail and whimpering.

Frieda opened the drawer. It was large; there were indeed several bundles of letters, all tied neatly together with red tape; and next to them, in a little brown paper bag, half open, were a few of the biscuits that Mr James kept as a treat for Max. Frieda extracted one and gave it to the dog. Max swallowed the biscuit apparently without chewing, and sat waiting for another.

Frieda could identify the correct bundle quite easily: the top letter was addressed to Mr James in the handwriting that she recognised as Mr Fullerton's, and bore a Paris postmark. Frieda did not recognise the handwriting on the other and much larger bundle: she assumed these letters to be from Mrs Wharton.

Max barked again and, reaching out for another biscuit, Frieda could quite easily remove the little bundle and secrete it in the pocket of her jacket. As she did so, she heard the front door open, then Mrs Paddington's voice ushering in Dr Skinner. Max rushed down the stairs to investigate and Frieda turned round to follow him. At the threshold, she turned and glanced at the motionless figure of Mr James. His large, dark eyes were open and looking at her – not in anger or accusation, more as if in curiosity or wonderment.

Chapter Twenty-three
July 1909

Frieda, walking away from Mr James's sick-bed with the letters in her jacket pocket, knew that she would be haunted by that strangely enquiring and recording stare. Not that she could have stated with any certainty what it was that Mr James had recorded: even assuming him to have been fully conscious, he might have taken her to be heeding Max's demand for a tit-bit. In short, only Mr James knew what Mr James had seen, and Frieda's part was to wonder what he knew. She secreted the letters in her private drawer in the Green Room, resolving, as a forlorn gesture in mitigation, not to read them.

Dr Skinner pronounced the cardiac incident, though alarming, not to have been as serious as its symptoms had seemed to suggest. He was, however, nervous of taking upon himself the full responsibility for such a diagnosis, and suggested that Dr McKenzie, the man whom Mr James had seen in London, be asked for a second opinion. This was done, and in a surprisingly short time the great man arrived, escorted from the station by Burgess Noakes. Again Frieda was dependent upon the communicative Mrs Paddington for her information; the housekeeper let it be known that the distinguished physician had *hummed and hawed a great deal over Mr James and then allowed as how one could never tell with absolute certainty but insofar as one could, he was doing as well as could be expected, which of course doesn't mean that much, does it, only it seemed to cheer up Mr James, which is the important thing, isn't it?*

This somewhat inconclusive verdict was yet deemed favourable enough to allow Mr James to resume his usual routines, which, again according to Mrs Paddington, he was *fretting to do what with having lost so many days with visits and jaunts.*

Frieda awaited his appearance, four days after his indisposition, with some trepidation. And yet, as he appeared in the Garden Room, as spry as ever in terms of waistcoat and cravat, only slightly more pale and less confident in his movements, she asked herself what on earth she had expected: Mr James was the last person ever to make anybody a scene, and it was not to be imagined that he would confront her there and then with her felony, as if she were a maidservant caught filching the silver. He was, allowing for his weakened state of health, just as he had been before, treating her with his habitual courteous formality. It was a manner designed to facilitate social living, not to broach awkward questions; it could cherish the warmest affection or mask the deepest antipathy: it was the acme of civilised living and the ultimate refinement of barbarity; it inflicted no pain and afforded no comfort. It was, this manner, to be her absolution and her torment. It was with this manner that Frieda had to arrange to live in future, or at any rate for as much of that future as she spent, as it were, under Mr James's roof. Having taken, she considered, the great step in purloining the letters, the next – to arrange for her flight to France – was a relatively mild one.

She could have asked Mr James for a holiday: since starting to work for him she had not had more than a few days. But there seemed to be something ignobly pusillanimous in that, like applying for permission to blow up the Houses of Parliament: a gesture such as hers depended for its validity entirely on its not being sanctioned by the authority it was defying. Since she was to betray Mr James, she had better make her betrayal as complete as possible; there seemed little point in holding back, once one had committed one enormity, from committing a second. It was curiously also as if, having robbed Mr James, Frieda felt obscurely wronged by him: what had she done but what had been urged upon her by her situation? And what was her situation if not created by Mr James? If asked to elaborate on the nature of this situation in whose name so much was sanctioned, Frieda could have been eloquent: could have expounded with passion on the invidiousness of a situation that placed her day after day face to face and nose to nose with flights of imagination, with a range of human possibilities so other than hers that they seemed to take place in another dimension, only to remind her that her place in all this was as typewriter. Surely anybody so deprived, and so conscious of deprivation, was justified in grabbing at whatever was offered her of that vivid life that she dealt with daily at second hand? Disregarded, or regarded only as a medium of transmission, she needed to demonstrate, as much to herself as to others, her own agency, her own capacity for independent action.

It was as part of this process of reasoning that she did not want to mention her intention even to Mr Fullerton. Apart from anything else, she had, since her elucidation on Camber Sands, suffered a revulsion from any indirect manner of communication: if she could not see him face to face, she did not want to make do with the mechanically mediated consolations of the typewriter. But above all she did not want to seem, even to herself, to be consulting anybody else, even Mr Fullerton, in this, the single most serious act of her life. She would take the decision and bear the consequences, whatever they might be, without reference to anybody else. If she had wanted guidance on how to run her life, she could have had it from Mr Dodds.

Frieda was not so impassioned with the theoretical virtues of her intention that she was incapable of considering the practicalities. These were relatively few but stringent: she needed money and, once in Paris, a place to stay. Money she considered she had enough of for a sojourn of about a month: she had managed to put by a certain amount of her earnings every month for the past two years. This would enable her to stay in a modest hotel until she could find lodgings somewhere. Sacrificing to this degree the excitement of unreflective action to the prudence of planning, she confided in her Aunt Frederica, at least to the extent of telling that good lady that she was planning 'an excursion' to Paris, and asking her for recommendations as to accommodation – Aunt Frederica having marked her accession to widowhood by an extended sojourn in that city, to which her late husband the banker had had an irrational aversion. Aunt Frederica replied promptly, full of advice and caveats, mainly to do with the Parisian transport system and French drains, the efficiency of the former being sadly offset by the almost total inefficacy of the latter. She sent also the name and address of a Madame Todd, the widow of an English journalist who had been shot in one of the last duels to take place in the Bois de Boulogne; the lady, though understandably ambivalent about the English as a people, spoke the language 'as fluently as French people ever do'.

Frieda sent the redoubtable Madame Todd a reply-paid telegram – the first she had ever dispatched on her own account – and received confirmation that a 'proper chamber' was at her 'disposition' for the dates mentioned. She had fixed on the first week of August for her flight, for no particular reason other than that it had better be sooner rather than later; this in the face of Aunt Frederica's express opinion that August in Paris was 'not to be thought of, except by American sightseers of the most undiscriminating kind'. Frieda thought that she could brave the American sightseers: she did not imagine that she would be competing with them for admission to those haunts of pleasure and culture that American sightseers were reputed to be addicted to. Mr Fullerton, she knew, would be in Paris; he had made such a point of the need for his return to that city. Beyond that she had few preconceptions or expectations: Paris had always figured to her imagination as a state, a condition, rather than a precisely designated destination, resembling, in this respect, Heaven itself, though its actual existence was of course more reliably attested. And now, at last, it was within her range of possibilities.

Towards the end of July, Frieda arrived at Lamb House one morning to an unwonted air of activity. Where, at this hour, she usually found only Burgess Noakes and Max stirring, there was a sense as of all of Lamb House being congregated in the garden. Her first thought, prompted by the great acrid gust of smoke that met her as she entered the garden, was that the house was on fire; but, turning the corner of the house, she found only a large bonfire burning in the far corner of the garden, next to the little plot where Mr James's dogs were buried. Max, as if in defiance of the fate of his predecessors, was barking at the fire, and next to him, apparently feeding the blaze, was Mr James.

This latter was the really unusual aspect of the little tableau: bonfires were a common enough occurrence in the garden of

Lamb House, George Gammon seeming to find an intense if morose satisfaction in consigning large piles of leaves to the flames, but for Mr James to be manually involved in horticultural activity was unprecedented in Frieda's experience. As profligate as he was of advice and instruction to the unheeding George Gammon, so reticent was he in usurping the actual performance of the tasks.

Mr James, dressed as if he were about to step out into West Street on a round of visits, was feeding the fire, not with the fallen leaves of autumn, but with papers that he was taking from a small stack next to him. George Gammon was standing to one side, his very posture registering protest against this invasion of his garden. Frieda paused, intrigued by this unusual division of labour, and while she watched, Burgess Noakes appeared, carrying another pile of papers to add to a stack already in place on the handcart that was evidently serving as temporary table.

Mr James seemed not to have noticed Frieda's entrance; seemed, indeed, not to notice anything other than the papers he was methodically placing in the flames. The air inside the walled garden was thick with smoke and the smell of burning paper. To Frieda there was something final, almost apocalyptic about the conflagration, an impression to which Mr James's immobility and set expression contributed not a little. She could have gone to the Garden Room without attracting attention to herself, but there was something so unusual about Mr James's air, something she would have called *forlorn* in anybody else, that an unusual impulse of pity took hold of her. Normally, in his self-contained urbanity, the least pitiable of human beings, with his implication of having dealt with all crises long ago, Mr James now had an air of leave-taking about him, almost, Frieda fancifully conjectured, as if he were standing by a funeral pyre. Without reflecting further, she went over to him; he did not notice her until she was next to him, in the smoke and the heat of the burning paper. Only then he looked up at her. His eyes were red from the smoke, but he smiled at her, gaily enough.

'Ah, my dear Miss Wroth, you don't want to get your clothes... *fumigated* with my fire.'

She hardly took note of his words. 'You... you are burning your papers,' she commented, at a loss for anything other than the self-evident. But Mr James ignored whatever there was of the obvious in her little speech, merely nodded, and said, 'I am divesting myself, in a manner of speaking, of an accumulation of almost forty years. There comes a time when one must clear one's cupboards and empty one's drawers.'

Frieda resisted an impulse to extend a restraining hand. 'But... there must be so many such precious papers there, with all the people you have known and situations you have witnessed.' She had, after her sporadic explorations of the previous few months, a vivid sense of the value, historically but even in mere vulgar monetary terms, of what Mr James was destroying. He had known, over several generations, so many people, people whose genius was exactly of a kind to be captured, however partially, by pen and paper. The loss to posterity of what Mr James was burning was immense: Flaubert, Turgenev, George Eliot – perhaps even Mrs Wharton would be prized in the uncertain tribunals of the future.

'Precious to whom, pray?' he almost sharply inquired.

'To... future generations, posterity.'

Mr James blew a speck of ash from his sleeve. 'I do not consider, you see, that I have a duty to posterity other than to leave it the best novels I know how to write. The rest – this –' and he threw another handful of letters into the flames as if to emphasise his point, 'was never intended for posterity, and posterity, for all its impertinence, has nothing to do with it.' He paused, a sheaf of letters in his hand; Frieda recognised, in the slight narrowing of the large gaze, the concentration of his mind on a topic. 'The hunt for letters, papers, memorabilia,' he at last asked pensively, almost meditatively, 'what is it all but a kind of literary journalism, with the researchers reporting on the lives of the artist with all the art and avidity of a hunter tracking his prey?' He threw another sheaf of letters on the fire and faced Frieda, his expression now almost grim, his face livid with the heat of the fire and the passion of his conviction. He could have been standing on a rampart inciting a revolutionary mob to plunder and burn, or on a cannon inflaming an invading army. 'It is time that the hunted creature, in pursuit only of privacy and silence, adopted something of the art of the hunter. Let privacy and silence only be cultivated, on the part of the hunted creature with even half the method with which the love of sport – or call it the historic sense – is cultivated on the part of the investigator; then at last the game will be fair and the two forces face to face; then at last the pale forewarned victim, with every track covered, every paper burnt and every letter unanswered will, in the tower of art, the invulnerable granite, stand, without a sally, the siege of all the years.'

As if to punctuate this militant declaration with his own act of barbarity, Mr James, Frieda was shocked to see, threw onto the fire a book. She recognised it, as the flames seized its flimsy covers, as Alice James's diary.

Frieda was aware of George Gammon gaping and of Burgess Noakes, appearing with a further bundle of papers, staring; but she felt herself to be no less gaping and staring at the passion she had unleashed. Mr James's peroration ended as unexpectedly as it had begun, with a return to his customary mildness. 'You will forgive the relative heat of my convictions, my dear; but it does so cheapen the concept of posterity, to figure them as pawing over one's letters and ignoring one's art.'

He took the proffered bundle from Burgess Noakes, and when the butler had disappeared into the house again, turned to Frieda. His outburst seemed to have opened a reserve of confidence; he said, his manner now almost conversational, 'The truth is, my dear, that I have realised afresh the essential incompatibility of one's art with what most people would call life. I believed, in my youth, that in order to dedicate myself to my art I had to sacrifice life, or that considerable part of it that is constituted out of one's intimate relations with other people – or, to be more precise even, with one other person.'

He paused again to add another priceless bundle to the fire, and Frieda took advantage of the interruption. 'And yet you said,' she pointed out, 'or your character said, surely with your sanction, *Live all you can, it's a mistake not to.*'

He looked at her, it was difficult to tell whether most in surprise or pleasure. 'You remember *The Ambassadors*? Oh yes. I am sure the advice was excellent, as far as it went, that is, as spoken to a young man not irresistibly gifted with artistic talent.' He paused, and his face assumed the ruminative placidity that marked his reflections on literary matters. He could have been holding forth after supper in front of the fire of his dining room. 'As coming from Strether to Little Bilham, it was *dramatically* the right advice. But I was not Little Bilham, and I pledged, at an early age, my allegiance to art; she is a jealous mistress, suspicious above all of life – though knowing of course that she cannot do without it. Oh, I made my vows, of chastity, poverty and obedience, and I served her to the best of my ability, believing that that was the only condition on which really to do anything worth doing. Nor was she ungrateful: she rewarded me with the unadorned laurels that she reserves for those she wishes to test, the bare critical respect that for long enough assuaged my young vanity.'

He looked around him, almost complacently, at the fine old red brick of the house, indistinct in the smoky haze. 'And even from a material point of view she has not dealt too harshly with me: it is something, after all, to be able to end one's days here, and contribute something to the history of a house that will survive to tell its own little tale to generations to come. But later in life, I had doubts; I wondered whether I had not, in spurning life so arrogantly, made a mistake. Life, at any rate, from time to time, still beckoned, as witness' – he held out a handful of letters before placing them on the fire – 'as witness these mute emissaries from her fair courts. I have been faithless and this is the record of my infidelities.'

Frieda thought it would be permissible to comment. 'But there is surely no infidelity to the practice of your art in the writing and receiving of letters? What are they but another form of art and another medium of expression?'

Mr James gave her his intensest attention, then moved his head obliquely, it was impossible to say whether in assent or dissent. 'It would not have occurred to me to see these poor letters in just this light if I had not somehow, very recently, lost a bundle of letters that I had regarded as precious above all else, in coming from a person who has mattered above all else to me. My devastation has brought home to me the folly of trying to change allegiance now. It has reminded me of the price life exacts, in terms of anxiety, perplexity, vexed relations, mistakes, vulnerability to loss.' He paused, as if wondering whether to continue; then he visibly braced himself as if for some task requiring fortitude, and continued: 'The loss of the letters happened to coincide with another great shock to my belief in those I had looked to as my most precious friends. I had believed Lamb House to be my stronghold against betrayal, to which I admitted only those whom I had selected on the basis of trust and affection; and I found that I had welcomed to it those who did not scruple to use me as an element in their own designs. To be mistaken in one's own abilities and potential is common enough; but to be mistaken in the capacities of one's friends shakes one's belief in more than oneself. It makes one doubt the value of life itself.' He pushed a recalcitrant shred of paper back into the fire with the toe of a well-polished boot. 'One should try, perhaps, in this respect to emulate the dead, and have nothing to lose. Life plays one false; all that does not let one down is art. So this fire, if you'll forgive the portentous tone of my peroration, is my little ceremony of sacrifice, and of my rededication to my art.'

Frieda gazed at the blazing fire; she could not bring herself to look at Mr James.

'Having suffered,' he continued, 'so recently and so vividly, the brush of the great wing of the harbinger of our mortality. I must see my life, both the vast sweep behind me and the short tract ahead of me, in the dark light of that visitation. What must remain of that life is not here –' he added, inexorably, a handful of letters to the fire, 'in these poor tokens of transient passions and affections, but there –' he gestured in the direction of the Garden Room, 'in what I have transmuted into the immortality of art.'

A light gust of wind, all unexpected in the serenity of the day, blew smoke from the bonfire into Frieda's face, and for a moment it was as if she tasted the acrid ash and sulphurous flame. Her eyes watered and her throat burned.

Mr James looked at her as if he had momentarily forgotten about her presence. 'There, I think you had better go indoors, my dear. You don't want to ruin your clothes for the privilege of listening to my philippics.'

'I do believe you're right – I don't mean about your philippics, of course; about my clothes,' Frieda said; but she was hardly aware of what she said. She felt suddenly weak – not with the smoke she had inhaled, but with the knowledge, so strangely chilling in the midst of the smoke and the heat, from which she could not avert her gaze. She had to take full in the face the knowledge of another's loss, as a consequence of her deed and of the injury she had inflicted. This was what Mr James made her see now, in his desolation and renunciation: the destitution of conscious betrayal. Oh, she had not been the only one to betray him, but that was not available to her in mitigation of her own guilt; it could serve only to make him feel how conditionally he had been loved by those whom he had loved unconditionally.

Frieda stumbled up the steps of the Garden Room, where once, it seemed years before, she had appeared in all the power of her indignation. There was only one way to deal with her situation, from the moment that she accepted that she lacked the courage simply to confess the truth to Mr James. Mr Fullerton would understand, would have to understand.

She opened her drawer. At the back, hidden behind her transcripts, was the little bundle – the slender record of a friendship of so many years. Measured against the bulk of the New York edition of the Novels and Tales, ranged in their handsome bindings on the shelves cleared for them and for their companions still to follow, the letters were as nothing; and yet they represented, to Mr James, a counterweight, imponderable but irresistible, to all that lifetime's achievement.

She closed the drawer and sat down at her typewriter. She had not communicated with Mr Fullerton since the last time she had seen him, but in the intensity of her emotion she did not doubt for a moment that she would establish contact with him. Usually she waited until he signalled his presence; today, confident of the power of her emotion, she simply started typing.

```
Receiver:        I have not been in touch with you all
                 these weeks, because I have planned to
                 come and see you in Paris.
```

She waited. There was a lull, during which she wondered whether she had been mistaken; then, abruptly, without even a preliminary sense of an alien presence, her fingers assumed control of the machine.

Transmitter:	That is excellent, of course.
Receiver:	But I need to establish the basis on which I shall be taking such a decision.
Transmitter:	That, too, is excellent. Unreflective action has its charms, but also its limitations.
Receiver:	That is why I have wanted to confer with you before leaving.
Transmitter:	I am happy to be conferred with, of course, as long as we both realise that any conclusion you reach will be your own entirely.
Receiver:	Yes, that of course; but I need to know, as truthfully as possible, what you feel about my coming.
Transmitter:	When you ask for the truth, are you sure you want it?
Receiver:	I would not ask for it otherwise.
Transmitter:	Excuse me, you would. In my experience, and I regret to mention that it has been extensive, people asking for the truth are in fact saying, please lie to me. Most people collude in their own deception, which explains the extraordinary success of spirit mediums and kindred charlatans. It is not even necessary to lie; all that is necessary is to remain quiet and people will invent their own lies and make their own mistakes. The surest way of invading a fortified city is to find an accomplice within the gates. This is why I have, if I may say so, been so successful: I know not to contradict the lies people tell themselves.
Receiver:	Are you saying that I was mistaken in believing that you said, on that afternoon in Folkestone, that you wanted me to come to Paris? Or that you did not

mean it when you said it?

Transmitter: If you believe that I said it, it is
likely that I did say it. And if I said
it, I must have meant it, for I seldom
tell a lie outright if it can be avoided,
not because I am an unusually moral
creature, but because lies lead to so many
complications. I must have found you so
satisfactory that it occurred to me that
it might be pleasant to show you Paris
on my terms. But my dear Miss Wroth, you
must not make too much of pledges and
professions made on a summer's afternoon
in the afterglow of passion. Of course I
meant what I said; but I did not undertake
to feel just like that for ever. It is
of the essence of life to carry on, to
change, to shift; it is only in death that
we become changeless.

Receiver: And yet we believe in fidelity,
constancy, permanence.

Transmitter: Do we? We say we do because we want
to believe in these things: they give
us security. But no sooner do we have
security than we begin to look for
variety and change. Again this is
something I know because I have often
used it to my advantage: most of my
admirers, for want of a better term, have
been married people, people committed
to the idea of fidelity, constancy and
permanence with other people, and who
then expect the same things from me in
relation to them. Having been unfaithful
to their husbands, their wives, the loves
of their lives, even their employers —
they look to me for fidelity, and resolve
to be faithful to me at least.

Receiver: I take it that you are telling me that it

would be a mistake to come to Paris.

Transmitter: I would not presume to tell you anything
as blighting to the imagination as that.
Paris is a magnificent city and everybody
should endeavour to come to it at least
once; if it is a mistake, it is at least
a considerable mistake. And if mistake
is the basis of all tragedy, it is also
the soul of comedy. It is even possible
that if you were to come, I should take
advantage of your presence here. The last
time I saw you, in that dreadful little
hotel in Rye, I realised again what an
attractive woman you are. But I would not
give you any encouragement, as coming
from me, to come here, lest you should
interpret that as a promise that I will
look after you — which I am naturally
not in a position to do. You would be
essentially on your own — and I would
be misleading you if I did not add that
Paris can be very lonely.

Receiver: Lonelier than Rye?

Transmitter: Oh, I should think so. We measure our
loneliness by the contrast between our
opportunities and our achievements;
now Rye strikes me as having so few
opportunities that quite a modest
achievement would constitute success.
But I am not, of course, advising you
not to come to Paris; I am merely
cautioning you about the realities of a
city that suffers more than most from
romantic distortion.

Receiver: And the letters?

Transmitter: Which letters?

Receiver: The letters that you wrote to Mr James and
that you asked me to retrieve for you.

Transmitter: Miss Wroth, you surprise me, remembering

that detail, after all this time. I
do now remember asking you that, and
feeling almost ashamed of myself later, a
sentiment I do not often permit myself.
I asked you, because at the time I was
anxious about the fate of my letters,
in the light of a bad experience I had
lately had. But since then it has seemed
to me an unnecessary concern; I seem to
remember that at the time I considered
that if anything were to happen to Mr
James, the letters might pass into the
possession of Mrs Wharton, whom at the
time I did not wish to know quite as much
about my early life as those letters
would have told her. But since then it
has ceased to matter very much what Mrs
Wharton knows about my early life; her
own life with me has rather superseded
those incidents.

Receiver: Then it is true that all this time — you
               have been intimate with Mrs Wharton?

Transmitter: I could say that that depends on what you
               mean by all this time and by intimate;
               but that would be an evasion. To all
               intents and purposes, that is, in the
               sense in which you use the term, it is
               true that I have been intimate with Mrs
               Wharton all this time. If it is any
               consolation to you, she does not feel
               that it has been enough. She is today,
               probably, an unhappier woman than you.

Receiver: Am I to take pleasure in another's
               unhappiness?

Transmitter: Not pleasure — consolation. Unless you
               are very unusually constituted you will
               find your own unhappiness more bearable
               in proportion as it is less great than
               someone else's.

```
Receiver:      How would you know? I don't think you can
               know what unhappiness is.
Transmitter:   Oh, but I do, if only because Mrs Wharton
               has so often and so eloquently told me.
               Unhappiness, as Mrs Wharton suffers
               it, is a state of unsatisfied desire.
               It is distinct from the unhappiness of
               deprivation or loss, hunger or thirst.
Receiver:      And as Mr James suffers it?
Transmitter:   Mr James does not suffer unhappiness,
               he experiences it, which is a far
               more active process altogether. For
               him, unhappiness is part of his
               subject matter, and the condition
               of its production. His is an art of
               renunciation.
Receiver:      That is very convenient for you.
Transmitter:   True, but in the long run also for you.
Receiver:      Then are you advising me to cultivate the
               art of renunciation?
Transmitter:   I would not presume to advise you. You
               have made your life thus far very well
               without my counsel. I am saying that some
               people have a talent for life and others
               have a talent for renunciation. The trick
               is to know where one's talents lie.
```

Frieda got up from her typewriter. She could not even find relief in anger at the waste of so much effort and anxiety and the sacrifice of such loyalty as she had owed Mr James; anger implied a claim that she could now see she never had. Nor did she find her unhappiness rendered more bearable by the knowledge of Mrs Wharton's unhappiness. If there was any consolation, it was not in sharing the other woman's deprivation in some camaraderie of resentment; consolation, such as it was, was out there, with Mr James and his bonfire. Perhaps that was what Mr Fullerton had meant by unhappiness as an *active process*; she failed to see what it could mean, in her case, other than active renunciation.

She opened her drawer again. There was the pile of typed transcripts of her conversations with Mr Fullerton, her tribute to Life, as she had judged it. She took out the little pile and paged through it, then placed it carefully with the bundle of letters and went outside.

Mr James's bonfire was still smouldering. Burgess Noakes had stopped carrying out papers, and was watching the fire die down, from a distance, with George Gammon. There was thus a little audience as she appeared with her bundle of papers. Mr James looked up as she approached.

'Do you want to burn those?' he asked.

'Yes, if I may. I find I also have material that I want to dispose of.'

'I see.' And he nodded as if he did see. 'Fire does not discriminate. You are just in time. There are still some flames over there.'

Frieda held out the little packet, with no attempt to hide its identity. If Mr James recognised the bundle for what it was, he did not say so nor acknowledge or assert in any other way his ownership of what Frieda was about to consign to the flames. He merely stood back slightly to allow her free access to the dwindling bonfire. She stepped forward and began to feed the letters into the fire.

As Frieda lent over the fire, she felt Mr James's eyes on her; but that was a small part of what she felt. She felt that they were looking at the truth together, that Mr James recognised her at last as an equal; not an equal in that high art in which he was supreme, but as a sentient being who had but this life to live, and was trying to do so on her own terms. Their equality was the fellowship of loss and renunciation.

She placed the letters on the fire one by one. I too, have lived, her gesture said, and have had my dreams and passions; and I too have had to recognise their futility. But where you made the sacrifice in the name of the greater good that is art, I am making it in the name of hard necessity. I renounce not in some high-minded turning away from life, but because my poor grasp at life has failed. I have not chosen, because I have had no choice. Insofar as my burning of these letters constitutes a choice, it is only an acceptance of the inescapable. I believed they were a charter granting me admission to the citadel, but that was a mistake: they are fraudulent, not valid for that purpose, valueless.

Frieda ignored George Gammon's evident displeasure, and placed the few letters, then the sheets of her transcripts on the fire one by one, two by two and three by three. The last to go was the sheet so recently typed: *to know where one's talents lie.* She watched it catch, flame up, blacken, curl, disintegrate. There were some charred remains of Mr James's letters to the side of the fire, not wholly burnt. Her eye, adept now at stealing quick impressions, caught the signature, and fixed it, because it was so much more laborious, so much more emphatically legible than the run of Mr James's correspondents. It said *(Mrs) Lavinia Tumble.* Apart from the signature, all that remained was a fragment: '...*trust there will*... *repetition of this unfortunate*...'

She looked up. Mr James was watching her, his head at an angle, the smile still hovering on his expressive mouth.

'Then there we are,' he said.

'There we are,' she answered, and went back to the Garden Room.

In her other drawer she had her poor little attempt at a novel, abandoned – how long ago? – in the interests of her recording of Life. She looked at the few pages remaining of her novel; she might now revive them; but they seemed insipid, imitative of Mr James's style and subject matter, self-conscious. She would start anew, write her own tale, not his. She inserted a fresh sheet, sat with her fingers poised. For a moment, she expected the familiar glow to enter her, announcing the presence of Mr Fullerton. But there was nothing, only the sheet of paper, blankly waiting for her.

But she, in her turn and in her place, waited. She was used, now, to waiting. She cleared her mind of all thoughts of herself, of her expectations and disappointments, her longings and disillusionments. She could do that, now; she knew how to become purely passive and expectant, a medium to another mind than hers, welcoming the invasion of an alien power.

Her fingers moved, a tremor, an impulse, a stirring. There was, after all, something, a presence taking possession of her thoughts, moving her fingers on the keys, forming words, sentences:

The worst part of taking dictation was the waiting.

And Frieda, following the prompting of her fingers, began typing – for life, as it were.

Author's note

This is a novel drawing on historical material, and I have blended fact with fiction promiscuously. I am indebted to the following sources, studies and collections for the information that I have annexed, incorporated and in some instances adapted to my purpose. The authors and editors are not to be held responsible for the considerable liberties I have taken with the literal truth. My young typewriter is based on Theodora Bosanquet, who was in James's employ from 1907 to his death. The thoughts and actions I attribute to Frieda are entirely fictional, indeed unthinkable as applied to Miss Bosanquet. Frieda does, however, have in common with her model an interest in thought transference: after Henry James's death in 1916 Miss Bosanquet regularly established contact with him through a spirit control called Johannes. For a history of Johannes and Theodora, and a more general consideration of the connections between typewriting, telepathy and automatic writing, see Pamela Thurschwell's *Literature, Technology and Magical Thinking, 1880-1920* (Cambridge University Press, 2001).

Morton Fullerton's affair with Edith Wharton, as well as his other involvements, including the saga of the purloined letters, has been exhaustively charted in Marion Mainwaring's extraordinary piece of literary detective work, *Mysteries of Paris: The Quest for Morton Fullerton* (University Press of New England, 2001) – essential reading for anybody interested in this fascinating if unreliable man.

For details of James's daily life and working habits I am indebted to H Montgomery Hyde's *Henry James at Home* (Methuen and Co, 1969) and Theodora Bosanquet's pamphlet *Henry James at Work* (The Hogarth Essays, n.d.); for Rye at the time of the novel to Geoffrey Bagley's invaluable *Edwardian Rye from Contemporary Photographs* (Rye Museum Association, 1991).

For background on the James family I have consulted *The Diary of Alice James*, edited by Leon Edel (Penguin, 1982).

The story Henry James dictates in Chapters 1, 5 and 9 is his 'Julia Bride' (published 1908).

The source of the dictation in Chapter 10 is the Preface to the New York Edition of *The Portrait of a Lady*.

Henry James's diatribe against biographical research has been adapted from a section of his essay on George Sand.

I owe the person and some of the characteristics of Mrs Mabel ('Pansy') Tuke to Sylvia Pankhurst's *The Suffragette Movement: An Intimate Account of Persons and Ideals* (Longmans, Green and Co., 1931). Her speech, however, and indeed her presence in Rye, are entirely of my devising, though the sentiments expressed were of course prevalent at the time.

Most of the letters in this novel are of my devising. The following, however, are copies of originals, held in collections at the institutions named:

William James to Henry James (p.72), 30 November 1907 (Harvard University).

Henry James to William James (p.90), 13 November 1907 (Harvard).

Henry James to Theodora Bosanquet (p.97), (Harvard).

Henry James to William Dean Howells (p.154), 17 August 1908 (Harvard).

Henry James to Edith Wharton (pp.165-67), 13 October 1908 (Yale).

More generally, I have consulted the following books:

Leon Edel (ed.): Henry James *Letters, Volume IV: 1895-1916* (Harvard UP, 1984).

Leon Edel: *Henry James: The Master 1910-1916* (Volume 5 of the biography) (Rupert Hart-Davis, 1972).

Fred Kaplan: *Henry James: The Imagination of Genius* (Sceptre, 1993).

RWB Lewis and Nancy Lewis (eds.): *The Letters of Edith Wharton* (Macmillan, 1988).

Lyall H Powers (ed.): *Henry James and Edith Wharton: Letters: 1900-1915* (Charles Scribner's Sons, 1990).

Skrupskelis, Ignas K and Elizabeth M Berkeley (eds.): *The Correspondence of William James, Vols 1-3; William and Henry 1861-84; 1885-96; 1897-1910* (University Press of Virginia 1992, 1993, 1994).

Edith Wharton: *A Backward Glance* (London: Century Hutchinson, 1987).

I have in general kept to the actual time frame of events and visits, as recorded in these sources. In addition to the mistakes I may unwittingly have made, I have committed the following conscious inaccuracies:

Frieda could not, in 1907, have met Horace Fletcher at Lamb House; his only visit took place in 1910.

Frieda could not have witnessed Henry James cycling: he gave up the practice in 1901.

Morton Fullerton spent the night of Saturday 8 November 1907 at Lamb House, not the Friday night. He seems to have confessed the theft of his letters and the content of those letters to James in a letter written soon after this weekend, not in conversation during the weekend, as I imply.

The letter from William James that Frieda reads on 11 November 1907 was written later, on 30 November.

The important letter to Edith Wharton of 13 October 1908 was written by hand, not dictated, as I have had to have it.

The James family did not return to America in 1908 from Rye but from London: I sacrificed historical accuracy to the temptation of describing the family's departure from Lamb House.

Henry James burned his letters 'in the autumn of 1909'; I have moved this to late July.

I have been consciously unfair to the James family and to Edith Wharton: they are here represented not as they in themselves 'really' were, but as they might have been experienced by a sensitive and marginalised young Englishwoman.

As dedicated Jamesians will have noticed, I have found myself at times appropriating phrases from the writings of Henry James. I have retained these borrowings, not as plagiarism, but as homage to the works to which this novel is above all indebted.

This novel was written as a contribution to Marlene van Niekerk's Creative Writing course at the University of Stellenbosch. I am grateful to the University and the Department of Afrikaans and Dutch for permission to attend these seminars. More particularly, thanks are due to Marlene and to my fellow students for their critical but supportive comments.

www.michielheyns.co.za